MW01658205

I screamed as the heavy [illegible] in my hand and fell to the ground. The bear moving toward Scout dropped, and I raced to scoop up my son before he toppled into the cold black stream. Looking startled, he managed a weak cry before I smothered him into my chest muffling both our cries against his thick scarf. The dog shoved something wet against my leg and began to bark, running from me to the Beaverwoods, now cautiously circling the bear. The boys were armed with pieces of thick deadwood and Chuck picked up my smoking gun, cocked the trigger and ordered his sons to stand back. He aimed the gun at the animal to finish him off, then suddenly dropped his arm and knelt beside the still lump of fur. Tommy grasped the growling dog by its collar, and in the sudden silence, I could hear a collective gasp. Someone uttered "Jeesus" like an invocation.

Still cradling my son, exhausted by fear, I ventured closer and could see at once that it was no bear I shot. A man in a bearskin poncho lay on his side. Chuck rolled him over and pulled off the man's hood. A mass of dark matted hair covered the part of his face that wasn't blooming with blood, pooling into his left ear, running down his cheek and into his thick beard.

"Is he, is he dead?" I whispered.

Chuck took off his glove and wiped the man's neck with it, then fumbled for a pulse. We all started when the man groaned and his eyes fluttered open.

Green! His eyes were green, the rarest of all eye color. The fear in them more than the color registered with me as he searched our faces.

Praise for Cj Fosdick

THE ACCIDENTAL WIFE was:

A finalist for the Golden Quill Best First Novel, and in the Top Ten for both Best Romance and Best Author in the annual Preditors & Editors Reader Poll of 2015.

She was voted Top Ten for Best Author in 2015 in P & E Reader Poll.

~*~

"…well described...well told...Fosdick is a talented writer."

~Historical Novel Review Magazine

~*~

"The Accidental Wife is a well-written book that is both entertaining and entlightening."

~Florence Osmund, author of Regarding Anna

~*~

Other review briefs:
"Mesmerizing!..."
"Part mystery, part romance... Written with a style of its own..."
"Much more than a time-travel..."
"Loved the characters, ached at their dilemma..."
"Every chapter is an incredible journey..."
"Couldn't put it down or out of mind..."
"I laughed, cried, bit my nails..."
"Ranks with best-selling tomes like *Somewhere in Time*...Fosdick makes readers understand the transformative power of love...Highly recommended..."
"Can't wait for the sequel!"

The Accidental Stranger

by

Cj Fosdick

The Accidental Series

This is a work of fiction. Names, characters, places, and incidents are either the product of the author's imagination or are used fictitiously, and any resemblance to actual persons living or dead, business establishments, events, or locales, is entirely coincidental.

The Accidental Stranger

COPYRIGHT © 2017 by Cj Fosdick

All rights reserved. No part of this book may be used or reproduced in any manner whatsoever without written permission of the author or The Wild Rose Press, Inc. except in the case of brief quotations embodied in critical articles or reviews.
Contact Information: info@thewildrosepress.com

Cover Art by *RJ Morris*

The Wild Rose Press, Inc.
PO Box 708
Adams Basin, NY 14410-0708
Visit us at www.thewildrosepress.com

Publishing History
First Mainstream Fantasy Edition, 2017
Print ISBN 978-1-5092-1241-5
Digital ISBN 978-1-5092-1242-2

The Accidental Series
Published in the United States of America

Acknowledgments and Dedication

Research always involves wearing many hats. For this book, my "figurative" headgear ran the gamut of historian, detective, journalist, photographer, and genealogist. In the journey of this book, I actually wore baseball caps as we traveled to most of the settings, including a local bar and restaurant in one historic western town. Human resources were often unexpected, but consequential pennies from heaven rained over all my hats.

A bad strep throat during last summer's research trip landed me in the ER of Platte County Memorial Hospital in Wheatland, Wyoming, where I met Dr. Jim and several nurses who gave me a tour of the hospital. (Yes, it has bright blue vinyl chairs.)

After a tour of Ireland with a gifted Irish guide named Deirdre Byrnes, we had to buy extra baggage to lug books and souvenirs home, including Claddagh rings and Irish dictionaries. The biggest Irish treasure I found after returning home, however, was April Hollingworth who lives in Clonakilty, West Cork. Among other things, April—who also writes for the wonderful Wild Rose Press—clued me in about placing foda marks on many Irish words, what a *gobshite* is, and how to say Love you (*grá agat*) in Irish Gaelic.

Details, like the name and photographic layout of a Tuke Fund Immigrant ship leaving Galway in 1883 required a broad search for books from inter-library loan. Susan Hansen of the Rochester Public Library was my diligent go-to gal for this.

The historian at the Fort Laramie National Parksite, Sandy Lowry, has been my go-to gal for several years, supplying me with historical bits for both *The Accidental Wife* and *The Accidental Stranger*, including the name of the huge hundred-year-old tree in front of the cavalry barracks: a Peach Tree Willow.

My dear friend Darlene Vowels has been a tireless researcher—writing about her family genealogy since she retired from teaching school. Quizzing her on general procedures netted me several pages of resources.

Laurel Winter, the talented writer/artist/editor I collaborated with for a Minnesota Anthology thirty years ago, has always been one of my biggest cheerleaders as a first reader and editor. Her encyclopedic mind clarified the true definition of a "wet willie."

Of course, my greatest technical resource has been the hub of my life—Eric Fosdick—who created my website and readily answers daily "how-to" questions. Control "F" replaces words? He also makes me protein shakes and gives honest critiques that end in hugs.

To all of these gracious people, I dedicate this book and my heartfelt thanks. *Grá agat!*

~ Cj

Prologue

He melted into the shadows, drawn to the sound of another human voice. He had never come this far, never dared to put himself in such danger. In the spangled light of sunset, he watched her bend over the child, like the graceful arc of a bog violet. She was singing a ditty that drifted on the wind, tugged at his heart. He closed his eyes and tried to remember his mum's voice, light as faerie strings, singing to him so long ago. When life was simple and true, but for the want of food.

No hunger now. Not in the physical sense. There were always rabbits, fish from the river, even deer he might hunt with the primitive bow and arrows he carved some winters ago. He hungered more and more for the sights and sounds of humanity, even the touch of another living creature. For a while, he toyed with the idea of finding a pet he could tame—maybe a bird or even a lone wolf. Anything to break the isolation and fill the lonely hours. But a pet could give away his presence, put him at risk.

The woman set the child on the porch step, then demonstrated how to hold hands, palms together, fingers pointed in the prayer position. Blowing between her cupped thumbs, she produced a weak sound. The child mimicked her and made her laugh. She was tall and when the wind whipped her thin shift against her body, he could see that she was slender…curved in all the right places. Her hair was lank and loose on her shoulders, as if she had just washed it. He couldn't make out the color. In the fading glow of sunset, it looked violet.

The child stood, teetering on the step with arms forward, reaching out for her. Too daring for a girl—yet the long curls made him wonder. With a high-pitched whoop, he—or she—flew into the woman's arms, and they twirled in a circle, laughing in harmony. Another sound that cut into his memory; like the sweet chords of the cruit his folk played.

The house was made of stripped logs, with an eyebrow porch that looked like it ran around two, maybe three sides. Well-built…new, judging by the patina of the wood. Where would such logs come from? Wyoming pine stands, even in the Bows, were plundered for miles around the fort. Finding such uniform logs without going a great distance…then hauling them to such an isolated spot…? He stroked his beard. Not even a wagon or barn in sight.

Maybe he was drifting again? Conjuring up the visions he missed, the undeserved comfort he craved, even as a watcher. His mum had visions. With her last sendoff, she told him he would find his people living in wooden houses with glass windows and fenced yards.

He patted his chest, feeling the secret pocket that held the fading image of his father. His father in uniform. It was a good thing both his parents were fading memories now. The shame of knowing their son…. He caught his breath. Best not to go there.

A shrieking nighthawk diverted his attention, circling high above him. The woman must have heard it, too. She looked upward, shielding one eye like a salute, her gaze drifting toward him. He crouched deep in the thicket. She was real, no faerie hallucination.

Marking a path for the quickest retreat, he checked his bearings. When he heard a door slam shut, he held his breath and listened for footfalls. Nothing but the night wind ruffling through the sage. When he looked up, the porch was empty and yellow light—like the eyes of a demon—poured from two of the nearest cabin windows. He crossed himself, then crept slowly away, a phantom in the night.

He would be back.

Part One

Return of the Native

Chapter One
The Last Raspberries

Wyoming, Present Day

"Damn, another one missing!" The ledge was empty, no sign of pie or tin, not even a telltale stain or trail of crumbs. I scanned the yard and followed the deck around the house, trying to ignore the little voice that trailed after me.

"Dam-dam-dam," my two-year-old repeated in singsong mockery.

At the back door, I scooped him up. "Little scouts don't say damn."

"Dam-dam," he repeated, poking a pudgy finger into my mouth. I kissed him soundly on his forehead and peered into his gorgeous green eyes.

"Oh God, you are such a replica." Retracing our steps back to the front of the house, I settled on the porch glider, cradling the little mimic in my arms. When he plugged his thumb into his own mouth, I knew it was naptime.

It had become a welcome midday routine for both of us, rocking gently on the glider angled for the best panorama of the Wyoming vista I loved: the distant mountains, fields of speargrass and sage dotted by sweet yellow clover and prairie primrose, our driveway leading down to the new bridge over Fish Creek. Closer in, my garden and the old Burr oak that sheltered birds, squirrels, and an occasional deer lured by the dried corn and stale bread I routinely scattered beneath it. The corn tree, Scout called it.

I inhaled deeply, savoring the fading scent of beebalm that lingered around the porch. The fall perennials were already blooming in the garden and among the creeping vines—even at a distance—I could count the global promise of a few large pumpkins amid a tangle of overgrown zucchini.

The garden, like the swing, was my sanctuary. Respite for any niggling troubles that worried my orderly world. Being in the right place at the right time, feeling soothed and safe with my son beside me, this lens of nature was my visual mantra.

Another missing pie was troubling, however. Jake and his girlfriend were coming for dinner and I was now without the dessert especially requested. It wasn't the same, but a frozen cheesecake would have to do—topped by what was left of the garden raspberries I thawed this morning. What worried me more was the fact that some animal large enough to abscond with a whole pie and tin was turning my porch into its personal commissary.

Pies weren't all that had gone missing. A lap robe, mug, utensils, even two of my curing soaps had vanished from the porch in the last few months—all too cumbersome for a thieving magpie or nesting squirrel.

Perhaps a larger animal?

Thinking Jake or Scout had absently wandered off with them, I had wasted time searching the house and yard until I let it go—chucking the mystery into my growing abyss of illogica.

I gently laid my sleeping son on the cushioned bed of our swing and watched the rise and fall of his chest. His fine dark hair curled at the ends, matching lashes feathered against his pudgy cheeks. A cherub's face that would lengthen and grow more faithfully into the visage of his father.

Proof. He was the tangible proof I needed, at least to explain the illogical to myself. Nobody else would understand. Not even Cousin Jake. Raised as my sibling by our beloved grandmother after we were both orphaned as children, Jake was the only man in my life before and after that summer. Nobody knew me as well as Jake knew me, but when I had tried to explain things to him after I returned home, I quickly recognized the look of disbelief that questioned my sanity. I had seen the same look on Mitch's face. Simple logic had become an oxymoron. I had joined the ranks of fictional characters transported in time.

I dropped my head against the high back of the swing. One summer. A mere blip in the course of my life that changed everything I thought I wanted and needed: Independence, emotional freedom, a career that utilized the degrees I had accumulated in college. There had been no room in my life plan for the demands of a husband…or children. I didn't even care about the legacy of our family. Jake could marry, have children, and take responsibility for all that. Men and children—I used to think—were an encumbrance. Not for the professional agenda of Jessica Brewster. Not even an afterthought.

Until that summer.

Four months in a hardscrabble era with a simpler agenda—taught me what it meant to love, really love in a heart-thumping, tear-jerking way that would shred priorities and soften the biting edge of any determined realist. Scout, the gift of that love was sleeping beside me, snoring softly as his father did beside me in 1886 when I woke up on my thirtieth birthday in the log cabin that once stood on this very spot.

Though named Mitchell after his father, Scout became the favored nickname when he began to walk and explore the perimeters of his own little world. It suited him, and reminded me that his father was once a scout for both sides of his people. Mitch was half Sioux, half white—which made his son a quarter Indian. With lighter skin and his father's green eyes, all evidence of his native blood was lost in our mix, however. Not that it mattered either way. Scout was my miracle: the smartest little charmer on earth.

My organic miracle.

I pushed a long dark curl behind his elfin ear and traced the shape of his cheek with my finger. Yes…living proof of my sanity…and all that I might have missed of heart-clutching, prideful mother love. As long as I lived, I would have this piece of his father with me. Tucking the new fleece lap robe around both of us, I closed my eyes and made a mental note of the changes in tonight's menu. Salmon, quiche, white wine…the last of the garden raspberries?

Chapter Two
Whatever Pops Your Cork

"More," Scout demanded, after squishing the last raspberry between his tiny front teeth. Jake was quick to sop up the juice that ran down his chin, staining one of my linen napkins. Meredith's cringe caught my eye before I went for the wipe kept handy for just such purposes, wondering if the cringe was for the napkin or the slobbering child.

Meredith Morgan was put together well. Since she started dating Jake, I had never seen her without makeup or nail polish or clothes that looked boutique-bred. I couldn't imagine her manicured hands ever mopping up any messes, much less changing a diaper.

I laughed as I scrubbed the baby face and sticky hands, noticing raspberry juice had already stiffened the cowlick in his hair and embroidered the neckline of his terry bib. "Half of what goes in the mouth leaks out somewhere…sooner or later."

Meredith's eyebrow quirk unleashed my tongue. "You don't have any nieces or nephews—no babies in your extended family?

"I was an only child," she replied with no remorse in her tone.

I looked at Jake, preoccupied now with making rubber faces at Scout. Though we were never babies together, Jake and I did grow up together, more like brother and sister than cousins. I had so many "messy" stories I could relate about Jake's room, his clothes, his eating habits, but I didn't know Meredith well enough to embarrass Jake. Officially, a couple for less than a year, both were taking things slow, probably because both suffered PTDS—post traumatic divorce stress.

I was fond of Jake's first wife, but the marriage only lasted a year, and Jake never wanted to talk about why it failed. The hurt probably made him cautious…and picky when he resumed the dating game. Meredith was a surprising choice. Opposites attract, though, and I could see that she had rubbed some serious "polish" on Jake's rough exterior. New clothes, new haircut, new aftershave. Jake was visually morphing into the professional he was supposed to be—as Sales Manager for the Sugar Beet Co-op in Torrington.

Jake was with me when Meredith became my realtor—showing me the property I now owned. She also helped me sell Granny Lou's little bungalow in Torrington for a good price in a bad economy. Bright and ambitious, she was a good example of the career women I always admired. The kind of woman I might have been…before messy love child.

Jake plucked Scout out of his highchair. "Time to turn this guy loose," he said as he bounced him on his knee. Baby giggles produced more juicy leaks, and this time we all joined in with a few chuckles.

"The last of our garden raspberries," I said.

Wide-eyed, Jake exaggerated his alarm. "What? No more raspberry pies?"

"Not with garden raspberries."

"Nothing compares to garden-grown, Jess. You've

got me hooked."

"I can agree with that," Meredith said, "Can you part with your tomato quiche recipe? It was delicious with the salmon and dill biscuits."

Jake winked at me. "This girl has finally learned to cook. I used to toss her burnt biscuits into the backyard compost." He chuckled. "Even the squirrels and birds avoided them."

No reluctance there to embarrass me!

I gave him a playful cuff on the head when I rose to clear the table. "More coffee or wine? Coffee's decaf—of course."

A buzzing cell phone commanded all attention. Meredith sighed as she drew her smartphone from her belt holster, like a sharpshooter practiced to the art.

After rinsing plates for the dishwasher, I grabbed another bottle of Moscato and rejoined my company in time to hear the end of a whispered conversation.

"I have to," Meredith said. "This closing's been canceled twice already. Tonight's the best time to get all parties together."

Jake frowned. "Did you know about this today?"

"Of course not. Maybe it won't take long. I can come back…"

"No, I'll just bunk here tonight." Jake glanced at me and held his wine glass up for a refill—"if that's okay with you, Jess."

I nodded. "I have some produce for the Farmer's Market in Torrington. I can drive you home tomorrow."

"I'm so sorry to put you both out like this." Meredith squeezed my hand with a delicate grip, looking mournfully at Jake. "What about your clothes?"

"No problem," I interjected. "Jake still has closet

space in Scout's room." Before Meredith, Jake was around more often than not, helping with Scout. It was Jake who taught my son to drink from a cup, Jake who got down on all fours to play piggyback. Having Jake around never put me out.

I watched them kiss at the door with Scout still in Jake's arms and Meredith's expensive leather tote between them. No space for close contact.

We waited until we heard the car crunch down the gravel driveway before gazing at each other. "That doesn't happen very often," he said, with an apologetic smile. "I mean, she brings work home, but extending the day…"

"You don't need to make excuses to me. I would have done the same thing," I said. "Her commission could be at stake here. Realtors have to bend with client needs."

"You don't like her, do you?"

I flinched. "Not true. She makes you comb your hair and wear matching socks."

He laughed. "Is that all you can recommend?"

"It shouldn't be what I think. If she pops your cork, that's all that matters."

He grunted like a caveman.

"Seriously, you know what makes you happy makes me happy, too. I would never discourage you from loving anyone."

"I do love Meredith, Jess. I just wish you could find someone who 'pops your cork,' too."

"I have my son. And you…on loan now and then, but I do love Scout's favorite uncle."

"Only uncle," he corrected. He set Scout on the floor amid a puddle of toys and crossed the room to give me a close-contact hug. "Jess, you're such a great mother. I only wish you'd find someone to be a father to Scout—and for you—to, to know what it feels like to love a man." Blushing a little, he grabbed the bottle of wine on the table and poured me a glass.

I couldn't tell him that I did know what it was like, that I had run the gamut of love found…and love lost with Scout's father. And brief though it was in another era, maybe the concentration of that summer…like fine perfume…was enough to scent the rest of my life. Jake believed what I told him about conceiving Scout via a sperm donor. To him I had sacrificed much to insure Granny's legacy, yet I was still the little sister he needed to protect.

Looking back, those four months were now the fantasy of dreams, beyond all reason and explanation. Even Jake would have viewed the truth as the ravings of a mad woman brought on by head trauma—not a mysterious teacup. Technically, I had been a thirty-year-old virgin, and determined to remain so, in spite of the family history that encouraged our unique legacy to pass on. I didn't plan to fall in love with anybody, much less with my ancestor's first husband and his nine-year-old daughter.

Tallie, the precocious little charmer who turned every creature into a named pet—all starting with the letter "F". I missed the dimpled smile and can-do attitude of the little girl who was destined to become the mother of dear Granny Lou. My memory was foggy when it came to anything Granny reminisced about her mother. I only knew that Tallie had become a teacher and an activist for women's rights. Probably animal rights, as well.

"To love," Jake said, and we clinked glasses in a toast. Jake threw back the wine like a careless shot of bourbon while I was beginning to feel my two-glass limit kicking in after a long swallow. When I gave the bridge of my nose a two-finger rub, he noticed.

"I'll give the raspberry kid a bath and put him to bed."

"You are such a catch, Jake. You'll make a great father, too."

"I may have to be content with uncle status. Meredith isn't gung-ho on the kid idea."

"Well, screw that," I said, and we both laughed.

He stooped to Scout's level. "Your mommy has a potty mouth," he whispered.

"Reminds me…put him on his potty chair before bedtime." I smiled, clearing the table and balling up the tablecloth. "We're in serious training now. Big boy pull-ups and all that."

While Jake sprawled on the area rug, making car noises and laughing over Scout's mimic, I stuffed the tablecloth and soiled napkins into the washing machine, and began to stack the dishwasher.

"Last piece of cheesecake?" I paused at the refrigerator.

He shook his head. "I was hoping you'd make your dessert specialty tonight."

"I did. It went missing this afternoon." He frowned through my explanation.

"This has happened before, Jess?"

I nodded. "Other things disappeared, too, but I imagine they'll turn up somewhere—probably in a toy box or hidden in some bushes. I may have to add a fenced yard to my handyman list."

"You found a handyman?"

"Not yet, but now that fall is here, I'll look for business cards in hardware stores in Wheatland and Torrington, and ask around at the gift shops that take my soaps. Labor's cheaper in fall and winter. Better prices on lumber, too."

"I could probably take a week off to help turn the carport into a garage."

"You've helped too much already, Jake. Without your loan for this acreage, and even Meredith selling Gran's bungalow, I would not have been able to afford what I have. The bathroom alone nearly broke my budget."

The builder had cringed over my changes, usually to downsize his ambitious plans. No granite counters, no mudroom, no *ensuite* or fancy fireplace. To save money, I gathered rock and stones that sprouted like sage chicks on the Wyoming landscape. With a deadfall oak found in the woods, I had a slab mantel made for the wood fireplace—to resemble the fireplace that once dominated Mitch's little 1886 cabin. To re-create the rustic look, even the stairs leading to the loft above the kitchen were made from half logs, just like the ones that once led to Tallie's bedroom. My floor plan duplicated the same open floor plan of the 1886 cabin, maybe a few hundred square feet larger with the extra bedroom and indoor bathroom.

Small and remote as it was by today's standards, my version of a log cabin was perfect for a starter family—with just enough convenience to save time and work. Living without modern conveniences for four months gave me new appreciation for indoor plumbing with a dishwasher, refrigerator, and stackable washer-dryer. What I didn't skimp on was the solar roof panels and a tiled bathroom with a steam shower, whirlpool tub, and counter with a sink large enough to bathe a toddler. Luxuries. Never to be taken for granted. Even the indoor toilet.

I carried the bottle of wine into my bedroom, stripped to my pajamas, and sank into the feather pillows stacked against the headboard. Amid squeals and splashes, I could hear Jake bantering with Scout in the bathroom.

"Rub a dub-dub, little man in a tub," he sang, and Scout's little voice echoed with mimicry. I picked up the latest Outlander novel on my nightstand and clicked on the reading light. I had to smile. Nothing could ever be taken for granted…especially for a time traveler.

Chapter Three
Hawkers and Stalkers

With Jake's help setting up our stand at the Saturday Farmer's Market, we stayed until closing at noon, selling a good portion of the squash and gourds and soaps I hauled, then headed for Bunny's Café that had once been our favorite for Spanish omelets and great burgers. At the edge of town, with plenty of parking, good coffee, and western home cooking, the café especially drew trucker trade. Bunny and Fred Torres, the proprietors, were another attraction, glad-handing or stopping at tables to chat with familiar customers or welcome new ones. Like their café, they were an institution in Torrington, and their adjacent gift shop—opened recently—attested to their folksy success.

"Land Sakes," Bunny crowed when we slipped into a booth with a booster seat for Scout. "Haven't seen you two since this little one filled an infant seat." She chucked Scout under the chin and was rewarded with a toothy grin.

"Has it been that long?" I smiled, tugging off my son's jacket.

"We heard you raised your prices," Jake teased.

Bunny smacked him on the head with a menu. "Normal inflation. Coffee and Bunny beignets are still four bits apiece. And you know we have the best breakfast menu in town."

Jake looked around. Most of the booths and tables were already filled for the lunch trade. "No price hike would thin you out, Bunny. You have a loyal following any time of day."

I nodded in agreement. "How's the gift shop doing?"

"Not as well, but we just hired a new girl from Casper to perk it up. She comes with some experience—buying and promoting and such."

Jake smoothed his hair. "Maybe you need Jessica's line of natural products?" He didn't miss a beat when I kicked him under the table. "Soaps and such," he continued. "Pure Wyoming ingredients. She has them in spas and gift shops, even at Fort Laramie."

Bunny paused, looking thoughtful while she hailed one of her waitresses over to take our order. "Not a bad idea. Louisa is looking for a local touch. I'll give her a call."

"Louisa?" Jake and I said in unison. Louisa was our late grandmother's name.

"Louisa Johnson, the new hire running the gift shop. Stop in to look around after you eat. I'd love to hear what you think of the new setup…and the new girl in town."

"Keep that up and I may have to put you on commission," I snapped after Bunny moved on to another table.

"Jess, every opportunity…"

"I know. I have to push more. I'm just not the sugar salesman you are."

"Don't sell yourself short. The whole natural soap idea is perfect—for a stay-at-home mom."

"Perfect for now," I agreed. "I would like to ramp up my income and pay you back."

He rolled his eyes. "Tell you what. I'll make the loan a wedding present when you get hitched."

I laughed. "Better not hold your breath on that one, hitched is not for me."

I tore open two cream packets and poured them in my coffee. The diner cup was white with a blue collar. Same color, wrong design. The mysterious china cup that sent me back in time was more delicate: porcelain with a scene of blue trees camouflaging a flock of birds that blended into the design, like the famous Doolittle prints of Paint horses in a rocky landscape.

Suspicious now over all cups with saucers, I had packed off a box of them for Goodwill and began to collect plain coffee mugs with humorous sayings—no designs. But for the rest of my life, I would hesitate to circle my finger around the rim of any cup, a habit Granny Lou had passed on to me. Granny Lou often demonstrated her talent for producing a hum by gliding a finger around the rim of a water glass. I was never able to produce a single decibel with water glasses or cups until Granny died and I found the mysterious blue and white antique cup locked away in an old desk in the basement of her bungalow.

My journey began and ended with Granny's hidden teacup. After learning the cup had little value as an antique, I used it as a prop in a living history skit at Old Fort Laramie where I worked part time. It was supposed to be a temporary position until I could find a teaching post that would put an end to my status as a perennial student at Eastern Wyoming College.

I was still working part time at the Fort, reluctant

now to give up the history I lived firsthand. The soaps I learned to make in 1886 had grown from hobby to business, affording me that stay-at-home luxury on most days. Jake and a friend at work always pitched in when I needed day care for Scout. Even without a mortgage or car payment, thanks to my inheritance and Jake's loan, selling garden produce and scented soaps was barely enough to support myself with groceries and gas.

****

The 'new girl in town' had all the personality I expected from a creative salesperson. Her smile and flashing blue eyes radiated friendly warmth. I left Jake to most of the social amenities while I browsed the shop. It was cozy, but well laid out with inviting fall colors and artistic displays stocked with local jams, homemade fudge, quilted crafts, and hand-painted greeting cards. Souvenir mugs decorated with the Torrington symbol of the ring-necked pheasant were stacked among feathered jewelry, silk scarves, and boiled-wool clutch bags. She was capitalizing on local talent more than cheap souvenirs of the West. A good idea from the perspective of someone who had scented soaps to marry with a display of sandalwood candles!

We left the shop with a consignment contract and two taffy twists, one for Jake and one for Scout. "An explosion of charm," Jake mused as I drove him to his apartment.

"Hers or yours?" I laughed, wondering if I would have been as convincing. Louisa even agreed to take what remained of my soap stock from the Farmer's Market after Jake told her what a magnet they were to tourist and local trade.

"You do have a knack for exaggeration. I may have to hire you."

"For you, I'd work cheap; maybe just a raspberry pie now and then."

"Wassberries!" Scout shouted from his car seat, and we both laughed.

Jake's studio apartment wasn't far from Meredith's realty office, or her own apartment where, I imagined, Jake spent most of his time. Moving in together was probably the next step in their relationship, but I didn't want to pry into logistics. They were both thirty-something adults, both professionally successful and capable of planning personal strategies without my consent or approval.

After dropping Jake off, I stopped at the local hardware store to pick up two business cards from prospective handymen. One of them stood out: No job too small or too large—for reasonable rates—call Beaverwood.

Beaverwood. Amusing name—easy to remember. I pulled into the Conoco station on Main Street for gas and a few groceries at the convenience store. Scout was fast asleep and drooping in his car seat by the time I turned west on Highway 26, heading for home. Midafternoon traffic was sparse enough to chance a cell phone call to Beaverwood.

When a cheery male voice answered with "Chuck here. How can I help you?" I laughed.

"Chuck Beaverwood?"

"Yes ma'am. How can I help you?"

"I'm sorry…your name…"

"Your reaction isn't new." He chuckled. "Makes me unforgettable."

I swallowed my amusement and told him I needed an estimate for a garage I'd like to have up before the snow flies.

"I'm finishing up a cabinet job in Wheatland this week. How about Monday afternoon?"

"Sounds good. I live on Fish Creek Road a few miles south of Guernsey. Just look for a low bridge with a red mailbox on one of the stone pilasters at the entrance. J. Brewster is the name on the box."

I plugged into my iTunes for the rest of the drive home and timed it just right, finishing up with my favorite song as we crossed the little bridge over the creek. "I Will Always Love You" always dampened my eyes.

I blinked away a tear when I saw the empty pie tin on the porch steps. A single Coreopsis was curling in the tin, some of its trumpets looking a little limp. I had planted several of the yellow perennials around the house, knowing they attracted butterflies, bloomed late, and were deer resistant. My hand trembled as I held the flower to my nose. Someone picked this flower…and returned the missing pie tin. No Wyoming animal I knew of had opposable thumbs to accomplish such a feat. I plunked onto the porch swing with Scout still sleeping in my arms, wondering what I should do. Call Jake? Call the sheriff in Guernsey? Load the little pistol Jake had given me on my birthday?

"You need this for protection if you insist on living remote," Jake told me, when he demonstrated how it worked.

Living remote always made me feel safe. With no neighbors closer than a mile, I never even bothered to lock my doors. Oh God, the house! Had someone been in my house? I laid Scout on the swing and grabbed his little orange plastic bat leaning against the house.

Right. Formidable protection—a child's plastic bat. I sidled around the porch deck, peering into the windows for any sign of an intruder before entering through the back door at the kitchen.

Barely breathing, I scanned the room. My half-empty coffee mug bearing the *Life is an Adventure* slogan was still on the counter, Scout's tippy cup in the sink, a dishtowel draped over the back of his highchair, newspapers and magazines stacked on the island. Nothing seemed out of place. I traded the bat for a serrated knife and slipping out of my shoes, I padded into each room, checking for anything out of place, second-guessing why a towel was on the bathroom floor, Scout's teddy bear on a window ledge.

Tiptoeing up the loft steps in my sweat socks, I noticed a fly on the handrail. A fly that turned into a smashed raisin. My eyesight blurred, darting from detail to detail. The silence was eerie, but it sharpened every sense. The tables in the loft held my soap molds, trays, and baskets of dried lavender and herbs. Pungent. Strong. Comforting. I began to relax. How could I even tell if anything in my workroom was out of place? Everything was scattered haphazardly in a craft room only I used.

My gaze drifted to the floor below and I noticed how light from the windows changed everything, brushing shadow into corners, highlighting objects into a still life painting. I sat down on the top step, and breathed deeply. Safe. I was the only animate intruder here. I closed my eyes and listened for my heart to return to normal. When I heard the mewling cry, my heart began to race again. Scout. It was rare for him to cry about anything. I raced down the steps with the knife handle tight in my fist.

He had rolled off the swing and the short drop to the porch deck woke him. I gathered him into a cuddle, both of us relaxing into the rhythm of the swing. But even while I hummed, my mind was racing, searching for probable explanations that weren't there. I scanned the landscape I knew as well as the interior of my home. The sun was descending over the mountains in a fiery glow and the woods were already deep in shadow. I shivered. Was someone watching me even now? I decided to call Jake.

Chapter Four
Plinking Makes Perfect

Jake stayed the rest of the weekend, and two minds hammering out every possible scenario for the reappearing pie tin forged no advance to logic.

"You say this has happened before? Why didn't you tell me all this before last night?"

"I figured it was just an animal. I've been leaving bread and food scraps out for the deer and squirrels. They—or even a stray dog could have carried off a fresh pie cooling on the porch."

He frowned. "But they wouldn't return it with a flower."

"Not if they didn't like the pie."

"This isn't funny, Jess. I think we should call in the authorities. I went to school with the sheriff from Wheatland. Clyde Lewis might have some ideas."

"Right. Yellow tape the crime scene. Put another pie out for bait…maybe post a guard."

He shook his head and rolled his eyes. "I thought you sounded frightened when you called me."

"I was…I am. But I don't want to blow this out of proportion. I've met Larry, and he has his plate full with domestic abuse, drug running, even missing people. He'd get a belly laugh over the case of the missing pie."

"My God, Jess, someone could be stalking you."

He waved both arms, encompassing the world from our porch. "Even watching us now."

I laughed, more from his dramatics than any implausible truth. "Stalking me? Because I may be a threat to Betty Crocker…or creative soap makers everywhere? Right."

"Stalkers never have good reasons for their obsessions, and you are still an attractive woman."

I laughed even harder. "Well, if it makes you feel better, I could throw out my makeup, lock my doors and cool my pies in the house from now on." I shrugged when he groaned. "I thought as long as you're here, you could also refresh me with some pistol practice."

"Great idea. Maybe I'll leave my slug gun here, too."

"Right. Can't have enough arsenal for a pie pincher."

He rolled his eyes at me again and mouthed a silent expletive.

****

My aim definitely needed improvement. Even after Jake showed me the stance, grip, and how to sight my target, it took five rounds before the revolver grazed the empty wine bottle just six yards away. Jake stood behind me, calling out encouragement each time I flinched with the recoil. My hand was sweating, and my trigger finger was beginning to hurt. When I suggested the gun was probably too big for my hand, Jake told me a heavy trigger was typical of any revolver, whatever the size. "It's a safety feature. The .38 double action is a great snubby to start with. It also has an internal safety and lock. More kid-safe for Scout. Less likely to go off by accident."

I remembered Mitch gave me a smaller gun to use in wolf territory closer to the mountains in 1886. I pretended to know how to use it, but luckily, it wasn't necessary.

"Aren't there smaller guns than this?

"Mouse guns." Jake snorted. "Like a derringer. It might not deter a 200-pound stalker."

He loaded a cartridge into his shotgun and handed it to me. "You'll find a shotgun or rifle has a lighter trigger."

I took aim and smashed what was left of the bottle. He was right about the trigger, though the recoil thumped my shoulder. "How do you know all this?"

He smiled. "While you collected college degrees for fun, I went plinking with boys like Clyde Lewis."

"Plinking?"

"Target shooting at inanimate objects is a big sport for Wyoming boys, especially those practicing for game seasons."

Come to think of it, there weren't many Wyoming boys who didn't own a truck without a mounted gun rack, or an NRA sticker pasted on the windshield corner.

"It wouldn't hurt for you to get some formal practice, Jess. Earn your own AFA sticker."

When I gave him a fish eye, he added, "Armed Females of America. That might put off a stalker who doesn't know about fierce redheads with college degrees."

I pointed the shotgun at him. "That sounds very sexist, Mr. Earp."

His face blanched when he pushed away the barrel. "The number one rule is to treat all guns as always loaded. This isn't the OK Corral, Jess."

"But this gun is unloaded now."

"Lucky for me." He sighed deeply. "Enough for today." After packing both guns in their cases, we headed back to the house. "Let's hope all this noise didn't wake Scout from his nap."

"Scout is a deep sleeper…just like his…" I caught myself before adding "mother."

Chapter Five
The Wood Man

Beaverwood and Sons was the name on the green pickup truck that inched up the driveway Monday morning. A middle-aged man in coke bottle glasses climbed out of the cab and looked around as if he was unsure of the address. I heard him yell "stay" before he slammed the cab door. The passenger he addressed was not a son, unless his son had long blonde hair and a cold black nose. I rose from the porch swing with Scout on my hip and held out my hand.

"Chuck, I presume?"

When he smiled and nodded, I couldn't help noticing the gap in his front teeth. Thank God, no beaver teeth. He shook my hand, looking around rather distractedly.

"You've come to the right place. I'm Jessica—the 'J' on the mailbox at the bridge. This is my son, Scout."

"You live out here all alone, then?"

I hesitated, thinking maybe I shouldn't be so quick to acknowledge that fact. "Well, I was the one who called you about an estimate for a garage." It always amused me in this enlightened age to find that some men still expected a woman with a child to be somebody's wife—as if I was the appetizer to the main course—or the secretary to the man in charge. If I was being stalked, I would at least need the illusion of protection. A gun could go just so far, but even I had to admit that a Wyoming man holding a gun might suggest more protection. Especially for a novice like me who was more threatened than threat—with a gun in hand.

I directed him to the car port and explained what I wanted, asking if it was possible to have a narrow hen house incorporated into the rear of the garage with access to the backyard. "There's nothing like fresh eggs for breakfast."

He seconded that opinion, telling me he had several hens of his own. "You may need a rooster if you want to insure your stock. Roosters not only breed; a smart one will look after the hens and warn you if a fox or wolf is near."

"Good to know. They can be noisy, though." I remembered how Frank, Tallie's rooster, became a living alarm clock, announcing the dawn of every new day in my 1886 summer. It was a jarring wake-up call—one you couldn't turn off with the touch of a button.

Chuck pulled a small notebook out of his back pocket and scribbled off an estimate, then handed me the paper. When I sucked in my breath, he told me it could be less if I wanted to start immediately. "I have some low grade lumber from my last two jobs that I can discount if you want it. Good enough for hen roosts."

No formal contract, but the man seemed honest and Mitch once told me Wyoming deals on the frontier were often made with a spit and a handshake. I swallowed the spit. "For ten percent less and maybe a couple of your hens, you've got a job," I said.

He glared at me over the rim of his glasses and

pursed his lips. When he looked upward, I knew he was mentally calculating. Was I was asking for too much?

He finally sighed. “Lady, you drive a hard bargain,” he said as he gripped my hand with a firm squeeze. I wondered if such easy capitulation meant he was short of work or just wanted to get started before the weather changed. October was never too early for a snowfall, especially when living near the mountains.

He told me he would have his sons haul up the lumber tomorrow. “We’d have to get a concrete base and some footings poured soon. If we can squeeze another week of Indian summer out of this fall, we’ll be set to start construction next week.”

“That would be perfect. The weatherman predicts an early winter this year.”

Before he left, he introduced me to his dog, a Golden Retriever named Sadie. Scout wanted to pet her and when he latched onto a handful of fur, Sadie washed his face with her long pink tongue.

We laughed when Scout squealed with delight. “Puppy kiss,” he cried.

The deal was sanctified, after all, with a little spit.

Chapter Six
Motherless Boys

The weather cooperated. I had a concrete slab by week's end, and a pile of lumber stacked beside it. Mr. Beaverwood's sons reminded me of young versions of Laurel and Hardy. Caleb, the leaner one, looked barely out of high school, but he had a shifty look about him, piercing dark eyes and long hair. Tommy, the portly one, was a jolly version of his father, more intent with teasing his younger brother, or the dog, than actually working.

Scout was fascinated with the dog and vice versa. Or maybe the dog was just happy to get away from the Beaverwood boys. When she retrieved the ball Scout threw—all of three yards—my son giggled as if it was the funniest thing imaginable. When his attention waned, the dog followed him, as if eager for any new adventure the toddler could deliver: picking wildflowers, collecting acorns, or lining small blocks of scrap wood along the porch. When Scout took his afternoon nap indoors, Sadie sprawled on the porch, head resting on her front paws, with a sleepy eye on the door.

I offered water or coffee to the men throughout the day, but the fresh-baked chocolate chip cookies were a singular hit early in the week. Beaverwood "Hardy" wolfed down three cookies to every one "Laurel" nibbled. At least Laurel shared his cookie with the dog.

"Your boys are very different," I said to their father one brisk day as I joined them on the porch to slug down a mug of coffee at noon. He was peeling a tangerine with fingers still stained from his work. The smell was intoxicating, but I declined when he offered me a section.

He wiped the juice from his mouth with the back of his hand and looked at me. "There's no guarantee same genes give same results with kids. You'll find that out if you have a second child."

I wondered if he lowered his tone out of disappointment. *I'll never know that comparison,* I almost muttered out loud. "Does your wife share that opinion?"

He hunched over his cup and smiled sadly. "She saw the best in both of them before she died." He peered up at me over his thick glasses. "Cancer."

"I'm so sorry. How long have you been a widower?"

"Coming up three years now. It was hard on the boys. If they turn out well, it will be a testament to their mother." He sighed. "I don't have her touch."

"Every child is a gift, someone once told me. We all parent with good intentions."

His thick fingers tapped lightly on his cup. "I work with numbers, missus. Good intentions double with two parents."

I thought of my family. Jake and I were both orphans raised by Granny Lou. If I looked backward, not many children among my ancestors had the two-parent gift for most of their lives. There weren't many parents, either, who had more than one child. Jake and I were only children. Mitch's daughter, Tallie, was also raised as an only child. The thought gave me a frisson of anxiety. *Will I do a good job as a single parent?*

Mitch was a wonderful father to Tallie, but he never knew his own father. On our last emotional night together, he told me how he learned of his white father's identity in a letter containing a hundred dollars. Guilty compensation from a man already in his grave. Mitch was raised by his Indian mother and grandfather. He talked about having a son our last night together. We both knew I was pregnant, and the Birdwoman had predicted a boy. Mitch's vow became mine when he told me then that if he ever had a son, he would see that the child never measured his worth by what one hundred dollars could buy.

One hundred dollars in the nineteenth century bought Mitch a horse and a pair of good leather boots. In today's market, you might get a pair of Gym shoes and a Breyer model horse for that amount…or maybe a load of inferior lumber to build a hen roost?

Raising a child without a father was daunting, but that trail had been blazed for centuries and I knew I could do it. If I needed help, there was always Jake. I drained my coffee and turned to Chuck Beaverwood when I noticed the wind picking up. We made a little small talk about the weather before he buckled on his tool belt and noticed his hammer was missing. We both made a cursory search before he shrugged and suggested maybe one of the boys had it. I inspected his progress with sufficient praise and asked about the garage door on order.

"It should be here by the weekend," he said. "Installation is easy enough for the boys to do it alone, but we all may need to pitch in."

He then said something strange that made me wonder. "I take it you found some use for the leftover lumber."

"What lumber?"

"Last night the boys stacked the boards left from the hen house on your porch—for you to use for firewood or fencing."

"I didn't see any extra boards this morning."

He scratched his head. "A box of nails went missing last…" He stopped when he saw my jaw drop. "You know what happened to them?"

I closed my mouth and shrugged, hoping he didn't notice the flush that must have stained my face. For some reason, I didn't want to tell him about the other missing items or the pie tin with the flower. Perhaps his boys were merely playing tricks on their dad?

Chapter Seven
Footprints in the Snow

As promised, with the garage finished, two speckled hens were installed in their new insulated roost that spanned the back width of the garage. Jake helped me install a doggie door, and together we wrapped chicken wire around the posts that were drilled into the ground from the extended roof of the garage. The chicken suite was complete: Fresh air and no fear from predators.

The garage door arrived a week later, along with our first snowfall. While the Beaverwood men installed the door, I sat on the swing watching Scout and Sadie frolic in the new snow. Scout wore the secondhand red rubber boots I picked up at a garage sale in town, along with a new purple snowsuit that made him look like a Teletubby. With a red wool hat and scarf wrapped around his neck, his giggles were muffled as he threw the ball, then lumbered after the bounding dog.

October was never too early for snow near the mountains, but I was still unprepared for it frosting the last of the garden squash and pumpkins. Jake and I had already carved three of the largest Halloween pumpkins, with Scout “helping” to clean the pulp and seed from each one with his chubby little hands. I boiled the seeds, then spread them on a cookie sheet to salt and bake for an hour while we played a counting game with smaller garden gourds that looked like miniature pumpkins. Halloween with Granny Lou's pumpkin seed recipe would be a tradition I intended to pass on to Scout. Jake and I grew up with so many "normal" traditions; it was hard to wrap my head around her teacup legacy.

I pulled on my parka and boots and followed little footprints to the garden where I filled my pockets after plucking a few squash and late onions from their dusting of snow. Elsewhere, the snow was wind-whipped, less than a few inches deep, smelling fresh and clean, brightening the landscape and amplifying all sound. I could hear Scout calling the dog, but I couldn't see them or judge their distance. A hazy sun meant more snow was coming our way.

The Beaverwoods hailed me to the garage to demonstrate how the new opener worked. After oiling the metal runners, the door sprung up and glided almost soundlessly overhead. We all laughed when the two hens seemed to cackle approval along with the final rumble.

I congratulated them on getting the job done by the first snowfall, and they eagerly accepted my invitation to come inside for cookies and coffee while I cut their check. When it began to snow again, I asked Tommy to help me round up Scout and Sadie. He let out a two-fingered whistle that rose to a shrill echo that must have been heard clear to the mountains. Silence followed. "They can't be far," Chuck assured me as he joined us. "Good thing about snow. You can always track the footprints."

Caleb threw him a look when he gave him orders, but followed his brother into the woods. Chuck and I scattered in opposite directions, picking up footprints that careened around the house in dizzy loops that bisected several track lines. Several minutes later one of the boys shouted when he found something and we converged in the woods about three hundred yards south of the house. We found Sadie's paw prints, followed by Scout's rubber-ridged boot prints, but there were older signs noticed when we spread out. Sled runners? And between them, a set of larger footprints.

After I caught my breath, I raced back to the house for my new gun.

Chapter Eight
The Bear Trap

Snow amplified every sound. The hammering he had heard for two weeks sounded more like gunshots than the *tap tap tap* of woodpeckers. He used his fur mittens to muffle his own hammering in the tree, though it was unlikely that anyone would hear…or ascribe the sound to his new tool this deep in the woods. Still, the years had taught him to be cautious.

It was the tallest oak he could find, near a bend in the creek just beginning to frost over. Remnants of an abandoned eagle nest already bridged a trio of sturdy branches, perfect for his own "eyrie."

Gouged out footholds in the trunk and several crosspieces of wood made access easy. The lumber would provide a sturdy platform; perhaps even for sides that would keep him from rolling off if he slept here. The wood was already weatherworn, gray as tree bark, he noticed, as each board was hauled up the massive trunk with the rope pulley he devised. Draped and padded with thick riverweed and pine boughs, it would almost look like an eyrie from the ground. It was not a substitute for the cave, but it was closer to the sun…offering fresh air and light, and from such a height he could see miles in every direction, even without the scope on his rifle.

Bracing himself between the cross-branches last

week, he had already observed ribbons of river and uniform roadways snaking through the flatland, winding around hills and into the mountains—track for the funny little horseless traps running on black wheels. From height and distance they looked like water bugs swimming a channel. She had one of them. A red one—with doors on the side and strange lights on both ends. She ran it fast and made it growl up the hill and disappear into the new shed beside the cabin. He could even see the roof of her cabin, with rows of odd glassy rectangles sticking on it and a wisp of smoke curling from the chimney more often now since the weather changed. After more trees shed the last of their wind-dried leaves, he knew he'd have a better view of her dooryard.

He pulled the bearskin poncho around him when the wind suddenly changed direction and a few snowflakes drifted into his eyelashes. He would have to put up some kind of a roof if he meant the lookout to service him through the winter. The creek below was a dark mirror, starting to frost at the edges. In another week or so, it might be solid ice. Early winter this year.

It took a while to register the new sound when the hammering stopped. He had memorized birdcalls and the language of wildlife prey and predators in their quest for survival. Was it a wolf in distress? More like a barking dog. A dog? He scanned the ground for movement, and the scope settled on a yellow dog about three hundred feet away at the edge of the creek. It was barking at something caught in floating debris on an open ridge of water. Then he saw the elfin figure in red and purple approach the dog, pat it on the back, point to the object in the water. A ball? The dog stepped gingerly into the creek, cracking the rim of frost at water's edge. The ball was drifting out of reach, inching slowly downstream. Whining, the dog hesitated, pawing the glassy surface, churning up a splash of water, then darted after the ball. Showing no such wariness, the child followed, wambling along the bank until his red boots grew heavy with mud, dragging him to a tipsy stop.

Reacting instantly, he shinnied down the tree, skinning his bare hands and breaking branches too thin to hold, hitting the ground with a jarring thud. He lumbered to his feet and called out to the child, and the sound of his own voice, spoken aloud was deep and foreign. More voices, a scream, and searing pain stabbed his head before the ground slammed into him and the force of his breath in the cold air shrouded him like smoke from a pipe.

He was caught.

Chapter Nine
"Don't You Dare Die!"

I screamed as the heavy revolver exploded in my hand and fell to the ground. The bear moving toward Scout dropped, and I raced to scoop up my son before he toppled into the cold black stream. Looking startled, he managed a weak cry before I smothered him into my chest and both our cries were muffled in his thick scarf. The dog shoved something wet against my leg and began to bark, running from me to the Beaverwoods, now cautiously circling the bear. The boys were armed with pieces of thick deadwood and Chuck picked up my smoking gun, cocked the trigger and ordered his sons to stand back. He aimed the gun at the animal to finish him off, then suddenly dropped his arm and knelt beside the still lump of fur. Tommy grasped the growling dog by its collar, and in the sudden silence, I could hear a collective gasp. Someone uttered "Jeesus" like an invocation.

Still cradling my son, exhausted by fear, I ventured closer and could see at once that it was no bear I shot. A man in a bearskin poncho lay on his side. Chuck rolled him over and pulled off the man's hood. A mass of dark matted hair covered the part of his face that wasn't blooming with blood, pooling into his left ear, running down his cheek and into his thick beard.

"Is he, is he dead?" I whispered.

Chuck took off his glove and wiped the man's neck with it, then fumbled for a pulse. We all started when the man groaned and his eyes fluttered open.

Green! His eyes were green, the rarest of all eye color. The fear in them more than the color registered with me as he searched our faces. When his eyes collided with mine, his jaw twitched and his beard moved. A flash of memories washed over me, and my heart began to thump wildly in my chest. I set Scout down when my knees began to buckle, and I thought I was going to be sick. My legs were crumpling beneath me as I threw out my arms to catch myself from falling onto the body. One of my hands slid into blood dripping in the snow and the touch prickled my bare fingers.

So red against the white snow. His eyes, so…green. Every shade in a spectrum of emotion raced through my memory; joy, frustration, anger…love. I knew only one man who owned eyes like those. He had come back to me.

Fear jolted into purposeful clarity. I took a deep breath and unwrapped Scout's scarf to sop up the blood on Mitch's neck. He groaned again and closed his eyes. "Mitch, look at me. It's Jessica. I didn't mean to shoot…look at me." I sobbed, unable to complete the order to myself, maybe to him. *Don't you dare die!*

I felt Chuck's broad hand on my shoulder. "You know this man?"

I could only nod, imploring him with my eyes. "We have to save him."

The boys dumped a few boards off a makeshift travois they found below a big oak tree and with a rope, they managed to secure Mitch to the stretcher. Caleb carried Scout while Tommy and Chuck hoisted each end of the travois. I stumbled alongside, trying to press Scout's scarf against the blood still dripping from his neck. Only our footfalls broke the silence of urgency as we raced through the woods, snapping branches and trying not to slip in the snow. I prayed all the way back to the cabin, a stream of every Catholic litany I remembered whether they applied or not.

The occasional snowflakes we felt in the woods were heavy as hail when we made the clearing. Mitch was still alive when we loaded him into the pickup bed, but his breath was shallow and the scarf I pressed against his neck and ear was stiff with blood. He looked like a Neanderthal, his hair wild and grimy with thick brows peppered with snow. I cradled his head and leaned over him, trying to shelter his face from the heavy flakes that spread over us like a veil of lace. The bearskin he wore smelled rank and feral as the animal it came from.

Tommy drove my Wrangler while Caleb and I took turns doing CPR when his breath grew shallow. Chuck drove the pickup, sharing the cab with Scout and the dog. Scout's nose was pressed against the window that separated us and when he waved to me, I formed a steely smile of reassurance I couldn't feel beyond my lips. A voice in my head told me I had killed his father…the only man I ever loved.

Because Chuck cell-phoned ahead, a trauma team was ready to take over when we arrived at the Wheatland hospital. I watched helplessly as they transferred him to a gurney on the ramp and wheeled him down a corridor to the right, shouting medical orders that sounded like a foreign language. Someone pulled me back when we reached the ER and the gurney disappeared through swinging doors.

I had an unsettling feeling that my perimeter of life was about to change, once again.

Chapter Ten
An Accidental Husband

Two and a half hours later, the doors opened again and a doctor wearing a dark blue hospital shirt, jeans and cowboy boots approached us. The Beaverwoods graciously stayed with me in the small ER waiting room, entertaining Scout at a child-sized table with coloring books and Winnie the Pooh stories. The room was equipped with a sink, TV, water and coffee dispensers. I set my Styrofoam cup down and rose to face the news, holding my breath.

The doctor pulled off his little scrub hat, revealing a gray crew cut, and introduced himself as Dr. Hawley. "Are you the wife?"

The wife? Did I tell the nurse who filled out a report that I was the wife? I nodded dumbly. Whatever I must have said mattered less than what I needed to hear. I watched his lips, willing them to move with the right message.

"He's going to be all right."

I collapsed into one of the blue vinyl chairs in the waiting room and permitted a deep sigh of relief. The doctor perched on the chair beside me and put a hand on my arm. "The bullet clipped off his ear lobe and grazed his jaw. We cleaned out all the shrapnel we could find, even some in his temple. An inch to the left and he might have lost an eye…or worse. If the damage had been more invasive, we would have had to air lift him to Cheyenne or Denver."

"Alive. He's alive, then?" I repeated.

"You got him here in time." He squeezed my arm. "He's a lucky man. But he's lost a lot of blood. We stitched him up and he's on an IV drip and monitor. How old is your husband?"

Husband. Did he say husband? Lost on the word, I forced some mental calculations. One hundred and seventy? Oh Lord, he was 43 that summer. "Mid-forties," I heard myself say.

"Well, his heart is strong, but he's badly dehydrated and still unconscious. He may have lost hearing in the damaged ear, but we won't know that until he wakes up. He also has abrasions on his hands and x-rays show a broken rib and signs of older breaks. What does he do for a living?"

"I need to be there when he wakes up," I said, rubbing my forehead. "Wood," I added. "He chops wood…trains horses."

Dr. Hawley patted my hand. "Are you okay? Can the nurse get you something? We have a wide lounge chair in his room if you want to wait there. It's meant for overnight family if you care to sleep over." He scanned my outfit, taking in the dried bloodstains on my jeans and jacket, and the muddy boots I had tried to shove under my chair. "We can get you a sterile robe to wear, and a pillow and blanket, of course."

I nodded slowly, and summoned up a weak smile.

Scout sidled onto my lap with an open bag of Cheetos Tommy bought him from a vending machine, and stuck an orange thumb into his mouth as he eyed the doctor. "My son," I said. "I'll have to call his uncle to come for him."

"That would be best." He patted Scout gingerly on the head. "Children this age can be frightened by the machines, and the look of the patient. We had to shave your husband before we cleaned and sutured the wounds. Is your husband a hunter?"

The question startled me until I remembered the bearskin coat. I nodded again. Was this all a dream? The doctor's voice was deep and wary, muffling into my consciousness. I stared at his mouth.

"Well, his clothes are bagged for you to take home." The mouth widened. "He's been sponged off and gowned in our dress code now. When he's out of post op, we'll wheel him to his room." He glanced at the wall clock. "Maybe another hour, but with any head wound, he could remain comatose for days."

I closed my mouth and took a deep breath, following his gaze to the clock. His hand was warm and soft when we shook hands, and I heard myself thanking him. *A healing hand?* His blue eyes studied me with sympathy.

Another dose of coffee cleared my head and braced me for calling Jake. When I told him where I was, he grilled me with questions. After assuring him that Scout and I were fine, I told him I would explain everything when he got here.

With profuse gratitude, I managed to dismiss the Beaverwoods with little explanation about Mitch beyond the doctor's decree that he was going to live. I told them I would be staying here overnight, but they could collect their check from Jake in the morning. Chuck assured me there was no hurry, but leaned close to murmur something about the gun still in his truck.

Murmuring back, I told him to put it in the glove compartment of my Wrangler. He blinked and when the furrow deepened between his eyes, I knew he wanted to say something…or maybe hear something more. I didn't know how to respond, and hoped a hug would translate my thanks better than any explanation I could fabricate. I hugged the boys as well, thanking each of them for their part in the drama and especially for taking care of Scout, who was now decorating the wooden arms of his chair with orange fingerprints.

Jake arrived forty minutes later, bursting through the hospital doors like his shoes were on fire. Covered with my stained parka, Scout had already fallen asleep in the blue settee that matched the waiting room chairs. Jake took one look at the stains and his face blanched. "You said you were all right."

"We are. That's not our blood." I took a long gulp from my third cup of coffee. "We need to talk." I hustled him across the room to another small settee. Thankfully, the room was ours alone.

He brushed aside my offer of coffee, looking grim. "What the hell is going on?"

I took his hands in both of mine and drew energy from their warmth, without looking at his face. How could I explain Mitch with any sort of logic? If I told him the truth, especially in this setting, he could have me committed to the psych ward, if such a small hospital even had one. I had to measure my words, call upon the lying finesse I thought I left back in 1886. "Remember when I told you I was pregnant?"

"Yess, a few weeks after you were released from hospice care after totaling your red Honda. You showed me the pregnancy test you took that fall and explained you had been inseminated to insure Granny's legacy."

I wrinkled my nose. "Well, that was a little twist of the truth. Scout's father was not a nameless test tube. He was real flesh and blood…and…and I was in love with him." I dared to look squarely at Jake, watching him gauge the information with a kaleidoscope of twitches.

"He's here," I said. "I shot him with the revolver you gave me."

"What?" His mouth dropped open.

"It was an accident…I thought he was a bear. It was snowing in the woods, and I thought a bear was going after Scout."

"What?" He repeated more loudly. Dropping my hands, he stiffened against the back of the settee and stared at me, his eyes large with incredulity.

"The gun just exploded in my hand—thank God I am such a poor shot," I rattled on. "The Beaverwoods brought us all here in their pickup and Mitch was saved."

Brows furrowed, he gripped the wooden arms of his chair for support, searching my face with laser precision. "Mitch?"

I turned from his scrutiny, watching my own knuckles turn red as I mirrored his grip on my own chair. "Scout's father. He's recovering in the ICU, but he's in a coma and I have to be here when he wakes."

Jake stared at me slack jawed and wide-eyed. When he was able to speak, he reiterated what I told him in a monotone of disbelief. "You accidentally shot Scout's father, thinking he was a bear in the woods?"

I nodded slowly. "I know it sounds crazy, but that's the truth. He was wearing a bearskin coat."

A staccato puff of laughter escaped Jake's pinched mouth. He eyed me as if I had just told him the worst joke in the world. "If this is some colossal prank, it's not funny, Jess. You shoot a man in a bearskin thinking he was a threat, only to discover he's your long lost lover?"

"I'm not joking," I mumbled, clasping my hands on my lap.

"All right, then where the hell was this man all these years?"

I glanced quickly at Scout, still sleeping peacefully across the room and pulled in a deep breath. *How do I double the shock to admit all those years added up to lifetimes of separation.*"Far away," I mumbled.

"Did he know you were pregnant?"

I nodded. "We, we had to separate. He was…he was married." Married to our mutual ancestor, Jessamine, had to be left out of my story. The truth was stranger than any fiction Jake would be able to comprehend.

"My God, Jess. Why didn't you tell me all this before? Is the man still married?"

I could safely tell the truth about that. I shook my head, knowing Jessamine had died more than six decades ago. Small detail that Mitch must have disappeared even before the turn of the twentieth century, and Jessamine had remarried my own great great grandfather, then outlived him to marry once again. Who in their right mind would believe all this?

"I guess I was ashamed," I muttered. "I never planned to marry or have children, but when Granny died, and I learned her legacy was specific to me, to the female line in our family, I felt the burden.

"Enough to lay with a married man?"

It was a gut punch, coming from Jake. "You make that sound so…so depraved."

He shook his head sadly. "Just so unlike you."

My eyes began to well. "I loved him. Can anyone help who they love? And look at the result. I can't think of life without the son he gave me." We both glanced at Scout, still sleeping across the room. Without looking at him, I could hear Jake breathe a deep sigh. For a long time we sat in silence, numb and lost in thought. With my forefinger, I swiped at a wayward tear running down my cheek.

"Can you…will you, take Scout home and stay with him tomorrow," I finally whispered. "I want to be here when…when he wakes…if he wakes."

Jake heaved another sigh tantamount to a balloon deflating. "Of course, I will." He covered my hands with one of his. "Jess, this is all so…so incredible."

If you only knew.

"How can I be sure these aren't the wild ramblings of someone who suffered a traumatic head injury? The accident. Your car was wrapped around a tree. You were pulled from the wreckage barely alive…in a coma for months."

I slumped in my chair. I owed him the whole truth. "What if that…that wasn't me, Jake. What if it was someone who only looked like me and we switched places in time? What if it was Jessamine, our great-great-grandmother?" I moved from my chair to kneel before him, pleading. "You have to believe me. You saw her pictures. You said she looked like my clone. I was at a living reenactment at Fort Laramie…a tea party. Then, suddenly I was living the history we portrayed. I became Jessamine in the flesh, and she, she somehow became me. She was the one in the coma, not me."

He threw his head back and made a strangling sound, then drilled me with a long stare that erupted into grudging laughter. "If what you're saying is even possible…you know you don't have to lie, Jess…you know I'd always have your back."

I looked up at him through a veil of tears, thinking yes, yes I should have lied. Slipping back in time may yet slip me into a warehouse for the insane, even with his support. Time travel was science fiction. A niggling little thought blossomed in my mind: As science fiction today as airplanes and computers were in 1886? Wasn't it Steven Hawking who even alluded to time travel as a possibility?

When I began to cry softly, he took my shoulders and rested his chin on my head. "Oh Jess," he whispered, closing his arms around me.

Chapter Eleven
Proof of Life

Green arcs danced on the heart monitor. Steady beeps. Blood pressure also steady at 130 over 70. The IV drip was equally mesmerizing, plinking crystal drops into the tube that was connected to his arm. Like the doctor said, it would have been frightening to Scout. It was frightening to me, knowing the beeps and blips of a machine they called a Dinamap was proof of life for a man that should have been dead a century ago.

I barely recognized the man I once knew so intimately. His hair and face were shaved and his head and neck were swathed in bandages. His scraped hands, like open claws, were spotted with iodine leaking through gauze wraps. I suspected the bulk under his hospital gown meant that his ribs were also wrapped. But even with the bandages, I could tell that he was much thinner than I remembered. His right eye looked hollow, the left one covered by another bandage slanted over his ear. How could one pistol shot do all this damage? I closed my eyes and could feel new tears collect in my lashes. I had caused this.

I reached out to touch his arm. *Cold.* Was that a good thing? Mitch was always warm to the touch. Didn't the body lose heat when it was shutting down? "Hang on," I whispered, bending over him. "Come back to me."

****

A nurse named Jennifer came in periodically to check his vitals and replace the drip bag. Thankfully, she ignored me as I pretended to sleep in the lounge chair by the window. It had stopped snowing, and the room was dark except for the Dinamap lights and dim bars of light filtering through the blinds from the parking lot lights.

I had questions, but I didn't want to talk, didn't want to hear anything that would crack my fragile glass of hope. I just wanted to be here, alone with my memories and prayers and the man that changed my life forever. The man who could give me the answers I most needed to hear. If he lived, would we have a future together? Or like the blip on the monitor, would this just be another cruel blip in time and circumstance that would wrench us apart once again?

A blue and white teacup had brought us together once before. I had it in my hands that last morning, watching the 1886 sunrise from the porch. I remember how stiff and unwilling my finger felt as I traced the rim of the cup. The next thing I remembered was waking up in a small room like this…without the cup. I was the patient in a bed and Jake was dozing in a chair beside me. I wasn't bandaged or connected to a monitor or drip, but I did have a splitting headache and my heart was racing. Had it all been a dream?

I remembered the living history role I played in the Burt House parlor at Old Fort Laramie. It was a tea party, and my costume reflected the last military era at the famous post. I forgot to change my shoes that morning, but my long vintage dress hid the purple Crocs on my feet. I remembered how stunned the tea ladies were when they noticed them. Annoyed by their reaction, I fled the house still holding Granny's teacup and noticed the changes outside: Picket fences, a boardwalk, new buildings that had materialized in an hour. A young boy thrumming a stick along the picket fence gave me the year when I dug my fingers into his shoulder. "Eighteen eighty six," he had stammered.

Everything went black when I crumpled, hitting my head against something hard, dropping the vessel that caused my time slip. *How did Mitch travel forward? Had he found another portal to the future? Did he abandon Jessamine and Tallie to come back to me? Was he the pie thief?* So many questions hung in the balance of life. Green arcs and blips eating time, bridging centuries. Questions only the body on the hospital bed could answer.

****

"Mrs. Mitchell." Someone woke me the next morning, invading my dreams with a gentle voice and a hand on my shoulder. "Would you like some coffee?"

I came to with a start, and my heart sank when I focused at once on the empty bed and the monitor gone blank.

"He's been moved," the nurse quickly said. "His vitals were steadily improving and he was mumbling…sure signs the coma was ending. The doctor thought he had improved enough to be transferred to a double room. You must have been exhausted to sleep through it all."

I breathed a sigh of relief and rubbed the cramp in the back of my neck, annoyed with myself for sleeping at all. "Take me to him," I said, rising to stretch.

Following her down the corridor to room 2220, I

hoped he hadn't awakened just yet. I had to be the first face he saw. A familiar face. I presumed he had never been in a hospital before, unless he had been in the one at Old Fort Laramie. He might be frightened, unaware even that he was living in my era. Ranting on about his century might convince the doctor his brain was truly injured. *Irreparable?*

He was sleeping when I tiptoed into his new room. Even in the thin light of morning, I could see improvement colored his face. He looked peaceful. The gray ash of death was gone, as well as the crease between his eyes. His face was thinner, paler than I remembered. With his vibrant green eyes closed and his long dark hair shaved, he might have been a stranger to me.

I pulled up a chair to sit beside the bed and touched his hand. *Warm.* When his long fingers moved ever so slightly, I picked up his hand and balanced the weight of it against my own. Solid bone, rough flesh, scraped knuckles, daubed with iodine. His nails were thick and squared, two of them hiding a bruise. It was the hand of a laborer…a farmer, used to the elements. A hand that once caressed me. I could smell iodine and lanolin when I held it to my lips. Someone had washed his hands, cleaned and trimmed the nails. I flipped it over and ran my forefinger along his rough lifeline, as I once did that summer. Was it as long then? *As unbroken?*

The solid feel of his flesh and bone was more proof of life than the beeps and blips of the Dinamap. My own heart was struggling, racing ahead of the beating metronome. "You are alive," I whispered, planting a kiss below his thumb. "You've come back to me."

Chapter Twelve
Truth and Consequences

"Practice," he rasped.

I leaned over him, fumbling for his hand. "What? What did you say?" The beeping Dinamap echoed through the room, spiking changes on the screen. I rang for the nurse, then bent over him, touching his forehead with the back of my hand. Warm. *Too warm?* His visible eye was still closed, but I could see a tiny flutter working under his lid and when I squeezed his hand, I thought I saw a faint smile cross his lips.

A nurse came running into the room and immediately checked the monitors and drip before taking a pulse reading. "He's waking," she said, smiling at me. "Shouldn't be long now." She cranked the bed until his head and shoulders were elevated a little more. "I'll notify the doctor."

When she left, I leaned over him, taking his hand again, and bringing it to my lips. I coaxed another faint smile from him. "Come back to me," I whispered, before I turned to grab a tissue from the nightstand.

"Liv."

I heard the word loud and clear this time, and when I turned back, I could see one green eye flutter open to stare at me. The green, so unforgettable to me, looked dull and confused.

"Liv," he repeated hoarsely.

The tightness in my chest deflated like a balloon. "That's right," I smiled, "you're going to live. You've come back."

"Back?" His gaze roved, circling my face, then the room, and the monitor began to beep more frequently.

I knew he had never been in a hospital like this, with beds that cranked and monitors that beeped. Even at the turn of the last century, hospitals would have been rare on the frontier. Strange surroundings to a man whose life just skipped over a hundred years.

"You're in a hospital," I said, squeezing his hand. "Welcome to my era, Mitch."

I moved aside when Dr. Hawley and Nurse Jennifer charged into the room and after a cursory check of the machines, timing his pulse, and taking his temperature, the doctor gave orders to the nurse, who then left. "Welcome back," he finally said to his patient, who looked more confused than ever. "We're going to have a look at the stitches. You have a slight fever and I want to make sure infection hasn't set in."

So much for bedside manner. When the bandages were cut away, I stifled a gasp. The lobe of his left ear was missing, with a line of angry stitches radiating from it like a vine curling from his shaved skull into his jawline and neck. His left eye was badly bruised and swollen. One misguided bullet did all that?

Dr. Hawley announced more to himself than his patient or me that the stitches looked good, but a course of stronger antibiotics would help. He asked Mitch to track his finger as he moved it from side to side and up and down just inches from his face. After flashing a small light into his eyes, he turned to me. "Probable concussion, as well. Did he hit his head when he fell?"

"I didn't notice," I said, regretting it at once when I told him I thought he was a bear.

"A bear?" It was the doctor's turn to look confused.

"His coat. You bagged the coat he was wearing."

"You shot your husband thinking he was a bear?"

"I didn't mean to. I thought I was protecting my son. The gun just went off in my hand."

The doctor stared at me his little flashlight suspended in the air.

"We were…in the woods. The bear was running toward my son." I stopped when I could see incredulity flood his face."

Still staring at me, he clicked off the light and pocketed it. "I see," he said. "You put all this in the hospital report?"

I shook my head. "Hardly had time, even if there was enough space on the paper."

"I'll have to report this to the sheriff, you know."

"This was a freakin' accident," I said a little too sharply.

"Of course, but gunshot wounds have to be reported. Hospital routine."

When the nurse rejoined us with a new IV drip bag, Dr. Hawley gave her a few whispered instructions, then left abruptly.

Oh Damn. My mouth is just as feral now as it was in Mitch's era. How am I going to explain all this to the sheriff?

****

I had another day to refine my story. Sheriff Lewis was either less skeptical with my explanation or had a lot of practice filtering expression out of his face. Mitch was improving by the hour. Two days out of surgery and he was off the monitors, sitting up in bed, drinking from a straw and even showing an appetite for the hospital food he was offered. He wasn't talking much, but then I thought maybe his wounds may have interfered with his speech. The tone of his voice when he did speak was not as deep as the one I remembered, but then, every trauma has lingering effects.

The concussion also affected his memory. When we were alone, I asked him how he got here and his green eyes glazed with bewilderment. His gaze followed me everywhere, drifting away only when I responded with a reassuring smile.

I thought the irony almost humorous. Under similar circumstances, we had met when I hit my head on a fence post after slipping back into his era. I had to fake the severity of my concussion almost from the start, blaming it on my loss of memory until I could exchange places with his real wife and find a way back to my own time…or give up the truth about who I really was. *Same scenario, different player?*

There was no reason for him to fake a memory loss, however. Unless…unless it was an accident that brought him back…or he regretted the decision that led him here. The only time I sensed his true understanding was when I warned him about the Sheriff coming and told him we had to keep our stories straight. Obviously, we couldn't say anything about his origin or my own time slip.

I also had to bring Jake into our collusion, in case the Sheriff—who used to go "plinking" with Jake—would want to question him. It was Jake who had given me the gun, helped me register it, and taught me to use it.

Sheriff Lewis remembered me right off. “You’re Jake’s little sister, aren’t you?” He pulled off his Stetson and combed his fingers through a shock of brown hair graying over his ears. “My deputy normally takes care of stuff like this, but this is his day off.”

I didn’t remember ever meeting Lewis before, and told him so after a rather limp handshake.

“That unforgettable, eh?” His gray eyes crinkled with amusement. He turned to Mitch. “I once had a crush on your wife, but she never noticed. Her nose was always buried in a book.”

One green eye darted from me to the sheriff and back again. My mouth went dry. I poured water from the bedside carafe into a glass and gulped half of it down.

The sheriff cleared his throat, and straightened his shoulders. “I just need a few statements from you, Mr. Mitchell.” Lewis took a small pad and pencil out of his pocket. “Can you tell me what happened?”

I jumped in before Mitch could answer. “He has a concussion. We’re working on the memory…and some speech loss.”

“Well, that’s kinda inconvenient for all of us, then. I was hoping to get statements from both of you. I wouldn’t want to tag this as a domestic violence shooting.”

I laughed without mirth. “Nothing like that. It was just a silly accident. Some animal was stealing my pies and Jake gave me the revolver to defend myself if it came to that.”

“What kind of gun?” Lewis gaped at me and the corner of his mouth twitched slightly as he cocked his head. "What kind of gun did Jake recommend for pie pinchers?"

"Jake called it a snubby, I think. A 38 double action."

"Good little piece to start with. Jake knows his guns."

"It seemed to misfire in my hand."

"The weapon is registered, I assume?"

"Oh yes, I have it in my car…uh, glove compartment if you need to check it out."

"To be sure." He stared at his notepad, then looked at Mitch, sitting ramrod stiff and close-mouthed, with an odd expression on his face. "This report says she clipped your ear."

Mitch shrugged, with a tight smile pasted on his face.

"Seems a lot of damage for a single shot." He snapped a finger against the notebook. "Possible hearing loss in addition to voice and memory. Sounds like you missed a dirt nap by so much." He spread his thumb and forefinger apart an inch or two. He definitely had a lot of practice filtering expression.

The lump in my throat was swelling by the second. I helped myself to the rest of Mitch's glass of water. "It was just a terrible accident. I thought he was a bear going to attack my son…our son."

Mitch looked at me sharply, rapidly blinking his eye, then slowly reached for my hand.

Lewis watched us impassively, then scratched his head. "I'd hardly mistake this man for a bear."

"He was wearing his bearskin coat and hat," I said.

"Well, that sure clears it up. Did your son think his Daddy was a bear, too?"

"He's a toddler. He was about to fall into the creek after the dog."

His left eyebrow arched. "So, there's a dog in the story, too?"

"Not our dog. She belongs to the Beaverwoods—who just built our garage. My son followed the dog into the woods while the garage door was being installed. When we couldn't find them, we followed their prints in the snow and that's when I saw the bear moving toward my boy.

"And where was your husband supposed to be when all this was happening?"

"He was, uh, deer hunting in the woods." Mitch blinked again several times.

"Deer hunting in a bearskin coat and hat?"

We both nodded in unison, holding hands in a united front.

"So when you saw your husband in his bearskin coat and hat, you naturally assumed it was a bear?"

"It was snowing," I said, raising my voice in exasperation. "One of the Beaverwood boys yelled 'bear,' and I panicked, thinking my son was in danger."

"Oh, the Beaverwood crew was with you then?" He scribbled something in his notebook.

"Yes, I told you we all were concerned. Missing dog and child, footsteps in the snow, wouldn't you…"

"Pack a double action revolver?" He smiled ruefully. "Good thing it was snowing and you were such a poor shot, Mrs. Mitchell."

I could feel Mitch's hand flinch in mine. To an honest man, a man with seventeen stitches in his head, memory loss and possible hearing damage in a frightening new century, this had to be unreal. I felt a fresh tear glide down my cheek and brushed it away. The dream of having him here...alive...was suddenly eclipsed by the twisted nightmare it had become. And I was totally responsible. I turned away to blot the new tears welling in my eyes.

The Sheriff who once had a crush on me must have noticed. He pulled his hat on while I poured another glass of water. Mitch sank back on his pillow and closed his unbandaged eye.

"Perhaps we should take a look at your gun, Mrs. Mitchell," he said in a softer tone. I've seen a few defective shells or gun chambers that cause excessive damage." He paused, then rubbed a finger under his nose. "And I do find it hard to believe Jake's little sister would marry a man she wanted to kill." He smiled when he added, "especially in front of so many witnesses."

When Mitch began to cough, I offered him the glass of water I had been drinking. He drained the glass and handed it back to me. I set it on the nightstand and bent to kiss him lightly on the cheek before Clyde Lewis ushered me out to the parking lot.

I was surprised to find the Wrangler was unlocked. More than surprised when I sat in the passenger seat to open the glove compartment. *There was no gun in it.*

Chapter Thirteen
Homecoming Surprises

Wearing a pair of Jake's jeans, a flannel shirt and a worried expression, Mitch sat stiffly in the passenger seat while I leaned across him to demonstrate how to buckle the seat belt.

"Why?" he whispered.

"For your own safety. Your poor head might crack like an eggshell if you hit the windshield." His bandages had been reduced to a neck brace and a patch on his ear and temple, covered mostly by a knitted ski hat. I pulled down the visor to show him the mirror. "Take a look."

He fingered his black eye turning yellow at the edges.

"That will probably take another week to fade out," I said.

He grunted.

I was getting used to his grunts and one word responses and hoped we could improve on that away from the hospital and heading home. We had a lot to discuss.

He braced his long legs and clutched the armrest when I accelerated once we were out of city limits. "Horsepower." I smiled. "Cars can even compete with a gallop." At 7 in the morning on the gravel two-lane that was sparsely traveled—even for Wyoming—I demonstrated.

"Whoa," he yelled, bracing his left arm in an Atlas pose on the interior roof.

Laughing, I eased off the gas and braked, then shifted into park at the roadside. He glared at the gearshift, then at me with a look of terror. "There's no way to walk into this century with ease," I explained. "You're going to have to swallow a lot of, er, improvements. Cars, trucks planes, cycles, have replaced horses for transportation. We have gas power, electricity…phones." I plucked my cell phone out of the dashboard holder and pulled up Jake's number with a couple taps, showing Mitch the lit up screen that was ringing the number. When Jake answered, I could hear Mitch suck in a quick breath. "On our way home," I reported into the phone. "How's Scout doing?"

"Better," Jake replied. "But he still asks for his mommy when I can't distract him."

Four days apart. "I miss him, too," I said with a little hitch in my voice. "We've never been separated this long."

"The sheriff was here yesterday."

My turn to suck in a breath. "What did you tell him?"

"We talked mostly about the gun, verifying it was a gift, registered at purchase, and that I couldn't imagine what happened to it. He was going to talk to the Beaverwoods about it." Jake paused a few seconds. "He did ask about your husband. You left that part out, Jess. You didn't tell me you married the man."

I quickly dialed down the volume and stepped outside the car. "What did you tell Lewis about that?"

"I imagine he noticed my surprise. When in God's

name did you manage to marry the man? Didn't you say he was already married?"

"I didn't marry him, but I said he was my husband when we got to the hospital. I was upset and worried, and I suppose maybe in the back of my mind, maybe I thought they wouldn't let me see him again unless I was next of kin."

"Jesus, Jess!"

"So, what did you tell him?"

"I told him you surprised us all by eloping. He wrote something down in his notebook. Probably what a great liar I had become."

"Jake, I'm so sorry about dragging you into all this. I don't know what to say."

"Well, the whole truth would be a great start. Lewis isn't going to let all this go, I'm certain of that."

The truth. I had started down that path with Jake, but he didn't know…everything. I still wasn't certain he could ever believe me. "Jake, you have to trust me. I know this is all so incredible…"

"Incredible is an understatement, Jess. I just hope you know what you're doing."

An alarming noise rose from the pit of my stomach. Loud enough that Jake must have heard. When I noticed the Wrangler's back window was rolled down an inch or two, I also hoped Mitch didn't hear any part of the conversation. "I have to go, Jake." For a moment, I sagged against the car, praying for a little guidance to set my direction. *What was I going to do?*

Mitch flinched when I took my seat and replaced the phone in the dashboard sling. I reached over to pat him on the leg. It was a familiar reaction from him since he woke in the hospital. The reaction of a man with memory loss, caught in a strange new world, a victim—almost killed by a woman he didn't remember once loving in his world. I could commiserate on some level. I had experienced similar anxiety in his world, just without threats to my life.

When he looked at me with troubled green eyes, I understood.

"I, I know how hard this is for you. Dr. Hawley said your memory will likely come back. You don't remember me now, but we…you and I…we were once…close."

He blinked, softening his eyes.

"I swear to you, I didn't mean you any harm. The gunshot was an accident. Your life will always be safe with me."

For a moment we locked eyes, each of us holding our breath. He hesitated, then moved his hand to cover mine and my throat tightened. "Best…" he rasped. "Best I drive then."

When the tease registered, I chuckled. It was the first glimpse of the teasing humor I remembered so well. And his longest sentence so far. I drove with caution the rest of the way, avoiding the ruts in the gravel road that seemed to jar the agitation in my stomach. Mitch was about to meet Jake. We were all victims of a delicate drama that couldn't unfold fast enough in any shift of gear or time. I thought of a Bible verse about time and a season for every purpose, and said a little prayer. Maybe everything will work out, in God's timing. Not mine. I needed patience more than I needed answers right now. Patience and a good stiff drink.

****

Jake met us on the porch, grimly assessing Mitch when I introduced them. They shook hands briefly, both turning to me for direction after an awkward silence.

I cleared my throat. “Well, maybe this calls for some refreshment.”

Jake headed for the liquor cabinet. I headed for the refrigerator. Mitch stood by the door, maybe looking for an easy escape route. I set a few bottles of beer on the island counter. Jake added an opened bottle of whiskey.

“Where’s Scout?” I whispered, taking three glasses out of the cupboard.

“Still sleeping.” He whispered back. “He was up late, working on a new tooth, I think.”

When I gestured to Mitch, he slowly approached us, both hands in his pockets, looking like a chastened schoolboy battered from a schoolyard fight. “Well gentlemen, what’s your poison?” My voice pierced the charged atmosphere. We all went for the whiskey…ignoring any kind of toast.

“Nice clothes,” Jake commented after another sweeping glance at Mitch.

“Yours?” Mitch patted the plaid flannel hunting shirt.

“Thank you, Jake,” I rushed to add. “They fit…in a pinch.” The truth was obvious to all of us. The jeans were loose at the waist and short in the leg and the baggy shirtsleeves stopped an inch or two from Mitch’s wrists. He had certainly lost a lot of weight since his ordeal. The loafers, at least, appeared to fit. Now that I had learned the joy of cooking, I would make it my mission to beef up the muscular body I remembered.

Whiskey in the morning churned up a smattering of

small talk, mostly between Jake and me once we settled onto the sofa. Mitch watched us from his perch on an island stool and shrugged or nodded with few words, as usual. His brooding gaze fell on me more often, and Jake was quick to notice. He abruptly finished his second round and looking at his watch, declared he had to leave. I silently rejoiced, hoping Jake had decided Mitch was no threat to me.

I walked Jake to the porch, thanking him for staying with Scout and when we hugged tightly, he murmured in my ear. "Take care, Jess. Call me instantly if…"

I hushed him with a kiss on his cheek and whispered back. "Mitch is a good man. Nothing will happen that I can't handle. Trust me."

He sighed and gave me a look. "I'd feel more secure if I knew you still had that gun."

I laughed. "With my aim? You want to trust that?"

He kissed me on the forehead. "I've always trusted your heart. Don't make me regret that, Jess. Any other man would have you committed."

I watched him drive away, hugging myself against the chill morning air. The snow had melted days ago, leaving a rock-mottled brown carpet of dying grasses and blown leaves swirling around the giant burr oak. Only the junipers brightened the landscape with any color. The air was sharp and crisp, mingling with the scent of whiskey when I gulped—and expelled—a deep breath. I was alone with the man of my dreams, happy, yet anxious for what the future might hold.

Mitch was examining a pillar candle on the fireplace mantel when I stepped back inside. I told him I had the fireplace modeled after the 1886 fireplace in his cabin. "In fact, the whole house is laid out like your cabin—on a larger scale, of course, with a couple rooms and more porch."

He gave me a blank look.

"You don't remember the cabin?"

He shook his head, sadly.

"It's only been a few days. A concussion can steal memory, but Dr. Hawley says time and rest should bring it all back."

He nodded curtly, with a twist at the corner of his mouth.

I felt like a salesman, showing off the kitchen appliances that would be new to him. He touched the inside wall of the refrigerator and smiled when he felt how cold it was. The gas stove and oven was probably more familiar, stainless steel now replacing a black iron shell. The dishwasher, clothes washer, and dryer required more explanation that led to a demonstration of electric plug-ins and the fuse box, switches and lighting.

"No candles?" he said in his raspy voice.

I showed him the kitchen drawer that held matches and my supply of votive and pillar candles with a couple of tapers and candleholders used for special dinners. He breathed deeply when I held the scented candles up to his nose. "There'll always be candles," I assured him. "Practical now for aroma…and romance." Like an owl, he blinked both eyes when I winked at him and for a moment, I wondered if he was trying to imitate me and forgot how to wink with one eye.

Chuckling, I lit a votive in a glass container, took his hand and led him to the bathroom. "This may be the biggest change of all for you." I set the candle on the corner edge of the tub, and turned on the faucet. His eyes grew wide when I demonstrated how the water jets worked. “No more bathing tubs set before the fireplace,” I explained. “The water is piped in from the well outside. For the shower, as well.”

He jumped a little when I turned on the shower in its glass enclosure. “There’s a steamer switch as well, virtually turning this into a sauna.” The commode was probably the most impressive highlight for him. He understood the concept at once and smiled broadly when I flushed a bit of toilet paper out of sight. “No more wooden thrones or outhouse snakes to intrude!” When he furrowed his brows, I added, “Freddie. Remember Tallie’s pet snake Freddie in the outhouse?”

Blank response.

“Well, maybe that’s funny only in retrospect? Indoor plumbing like this was just beginning to debut in your time.”

When I led him to my bedroom, I felt the atmosphere charge more awkwardly when we gazed at the bed. Mattresses had certainly improved with time, and closets now replaced pegs on the wall. I slid my closet doors open and cast a Vanna White gesture encompassing the poles and hangers draped with clothing. His eyebrows inched upward. Probably more wardrobe than he could imagine for a whole family!

I saved the closed room on the far side of the bathroom for the end of the tour. Quietly opening the door, I saw at once that Jake had made a cursory effort to make his bed. Holding my finger to my lips, I led Mitch to the far end of the crib. Scout was still asleep, sprawled on his back in his favorite green dragon PJs, vigorously sucking his thumb. He had kicked off his covers, as usual, and one arm was hooked around his favorite stuffed dog with the floppy gold ears. Scout spotted the dog at a garage sale and instantly called it Sadie, after the Beaverwood dog. An aura of dark curls swirled around his head. I could see movement beneath his eyelids and when they fluttered open, he focused his green eyes on me at once, blinking away the sleep.

"Mama." He smiled, and the room brightened at once. I picked him up and kissed him on the forehead.

"Mama's back, darling. I missed you!"

He stuck a wet finger in my mouth. "Mama home," he said.

I rocked him close for a few seconds, then turned to face Mitch, adjusting Scout on my hip. With a hitch in my voice, I said, "Meet your son."

"My son?" Mitch blanched and his mouth fell open. I compared the resemblance, mostly in the color of their rounded eyes and the shape of their mouths. Both of them wore the same expression, somewhere between surprise and fear.

Scout studied the black-eyed face, still crowned in a brown knit hat, the white edge of a bandage peeking below his left ear with a kite tail of stitches descending into his neck brace, then buried his face in my chest.

I closed my arms around him, savoring his scent and the brush of baby-fine hair against my chin, and when I was able to speak, I whispered in his ear. "Say hello to your daddy."

Chapter Fourteen
Building Family

It was a rare day in late autumn that the wind carried no reminder of the coming season. The sun was brighter than usual, and I thought it a good omen as I watched them from Scout's bedroom window. Mitch's brown knit hat was askew from the clutches of Scout riding piggyback on their circuit around the old burr oak. Even without an open window, I could hear Scout squeal as they galloped around the tree and my heart skipped a beat to the music of their laughter. Father and son were bonding. A happy tear trickled down my cheek. If everything was not exactly right, things were at least heading in the right direction.

Mitch had made up the bed he slept in—the same bed that Jake always used when he shared the room with Scout. Jake's robe and pajamas were still on the chair where I laid them last night. I smiled to myself, remembering how Mitch always preferred to sleep naked, and how uncomfortable that made me feel—perched on the far edge of the bed we once shared—knowing I was not the wife he thought I was. It had been a tricky business, distracting him with excuses to protect my virtue. *My* concussion and supposed memory loss worked—until he caught me bathing in the creek that hot summer day in 1886.

He owned the same excuse in my time, without a

reason for trickery. Truly, he didn't remember "us." If I didn't sense it by his shorthand speech and the confusion in his expressive green eyes, I could tell by his introduction to Scout last night.

Deer in the headlights surprise.

Obviously, he didn't remember our last conversation in 1886 was about the child I carried. The last night we spent together in his time, I was probably two months along. When I returned to my own time in the same condition, Mitch had no way of knowing for sure that his child would be born…or even that it would be a son as the gypsy had predicted. *Surprise warranted.*

There was so much to talk about. Three years…and several lifelines to condense. Slipping back in time gave me an advantage. I knew what the future held. Traveling forward, whether dream or nightmare, had to be a surreal shock to anyone. *Shock warranted.*

Take it slow, Jessica. I could almost hear the cautionary voice of Granny Lou—warning me to fight the impatience I always felt with any new task, a child's homework problem, or even re-producing the sound she made when circling a finger around the rim of a teacup. The sound that had changed my life forever.

I could tell Mitch was distracted at supper last night. Meatballs and tater tots were Scout's favorite finger foods, with a dip of mayo and catsup. It was always messy, but I thought maybe it could become a point of reference. Did the father pass any culinary tastes to the son?

He laughed.

It was the first time I saw his mouth open wide enough to show any teeth. Mitch laughed at Scout shoving the food into his mouth until his little chipmunk cheeks could hold no more.

I gave Scout a quelling look and apologized to Mitch. "His manners need improvement, you can see, but you can't fault his gusto when he likes something."

"I noticed." He patted Scout on the head and popped another tater tot into his own mouth.

Mitch's teeth were not as white as I remembered, and the corner of an incisor was chipped. He would be surprised at the new advances made since 1886 for cleaning teeth and refreshing breath. White teeth were the cornerstone of civilization, I told him then, leading to a more intimate tease about yellow teeth and potty mouths. I made a mental note to demonstrate the electric toothbrush in the bathroom.

Mitch actually did attack his food with the same gusto as his son, both asking for more before I brought out the tin of chocolate chip cookies I always had on hand. Perhaps the cookies would spark a memory. Broken bits of a candy bar had replaced the chocolate chips that were not yet invented for my 1886 version of the famous cookie. I continued to bake the older version.

I watched intently as he took a cookie and following Scout's lead, nibbled a bite. "Do these cookies bring back a memory?"

A slow smile followed his blank look. He examined the cookie more closely, then shoved half of it in his mouth. "These would be hard to forget," he mumbled. I took it as a compliment and refilled glasses of milk as the cookies began to disappear. Milk, I explained, came from the grocery store via local dairy barns full of cows.

“Not as thick,” he said.

While I cleaned up the kitchen and loaded the dishwasher, Mitch entertained Scout on the living room floor. My heart tripped again when I paused to watch the two of them playing with building blocks. We were building a family.

Mitch stood in the bathroom doorway watching me bathe Scout in the tub, handing me a towel when I finished. With some success, Scout used his potty chair before I sealed him in his overnight pull-ups and PJs. Our bedtime routine always ended with a read from one of his favorite storybooks. Clean and dry, with the lingering scent of baby powder enveloping us both, and the click of the rocker on the wood floor, it was a peaceful drift for my son and the daily reminder for me of the miracle I held. I brushed my lips over his baby soft cheek before laying him gently in his crib.

At the bathroom sink, Mitch was dry brushing his teeth with one of Scout’s ninja turtle toothbrushes. “I think you’re old enough to use a big boy toothbrush.” I smiled, showing him how to apply a fresh head to the electric toothbrush in the drawer, and demonstrating how to use it with paste, then rinse and gargle with mouthwash. “Some improvement, eh?” I could tell by his wide-eyed nod that he was impressed.

I handed him a clean bath towel and washrag. “You can take a bath like Scout, or use the shower if you prefer.” He nodded again with some enthusiasm. Before leaving, I showed him how to lock the bathroom door at the knob. In the hall, I heard the lock click and unclick several times behind me.

After an hour listening to the shower, then water filling the tub, I washed my face at the kitchen sink and retired to my own room for the night, locking my door. Sharing a modern bathroom with someone used to outhouses and creek bathing would be a new experience—for both of us. Sharing a bedroom as we did before…well, that might be pushing the envelope.

Take it slow, Jessica.

But did I have the luxury of time? I knew Sheriff Lewis wasn't through with his investigation. I could tell that he didn't believe me when I told him I probably left the gun in the Beaverwood truck when we raced to the hospital. He somberly promised to check it out.

There was no shortage of panic or confusion during that race to the emergency room. The weapon was not the focus while Mitch hovered between life and death. It could have been in the truck or still at the creek where I used it. I thought it was in the truck. I remember telling Chuck Beaverwood to put it in my Wrangler's glove compartment before he left the hospital that night. Strange, not hearing from any of the Beaverwoods since then. I made another mental note to call Chuck tomorrow. For some reason, Sheriff Lewis must have thought the gun was important. Maybe it was just one of those gender fetishes: Men and guns?

Chapter Fifteen
The Greatest Debt of All

After showing Mitch my "Soap Studio" in the loft the following day, and boxing up all the soaps that were cured and ready to sell, I decided it would be a good time to head back to Wheatland. The few places that sold my soaps were running out, and I thought any profit collected would be well spent for clothing that fit Mitch better than Jake's hand-me-downs. Mitch was all for the idea, until he saw how much a pair of jeans cost at the Country Emporium.

His eyes bugged out when he read the price tag. Mine bugged out when I saw the way the jeans fit him. The weight loss was evident at his waist, but the tight fit emphasized his long legs and dishy butt. When he protested the cost, I explained they were from the sale rack, and I had plastic money.

"Plastic money?" He gave me a fish eye.

I fanned open my wallet to tap the credit card next to my driver's license. "Plastic money. We don't need paper and coin." I decided to leave out the part about a bill coming at the end of the month until I could explain the concept without a clerk rolling her eyes at us. With only a little more protest, he allowed me to add another pair of off-brand black jeans, a couple tees, a pale green long sleeve shirt, socks and underwear, a new fall jacket, cowboy hat and some boots at half price. Even with most of the stuff marked down from last season, the total came to over $250. I grabbed the receipt before he could read it and shoved it into my pocketbook. I would have to ask for more hours at the Fort Laramie Visitor Center this month.

We stopped for lunch at Burger Boy where Mitch was also introduced to the concept of fast food burgers and fries, chicken nuggets, and a strawberry shake I shared with Scout. I hoped maybe he would remember the homemade fries I served in his time, but I saw no evidence of that when he followed Scout's lead by dipping them in the little cup of catsup with equal enthusiasm.

"You like?"

With a grin, he gave me a thumbs-up gesture as old as ancient Rome.

Our final stop was to a Maverik station for gas, milk, and a few groceries, before heading home. Mitch followed me out of the car to watch intently as I used the spigot to pump gas into the tank.

"That moves the car?" he asked, tracing the hose from spigot to the meter that calculated the sale. I let him handle the spigot to feel the gas flow through the line, and watched his eyes grow wide in wonder.

Once out of the city, I pulled over and asked if he wanted to drive. His face lit up again, reminding me of a teenager about to take the wheel for the first time. After adjusting the seat to his longer legs and a quick review of the pedals and shift, we moved forward with a minimum of chugging at a cautious 20 mph and a little editing from the car seat behind us.

"Faster," Scout yelled.

We both laughed, and with a nod from me, Mitch

doubled our speed the rest of the way home and braked in the garage with a jolting stop. I praised him for not hitting the chicken coop.

A broad smile creased his face as he tugged on the brim of his new hat.

Later that night, he insisted on reading Scout's bedtime story while I showered and changed into my blue velour caftan that doubled as a robe. My hair was still damp when I used the hair dryer and brushed it into a manageable shape loosely hooked behind my ears.

The night was cold enough to light a few logs in the fireplace, and I opened a bottle of wine and grabbed two glasses, pouring one for myself before I sat to read the Wednesday paper we picked up in Wheatland. He eventually joined me, standing at the fireplace, looking appreciatively at the small blaze I managed to produce. "He's asleep already."

"I've always counted my blessings for that. I've heard from other mothers that bedtime can be a hassle with toddlers. Scout is an easy child."

He turned to nod in agreement and I thought he was going to add something when I heard him clear his throat. His voice was low, still scratchy from his wounds. "A beautiful child."

"What did you say?

He studied me for a long moment. "I wish I could fall into sleep as easily."

Our gazes met and after an awkward silence, I asked him if he wanted a glass of wine. "It helps, you know—to nod off."

He shook his head and turned his back with one hand on the mantel, gazing into the fire. "Why are you doing this?"

"Doing what?"

"Taking me in…feeding me…" He smoothed the front of his shirt. "Fine clothes."

I swirled the wine in my glass, measuring a response. "Well, an apology for nearly killing my son's father didn't seem quite enough." I sipped my wine and gave him a weak smile. "But you must know."

"I, I don't remember you…" I could hear the frustration in his voice.

I felt a little bruised. Was what we had *that forgettable?* "Dr. Hawley said the memory loss was probably temporary."

"What if he's wrong?"

I shrugged, trying desperately to remain dispassionate. "Maybe it's a clean slate for you. Like Scout, you live in the present, until we figure out…what lies in the future."

I realized it was easier for me going back to his time. Living simple was hard work but not a hard adjustment. At times, I found it amusing, knowing telephones and autos were not science fiction in 1886, but part of the future I already knew. In my time, he had to play catch-up, learning *everything* was new.

My greatest source of anxiety then, and probably now, was Jessamine—the great-great-grandmother I resembled. The love of Mitch's life. They shared a past, had a daughter. For one summer, Jessamine and I were exchange students. I filled her shoes…and fell in love with her husband. I had faked my memory loss only to pull off the charade until I could find a portal back to my own time. When Mitch finally understood I was not Jessamine, he was conflicted. On our last night together, he had asked me if I knew of any man who loved two women at the same time.

He loved both of us.

Was I selfish enough to think that might keep him here, in my time? How did he get here? Would he want to go back? Was Jessamine waiting for him? So many questions.

He turned to face me, warming his back against the fire. “How am I to repay you?”

“You already did. Scout,” I whispered, with a break in my own voice.

He hung his head, muttering so low I strained to hear. “Greatest debt of all.”

The blaze crackled, sending a tiny spasm into my arm. I savored the sweet draw of Riesling sliding down my throat, while I considered a response. “Well…when your memory comes back.”

He looked at me sharply. “And if that never happens?”

I poured him a glass of wine from the bottle on the lamp table and swept across the room to hand it to him. “You once suggested we make new memories. Maybe we can toast to that.” In the firelight, I could see new hair sprouting at the edge of the knit hat he still wore, even indoors. A dark five o’clock shadow was already detracting from the bandage on his ear. We clinked glasses and sipped our wine in silence.

He clutched his glass, frowning thoughtfully. “I don’t deserve…”

“We’ll figure something out,” I said with more confidence than I was feeling. “I know this is all strange and new. Do you remember anything at all?”

For a moment, when our eyes met again I thought I saw a light flicker in his liquid green eyes, then realized it must have come from the firelight. I understood his duck-out-of-water feeling. I had been there. “I know,” I said softly.

He took my glass and carefully set both of our glasses on the mantel, then reached for my hands and squeezed them gently. “I’m in your hands, Jessica. May I call you that?”

“Of course.” I squeezed his hands back. “Everything else considered, we aren’t strangers, you know.”

Without taking his eyes from me, he lifted one of my hands and pressed his mouth against it. “You are a good woman.”

I met his gaze and trying to control the tremor in my voice, I answered. “And you are a good man.”

Even in the glow of firelight, his face darkened. He dropped my hands and bowed slightly before saying good night as he backed toward the room he shared with Scout. I watched him slowly open the door, hesitate, then close it quietly behind him. It had been the longest, most intimate conversation we shared since he crossed the timeline. I drained what was left in both glasses of wine before rinsing them off in the kitchen sink, corked the bottle, and picked up the paper before retiring to my own room.

Something was off. Could a concussion and memory loss account for all the changes? Alter a man’s voice, the way he spoke and gestured? Was I detecting a trace of an accent? It had only been a few years since we parted, but I could see that Mitch was…different. I left the door unlocked and fell into bed, hoping the wine would lull me into sweet dreams, memories of the man I left behind in 1886. I wondered if I had a place in his dreams…if somewhere deep in his subconscious, there were memories of me waiting to surface.

Part Two

Meirliún Manor, Ireland

Chapter Sixteen
The Duel, 1880

"*Buíochas le Dia!* What are ye thinking?"

Lewy shrugged Robbie's hand from his shoulder. "I'm thinking we can clear the fields of rooks or wood pigeons before they cop the seed crops."

"With these?" Robbie pointed to the brace of Rigby pistols in the wooden box. "Where did you get them?"

"Ye dinna need to know." Lewy picked up one of the pistols and polished the long barrel against his shirtsleeve, then pretended to sight a target on the stone fence in the distance.

"They belong to The O'Brien, don't they?" Robbie balled his fists, knowing the answer already. He never beheld such a fine pair of percussion weapons anywhere. Set in a sheepskin-lined box with tamp rods and balls, the fishtail handles were typical of John Rigby weapons. He once found a Rigby advertisement in a paper folded in a book on arms in the manor house library. Rigby's of Dublin had been in business for over a century, producing rifles and pistols valued worldwide. Only a man of means would be able to own one, much less a pair.

"You copped these from Meirliún, didn't you?"

"Borrowed them—for the afternoon. From the groundskeeper."

"Will Turner gave you leave, then?"

"Probably would have."

Robbie flat-palmed his forehead. "Have ye gone mental? These aren't his to lend. They likely never left the box."

Lewy waggled his eyebrows and showed a toothy grin. "Aye, Robbie, ours to break in. Time we had a little fun after years of tending the little shite."

Robbie swiveled around, searching the landscape for Olivia. "She'll tell her da."

"Nay, we're free of her for a few days. Me da drove her and The O'Brien to the railway station. They're off to Dublin to check out a finishing school. We may be free of the tagalong before long, I'm thinkin'."

"Yer not thinkin' at all, ye fecking eejit. If The O'Brien finds out you took his brace…"

"What's he going to do? Have us whipped? Stop us from guarding his precious *rua*? No loss to us there."

"Does she trouble you so much?"

"She anchors us both. Play acting she's one of us—asking stupid questions. We can't piss without her spyin'."

Robbie coughed up a spit, aiming his projection just short of Lewy. "That hasn't stopped ye, I noticed."

Lewy smirked. "Yer sweet on her, ain't ye?'

"She's just a wee lass…no one to amuse her but us. If ye gave her a chance…"

"I'd give her a good rub, if she wasn't the master's daughter. Put her to straw like the willing wenches at Gooseberry Coppice."

Robbie's backhand squashed Lewy's grin and caught him by surprise. The pistol flew out of his hand

and clattered to the ground. With a snarl, Lewy flew at Robbie like a bull in heat, knocking him down with a head butt to the chest. They scuffled in the Burren clay, trading gut punches, rolling and kicking, rising in a patch of heather, drawing blood with a flurry of awkward knuckle punches to the face and ears before Robbie pushed clear to suck in a breath.

Lewy smacked his fists together, trying to bob and weave like an experienced match fighter. They feinted sideways out of the heather, huffing as each lad circled his prey. A cut above Lewy's left eye dribbled blood into his thick brow. His mouth fixed in a snarl, nostrils flaring. He had weight and muscle behind his threat, not to mention experience. For two years now, Lewy was always up for a go, known as a bad egg outside of Meirliún. But he had never raised a fist to Robbie, who had height and might on his side.

Robbie swiped his bloody nose on his shirtsleeve, crouching with equal menace. "Take it back, ye *gobshite*. Have ye no decency?"

Lewy cupped his fingers, waved him to bring it on. "You *are* sweet on the rua. I knew it for sartin."

"Wrong. I know me place. A lesson is what ye need—to know yours."

"Who's to pound that lesson into me, boyo?" Lewy snorted. "Even me da has given up that sport." He pulled his fists into a guard and began a slow dance, stumbling sideways into a rock that threw him off balance.

Robbie muffled his laugh as he wiped his bloody nose on his sleeve once more. "This is cockeyed." He huffed. "You and I have been mates for seventeen year—since we were sucklin' babes." He ran his tongue over the metallic taste of blood on his teeth. “Our mams taught us right from wrong. Stealing guns and shooting insults is terrible wrong.”

Lewy scoffed. “So when did ye take up the pious life?”

“When did ye decide to risk life at Meirliún?”

Lewy dropped his fists and shook his head. “Ye actually think we live a good life here?”

“Better than most.”

“Blockhead, we were born to service. We’ll die servin’ the rich, never knowin’ what it feels like to own land, marry well or”—he jerked his thumb toward the box on the ground—“shoot a pistol fancy as those.” He slumped, tenderly touching the eye beginning to swell shut. “Geezus, Rob, we’re no really better than the darkies yer mum tol’ you ’bout in America. Worse off, maybe since it took a war to set ’em free.”

Robbie spit the blood pooling in his mouth. “You compare us to slaves? For years, we had the run of the farm, asked only to do light work expected even of well-born lads. Me mum always says we’re blessed to live here like kings.”

“Me mum says, ‘It is not the same to go to the King’s house as to come from it.’ We are not sucklin’ babes or young lads anymore, Rob.” Lewy thumped his chest and straightened his shoulders. “I say the man who can follow his own will is king.”

Robbie didn’t answer. He never once considered himself a slave, but he couldn’t dispute the argument. Life was hard for everyone in Ireland—unless you were gentry or owned land you could scratch a living from. Even then, you were a slave to the soil. But Meirliún was the only home he knew. Named after the stone falcon that hovered over the entry, it was originally a summer farmhouse built of native stone nearly a hundred years ago by O'Brien's granddad when potatoes were still king. After the Famine thinned out the population, sheep became the pre-dominant land crop, and wool and mutton churned up the county trade. Fishing the bays and islands of the North Sound sustained life, and kept homes like Meirliún safe for the Catholic O'Brien families that dominated County Clare.

His mother had started at the main house as a nurse for Olivia, was promoted to governess, and eventually hoped to become the housekeeper. As a lad, Robbie was expected to help where he could, dividing his time between fields and stable, along with his best mate—the cook's son, Lewy McDermott.

He scowled at Lewy as he bent to pick up the pistol and dusted it off with the only clean spot he could find on his shirttail. Below the barrel, a serial number was scratched through the stamp, 8636. He spit shined the numbers and carefully laid the pistol in its sheepskin mold next to its twin and snapped the lid shut.

With a black eye, bloody noses and bruised egos between them, they marched back to Will Turner's croft in silence. Robbie hugged the box of pistols against the hitch in his chest. Neither boy flinched when a flush of blue wood pigeons rose up from the heather beside them, calling their familiar *'ru-hoo ru ru hoo!*

The duel was over. No shots fired.

Chapter Seventeen
A Pretty Face Catches the Eye, 1881

Alive. It made a lad feel alive. No one ever scaling the ruins of the Ballinalacken tower would regret it, once exposed to the view from every direction. Today, the smell of fish was sharp in the wind. The Galway hookers were out in numbers, their dark red sails punctuating the green water like floating kites. From the tower ramparts, he could make out sea vultures circling the crafts, their laughing echoes bouncing off the cliffs of Moher. *He! ha! he!* The sun shone on the distant Burren, with brilliant blue gentian and woodruff edging the gray rocks like a quilted border. Further south, the inland vista was a living counterpane—earthy shades of umbra and green, some carpeted with mountain aven and primrose—colors bursting with spring.

She belonged. Her ginger hair was almost gold in the sun, a bright pop against the gray rocky trail as she bobbed up the hill on her pony. When the ascent sharpened, she stopped to tie her pony to a tree, and bent to pick some of the little blue and white flowers along the path. He had to smile when she hiked up her long skirt to hurry her stride. Wearing breeks were a thing of the past; she was growing up. When she spotted him watching her from the tower, she stopped again and cheerfully waved. He waved back and could feel the flutter of anticipation in his chest.

Was it Christmas Day when he saw her last? They had little opportunity to share more than a few sentences, or even re-connect beyond a few stolen glances and the touch of feet beneath the harvest table set for family and servants. Her mother was a vigilant hostess, and her father clearly doted on her whenever she was home from Dublin. Last Christmas, she was old enough to attend holiday parties and meet the social engagements that her parents required of her. Christmas week went by quickly, and even with excuses and errands that brought him to the big house, he never caught more than a fleeting glimpse of her.

Summers were different. Three months home. Her free time was less accountable and he knew that sunny days would bring her outdoors, especially to ride or groom her horse. She had found his recent note, tucked in her saddle flap in the stable tack room. A day later, she even agreed to meet him at the tower.

They shared a past, as well as the love of horses. When her pony foaled five years ago, she helped him deliver the colt on a stormy night in May. She had come to the barn every day that summer, imprinting the colt, asking questions he often found humorous, sometimes embarrassing. "How can ye tell it's a colt right out of the pocket? Does every newborn get the nasty *buinneach?* Does suckling hurt the mare?" Questions he thought no highborn lass should dare to ask. But Olivia Moire O'Brien was no ordinary highborn lass—full of questions and blunt as a wooden spoon as long as he had known her. He had to know if two years at a Dublin finishing school had ironed out the wrinkles in Olivia.

Even with her skirt, she easily climbed the old limestone outcropping, taking his hand when he met her half way to guide her the last forty feet of stone steps. She didn't let go of him until they reached the top and she gathered her breath and adjusted to the wind. The wildflowers tucked in her bodice dusted the air with a sweet scent, and he couldn't help gazing down at the new shape of her bosom when she bent to remove a stone from one of her boots.

"I almost forgot how grand this was." She spoke with breathless awe, twisting slowly to take in the panorama. They moved to the opposite edge of the crumbling ramparts and with one hand on her shoulder, he pointed out the landmarks and the stone-fenced sheepfolds spreading across the pasture grids as far as the eye could see.

Meirliún's blackface sheep were dots in the distance. "They're already fat as clouds, grazing on the spring turf," he said.

"Fat or ready to lamb," she snickered. "'Tis the season for such." She twisted to look sideways for his reaction.

He chuckled, plucking one of the blue flowers that matched her eyes and threaded it over her ear. "Aye, everything springs forth in May, on choice ground or no, with great due paid to the rain and sea mist."

The gesture seemed to surprise her at first, but she gamely removed another flower to plug it behind his ear. "Lucky we are then—to settle so near Galway Bay and the sea. No worries about drought."

The wind danced in her hair, a flame of red-gold fluttering against her face and shoulders. She closed her eyes as if savoring the scent and feel of the breeze.

"Have ye ever been out of County Clare, Robbie?"

"Only to market in Galway and Lisdoon. Have you been, besides Dublin, that is?"

She nodded. "Limerick and Galway, of course. And when I was eleven, we summered in the Reeks of Killarney. When the sea lay quiet, we even took a curragh to see the Puffins on Skellig Michael. One of the fishermen netted two of them for dinner but I couldn't eat a mouthful, picturing those funny creatures with the colorful bills and merry eyes."

He laughed. "In the old days they fed the climbing monks on Skellig, you know."

She sighed, shaking her head. "Their eggs should have been enough. The birds could have died off entirely."

"'Twas a good reason to abandon Skellig hundreds of year ago."

"So, you've never been south that far?"

"Unless we go to market, I've never been more than a day north, south, east or west of Meirliún. Your da keeps me busy on the farm these days."

"And what takes up your leisure by night these days?"

"I read most evenings. My mum encourages that since your Mum lets me borrow from the house library."

Her face lit up with approval. "What choices do ye seek?"

"History mostly. I like to read about the old chieftains and Celts, but there are a few tales of faeries and some poetry that catches me eye. Your mum has them scattered among your da's books on animal husbandry. I wish…I'd like to put the shelves in better order, but that's not my place. 'Tis trouble enough memorizing where to put them back."

She laughed. "Robbie, the logical. You haven't changed." She pulled his crumpled note out of her apron pocket and fanned it between them. "Though your hand has improved, I see."

"Me Mum taught me well, but I have little reason to practice a readable hand."

She shoved the note back into her pocket. "Yer mum was my first teacher, too. I wept, ye know, when I was to be finished in Dublin. I was told yer mum wasn't qualified to teach me lady manners. We had an awful row about it, until Da took me aside to explain it was for me own good, if I was to marry well."

"He said that?"

"He said that since I was the heiress to Meirliún, I would have to marry into wealth if we were to keep the estate in family. He came near to losing the farm more than once, he confessed—especially during the Great Hunger." She sighed heavily. "Da told me a son or a rich son-in-law would save our little family from a nap in a potter's field."

"You believe that?"

"Da never lies to me. But his face colored when I told him to breed a son, then, because I was not a sheep or a horse to be bartered off." She walked to the edge of the tower and leaned against the wind, pushing away hair that whipped at her cheek. "I can almost see the isles from here," she said in a small voice.

He closed the gap between them, pulling her backward against him. "Have a care, Livy. 'Tis a long journey down." He could feel her silky hair tickle his chin. For a long time they stood together, buffered against the wind and rocky ramparts.

"Judas, I almost forgot," she finally said, twisting against him. "Mum has invited company for tea and wants her poppet to play for them."

He remembered the sweet music she coaxed from the parlor harpsichord. Music that drifted even beyond the stable when a parlor window was left open in the manor house. "But you just got here."

"I forgot how far the tower lies from the manor." She punched down her skirt ballooning in the wind. "*Damnú!* And wearing this nuisance makes the trail twice as long."

It always amused him to think her fingers could coax the refinement her mouth never did, and planning ahead was never her way. Finishing Livy would take time, but time was on her side. She was only fifteen.

Damnú? He took up her hand and measured her long creamy fingers against his own, sun-weathered and blunt-rough from culling rocks and harrowing fields for planting.

"Ye may kiss it," she said, curling her fingers and offering her knuckles.

"What?"

"My hand. Isn't that what gentlemen do? Kiss the back of a hand when greeting or taking leave?"

"You think me a gentleman?"

She took a small step back to study him, taking in his full height from boots to brows and dark hair curling below his ears. His baby cheeks were gone and his nose seemed longer, his mouth wider, his chin stronger, but the eyes…the eyes were still the color of the deep green sea, lighter in the prism of sunlight. "Aye, you've smoothed out a few edges in the last few years. And your voice is deeper. You sound almost…well you've lost some of your brogue." She shifted her shoulders and offered a smile, along with the back of her hand. "It sets you even more apart from Lewy."

"You never fancied Lewy, did you?"

"The cook's son was never meant to be more than shanty Irish, but he was sometimes good for a grin when the three of us hung about. I knew he was fixed on getting rid of me—taggin' between two good mates—and it made him crude and mean." She smiled sweetly. "But you always treated me fair, Robbie, a gentle boy who is growing into a gentle man."

Preening over the compliment, he smoothed his hair and took her offered hand, chuckling as he bent low in exaggeration to brush his lips across her knuckles. "My lady," he murmured, catching her eye with a wink from his own.

He remembered the day six years ago when her da playfully knighted him and Lewy with an old sword he kept in his study. "Ye lads need to watch over my Livy when she follows you about the estate. Me only child is too old for a nurse and too young, in me mind, to be sent away to school," he explained.

Minding Livy was the last thing either of them wanted to do. The mates had extraordinary freedom for two Irish lads on a working farm. Once they finished their daily chores, they fished and collected masked crabs from the beaches of Galway, hiked the Burren, and explored the cave near Ballyvaughan, as well as all the old castle ruins in the county.

It had always been a cat and mouse game they played after chores, trying to avoid the freckle-faced lass with the unruly explosion of red curls. It didn't matter that she was the daughter of The O'Brien of County Clare—the wee lass who once burned her dolls and fancied wearing breeks to follow in their footsteps. Lewy did everything possible to discourage the alliance, but eventually, despite the four-year age difference, the three of them became grudging friends.

"'Tis good practice—kissing the hand," she said, retrieving her hand and dipping into a curtsy. "Perhaps if we meet like this again, I may even let you kiss my mouth."

His gaze fell to her lips. Full and ripe as a wild berry. *Was she coloring her lips already?* "Would a gentleman do that on short acquaintance?"

Hands on hips, she gave him a sour look. "Six year is a short acquaintance? Bah, me mum always says a pretty face catches the eye, but everything else takes practice."

He chuckled, looking around. "Is there a pretty face about? Your mum probably means practicing the harpsichord."

"Oh, Robbie, I do miss ye and all the fun we used to have." She captured both his hands this time and swung them at arm's length.

He grinned, pirouetting her to the stone steps. Was it even possible to meet again, knowing they were classes apart and she only fifteen? He was the stable boy; she was an O'Brien of the old Dalcassian families of the Scots Irish. His mother was also a descendant of the Claddagh fishermen of Galway, with a dram of Scots Irish blood, distilled through a century of intermarriage. "A dram of Scottish blood," she always crooned "was a lucky charm."

A lucky gentleman, then? When they reached the

bottom of the tower, he affected a formal bow at the waist. "'Til we meet again, my lady." Watching her skip down the trail to her pony, her skirt hiked to her knees, he had to laugh. Two years of school had not finished Livy.

Chapter Eighteen
The Bastard

"You're of an age to know," his mum began in a tone so solemn, he studied her mouth to make sure the words came from her. She had climbed on a chair pulled to the cupboard and reached for her sewing box kept out of reach on top of the valance.

Ten years ago, he took her scissors from the box she left on the table to cut away a curl hanging over his eyes. Caught in the act, she smacked his hand and raised her voice in an uncharacteristic curse. He ran from the croft and hid in an empty lambing shed. Never before had she spilled her anger on him. When he heard her calling for him, he plugged his ears and curled into a stained rug he found in the corner.

The damp stench of the shed, and a growling in his stomach finally drove him out of hiding at dusk. His mum had made his favorite stew, thick with potato and chunks of mutton steamed with the scent of rosemary. Clutching a handful of purple heather, he shifted from foot to foot in the open doorway of their croft. With a twitching smile, she closed the door behind him and put the drooping blooms in a jar on the table. "Well, then." She wiped her hands on her apron and ladled the stew into his wooden bowl.

No apologies were uttered between them, but he knew something had changed. The sewing box was kept out of reach after that. When she needed to mend or sew, she took care to do it after he retired to his cot at night.

Through the years, it became a habit to settle in his cot when she picked at her cruit, falling asleep to the sweet, sad lullabies she played. But sometimes he woke later, thinking he heard a mewling draft from the chimney. More often than not, she was bent in a weep over her sewing box, her profile edged in the light of a single candle. Still shy of forty years, she was always beautiful to him, but her brown hair had a touch of brindle now, and the flickering candlelight emphasized the hollows of her face and soft lines around her mouth.

After she became housekeeper in the manor house, he was alone more often. When feeling a dare, he pulled up a chair and reached for the box to examine the contents. The scissors she now used to trim his hair was there, among twists of colored thread, needles, a leather thimble, and squares of cloth she used to mend his shirts and breeks. Nothing in that box, not even an errant prick of a sharp needle should have brought on such mournful tears. Nothing…until the secret was revealed on his eighteenth birthday.

****

After his favorite supper of mutton stew and bannocks, she presented him with wrapped gifts from the manor house. An apple cake from the cook, the mistress's library copy of *Gulliver's Travels*, and a folding razor from the master. She laughed and smoothed the back of her hand across his cheek. "Almost bare as a baby's bottom. You'll not be needin' to scrape today, but it bodes well for the future. You're a man soon enough."

Blushing, he cupped his chin, feeling for the whisker sprouts he knew were there just yesterday. Lewy McDermott was already scraping his chin once a week, he pointed out.

"Have ye had a look at Lewy's da, me boy? The old Scot is hairy as a wild boar. His son is bound to be, as well."

Angus McDermott was an all-purpose man at Meirliún. Except for his wife, Peggy, the cook, everyone in service pitched in with double duties. Will Turner helped Angus with grounds and barn, and the boys were dutiful to both of them in pasture, barn, or gardens. It was even common to see the master roll up his sleeves in season to help with planting and harvesting his wife's beloved house gardens. The grain crops and the sheep tending and shearing were left to the tenants in the Gooseberry Copse.

With some hesitation and great ceremony, Robbie's mum also set her sewing box before him on the table, then slipped her fingers beneath a tear in the lining and pulled out a scratched sepia photo of a man in a strange uniform. "Your da," she announced, laying it on the table before him like the King in a deck of cards.

"My father?" he repeated stupidly. The man was formally posed sitting between two flags, one bearing the Irish Harp and the other, a large "X" starred from corner to corner. He wore a long-sleeved button-down jacket with contrasting shades on the sleeves and collar. A brimmed hat with a rakish feather covered most of his dark hair and shaded his eyes. His expression was somber, maybe even prideful in the tilt of his chin.

He had never seen the picture before, never heard

his mother talk of his father beyond telling him that he died in the American War. She rarely talked of any family, except to claim that she was blessed to be a distant…and poor cousin of Conal O'Brien, their benefactor.

"Lucky, we are, Robbie, to have a roof over our heads, a bed to sleep in, and plenty to eat," she oft repeated. "We must never upend our position at Meirliún, and always, always give praise for such blessings." As she did whenever God or Meirliún were mentioned, she dipped a knee and crossed herself. For a long time, he thought perhaps Meirliún was one of the holy places to venerate, like the hill of Tara, or Croaghpatrick.

He turned the picture over and saw that a short lock of dark hair was sealed in a smear of beeswax. "Why have ye kept this from me?"

"I dinna want to burden," she replied, looking away.

"What burden comes from a son knowing his da?"

"He died not knowin' about ye, and I, I gave my pledge to the saints…to protect ye."

"Protect me from what?"

"Your da and I…we were…unwed." She took the photo from him and slumping into her rocker, she studied the picture in hand. "Dawson was the youngest son of lace-curtain Irish, and I was then a poor kitchen maid with me own bottle-swilling da to support. When word came that your da had been killed, I nearly lost ye in my grief. When I took my cares to his mum, she was shocked, but thought only of the new shame I would bring to the family. Her husband, your grandda, had a roving eye, and she would have no such taint visited upon her sons."

She clasped her hands in her lap and tilted her head to study his reaction, her dark eyes glazed with entreaty. "I was sixteen, mind you, and my belly was starting to bloom when she sent me away with a purse full of coin, telling me the best use for it was a passage back to Eire."

"So you did as she wished then," he said tersely.

Again, she studied the picture she held and continued in a small voice. "In time. Me own da snatched the coin for a grand bender that drained the final life from him. Praise God, an O'Brien uncle in Boston took pity on me. He was a saloon fighter and collected enough in one match to pay for his brother's burial and my passage back here, even arranged for my indenture to our present master."

"Then I have an uncle in the States?"

"Aye, but he washed his hands of us. I never heard from him again. Boston Irish were waging another kind of war, even before America divided. The color of their skin pegged them only a wee step above the darkies. The Irish knew enough to band together—in war and peace—to fight for a better life in America. And they helped their own when fortune allowed and conscience nibbled." She dabbed at her eyes with a corner of her apron. "Scandal, perhaps, flew against better nature."

Silence grew between them for a long minute. "So you left for the homeland, then?"

"Aye." She nodded. "Ye were born on our way to Galway in the bowels of a merchant ship, midwifed by the ship's undercook." She tried a weak smile. "We marveled at how your first gusty howl pierced the ranks of the ship, but after you were swathed and settled, you seemed to like the sea-shift that rocked our berth like a cradle."

He sat stiff and motionless, his face blank. "I was born…on a ship?"

"Aye. The first of May, 1863." Her lips trembled around a thin smile.

Waves of emotion shrouded the room in silence until a pop in the turf fire warming the teakettle made them both jump. He watched his mother spring from her chair with purpose to attend the kettle and pour two steaming cups of tea.

He ignored the cup she offered him. "So then, I am old enough today to learn that I am not only a bastard, but the grandson of a drunk on one hand, an eye-rover on the other—with both sides of a family eager to crush the stench of scandal?"

Wringing her hands again, she stifled a sob. "I, I only thought you had the right…"

"To know my place? Yes, mum." He managed to push his voice through the clot in his throat and rise with an ache in his backbone. Fresh air. He needed fresh air. He slammed the door behind him and made a heart-pumping dash for the castle ruins. The rush of wind against his face dried his own eyes and with just enough breath left after running miles, he climbed the tower and collapsed at the top. Sprawled on his back, with fists tight against his ribs, he metered his breath until the painful thump in his chest began to subside. The crash of the waves breaking against the cliffs emphasized his thirst. The stars above winked like fireflies in the growing darkness, and he felt the rocky turret spin beneath him.

A bastard. He was a bastard. Born in a ship. No

country to claim. Was there any place in heaven or earth fit for him now?

Chapter Nineteen
The Festival of Good Wishes, 1882

Olivia was back in time for St. Johns Eve. The healing waters of Dublin's holy wells brought her mother some relief from the heart ailment that had turned her into an invalid the last two years. The midsummer Festival of Good Wishes at Meirliún could only accelerate a cure. Bonfires dotting the country from sunset to dawn were meant to bless, protect, and nurture every living thing, even beyond the human spectrum—livestock, crops, fishing boats, homes. The all-purpose flames even fanned the hopes and dreams of maidens willing to jump embers to the man of her choice.

Beyond answered prayers, jumping the embers intrigued Olivia most. Miss Finnegan's Girls joked of little else while packing for summer leave. Olivia's blonde and beautiful roommate had circled June 23 on the hall calendar, crossing off every day used up 'til then. Everly Halpin was from Wicklow, just a day's coach ride south of Dublin. Her father was a sea captain, anxious to educate his daughter enough to see her married, even above his station.

"He tempts me, Livy, with all the strong, ruddy-faced seamen he brings home to dine, but tells me none are worthy of my hand. I'm thinking I may have to jump embers to find a man of me own choosing."

Olivia laughed. “You have such a lad in mind?”

“I have. For the last few years, the shoemaker’s son has shown me some attraction.”

“You or your pretty little feet?”

Everly’s laugh was as diminutive as the rest of her. “You know how I love a well-fitted slipper. Happy feet make a happy lass and what likely suitor isn’t up for a good natured wife?”

Most of the girls were already gone by the first week in June, giving up the usual term end repetition devoted to those who had missed classes during the school year. Olivia was one of the stay-behinds, having missed time before winter break when her father called her home early to help relieve her mother of duties required at Yuletide.

Like Everly, she began to mentally check off the days, knowing that her parents would soon be fetching her home after her mother’s pilgrimage to the healing wells of Dublin. Was it a coincidence that Dublin’s major well was named for St. John? Another coincidence that St. John was the patron saint she chose at first communion?

The soft cowhide book she received in the Kinvara parish on that special day was meant for penning words to favorite hymns and supplications to the patron saint. Olivia’s sporadic devotion to her entries had more to do, however, with every facet of St. John’s annual festival, recording the lore and lure of it, along with a who’s who of participants. Who was the chosen *Giolla* tending the fires, who spoke the prayers, who’s health and family increased, who jumped the embers for a sweetheart, a new baby or a new home? Tenant farms surrounding Meirliún were always fair game for tradition…and plenty of chinwag.

Her cowhide book became a ledger and tally of sorts when she compared it year after year, registering when she was younger how many pennies she collected for sweets, who collected the most fuel for pyres, and when she was older and more privy to the gossip, whether it rang true or not for the wishes.

Among Finnegan girls, a singular interest in who's jumping the embers was natural by virtue of their finishing goal. A lady of good repute and social skill, who could embroider well or play an instrument was a desirable bride, but too often in an arranged marriage. Having recourse for their own choice on St. John's Eve was an exciting alternative, even if it didn't amount to a lasting attachment.

Olivia remembered what her mum told her the day of her first communion at St. Colman's. Dressed in the purity of white, it was the first time she eagerly donned a costume of lace and petticoats and fine kid slippers over white silk stockings. Her parents made much of it—even hiring an artist to paint her portrait. Olivia in a dress was a rare occasion.

"You are the Lord's little bride," her mother told her that day. "Someday, you will be grown enough to walk the aisle with a man of great standing."

A man of great standing. What did that mean?

At the age of eight, she thought maybe it was a portly man, like Angus McDermott, who never missed a meal or a sampling of his wife's puddings and cakes. By twelve, after the heiress conversation with her father, she understood it to mean a man of wealth. By sixteen, she knew "wealth" might include a title of some regard. Her parents had certified hope for such a union by sending her away the last few years to Miss Finnegan's Academy in Dublin.

"Time to polish your manners and act the lady born to the manor," her mother told her one evening as she bathed in the carved brass tub set before the fireplace in her room. "Your father has indulged you enough, tagging after low boys."

Olivia's mother was born to the manor by virtue of a line of minor chieftains who once ruled Ulster until the Gaelic order collapsed in the seventeenth century. Margaret Moire O'Donnell may have been a sheepman's daughter who dyed wool for her own shawls, but she had the proud bearing of a princess and never let anyone forget her ancient ancestry, least of all Donal O'Brien when he came to court her twenty years ago. She was polished and ready at seventeen. Her daughter would soon be that ready, as well—if she had any say about it.

Summers back home at Meirliún tarnished Olivia's new polish at first. Lewy and Rob saw to that when she was able to sneak away from supervision. It became a serious tug of war when her ailing mum commandeered even more of her daughter's time with new tutors.

"I know how to play the harpsichord," Olivia protested. "I don't need a music coach, and a lady doesn't need to cook like a pastry chef. She only needs the means to hire one—if soufflés and whiskey pies can seduce a man of good standing." Her mother took the impudence as she always did, throwing back her shoulders to glare at her daughter with narrow eyes and a slow shake of her perfectly-coiffed head.

Olivia never forgot the time her mum spilled her anger openly, railing at her father for turning a blind eye to his daughter's flagrant behavior. Coming late to dinner, barefoot and still wearing breeks after a day spent with Rob and Lewy, Olivia was sent to her room without a tray for such grave offense. She had lingered in the hallway long enough to hear her father's booming laugh when her mum declared, "the child is a few quarts shy of O'Donnell blood."

Nearly seventeen now, wearing breeks was a thing of the past. Olivia did understand that the freedom she once enjoyed was a bridge burned, and her duty to the legacy of her family…and Meirliún…was as inevitable as the day's sunset. St. John's Eve in 1882 could be her final chance for mutiny, and she already had her mind set on the only boy she would jump the embers for.

****

In Galway and Lisdoonvarna, the elaborate bonfire celebrations focused more on merrymaking than prayer, and were directed by a man from the community selected for the honor. The *Giolla* in Kilfenora was old Father Monahan who led prayers over the cathedral bonfire for twenty-five years, and supervised the burning of worn out scapulars, statues, and rosaries on the occasion.

"I'm for Lisdoonvarna," Lewy said, when the three of them met in the stable early in the day. "A clean spoon is all you need to dip into the goody pot the widows set on the coals there."

Robbie scraped a thatch of dark hair from his eyes. "Doesn't your mum see that's provided here at Meirliún?"

"She did, until someone flavored the bread pudding with too much rum last year. The mistress complained when she saw the neighbors tromp her flowerbeds to get at the goody."

"Your mistress won't be objecting to much this year." Sitting on a hay bale, Olivia knotted a colorful scarf beneath her chin and pulled it over her hair. "My mum asks only for a small family fire for protection of farm and the good health of every man and beast that bides here."

"Is she well enough to attend even that?" Robbie asked.

"Da will bring her down 'til she tires. I'm thinkin' that won't be overlong from sunset." She looked from one solemn face to the other, wondering if it was pity or disappointment she encountered. "It's a long night. I'd be free to go elsewhere once they retire."

"I'll stay with Meirliún, then," Robbie said, leaning his chin on the handle of a pitchfork. "Me mum would wish that I do…out of respect."

Lewy turned to spit in the soiled straw he was forking into a wheelbarrow. "Me mum cares not where I go, as long as I bring no shame to her again.

Robbie squashed a look at him. "So that business with the lass from Ballyvaughan is over?"

"Over and done. I've a new gal wanting to jump the fire to me arms tonight."

"Would she be from Lisdoonvarna, then?"

"More than one goody pot there." Lewy's half grin was sardonic. "She has a friend who fancies to meet you…"

"I'll pass." Robbie rolled his eyes. "But I could drop ye off there. I'm to pick up a moveable chair for the Mistress in Lisdoonvarna this very afternoon. Could ye be finding something to do there 'til sunset, and make yer way back in the morn?"

Lewy pretended to think a bit, scratching his shaggy beard. "I can manage that, to be sure." He forked up a ripe pile of manure. "I've orders to cut some turf for the pyre tonight. I suppose I'll be having to shave and clean up after. Can't be smelling like *seascann* on St. John's Eve."

Watching his friend cart away the wheelbarrow, Robbie absently rubbed the back of his fist across his chin. He caught all his whiskers this morning, trimming his sideburns and the irregular patch that had started to grow beneath his nose. He was dressed in his mucking clothes, and suddenly aware that he reeked no better than Lewy.

Olivia smirked at him, pointing to Lewy with the limp cluster of meadowsweet she had picked on her way to the barn. "Poor Lewy. He'll always be a *gobshite*, no matter how well he scrubs free of the stench."

Robbie laughed. "Lewy's good for a chuckle if you don't take offense at the devil in him."

"I think he'd do better going for the bonfire at Kilfenora. Old Father Monahan has had practice, I'm told, exorcising demons on St. John's Eve." They laughed together before parting, each mindful of tasks that would whittle away the hours 'til dusk.

Chapter Twenty
Jumping the Embers

Angus McDermott lit the small fire in the garden pit, and in unison, all spoke the common prayer from memory: "In the honor of God and of St. John, to the fruitfulness and profit of our planting and our work, in the name of the Father and of the Son and of the Holy Spirit."

The mistress mouthed an occasional word from the sling chair that seemed to enfold her, and when her hands baffled the air at the Amen, everyone automatically made the sign of the cross. Nothing but the crackling flames broke the silence that followed. It was the smallest gathering for St. John's Eve in Olivia's memory. Only the housekeeper, cook, and herder, Will Turner, were invited with their families. The rest of Meirliún's tenants between the Burren and the gooseberry coppice were doing their usual *craic* near Cottage Row a mile north.

The Turner's little blonde daughters, Faith and Hope, anchored each side of their mother on a low bench across the fire from Olivia. Prudie Turner, looking careworn and pensive twiddled her fingers on her distended belly. *Charity?* Olivia wondered—*if the child within the bump comes out another girl?*

The children were as mesmerized as their mother by flames that troubled to rise when their father tossed a few noxious weeds on the pyre. There wasn't much of a stockpile of dry turf and weed since the coastal downpours last week. It would be hard to keep even a small fire going 'til midnight without a cache of dry tinder. Lewy had either failed to cut enough turf, or the stockpile had been pilfered by mischief-makers near the gooseberry coppice. Will and Angus discussed both prospects, both scowling into the cheated fire. Olivia wondered if thirst deepened the scowl. There was no bottle in sight.

Olivia glanced at her mother, already dozing between her father and Robbie's mother. She had noticed the new reliance her parents had on Sarah O'Brien, who doubled the past year as head housekeeper and companion to her ailing mum. She wanted to ask about Robbie, but thought better of it. He promised he would be here, and the night was still young. Something must have delayed him in Lisdoonvarna. Robbie never made idle promises he couldn't keep.

There was small chatter among the group until Olivia's father began to snuffle when his head lolled to the side. Angus offered to help his master retire, carrying the mistress back to the manor. Olivia kissed them both goodnight and said she'd stay 'til midnight. With a catch in her throat, she watched their slow retreat to the house. Both her parents had aged.

She remembered the general belief that even the very ill who survived 'til midsummer would survive at least until fall. It was a good sign that her mother had dressed herself and powdered her face for the bonfire appearance. The trek to the holy pools had given them all great hope. With care and prayer, the weak hearted often lived long into their half-century mark and her mother was only thirty-eight.

With the O'Briens gone, the Turner girls lost their shyness, leaving their mother's side to throw handfuls of grass into the ebbing fire. Olivia beckoned them to her with a couple of sticks she found to poke at a lick of flame. When an owl hooted, she held a hand to her ear. "Did you hear that? The cuckoos may stop their cry at midsummer, but not Mr. Owl."

"What happens to the cuckoos?" Five-year-old Faith asked, her dark eyes round as blackberries.

"They seem to lose their voice at midsummer, but some stay 'til September."

Three-year-old Hope sidled up to ask, "Where do the coos go?"

"To Spain," Prudie Turner chimed in. "Is that not the legend?"

Olivia nodded, assuring the girls that they come back in time.

"In time for what?" Faith persisted.

"They like our spring, especially on the Burren, I'm told."

"Marshland, too," Will added. "Wherever fat caterpillars are found." He picked up his youngest daughter, snatched her thumb and pretended to eat it. "Yummy white caterpillars."

Both girls giggled, along with their mother who rose to rub her backside in a stretch. Her husband noticed and asked Olivia's permission to retire, as well. The small fire pit was nearly a pool of ash, wafting a smoky peat fragrance that at least chased away night flying insects. "I can manage." Olivia smiled.

Alone with her thoughts, Olivia wondered what

had happened to Robbie. She poked a few embers with a stick and watched them blink half-heartedly back to life. This was supposed to be a night for merrymaking and it had turned solemn as a deathwatch. She could feel a tear roll on her cheek and brushed it aside like a pesky midge, then tore the sprig of yarrow from the ribbon in her hair and threw it in the fire pit. Cradling her chin, she braced her arms on her knees to stare into the winking embers. How did the divination go?

"Good morrow, good yarrow, good morrow to thee
Send me this night my true love to see
The clothes that he'll wear, the color of his hair
And if…"

The rest of the words stuck in her mouth like dry breadcrumbs.

"And if he'll wed me," was only a fantasy, caged in silence.

She poked the embers again, oblivious to the shadowy figure that studied her.

"And if…?" he said.

Looking up, she caught her breath, then leaped across the pit into the circle of his arms. "Robbie! You're back."

He took the onslaught with a little grunt and when a shaft of moonlight speared his face, she could see that his mouth was swollen and his brow was caked with dried blood. His shirt was torn and bloodied as well.

"Judas, what happened to you?"

He gave her a half-frozen smile. "Trouble with Lewy."

"Did Lewy do this to you?"

"Defending Lewy," he answered carefully. "Lewy's Lisdoonvarna lass had four brawny brothers—

defending her. It was two to one, for each of us."

"Where's Lewy, then?"

"Sleeping it off, still in the trap at the barn. He'll be all right when he comes round. He made me promise not to alarm his folks."

"If he looks as rough as you, his mum will go gray as midsummer ash."

"Well, I'm thinking she has to be used to seeing her boy as such. Lewy has a deal of experience claiming fights."

"Lewy may, but you don't. What will your mum say? She was restive, too, when you didn't show for the bonfire."

He gazed at the small fire pit. "That was a bonfire?"

"Well…scaled down a bit."

He peered at her through a swelling eye. "So you worried about me, did you?"

"Of course. Two year's we've spent together on St. John's Eve."

"You've been counting the years, then?"

"You haven't?"

He made no reply, looking up at the moon. "It can't be midnight yet. We have 'til then, if you're not to be home."

She slipped her arm through his, following his gaze. "The night is young still. Your mum is tending mine tonight at the manor house. She won't be seeing you like this if you clean yourself up at your croft."

His eyebrows shot up. "You've got plans?"

"If you're up to it, we can find another bonfire," she said, "maybe the *craic* at Gooseberry. Are they not known for their merrymaking?"

“Tenant society isn’t up-country, you know.”

“But on St. John’s Eve, all of Eire—high and low—celebrate equally.”

He clucked her under her chin. “Always the schemer, Miss O’Brien. School has sharpened your thinking.”

She tilted her chin up. “I always knew my own mind.”

He patted her hand. “I never doubted that, but you grow more dangerous with age, I think.”

“I’m seventeen…well near enough.”

He gazed at her peasant jumper and sighed. “I should think that is old enough for a taste of Gooseberry fun. Maybe in that disguise, they won’t recognize the O’Brien daughter. Do you have a hat or shawl?”

He groaned when she threw her arms around his waist. “What fun! You shall call me Lucy, the new kitchen maid at Meirliún!”

“Go then, Lucy, find a hat before the night ages.” He watched her lift her skirts to run more freely and held his ribs to keep from laughing. After Lisdoonvarna, he was feeling twice the age of Lucy.

Chapter Twenty-One
The Gooseberry Gang

A smoky drift of bonfires painted the night sky gray. Enveloped in a scent of ash, they rode double on a broad-necked bay horse named Jewel who flared her nostrils and snorted in protest. Robbie worked hard at the reins to keep her from turning back to the barn for most of the way to the coppice.

A tub of poteen was nearly consumed by the eight tenant families when Robbie and "Lucy" arrived at Cottage Row. Two pots of goody were also scraped clean by the tenants' children—seventeen in all, though most were already abed. On a trestle table scattered with empty crockery, only a small heel of brown bread, a wedge of cheese, a half-eaten apple, and an empty honey jar coated with ants, remained of the common repast that had been offered early in the evening.

Robbie was welcomed by most of the men and women who were still ambulatory, and even a few propped against a bench or cottage wall called out a greeting to him. Even without the straw hat and plain clothes that Olivia wore, no one in their present state would have recognized her as the landlord's daughter. Most likely, she would have been accepted.

The present O'Brien was Catholic, like his tenants who were loyal to him. Only the very elderly would remember that his grandfather had declared he was

Protestant. Some understood and forgave the conversion, knowing the circumstances. Catholic landowners in Ireland were supplanted by the Penal Laws of England unless they converted.

The conversion saved Meirliún from falling into the hands of an English Duke at the turn of the century, and from subsequent Catholic boycotts until the present O'Brien married an heiress and secretly reverted back to his grandfather's religion. Conal O'Brien was cautious with tenants, knowing his sincerity would always be suspect. Protestant landowners appointed by England still lived in fear for their lives as well as their livelihoods. The Irish had memories not easily watered down.

Robbie offered Livy a mug of the watered-down poteen. Olivia coughed, and wondered how it could have been any stronger. "Paint peeler," she whispered to Robbie, as he gulped down his drink.

Robbie introduced her to the Mayo family, Dick and Josie and Colin, their eldest son who was either too shy or near comatose to do more than offer a limp handshake. "Me boy is sixteen on the Saint's day—old enuf to test the honeyed waters," Dick grinned, slapping his son on the back. The boy's eyes rolled back and his long legs folded under him. Laughing, his mother and grandmother each grabbed one of his arms and with his bare feet digging tracks in the ground, they dragged him into one of the stone crofts of Cottage Row.

Robbie steered Olivia clear of a group of singers around the bonfire belting out a bawdy song to the beat of a makeshift drum.

"*I saw that she was coxy, no lovin' here by proxy?*"

Olivia nudged him "What does that mean?"

He answered her only with a lopsided grin and joined in the refrain,

"*As pretty a piece of mischief as never I saw.*"

A couple of teenage boys were competing to see how high they could toss a lighted stick in the air. A few women were squabbling over a pile of weeds, deciding which was noxious enough to burn and which should be separated as figwort, used to combat itching and swelling.

An old man was trying to wrest a bone away from a large dog. "Jack's got him a Protestant rib," he huffed to a man with a corrugated face. I'm thinkin' no good can come from chewin' one o' them."

"How do you know it be a Protestant bone?"

"It comes from an Ulster bullock."

"Don't make it a Protestant bone. Cattle don't pray one way t'nuther." Olivia didn't hear the low reply made before the two men laughed heartily.

Someone with a cruit plucked a few strings and the drummer joined a kilted bagpipe player for the start of a ring dance. This drew some interest from a few younger people surrounding the bonfire. The circle of dancers grew, along with the levity of clapping and whistles. A young man approached Olivia to pull her into the ring.

Robbie watched her, circling hand in hand between the forge boy and an older lad he recognized from Galway. She scarcely noticed when her straw hat flew off, freeing her long hair to bounce on her shoulders, gleaming like flames from the fire pit. He retrieved her hat before it could blow into the fire and settling on an empty keg, he fingered the brim with a slow smile. It was a rare pleasure, watching her blend into such exuberance. Even those poorly dressed hard-working, hard-drinking souls—always scuttled by the promise of a better day—were always ready for a *craic*. Was it an Irish thing? He didn't see it among the gentry. But then, he would never be part of that gang.

The dance ended and before everyone pulled in new breath, someone yelled "Trenchmore." The music found a new beat, and partners were chosen for the Irish line dance that was favored for centuries. The boy that had chosen Livy grabbed her arm again, just as his was grabbed by a cow-eyed, brown-haired lass. "Settle off." She snarled. "He's my jump tonight."

Livy curtsied low, understanding exactly what she meant. The boy's ears turned red and he rubbed his nose with a sly look at the girl, then at the campfire. It was still too inflamed for an ember jump, but he didn't lag when she pulled him toward the dance line.

Robbie was at her side before anyone else could claim her, and hustled her into line as well. There were few steps to remember, as they bridged and ducked, scampering down the line and swinging the reel. Sweat mingling with the pungent scent of poteen and burning wood became a heady fuel to keep step in line. Her hand was light in his, careful of the swollen knuckles she must have noticed. He winced a little when they fell against each other in the final round, laughing and breathless. Still holding hands, they retreated for another drink and crumbled on the ground to watch another set.

Two boys about ten were lighting hocusfian stems plucked from marshland, and parried them like swords until an elderly woman stepped in to separate them. "Here then," she warned, holding each boy unsteadily by his collar, "these are to protect you from evil, not set it free. You tap your man, then burn the shafts if good health is your aim." The boys wiggled out of her grasp and pitched the firebrands high in the air, narrowly missing the fire and Robbie standing beside it. With a bear growl, Robbie pretended to give chase.

"I think this boilin' is too far along for you Livy." He took her arm and guided her toward Jewel, tethered to a tree neatly stripped of a line of bark. "We should have come earlier."

"I don't want to leave," she said, with a little slur in her voice. "Just one more dance?"

A husky man in the shadows of the tree heard and approached. "If dancing is your fancy, lass, I'm your man." He clucked her under the chin and fingered her hair with a grimy hand.

"She's leavin' with me," Robbie said, taking Livy's arm.

"Hold up, boyo. The lass says no." The man glared at Robbie with a liverish eye, noticing his swollen eye. "You're the fighter from Meirliún, ain't you?"

Robbie stiffened, clenching his hands, meeting the man's dark gaze without answer.

Livy shrank back, steadying the horse with a stroke on her neck. "Perhaps we'd best go."

It happened so fast, she couldn't tell who took the first swing. The sound of fists slamming against something hard was counterpoint to jabs that blew grunts of wind. They were on the ground then, rolling with wild punches and snarling holds that brought the attention of two women. One yelled, "Fight," and spectators gathered like flies to honey.

Livy could see that Robbie's opponent outweighed him by at least two stone, though the man was shorter.

Robbie's swollen eye was freely oozing blood. *Two fights in one night could blind him*. Jewel was stomping and shifting around the tree, ears flattened to her head, ready to rear or trample. Trying to settle her, Livy's own fear was stoking the panic of both of them. Her head pounded with every jab that Robbie took.

The crowd encouraged the fight, even cheering when new blood was drawn. When the horse nipped at her, Livy picked up a cast-off hocusfian branch and slapped the horse's nose, then went after Robbie's attacker. Some of the spectators laughed, shoving her out of the way.

"Stop them," she cried. "Can't anybody stop them!"

Robbie rallied for one last punch, putting to ground a hefty man weakened by drink. He collapsed beside him, on hands and knees, rocking unsteadily while his nose dripped blood. Jeers and cheers whistled around him as he struggled to rise. While the man on the ground was tended, someone helped Olivia mount the skittish mare and two other men hoisted Robbie up behind her.

"The girl isn't from around here," she heard one of the two say. "He'll be having that one in the straw for no thanks," his companion replied. One of them slapped the horse's rump and Olivia grabbed Jewel's neck as they spurted away.

Chapter Twenty-Two
Unholy Bliss

She knew where she was going before they hit the crossroads to Kinvara and Dort. The smoky sky was clearing to reveal a misshapen globe of amber light above, and the dying embers of torch fires in fields of barley and corn lit her way like votive lights in a giant framework. Once the gooseberry coppice was far behind, she paused to circle Jewel on a slight elevation and pointed out a few glowing lights marking the fields they passed. She could feel Robbie's breath on her neck, more even at last, but he held himself back from his previous slump against her back with a fierce grip on her waist. "Like glow worms." She pointed.

He grunted in agreement.

"How do you fare?" She caught a strong scent of blood, and whiskey when she twisted in the saddle.

"Foolish," he muttered. "I should not have brought you…"

She patted his leg. "My idea, was it not?" Changing the subject to lighten his mood, she asked why the small fires dotting the fields never burned the crops they were meant to bless and protect. When he didn't answer, she rattled on. "You know midsummer is truly a festival of light, nearly as old as the land itself, when the ancient cave dwellers dotted the land with mounds and henges built of wood or stone and fire-loving druids worshipped the sun and moon."

He grunted again, leaning heavy, once more, on her back.

They traveled slowly on until the smell of the sea was unmistakable, and the sound of it spraying against the cliffs, as comforting as the rustle of thick petticoats.

His hands shifted on her waist as he sat up straighter, mumbling like his mouth was full of rocks. "Are we losh?"

"I'm not for home just yet. We are not far from the smuggler's cove that drew us when we were young. A good place to clean you up."

Moaning, he sagged against her back once more.

It took no prodding for Jewel to skirt around the untended remnants of a fire in the path leading down to the cove. Someone had already been here, hoping to block the midnight passage of noisy sprites. Older Kinvara natives declared the cove was a faerie haunt, and St. John's Eve was the perfect occasion to protect the seaport with a blessed fire.

Olivia swung a leg over the mare's neck and slid to the ground. "Do you think you can make it down to Pirate's Cove from here?"

Robbie braced forward on the horse and carefully drew a long leg over Jewel's rump. Both feet hit the ground with a grunt. He took a deep breath and forced himself to straighten up, leaning heavily against the horse. "Nothing wrong with my legs." He waggled his jaw and traced the ridge of his nose with his forefinger before his hand trailed over his left shoulder and down his ribs. "Can't say as much for the rest of me."

She helped him walk, wedging her shoulder under his left arm until she could feel him summon enough resolve to drag slowly on his own.

They left Jewel picketed in a patch of tender turf before they carefully inched down the path to the beach. The tide was low, exposing the remnants of a rocky quay. Seaweed, rocks, and shells dotted the new expanse of sand floating inland by the push and pull of dark water that chipped at their feet. The cove never took the violent pounding of surf that crashed against the Cliffs of Moher to the southwest, but in daylight, the tide covered all but a ribbon of beach no wider than a few yards.

She eased him to sit on a boulder on the beach. “Remember how we used to gather clams and pilchards in season and roast them over a fire here?”

Robbie nodded. “When we could fix a fire in the damp. Lewy had that talent.”

She thought he grinned when she added, “Talented for peeing it out, as well.”

His grin slipped when he watched her remove her shoes and stockings, then unlace the ties of her cotton jumper and slip it over her head. “What are you about?”

“A night swim.” She folded the dress over a rock and spread her arms, circling to model the muslin blouse and drawers she had exposed. “Can I help you with your boots?”

The blouse hung loosely below her waist, baring a shoulder, but showing little definition of her figure in the dark. “Liv, we are no longer children. Wading is one thing…”

Ignoring him, she pulled off his boots to stack beside her clothes. “A swim will wash the blood away. A cold soak will take the swelling down, as well. Do you want me to undress you?”

He hugged his chest to stifle a gasp. "I can't swim. I can barely raise my arms."

"Then wade in your clothes. It doesn't matter. I…I just assumed all boys sea-bathed naked."

"We do…when we are with boys."

"That didn't stop you when we came here as children. I always envied you and Lewy swimming further out in the all-together."

"We were wrong to do that with you about…Lewy taunted me…he wanted…"

"To shame me into leaving. I knew that, and it made me more determined to watch."

"Oh, Livy." Gauzy moonlight couldn't change the profile of the stubborn chin he remembered so well. Her neck was longer, more graceful now, rising out of her white shoulders like the bloom of a night flower. "Your da would have skinned us alive if he knew how we tried to humiliate you."

"I think Da wanted to forget I wasn't the son he desired. It always amused him when I related our adventures at the dinner table. Even more when he saw mum cringe."

With great effort, and some help, he pulled his bloodstained shirt over his head. "You didn't tell him…everything?"

She stared at his chest, broad and golden tan even in the moonlight. "I left out details." She snorted, looking away. "If I told all, I knew it would be the end of my romps, and I'd be back in skirts doing needlework with mum—or sent away to school far sooner."

They began to walk the shoal, feeling the cool sand give beneath their feet. He felt sudden shame for his part in humiliating her. "We were careless lads back then, making a joke of the freedom we enjoyed…at your expense."

"I envied that freedom, watching you dive in the surf like brown and white gannets and when ye came bounding back to shore, I pretended not to notice…the differences."

"I thought you were embarrassed, collecting shells to avoid us while we dressed."

She snickered. "I didn't always avoid a peek."

He stopped. "*A Dhia!* The scandals of wicked youth."

She smirked up at him, tossing her hair. "Do you remember when we came here last?"

"Three, maybe four years ago, wasn't it?" He took her hand when they started treading the uneven rocky quay and felt the water lap at their ankles as they followed it out. The water was deep enough at the end to dangle legs in the salty brine. He groaned when he bent forward to splash his chest with cold water.

"Night hides the colors I remember," she said. "The water was always so green and blue in daylight, sometimes even shades of mauve, with shadows like dark eels squirming in the wake."

"Seaweed shadows, probably. Lewy and I found a lot of it further out in the inlet. Galway is noted for the export of seaweed."

"Is that what the coastal hookers traded with?"

"Still do. It makes for great manure. But Kinvara markets also trade field crops and limestone and wool."

"This quay was thought to be a favorite of smugglers, was it not?"

He nodded. "Lewy had ancestors among them. He

told me his great-great-grandfather was caught by English revenue men and hung for his part intercepting French bales of tobacco and kegs of brandy."

She laughed. "So Lewy comes natural to his scandalous ways."

He cupped his hands in the water and splashed it over his face and neck. "Aye." The cool water felt good against his jaw and the swelling he fingered around his brow. He slipped in the water to submerge his throbbing head, then came up shaking the curl out of his wet hair. The salty water burned in his nose and the cut above his eye. Even his hands hurt.

Olivia followed his example, and found the water just deep enough to swim, and her feet touched off a slippery bottom.

"Have a care," he called after her. "There may be eels looking for a nibble."

She turned instantly and swam back. "Eels, you say?"

"So, there is something here that scares you?"

In a sliver of moonlight, he saw her blue eyes blink and her wet lashes fan over ivory cheeks. She touched his shoulder and spread her fingers. "I fear some things."

He pushed her hand away. "Livy, you cannot test me in this state. I…we both have had too much swill tonight."

"I jumped the embers at Meirliún. To you, Robbie. I've wanted to do so for two midsummers."

"Two years ago, I might have welcomed that."

"What has changed in all that time?"

He looked away. "You don't know me."

She laughed. "I've grown up with you. You were

like a brother…"

"I am no brother, and I can't be anything more," he said, still avoiding her eyes.

She came closer and placed a hand on each of his shoulders, threading them around his neck. "I don't believe that. You kissed me at the tower. More than once, if I remember it rightly."

"You asked for practice. I was young and foolish in my weakness to serve."

"Then serve me again." She stood on tiptoe in the water, brushing her forehead against the stubble of his chin. "Practice makes perfect."

Reluctantly, his lips covered hers and standing waist deep in the cool water, an eddy of warmth enclosed them, melting whatever resistance remained in his battered body. He could hear the ocean roar in his ears and their tongues touched, mingling the scent of liquor with the salty tang of the sea.

When he pulled away, his gaze locked hers, and his voice was deep when he muttered, "This cool night could turn us both to fool and madwoman."

She nestled into his chest with a deep sigh. "I know that phrase."

He peered down at her. "There's a small bust of the writer in the library at Meirliún."

"The Bard of Avon? I know the bust. Shakespeare was a true romantic. Listen to the surf, feel the night air, Robbie. Is this not a night for romance?"

They undressed on the beach and lay on the skirt she fanned over the sand, away from the fingers of tide. The moon had ducked behind a bank of clouds and in the dark, they caressed the cold from each other, warm hands and mouths surfing forbidden landscape. A chorus of moans and sighs broke the silence between them in the urgency of discovery. It was over when she gave up a cry as shrill as a gull and he shuddered with release, collapsing against her. Quickly withdrawing, he braced himself beside her and drew in his breath.

"Have I hurt you?" He sighed.

"Yes…no, it matters not. I think that is normal."

"That may be."

"You don't know?"

He groped for her hand and squeezed it. He didn't want to admit that his lovemaking expertise was based only on the *Bard of Shallow Confessions.* Lewy had taken a pig farmer's daughter to straw several years ago. He gave up boasting details of further conquests when Robbie refused to cover up his lies to broken-hearted lassies who showed up at the Meirliún stable with some regularity.

A long silence fell between them. The wind was picking up as they listened to the bubble and slide of the water washing the beach.

"Did…did I hurt you, too? Ye quailed."

He found it painful to laugh even a little. "I think I may have cracked a rib, but no fault of yours."

She sat up. "Robbie. Why didn't you say?"

He drove two fingers into the cool sand. "You did mean to jump the embers at Meirliún—to me, didn't you?"

"I've thought of nothing else all month."

He kissed her quickly and groped for her hand. "I don't take that lightly, Livy. For years I waffled, wishing for a sign, dreading a sign, wishing for a sign…something that meant you…well, I dreamed in another world we would be measured equal. And if there ever could be something between us, I didn't want to disappoint."

"You have never disappointed…"

"Well, I never expected to get jumped by you"—he squeezed her hand—"as well as several thugs on St. John's Eve."

She caressed his cheek, feeling a stubble of whiskers. "Poor Robbie, I was drawn to you when I was a child, just hoping we could be friends. Does this mean we can be more?"

He sucked in his breath. "I don't know. An ember once sparked can hardly deny the flame."

"Is that also Shakespeare?"

"Nay, that's Robbie O'Brien on St. John's Eve." He pulled her hand to his mouth and kissed her fingers. For a long minute they lay connected side to side, lulled by the surf and the occasional call of a cliff swallow.

"Everly said this, uh…the first time…would be locked in memory forever."

"Who's Everly?"

"My Dublin roommate. She was taken in Wicklow by a seaman."

"She told you that?"

"I wanted to know what to expect."

He was silent again. "So…did I, did I measure up to…expectations?"

"Yes, but I would like to try it again. To be sure."

"That isn't possible just now."

"Why not?"

He held an arm over his ribs. "Maybe you should ask Everly."

"Did I measure up…up to your…what you expected, then?"

"You rarely do or say what anyone expects of you, Liv."

"You are disappointed, then?"

"Disappointed, no, astonished, maybe." He groped for her hand. "Enchanted, always."

"You…like me, then?"

He tried again not to laugh, sucking in his breath. "I think I always have."

She rolled into him and feeling for his chin, pushed herself up to brush her lips carefully over his battered face. "I like you, too."

He closed his arms around her, feeling goosebumps. "You're cold."

"No, but I am beginning to feel my backside will be imprinted by snail shells and sea rocks." She sifted a handful of sand over his chest. "There may be some advantage to being taken in straw."

He chuckled, and after a quick groan in a ragged voice, said, "I think we'd be well to beat the dawn home. Were you not expected in by midnight?"

"I left me bed with a rolled bundle of nightclothes beneath the quilt if anyone dares to check. Mother sleeps sound with medicine in her tea and Da sleeps as soundly with his own nightcap of brandy."

She rose to shake out her skirt, fastening it across her chest beneath both arms, leaving her shoulders bare. He pulled on his dry long shirt and rolled the rest of their wet clothing into a bundle to carry back up the path to the horse. Jewel, well fed on sea grass, greeted them with a soft nicker. The leisure journey back to Meirliún was quiet with repletion.

Lewy was gone when Robbie checked the wagon in the barn. He led the horse to her manger with a bucket of water and patted her thick neck. Livy waited for him, drowsy on a hay bale, then followed him to the croft he once shared with his mum. Now indispensable to Livy's mum, Sarah O'Brien was rewarded with her own room that adjoined the Mistress's bed chamber in the manor house.

After lighting a candle, Robbie unrolled their bundle of damp clothes and spread them over a huckaback towel on the trestle table. "Not dry yet, but by dawn, most likely. Do you want to wait here 'til then, or can I escort you home like so?" He ran the light of the candle over her makeshift dress. The skirt came below her knees, within a foot of her gaiter tops, giving him a short glimpse of her shapely legs. Scanning upward, she held the waistband of her skirt protectively over her breasts. Her wet hair had dried and sprung into soft curls against her creamy shoulders, and she blinked with sleepy eyes when the light flickered across her face.

"I'm thinkin' to wait until all is dry. If I'm seen by one of the servants sneaking like this into the house, they could mistake me for one of Lewy's brazen trollops."

"Do you thirst, then? We keep buttermilk in a stone closet."

"No, thank you." She bit her lip. "I am that tired, though."

"Take my bed," he said quickly, gesturing across the small room. "I can rest in the chair and wake you at first light."

She looked at the small bed with some misgiving. Not as large as her own feather bed. Nothing furnishing the little croft was as large as anything in Meirliún. She let him take off her shoes while she bounced a little on the edge of the mattress. “Is this…?”

“…filled with straw,” he finished, and they exchanged knowing smirks.

When he pulled back the quilt, the skirt she held against her chest slipped and by the light of the candle on the bed stand, he caught a glimpse of the canvas his hand had possessed on the darkened beach. He had never seen a woman’s bare breasts so close in spotlight, all cream and rosebuds, and when his hand reached out instinctively to brush sand from one of the rosebuds, she flinched at once and sucked in her breath. The skirt fell to the floor and his gaze descended with it. And when she closed the space between them, he could feel her breasts tickle his tender ribs.

“Your eye,” she said, lifting her fingers to brush his brow. “It’s all a-bruise, and your nose is swollen.”

He winced, catching her wrist.

She gasped, noticing how raw his knuckles had become. How had she missed all this. Had the salt water done more harm?

“But how will you explain…?”

“Explain what? Lads fight. Men…” he slurred in Gaelic, “*dhéanamh fir grá*—men make love.” He kissed her mouth, cupping her soft breast and in slow motion, they settled onto the straw mattress together.

****

They were both sleeping when Sarah found them twined beneath the quilt she had stitched with her own hand. She had come to the croft twice before, checking to see if Robbie was home and abed on a night that held such promise of good and evil. Lewy had staggered in hours ago, and she had helped his mother tend cuts and scratches with figwort for the swelling, and sealed his wounds with honey and aloe thinned by a few drops of the precious water brought back from the holy wells.

No, Lewy didn't know what happened to Robbie when questioned, but he knew that Robbie had driven him home in the trap that held the Mistress's moving chair from Lisdoonvarna. "Lighting the tenant fields," he guessed. "Or nursing his own bruises." Lewy was happy to stay the night in his own bed, with a cold compress over his swollen face, and his head pounding like a hammer against the feather pillow he was offered.

****

In the thin light of morning streaking through the windows, Sarah crept closer to her son's bed. Robbie's face was as bruised as Lewy's. His dark hair fanned against the white pillow, but he looked peaceful, content, even with his strong chin buried in amber tresses. He wasn't alone. The girl beside him moved, nuzzling into the curve of his shoulder. She gasped against the back of her hand. It was the mistress's daughter. He was abed with Olivia. The bruises were inconsequential to the shattering sight of them, sleeping in such unholy bliss.

Chapter Twenty-Three
The Wake

Whoever survived midsummer was said to survive 'til fall, even those desperately ill. Margaret Moire O'Brien did not receive the legendary reprieve. The priest at St. Colman's in Kinvara was called to give her last rites on August 30. She died before dawn the following day and was laid out in the parlor for the customary Irish wake. Sarah and the housemaid washed her and dressed her in a white linen shroud adorned with black ribbons at the neckline. Her favorite rosary and a small bell were entwined in hands set stiffly into prayer position. A candle was set at the head and foot of her coffin, clocks stopped at the hour of her death, mirrors covered, and only one mullioned parlor window opened nearby—to allow her spirit to escape.

Dressed in black faille, Livy sat beside her father opposite the coffin, receiving condolences from a half-dozen house servants, as well as tenants, neighbors and friends. Robbie and Lewy were dressed in green baize livery with white cotton gloves, serving now as footmen for the occasion. They ushered guests, carried food trays, and did as Angus McDermott, beefy and awkward in the role of Butler, ordered them. With the help of Prudie Turner and a kitchen maid, Peggy McDermott had turned out an array of soda bread sandwiches and tarts to complement cups of traditional whisky skin tea.

The master's liquor cabinet, under Angus's strict supervision, was open to The O'Brien gentry who appreciated something stronger. Relegated to the library where clay pipes and tobaccos were laid out, the men offered a puff of reverence between Irish toasts to the soul of the departed. Angus pulled at his collar and after ringing a bell, prompted several toasts with one raised glass after another. "To the O'Brien mistress and the protection of her soul in the hereafter."

"Until we meet again, may God hold her in the palm of his hand," Will Turner added, with a tear in his eye as the bell was passed to him.

In the parlor, the corpse held a similar bell—an emergency contingent—if by some miracle, life still remained. The sun's last rays were streaking through the mullioned glass, casting a tawny glow over the room when Sarah brought a silver tray of sandwiches and two cups of whisky tea to set beside Livy and her grieving father, who sat as immobile as the corpse in his tall-backed chair. Sarah replaced the dripping candles at the head and foot of her mistress while Livy nibbled at a sandwich, then folded it into a napkin and set it aside in favor of the tea. She leaned forward to whisper something to her father and he rose to stretch, drain his cup and with a parting nod to the mourners, adjourned to join the swell of voices emanating from the library.

Robbie and Lewy had already eaten, and in maintaining due respect in the viewing parlor, with simple gestures between them, they moved closer to the bier, taking the traditional stance that would keep them on watch through the night. Robbie tried to catch her eye, but Livy seemed transfixed, staring only at her mother's regal face.

Had the soul already departed? Livy had squeezed her mother's warm hand as she watched her take her final, almost imperceptible breaths, hoping superstition proved right. Would she utter a wild cry when the nearest kin touched her hand? Her mother had not cried or moved then, and her hands were cold as marble when she touched them now.

Only one parlor window was open for the soul's release. Was one enough? How long did it take? Would she know…see something rise like a dust mote…drifting on a current of air through the open window? Sarah had closed the window before replacing the candles. *Was that too soon, too late?* No one to ask now. Her mother had been a fierce believer of tradition and superstition, a living compendium of all that was proper and right. With the window closed, and the mourners departing, nothing stirred in the room but the flicker of candlelight and the heaviness of Olivia's own breath.

She had smiled and nodded for hours, accepting condolences, crossing herself with each memory, like blessings intoned. "Always in memory…a great lady…so kind and generous…too young to be taken…a sign that God wanted her…"

Her mum. Had she really known the woman who gave her life?

Most of her memories were stung by objections. Livy's objections to her mum's objections. Livy had won some of the battles: choosing her own clothes, tagging after Lewy and Robbie, laughing at customs, eventually refusing to consider "appropriate" suitors.

Waves breaking against cliffs. Anything to avoid the apprenticeship of a proper heiress. Her sentence to the finishing school in Dublin was her mother's last salvo.

She studied her own hands, so pale against her black dress. The mourning dress she wore had belonged to Margaret Moire O'Brien, hastily altered to fit her daughter's slender figure. Her mum would have approved the choice.

Robbie caught her eye when he moved in position at the head of the bier. Olivia knew he had been watching her through the day, but she had avoided him. Planned or not, they had carefully avoided each other for weeks, as the mistress took a turn for the worse. Once, when she came with his own mum to the croft for bunches of dried herbs and ointment, she had been awkwardly tense, uncharacteristic in her brevity. Until the mistress died and he was called to serve at the wake, their paths had not crossed again.

Their gazes met for the first time, and held. His heart clenched at the sight of her. The candlelight emphasized shadows circling her blue eyes, the only color in her pallid face. Her hair was pulled back into a bun, covered by a triangle of black lace that fringed her earlobes. She had been housebound for weeks—spelling his own mum with constant care in a lingering deathwatch.

Her lips stretched into a thin line as she closed her eyes and gripped the arms of her chair momentarily. He knew she was exhausted in her grief, and he wished he could help her. Say something. Do something. He straightened his back and leaned against the wall behind him, flexing one foot after another to adjust to his own stiffness. The black faille dress withered her like a raven caged in a wing-backed chair. This was not the Olivia he knew. Had the mantle of mistress already passed from one generation to the next?

By dusk, silence invaded the household until a clattering rose from the dining room as a kitchen maid began to clear away empty cups. Lewy immediately left his parlor post to help her, his friendly assistance happily motivated by draining what remained of the whiskey tea from one of the teapots. Not long after, Will Turner and Angus managed to carry their crapulent master from the library to his own bedroom. Angus was barely able to walk, himself, and the two men paused only long enough to order the two sentinels to keep watch until the morning burial.

"Only one day, the master decided. One day and night watch is all he can take, he sez, though she deserved a fortnight."

Will nodded, wiping his chin on a shoulder. "The mistress is done fer good, she won't be ringin' a bell in her box when she goes to ground in the morrow."

Robbie's mum had appeared throughout the day, supervising all service activity and pausing occasionally to cross herself as she perused the parlor scene with a housekeeper's detailed eye. His face colored when she whispered, "Straighten your cravat," as she stuffed a few extra candles into his livery pocket. On her final visit, she and the maid convinced Olivia to retire and arm in arm led the girl away, drifting between them with a swish of her long full skirt, as if she floated on air.

Robbie sipped at the cup of tea his mother had brought him, hoping it would keep him awake for the long watch. He followed the light of flickering candles into the shadowy reaches of the parlor. As a boy, he thought Meirliún was a mansion fit for an Irish Chieftain, with every room larger than the croft he called home. In truth, the parlor was more of an alcove to the dining room. A harpsichord and two easy chairs hugged the far wall, with a fireplace opposite, flanked by two settees. Odd tables and chairs had been moved to the dining room to make room for the wooden bier that held the mistress.

The smell of candle wax and roses mingled with the perfume and herbs that anointed the corpse. Two large urns of white roses bookended the fireplace, drawing his eyes to the portrait above the mantel. It was a much younger Livy, looking delicate in a white dress, her ankles crossed as she sat on a low garden wall, holding a book between lacy gloved hands. A short veil was pinned to the back of her long copper hair, anchored by a braid that arched her head like a tiara. Her blue eyes were clear and dreamy but her mouth was solemn, forming a pout, not unlike the grown-up Livy in mourning. He recognized the costume from her first communion, and thought maybe her parents had immortalized the occasion to remember their daughter in a dress she disdained. Until she was sent to the Dublin school, Livy was rarely seen in a dress.

Was it his imagination or could he paint a faint resemblance of today's Livy to the face in the coffin? The mistress's face was gray as the streaks in her hair, despite the effort to rouge her lips. No, he decided, there was no resemblance to her daughter, never was, except for the color of her hair before it faded. Illness had drained the mistress's bloom of life, but she had always been kind to him and his mother, remembering them both on name days and holidays with special gifts and invites to the manor.

A wake was only one of the Irish traditions with ancient origins. He thought about others. As long as he could remember, he had helped to clean up the ancestral graveyard each Christmas, pulling weeds and setting up candles for the traditional Christmas Eve homage. Afterwards, he and his mother had been invited back for refreshments to this very parlor decorated in holly, with cheery firelight and candles sparkling in every window. Every year, he had been invited to dine on black buns, skirlie and plum pudding.

On St. Stephen's Day, he and Lewy led the Wren Boys Procession with a stuffed wren atop a pole twined in holly. They traveled by wagon as far as the Gooseberry Coppice, dispensing jugs of cider, caraway seed cakes and satchels of fruit and nuts to tenant children in every croft, singing:

"The wren, the wren,
the king of all birds,
on St. Stephen's Day
was caught in the furze."

Olivia, dressed in britches, had often accompanied them, reveling in the camaraderie her disguise allowed. No one questioned where the third boy came from. The tenants were always too happy to receive Meirliún's gifts. No one but Robbie even seemed to notice when Livy's cap gave up a hidden braid of her long hair, or how the timbre of her voice changed when she laughed.

Livy was also well-disguised at her mum's wake, dressed for the occasion befitting mood and tradition, but with no small sign of the lass he knew.

Chapter Twenty-Four
Fire in the Soul

Lewy was already snoring softly in his chair, and Robbie was nodding off when he sensed a brush of movement in the room. Opening one eye, he focused sleepily on a halo of light at the foot of the bier. The candle had puddled into its pewter saucer, and the wick was struggling to maintain light. He fumbled a new taper from his livery pocket, lit it and carefully seated it in the melted wax before he noticed the candle at the head of the coffin was drifting toward the window. He rubbed his eyes…heard the latch break…felt a wisp of fresh air smudge his face.

The soul of the mistress, leaving her body?

Hadn't that already been presumed? The open window had been closed by his mum after the viewing. The light grew larger, multiplying, reflecting copper flames in the mullioned glass. He blinked again, focusing on a shimmery slip of white swaying in a new flood of air as the window creaked open.

The ghost of the mistress?

"*Saoirse,*" she whispered, leaning over the sill into the ocean breeze. The candle flame broke into tiny stars that caught in her hair. Robbie leaped to her side, smothering the sparks with his gloved hands. Her muffled scream startled them both, and she fell backward into his arms, both collapsing on the floor with a loud thump. The snuffed candle rolled out of her hands, splattering drops of hot wax on the blue and purple Donegal carpet.

"Livy, *A Dhia*, what have you done!" He cried over the limp body, frantically crushing her singed hair and sparks that blinked like fireflies across her shoulders.

Lewy woke with a start and stumbled across the room holding the new taper aloft "Wha, what in God's name?" he sputtered.

"Her hair, her hair was afire." Robbie tore off his jacket to cover the filmy nightgown she wore, then scooped her into his arms and twirled around, indecisive in panic. "To her room, there must be water in her room."

They fled swiftly down a darkened hallway, Lewy guiding with the candle. At the end of the corridor, he shouldered the door open and Robbie plopped Livy on a large canopied bed and smothered her hair and shoulders with a pillow until she began to claw the air.

Lewy grabbed a pitcher of water from her dressing table and shoved it at Robbie. "Easy Lad, you're suffocating the poor lass!"

She coughed as water dribbled over her sooty face and hair. Robbie peeled off his charred gloves and slapped her cheeks with his hands. "Livy, speak to me, look at me."

She opened her eyes and blinked, then coughed again, struggling to sit up. "Robbie?" Her gaze shifted to Lewy. "What are you doing here?"

Robbie gently pushed her back on the wet pillow. "You were sleep-drifting, Livy." With a corner of the damp sheet, he swept lines of soot from her forehead and brows. "Your hair caught fire from the candle you held."

She clamped a hand on her head and her lips quivered when she examined the clump of charred hair tangled between her fingers. "My hair…what…what have I done?"

"You whispered *'freedom'* at the parlor window. The breeze fanned the flame…"

She looked up at him, her eyes wide and glistening with tears. "I dreamt I had to free mum's soul. It was all on me. I put her in that coffin, Robbie."

"No, Livy."

She pushed herself up on her elbows, shaking her head. "It's true. We had words, even in her deathwatch. She called me careless and wild, a *cailín fiáin*. Told me I was unworthy to be mistress of Meirliún." Livy plopped back on the damp pillow and stared at him, her blue eyes puddling with tears that spilled down her cheeks. "I killed her."

"Livy, it was not your fault." Robbie took up her hand and picked at the hair still webbing her fingers. "She died of the weak heart. Your da told everyone…"

She fisted a sob. "A disappointment I was…to both of them. Not a son for Da, never the lady mum wished."

"Your da loves you, Livy. It was he who freed your spirit years ago, when he permitted you to tag with us." He gestured to Lewy.

"A grave mistake, mum said. No good could ever come to my soul from chasing low boys."

Lewy rolled his eyes and the candle he held wavered. "*Dhia*, are we in a confessional? All this soul and spirit *urlabhra.* Sorry I am, lass, that your mum has passed, but Rob is right. Not your fault. Disease takes low and highborn alike, at any age, unless they are kilt or take poison by error."

When Livy smothered a sob in her pillow, Robbie grabbed the taper from Lewy. "You are such a comfort, you sot." He gave Lewy a shove toward the door. "Go keep night watch. I'll join up ere long."

Livy was still sniveling when Robbie glanced her way. "Lewy was in his cups with whiskey tea by nightfall. Pay him no mind."

"I never do." She pushed herself off the bed, dragging the wet pillow and coverlet over to the fireplace where Robbie was nursing peat bricks into flame. "These can dry here."

"You keep fresh linens nearby?"

She pointed to a trunk across the room. The damp top of her nightgown molded to her breasts, and the firelight revealed the shapely silhouette of her body and legs through the fine linen.

Robbie pulled a flannel counterpane out of the chest, along with a small silver flask buried deep in the bedding. He covered her shoulders with the flannel. His eyebrow arched when he shook the flask. It was half-full yet.

She flushed. "Wild, I may be, but not a sot. That's been stowed there for years—for emergencies."

He smiled. "*Years?*"

"Canary wine. The taste warmed me when I was young."

He held the flask to her mouth. "This is an emergency. It may still warm you, unless it's turned to vinegar."

She took the flask in both hands and emptied the contents, then held a finger to her mouth to cover a small burp. "I am a poor sight," she whispered, combing fingers through her hair, and stricken once again by sooty strands caught between her fingers. She shook her head, raining more soot onto her shoulders. Robbie brushed it away, tearing thin material weakened by tiny cinder holes. The gown drooped over one shoulder, revealing a small purple birthmark shaped like a rose petal.

Looking into her liquid eyes, he tried to smile away the sorrow he felt for her. "Does it burn…do you feel any pain?" He examined her scalp, afraid to part the patches that remained. "I don't think the flame reached your scalp."

She shook her head. "I feel only light-headed…and careless as named."

"Your hair will come back."

"Aye, but my mam will not." She looked into the fire, bracing one hand on the mantel. "I am the careless poison that killed her."

"That is grief speaking."

"That is the truth, Robbie. What harm would have come from soothing her last days, honoring her last wishes." She looked up at him. "That is the least any common Irish daughter would do."

He wondered what those last wishes might have been, wondered what they had argued about. "But you were not born a *common* lass." He put his arms around her, letting her weep against him while he stroked her back, understanding but not knowing how to comfort her when he carried a similar shame. He was born a *common* bastard—a cold reminder of his own mum and the shame he caused her. Maybe not overtly his fault, but still… His mum had become distant to him, lately. Had he disappointed her, as well. Perhaps he was a reminder of the father he knew only from the fading photograph?

He nuzzled his chin over Livy's head, smelling the acrid scent of singed hair. He could feel her perky breasts poking his chest through two layers of clothing. Layers. There would always be layers between them—dividing, separating, quelling choices of the heart. He bent to kiss her forehead, and an involuntary sob caught in his throat. "I must go, Livy. Back to my station."

"No, Robbie." She locked her arms around his neck. "You can't…don't leave me." Stretching on tiptoes, she pulled him down to meet her mouth in a desperate kiss.

He wrenched her arms apart. "Livy, this isn't right."

"Love me, Robbie." Her blue eyes were wide with pleading. "In my state, this is the only thing that feels right now." She pushed her tattered nightgown off both shoulders, letting it slip down to puddle at her feet. "Body and soul, you alone have my heart."

He stood there, mouth agape, speechless and sweaty, rooted in emotion. He had never seen her full naked in firelight. On St. John's Eve, his hands had groped and caressed on a moonless beach, then he slept beside her in his croft bed, with a snuffed candle blinding him of the guilt he felt. She was gone by the light of dawn, and until today, their paths had not crossed again.

Before Livy, Robbie had never touched a breast or belly or slipped between a woman's legs. Standing before him now, Livy was a milky wraith in the amber glow of the peat fire. Her chin was up, her nipples taut and rosy and her slim legs parted. Nothing in her posture reflected the pity that clenched him when he beheld her ragged hair or the longing in her eyes.

His mouth was dry. He swallowed hard, fighting the thirst for what she offered. "Oh, Livy," he heard himself moan before offering token resistance when she began to tug at his breeks. When all that fell between them was his long shirt and the silence of denial, he could feel his heart pump wildly, and lower, the most eager sign of capitulation. He closed his eyes, took a step backward and sucked in his breath. "This is indecent, Olivia. Not now, there can be no…us…not anymore."

She placed her palm against his beating heart. "No, sweet Robert," she tossed back his full name, her voice low. "Nothing changes. I am *cailín fiáin*, the wild girl who jumped the fire to you. You can't deny what happened on St. John's Eve. I rescued you then. You rescued me tonight."

"Anyone would have done that. Lewy would have done that if he woke before me."

"Then rescue me again. One last time." With a throaty sob, arms locked around his neck, she pulled him into a frantic kiss. He could taste the sweet wine that lingered yet on her tongue. His hand slipped behind her back, caressing the bony ridge of her backbone, sliding lower to the soft curve of her bottom.

They moved, gliding toward the canopied bed, sinking into the feathery comfort. "Yess." She hissed like a flame touched by water, as she drew the bed curtains closed, plunging them into darkness.

Chapter Twenty-Five
God Only Knows

He woke naked, disoriented—darkness enclosing him. *Was he dead?* No, he could feel his chest rise and fall, his heartbeat prickling in his ears, throbbing in his temple. Ring the bell. *No bell.* He reached to his left, knuckles brushing against tapestry and the movement made the mattress ripple beneath him. *No straw.* Too soft. He could smell something acrid, burnt. He wiggled a foot, touching something. Warm flesh? *Not alone.* He groped to the right, sliding fingers along the warm curve of a back, and his heart began to hammer as it slowly came to him.

Had he been drinking? How could he? He had been standing at attention most of the day. A few cups of whiskey tea, maybe something sweeter. He licked his lips and swished his tongue around in the cavern of his mouth.

She shifted beside him, moaning a little, and he remembered her musical voice, whimpering, cajoling, little squeaks of pleasure muffled by his own deep voice, confined to the space between the curtains. Between the curtains? Oh God, what had he done? He tugged the heavy drape open, and blinked at the tentacles of blue-gray light sweeping into the room. It was near dawn and even in the thin light he could tell the room nearly doubled the size of his entire croft.

Rugs muted the plank floors, defining the room's perimeters with ornate chests and a chaise lurking in the shadows.

Edging slowly off the bed, he carefully closed the drapes behind him. Found his clothes scattered before the cold fireplace, his green livery coat thrown over a wooden chair. His heart was pounding as he dressed, pulled on his boots, and tiptoed out of the room, closing the door quietly behind him.

He slinked into the parlor like an outside dog, finding it cold and dim, smelling of death and wilting roses. The candles had melted long ago, leaving only waxy lumps in the sconces. Lewy was asleep in Livy's wing chair, chin to chest, chuffing snorts. He found a flint box and lit a fresh supply of wake candles. Orders had been explicit. Wake candles should never be allowed to expire. All night, they were to blaze according to tradition, and the corpse honored by attendants who stood watch for the last hopeful ring of life. The bell was unmoved, still in the porcelain hands of the mistress. The sound of Lewy's strangled sputters and wheezes were the only proof of life in the room. He started a peat fire in the fireplace, then lit every other candle he could find, until the room was bright again.

Lewy woke with the light, and after establishing nothing errant was afire, he pointed out with a smirk that Robbie's chin was gray with smudge and his cravat was missing. "You were overlong, boyo." Lewy fished in his pocket for a linen square and still smirking, handed it to Robbie. He then untied his own cravat and offered it as well. "Singed by her fire, eh?"

Robbie blushed, brushing his hands on his livery jacket and raised his chin to allow Lewy to adjust the cravat. “Thanks, Lewy, mum would spot me for sure, missing this.”

“Think I don’t know that? You’ve always been held to a higher court than me. How does she fare?”

“Livy? She sleeps well.”

Grinning, Lewy fisted him on the shoulder. “Well-sated I trust.”

Head down, Robbie gave him a narrow eye. “How do you know…if you’re in love?

Lewy shrugged. “Love and lust are two sides of the same coin, I’m thinkin.’ I’m glad you’ve rolled with her, though I canna see it ending well with the lass, even if ye were equals.”

Robbie slumped in the nearest chair, pinching the bridge of his nose. “What can I do?”

“Maybe what I always do, boyo. Put some distance into the match.”

Robbie looked up, searching his face. “You don’t mean leave Meirliún?”

“I do.”

“How could you? This is the only home we’ve known. It’s where we grew up.”

Lewy snorted. “You want to be a servant all your life, Rob? Doing someone else’s bidding. Do we not deserve a life, maybe a family of our own making?”

Robbie rubbed his forehead. He had heard this before. “But we have no means to build a life outside of Meirliún.”

Lewy made a rude noise, throwing up his hands. “We are no longer tree-pissing children. We have these, and a backbone, and, well, I know of no one who has more learnin’…than you, Rob. And you are an O’Brien…better named than myself, in this county, anyway. You will get on."

Robbie stared at his boyhood friend. Reckless, self-serving, foul-mouthed Lewy, and his throat suddenly felt the knot of his tie. Bastard tripped over many tongues describing Lewy, but he was not the real thing. Lewy, at least, had grown up under a father's care and guidance, however polluted that might have been. Suddenly feeling the need for fresh air, he rose and went to open the window. "You've given some thought to this, then?"

Lewy followed him to the window. "I've been sitting here all night in this *diabhal* uniform, staring at death. Thinking. The mistress had less than forty years—what if that befalls us? Not even twenty more years of life to taste freedom and choices only we can make. Think on it!"

"She died young, Lewy. Her heart was weak. I know folk who lived more than twice her age."

Lewy sighed. "That's not my point, boyo. Do we live to serve others or dare to serve ourselves?"

Robbie pinched the bridge of his nose again. "God only knows how much time we are allowed on earth." He gazed at what remained of a woman he had known all his life. "Her death has made ye eloquent," he said with a wistful half grin.

A ringing bell made them both start, and focus sharply on the bell in the corpse's frozen hands. Behind them, Angus McDermott laughed at his joke, holding the cord attached to a bell in the dining room. Despite the jest, his face was drawn, his hair and clothing disheveled. He nodded at Robbie. "Your mum sent me to spell you boys while you find some porridge and tea in the kitchen. She thinks you will need your strength to heave the coffin to the graveyard."

"We will have aid, will we not?" Lewy asked.

"Aye, son, Will and I, an mebbe two others will bear the thing out. I'll stand watch here while you break fast, but be quick about it." He squinted down at the corpse, combing his hair with his fingers and pulling at his collar. "Dead as yesterday's swill, our lady is. She'll not be ringin' any bell agin." Lewy rolled his eyes at Robbie as they hurried from the room

Chapter Twenty-Six
The Burial

Father Joseph from St. Colman's in Kinvara was invited to stay for lunch after Margaret Moire O'Brien was interred in her Meirliún gravesite near the rose garden. The eight-mile journey from Kinvara took him nearly two hours on a borrowed mule in a typical Irish mist. Arriving before nine in the morning, he expected to return for noon mass at St. Colman's. He didn't count on the rain, a recalcitrant mule, or the lingering O'Brien heiress.

When Olivia finally emerged from her bedchamber an hour later, on the arm of her doting father, she was cloaked in black from head to toe. The heavy veil she wore muffled her apology. He could barely see her mouth moving, but her scent was unmistakable, almost cloying of rosewater and mint. She held a single white rose in her black-gloved hand.

Her father left her sitting in the arbor while he apologized further as they waited for the bier to be moved into position. It was only a few hundred yards to the gravesite, and the tenants, servants, and some of the neighbors huddled in groups under umbrellas or tree branches, all eager to fall in behind the casket processional. They, too, had been waiting for Olivia, and chinwag among them ran the gamut:

"Poor thing—Grieving hard for her mum—Easy to

oversleep—Hard to fathom—Her mother was never tardy—So disrespectful—who does she think she is, veiled like a princess royal?"

Angus and Will Turner, Robbie and Lewy, and one of the tenants were all that was needed to carry the casket. The Mistress was small in stature and withered more by her illness. The polished coffin was built from the watertight wood of an Alder bench and table that graced the garden for decades. The Mistress herself had ordered the coffin made a month ago, after she fell in the garden and was found weeping with a bunch of daylilies in her hand.

The men lowered the coffin into the open grave with heavy ropes, greased to slide away more easily once positioned. A bench for The O'Brien and his daughter was positioned along one side of the grave. Surreptitiously, Robbie watched Livy settle at the far end, still clutching the rose in her lap. He arranged his thoughts as the rest of the mourners, including his mother, closed around the grave, giving respectful space to the priest at the head. He was relieved that Livy concealed her hair. No sense fanning the winds of gossip, though it might have circulated that she tore out her hair from grief.

The young priest opened the rites from the Book of Prayer he held close, sheltering it from the mist with the brim of his hat. He then invited the mourners to sing "Nearer My God to Thee" while he juggled books to open his Bible and read from Gen. 28, relating how the song was based on Jacob's dream.

Good choice, Robbie thought, connecting song to liturgy based on a dream. He had stopped attending church with his mum for some time now, and had never been to a formal funeral. Did it count when he and Lewy once helped a distraught shepherd bury his sheepdog? Over a small grave beneath a Rowan tree, Robbie shed a tear for the shepherd's loss. He knew Ennis, the dog, had seen him in action many times, marveling at the way he maneuvered his flock, and the fealty he paid to his owner.

Then there was old Danny O'Halloran who drifted around Galway with no kin, sleeping on a pallet in the ruins of Dunguaire Castle on an outcrop of the Bay. He and Lewy had been gathering shore crabs at the Southeast end when they came across the old man's bloated body covered by brown and green crabs. The smell of decay and rum was overpowering. The boys alerted four fishermen on the quay, and the body was hauled up to the castle yard in a canvas sail. Old Danny had been warned by Kinvara authorities to abandon his trespass, but the small castle was centuries old and some said it was haunted. Who could begrudge a homeless man from taking care of something so historic, begging for bread and ale in exchange for an informal tour and a tale of the overlords who once lived there?

The boys had trailed along to witness a hasty burial in the castle yard and were sworn to secrecy by the sympathetic men who cheated a pauper's grave in town. "It's the least we can do for the old beggar," one of the men had declared. "He was king of his final outpost, and should be consecrated in the grounds he loved so well."

The boys never returned to Dunguaire Castle, famous now for the new ghost said to roam there.

The young priest was now reading from one of the

newer Church of Ireland Bibles, embossed with gold lettering on the spine. It had stopped raining but the air was heavy with the smell of rain and fresh bloom, more like spring than late fall. There were even a few buds left on the rose bushes that bloomed so profusely, and so late in a season unusual for its warmth. The last of the roses had been cut for the parlor vases.

"When Christ…shall appear then shall ye also appear with him in glory. Mortify then your members which are upon the earth: fornication, uncleanness, inordinate affection, evil concupiscence…"

Laughter cut into the priest's words, stopping him mid-sentence as everyone looked confused, searching for the source of the interruption. Robbie could see Livy's shoulders shake, and at first he thought she was crying. When her father moved on the bench to console her, she pushed him away and laughed more shrilly. A collective gasp and a buzz of whispers drifted up from the mourners as her father beckoned to Sarah and she came at once, bending low to whisper something against the dark veil. Wedged now on the bench between the master and Robbie's mum, the small dark figure slumped in silence as the priest continued.

"For which things the wrath of God cometh on the children of disobedience…"

Another interruption, split this time between sob and laughter, cut through the heavy dampness, and with a look, the priest abruptly closed his Bible and loudly began the final intonation with the sign of the cross, "…dust to dust, ashes to ashes…"

Robbie held his breath, his gaze riveted on Livy and his mother, standing shoulder to shoulder now, heads bowed in unison with most of the mourners, save those craning necks to see what further drama might erupt. When the prayer was over, Livy placed her rose on the casket, and the veil moved slightly as she whispered something only Sarah and her father seemed to acknowledge. Her father reeled a bit before he whispered back. Sarah's arm coerced more than sheltered Livy as they separated from the mourners to move toward the manor house.

Donal O'Brien thanked the priest and took final condolences from those gathered. Robbie heard him making patchy excuses for Livy. "Doting child…sick with grief…deep in mourning…" The haunting music of a bagpipe interrupted, playing "Down by the Sally Gardens," and people began to disperse, those with horses penned near the barn in one direction, those on foot in another.

He stood stiff with emotion, his heart thumping in his chest. He heard what Livy heard, and shared the scripture's conviction. *Fornication, inordinate affection, evil concupiscence.* The words echoed in his head, burned in his chest. He tugged at his damp collar, feeling a tide of shame. He was complicit. Equally sinful. No, it was all his fault. She was vulnerable, riddled with guilt.

Táidhes on the eve of her mother's sacred burial? Had she confessed to her father? His mother? Surely, they saw her hair. How could she explain that without bringing him into it?

He wheeled around when Lewy clapped him on the back. "You all right, boyo? You look ready for the ground yourself."

Robbie pulled a hand over his face and took a deep breath. "'Twas all my fault."

Lewy opened his jacket and after a quick look around—pushed a small flask into his hand. "Take this, an go home, boyo. I'll make yer excuses."

Chapter Twenty-Seven
Shunned By Remorse?

She didn't go back to Dublin until after the holidays. For the next seven weeks, he caught only flashes of her, dark shadows behind a window, a kneeling figure in a black turban beside her mother's grave, and once, in a hooded cloak, quick as a raven skittering across a snowy dooryard with an armful of fir branches. He called out to her when he came upon her that day, his arms loaded with a box of cut turf for the manor, but she didn't hear him—or didn't want to—as she fled to the house and closed the door behind her firmly enough to make the black wreath swing on its twine rope. He straightened the door wreath and pressed his forehead into the cold stone frame, savoring the scent of a holly sprig tied alongside.

"Livy, we need to talk," he said, hoping she was listening on the other side. His voice echoed against the stone. Silence penetrated the door and chilled his heart.

When he finished his daily chores, he often found himself looking up at her window, watching for a moving shadow. His mum told him Livy often confined herself to her room, reading, doing needlework, even preferring to eat there alone. He knew she was still guilt-ridden, and by her gravesite explosion, he knew she was blaming herself, maybe blaming him for the *"evil concupiscence"* the priest spoke of. It wasn't like

Livy to belabor and retreat. She rarely apologized for anything she said or did. Small relief, it gave him, knowing he wasn't singled out in the shunning.

Sarah's duties as companion transferred from mother to daughter, which still required her to remain in the manor house, leaving Robbie to his own devices in the croft. She left behind her cruit, and in the long lonely nights, when sleep was a stranger, he plucked the strings and tried to remember the tunes she played that always lulled him to sleep.

Lewy sometimes joined him there for the night, as winter weather shortened days and hours of light. He often brought a flask to share and a deck of cards to play Switch by the firelight. Robbie was glad for his company and any report of a reclusive Livy, since she had become a celebrity source for local chinwags in and out of the manor house.

"The *rua* is more typical than we thought of Irish lasses. Me da calls them all 'drama afoot with swift tongues and swishing backsides.'"

Robbie cracked a weak smile. "Lewy, you know that isn't Livy. She lost her mum and…and she feels remorse for what never was between them. Besides, she doesn't swish."

Lewy raised an eyebrow and scratched his chin. "Well, maybe the wrong word falls there, but swish she did for you, boyo."

Robbie could feel the heat rise in his neck, but he said nothing. His concentration over the card game was broken and once again, he slept poorly, in spite of the advice and a prodigious amount of ale he consumed.

****

"Her hair has grown enough to cast off the turban

she fancied," Sarah reported. "We cut it to even the edges. Like new growth after a groundfire, I think it is even more lush in color." At least once a week mother and son supped together from the basket of food she brought to the croft.

"The girl comes out to the parlor to play the harpsichord, and for *Nollag,* she practiced a fugue and even "Curoo Curoo"—all good signs, I'm thinking."

Robbie smiled weakly. "Relieved to hear it."

Sarah fished in her pocket for a small satchel. "The master wanted you to have this for Christmas. There won't be a formal dinner for everyone in the manor house this year, but a meal or coin will be paid to all the staff. Things may change, once the mourning period ends. The young mistress grieves more strangely even than her father, but that may change once she's back to Dublin."

"Will you give her a letter from me, then?" Robbie pulled a small wrinkled envelope from his pocket and set it on the table beside her cup of tea, and their eyes met for a long moment. "It's just that I want her to know my sympathies are with her. We were friends that long ago."

Sara sipped her tea and chose her words carefully. "Aye, son, I know you and Lewy were charged with her care once, but she is grown now, educated in the ways of a lady, and nearly of an age to marry."

"To marry?" He swallowed his surprise. "She can't be more than ten and six."

"And in a year, when the mourning is done, she'll be old enough for a proper suitor."

"Did she, does she talk of this?"

"Not yet, but her father has told me there have been

inquiries."

"*Inquiries?*"

"She is the heiress of Meirlíun, Robbie. Saving it rides on her."

"Her father tells you this?

Sarah colored as she rose to clear the table. "He is a lonely man with the mistress gone. From time to time, he asks me to take tea with him, especially when his head hurts. My warm herbal teas relax him, he says."

Robbie snickered, stretching his long legs beneath the table. "Tea with the master, mum? You seem to be favored with several roles in the household. Were you not just the housekeeper after the mistress died, and now companion to The O'Brien as well as his daughter? Not so long ago, you warned me of *my* place, and said we should be grateful that we have been provided for."

Sarah's dark eyes blinked. "And so we should. I will always be grateful to Conal O'Brien for taking in the two of us. A clean house, a cuppa tea and a motherly watch over his daughter is small payment for his kindness."

"A motherly watch over his daughter?" Robbie gave in to a sharp twist of sarcasm. "You sure a matronly jailor doesn't better fit what you describe? Perhaps the master also means to elevate you as his bed warmer in time."

Sarah carefully set down her cup of tea and surprised him with a hard slap across his mouth. "Robbie, that's gutter gob…unworthy of you."

He sucked in his lower lip. "Well, mum, what can you expect from a bastard?"

She stared at him, blinking away the film in her

eyes. Without another word, she snatched his letter from the table and left with it, slamming the door behind her.

He picked up her teacup and threw it against the door with such force that a hailstorm of pieces flew back at him. He bent to pick up the pieces, choking back an acid mix of anger and remorse.

Sarah pulled her shawl tight against her and lifted her woolen skirt to run back to the manor house, scarcely taking in a breath of the cold wind that gripped her inside and out. When she reached her room, down the hall from the young mistress, she bolted her door, and lit the small coal stove that heated her through the night. She undressed, carefully laying her cloak and shawl over a chair, stacking her half boots beside the stove, and pulled her nightgown over her head before she took out her hairpins and brushed her hair with a vengeance.

When she remembered the letter in her skirt pocket, she was quick to open the seal and hold it to the firelight to read. Half way through the second time, she heard a soft knock at her bedroom door and hesitated only seconds before casting the letter into the firebox before she padded to the door.

Conal stood there in his dressing gown and cap, holding a candle, his dark eyes glazed by a familiar look.

Sarah pulled him inside and latched the door again. “Is it your head?”

“Not this time,” he said, taking her in his arms and burying his face in her unpinned hair.

She stood stiff and breathless, captured in his embrace, letting him kiss her forehead while Robbie’s cruel words rang in her ears. Slowly, her arms circled his waist, and she began to breathe again.

Chapter Twenty Eight
The Tuke Fund

"The what?" Robbie hoisted the last of the salt bags into the wagon, toppling over a keg of ale that rolled between bales of dried seaweed in the wagon bed. Lewy turned on the wagon seat, waving the *Galway Express* he bought from a newsboy on the wharf.

"Tuke. It's called the Tuke Fund," Lewy explained. "Part government aid, part private benevolence for relieving the destitute families in the western regions. It's *free* emigration, Rob, think on it. We could apply for it at Oughterard and if we qualify, we'll be in Boston in April!"

"Wrong County, Lewy, and we are not a destitute family," Robbie replied calmly as he rearranged the supplies in the wagon bed.

"I'm destitute, boyo, and we are distantly related, are we not?" Lewy frowned. "It can't hurt to apply for a certificate. They're taking whole families—brothers and cousins and grandparents, Irish, Scots, even Russian tenant farmers. All laborers—people like us, boyo." He doffed his cap and flung it at Robbie for emphasis. "This says there will be three emigrations sailing fer Boston or Canada, the first leaving Blacksod Bay with a stop in Galway at the end of March."

Robbie chuckled, tossing back Lewy's cap. He had

never seen him so enthused. He'd never seen Lewy even reading a broadside, much less a newspaper. He climbed into the wagon and grabbed the paper, already damp from the mist rolling over the bay. Under a woodcut of a three-masted ship named the *S.S. Nestorian*, he read about the proposed emigration made possible—with a private benevolence of 3,000 pounds from the Duchess of Marlborough.

"This says the ship will stop here after Blacksod Bay?"

"Aye, Galway! For a second pick-up from the islands and County Clare as well. Me own da came home last week from a trip to Inisheer and said the islanders were all abuzz with this. The Gilboys and Barrett families already have certificates in hand."

"Are your parents thinking of this for themselves?"

"Mum would never leave Meirliún," he scoffed. "She's wedded to her kitchen, and da with her."

"But you would leave *them*?"

Lewy adjusted his wool cap. "I would miss her for sure, but there's nothing fer me here but a tenancy near the coppice or a fisherman's life in the Bay district." He gestured with a two-handed appeal. "I want to see what's beyond the ocean. America is land rich and beggin' fer people to settle it from coast to coast. Johnny Nolan wrote back to his cousin that farmers can earn four to five pounds a month and railroaders get eight to ten schillings per day in America!"

Robbie rubbed his chin, rolling his thumb around a patch of new whiskers. "I don't know, Lewy. I'd have to ask my mum what she thinks."

"Geezus, Rob. You're a man now. You don't need your mum's permission to find your way."

"She's all I've truly got of family, and knowin' that she fled from America once, I don't see her wantin' to go back. And then there's…" His voice drifted off as he eyed the Galway Hookers drifting ahead of the weather back into port.

"You can't still be thinking of her? Boyo, that ship has sailed long ago. We both know that. Did she even respond to one of your letters?"

Robbie shook his head.

"How many did you write?"

He held up five fingers.

"Gossip has it that she is already in half mourning in Dublin—wearing purple and gray now, even gadding about at socials."

"Socials? She's not in school, then?"

Lewy shrugged. "A sorry school it would be if they dinna finish the girls with practice. You know, playing hostess at teas, teaching dance. Me mum heard the school sometimes invites naval officers to practice with. Like mock socials, she sez."

Robbie sighed. "They practice more with their own gender. Livy told me once how some of the girls volunteer to play a lad's role. She was always in that camp, and said they laughed at her when she remembered to take a tone and swagger like one of us."

"The little monkey imitated us?" Lewy laughed heartily. "We tutored her well then." He thought for a moment. "What's a swagger?"

"Puff talk and prancing," I think.

"I do not prance, boyo."

Robbie snickered, taking up the reins. "I'll think on this emigration thing."

****

Robbie paced while Sarah studied the newspaper he handed her. When she finished reading the front page, she set it aside and patted the settee beside her, urging Robbie to sit. He had not been in the Meirliún parlor since the funeral months ago, or even in the house except to unload kitchen supplies and stay briefly for a cup of tea offered by Lewy's mum. He was never formally invited, even with his mum living there in her own quarters. And since their recent fight, he lost even that hope for an invitation. Each week, however, Sarah continued to visit the croft with food, clean laundry and spotty news of life in the manor. News that now avoided any mention of Livy. She always shook her head sadly when Robbie asked if she had a letter for him. After the lass left on the railway from Galway, Livy's name was never again raised between them.

The furniture was rearranged and a table now stood below the window that Livy had opened the night her hair caught fire. A small table covered the spot on the Donegal carpet that may have been damaged by hot tallow. The portrait of Livy that once hung over the fireplace was gone, replaced by a pastoral scene of grazing sheep around a majestic Rowan tree.

"This, this seems like a great opportunity," she said, smoothing the folds of her apron over her gray woolen dress. "I thought the great migration was thirty years past, though."

"'Tis true, mum, but Ireland has not fully recovered from the famine. The northern districts, especially, are more rock than soil—too poor to support families. That paper says those who have already migrated write back about the opportunities in North America. Not just in farming."

"So you want to emigrate for opportunity?"

"I, I'm thinking on it, if you will consider it, too."

Sarah shifted her shoulders to clasp hands on her knees. Hands surprisingly smooth and dainty for a housekeeper. He couldn't quite put his finger on it, but he thought she looked…serene since she moved into the manor house for good.

"I never told you this, Robbie, but I was barely seven when I made the crossing with my family thirty years ago. We were crammed into steerage below decks with all our belongings, including my mum's precious books—some of the same books you learned from."

Robbie smiled, thinking of those weathered and worn old primers with words underlined and writing smudged in the margins.

"Your grandmum taught school to fisher folk who sailed the Bay, you see. Mostly women yearning to read and write along with their daughters. Sons took to the sea at an early age. Mum knew some English and expected to teach Irish immigrants in America." She paused, wringing her hands.

"*Coffin ships.* They were called coffin ships. The ones that crossed in the '40s and '50s were called that for good reason, Robbie." She paused again. "Mum and my wee brother died of the typhus two weeks before we reached the new land." Her voice hitched when she described how she stood beside her da on deck, "watching half my family bound together in a shroud…slip into a watery grave, along with two other poor souls."

Robbie moved closer to his mother, and covered her trembling hands with one of his.

"My da never recovered from the loss. I took to the

streets in Boston begging for schillings while he hobbled beside me with a cane, pretending to be blind. We lived in a drafty hovel near the marketplace and had a good meal when I was able to scramble with other waifs for leavings of rotted vegetables or fish at day's end.

"I thought we had it made when I was also hired to sell apples and cabbage a year later for three schillings a week. Da continued to beg, but whatever he made went for a pint." She smiled wistfully. "Oh, he took pains to hide the purchases from me, but I knew the stench. Whiskey and cabbage. Even a blind man would have known our stench combined. Da called me his cabbage girl and when he was in his cups, he was merry enough to promise me the moon. 'Someday,' he said, 'someday Sarah you'll be rigged in foine clothes and treated like the lady yer mum was.'"

Robbie patted her hand, noting the new dress she wore. "Not far from the truth, mum."

"Our fortunes improved when a pub owner named Kelly took him on to promote fights. With a pair of boxing gloves strung across his shoulders, Da walked the streets passing out broadsides announcing a weekly fight at Kelly's Oyster House."

"Did you go to the fights, mum?" He pressed her hand, urging her to continue when she stopped suddenly.

A tiny smile quivered on her lips. "Once. Females were never allowed, but one time I pulled my hair into a cap and wore knickers to squeeze in with the crowd and creep up the stairs to get a better view. The noise was rippling…and the language…O' Lord. Men already in their cups were placing bets, braying curses and taunts, encouraging the fighters, and giving them little room to dodge and parry on the plank floor. The smell of sweat and whiskey was everywhere. Hoots and whistles pierced the tavern when one of the fighters went down for the count. 'Twas then I saw my da across the room and thought he recognized me. I scampered up the stairs and ran into a room at the end of the landing."

Sarah checked herself, biting her lip with a glance at Robbie.

"Did you get away, then. Go on, mum."

Sarah flushed brightly, holding a hand to the side of her face as she looked away. "Well, I found I wasn't the only female in the Oyster House. There was a girl kneeling before a man. At first I thought she was prayin,' but the man had a, a look on his face and his trousers were puddled around his ankles. They were…concentrating, so I uh, I tiptoed over to an open window and climbed onto a small porch and shinnied down a post and ran all the way home. I slipped into bed and pretended to be asleep when da came home a little later."

Robbie bit his own lip to keep from laughing. He couldn't picture his pious mother—at any age—in any such circumstance. It was a rare glimpse of her childhood, rarer still to hear her talk of her parents—perhaps her longest reminiscence in any case. He didn't know how to respond, what to say to this demure little woman in a gray wool dress with a small cross pinned to her white collar. Most often, she spoke with an economy of words. He suddenly wanted to know more. What became of his grandfather? How did she come to be a maid in his father's Virginia house? Was she in love with his father? What he most wanted to know, he could never ask. Had she also forgotten *'her place'*?

She broke the silent string of questions, fiddling with the pin on her collar. "I tell you this now, Robbie, because I want you to know why I can never leave Meirliún." She looked up at him, her doe eyes wide with entreaty. "This is the only home in both countries that makes me feel…needed."

Robbie sighed deeply and leaned over to kiss her flushed cheek. Over the last year, he had come to understand the sharp difference between feeling a need and feeling needed.

"I have to go," he whispered.

She hugged him fiercely and her voice cracked when she whispered back. "I know."

Chapter Twenty-Nine
Even the Connemara Emigrated

Lewy deemed it fortuitous that the master would send he and Robbie to a horse farm in Oughterard to pick up a Connemara mare to replace Old Ned who died of colic in early March. Oughterard also happened to be the nearest county site taking applicants for the Tuke Emigration plan.

Edward Brady was a weedy man with the gift of Irish gab. He picked up all four of the mare's hoofs and with a sharp stick, dug out clods of manure. "Without this breeding stock of Connies," he said, "I surely would have lost my way years ago." The ponies he sold each spring were tough as the turf that fed them, a breed known all over Eire for their endurance and willing nature.

The dapple-gray whinnied shrilly and tossed her black mane when Brady fitted her with a coarse rope bridle. From a distant pasture, a half-dozen horses ran the fence line, some of them returning the call. The horseman laughed and ran his blunt fingers through her mane and over her arched neck. "There, there, girl," he gently soothed, and after the horse settled, he pushed back his straw hat and winked at the boys with eyes that matched the color of the mare.

"This girl has had her run of the pasture for nigh onto four year now. She be ready for plough or cart with some training." He looked from lad to lad. "Ye know how to train a Connemara?"

Lewy shrugged but Robbie smiled, rubbing her hindquarters at the top of her tail, like he always did to calm Livy's Connemara pony. Frosty grew fat and foundered when Livy first left for school. Robbie built a dry pen for her and learned how best to trim her hooves. When she lost some weight and moved with her former ease, the master sent her with Robbie to the Clifden horse fair to trade for Ned, a large muscled plough horse. Livy was furious when she found out and boycotted her father the whole summer, refusing to speak to him. She had a few sharp words with Robbie as well, until he told her about the children who were the beneficiary of the sale.

Robbie dug in his pocket for the bank note the master had endorsed as payment for this new horse, thinking how coincidental it was for Meirliún to have two plucky Connemaras before and after old Ned.

"Ride her easy, me boy. Sheba may even be droppin' a foal this summer." Brady ran his hand over her chubby flank and chuckled. "Then again, she may be showin' the seaweed treats me wife feeds her. In any case, tell the O'Brien he's made a rich bargain. A Connemara is the smartest horse in Ireland. She will live long and work hard to please—however you use her." When the mare added her voice to the testimonial, they all chuckled.

Brady showed little surprise to hear the boys were bent on emigrating themselves. "'Tis a sweet deal for able-bodied young men. Major Gaskell's been processing applicants from all over the District. You'll find him in the Garda Barracks in Oughterard." He gave

Robbie a leg up and handed him the rope reins. "Did ye know some think the Connie was an emigrant herself? Centuries ago, Viking stock 'tis said."

Riding a new-broke mare, Robbie had to concentrate, careful with his leg cues and light with his hands, even without a bit. The mare arched her back at first, giving his balls a hard bounce at the trot when she sprinted well ahead of Lewy on Jewel. They stopped to water the horses at an inlet of Lough Corrib, glistening under the sun with the brooding Connemara Mountains in the background. Neither boy had seen the Twelve Bens this close. Lewy agreed their gentle slope was no match for the sharper rise of the Cliffs of Moher. "Och, they are swollen hills," he snorted. "No challenge to anything 'round Galway."

Stiff and sore from the ride, Robbie was relieved when they approached the Garda barracks at the edge of Oughterard. After tying the horses to a rail, he rubbed his backside and each boy scrubbed a sweaty hand through windblown hair before taking a rather limp handshake from a portly man with a brushy moustache and a crooked nose.

"You lads know about the Tuke man?" He invited them to sit on a bench at a trestle table piled with notebooks and papers, then eased himself between the arms of a large wooden chair opposite them.

"James Hack Tuke, is a Quaker and a Brit from York," he explained. "The Quakers care much about social injustice, ye know, so we can't hold it agin him for being a Brit." He laughed at his joke, ignoring the way the table shook when his belly quivered against it.

Lewy rolled his eyes and Robbie grinned when they glanced at each other.

Gaskell tweaked his moustache. “Well now, Tuke was aghast at the poverty he saw in Ireland, quite right to call our regional poor houses warehouses for the dying.” He pulled from his pocket a pair of folded spectacles and used them to gesture broadly. “You lads are too young to remember the Great Starvation that took half of Ireland, but Tuke knew of it and not so long ago he toured the West and saw fer himself that famine still lingers where Irish soil is sterile as an old crone five ways from Sunday.”

Again, he paused to chuckle, tapping his spectacles against a pad of pink papers before he continued. “Well then, Mr. Tuke persuaded Parliament to pour 100,000 pounds into his plan to send three ships of our poor Irish to America. Seems it costs the government less to transport than to provide care in a poor house. After seeing the wisdom of it, private benefactors have jollied up with contributions as well.”

Noticing the boys had little reaction, he cleared his throat, and with his glasses now perched an inch from the end of his crooked nose, he peered from one to the other. “Well then, you lads from County Mayo or Galway?”

“Clare,” they answered in unison.

Major Gaskell jotted their names and ages down on the pink pad of paper and added the particulars while interviewing. Did they have means to pay for transportation? Any holdings or debts? Guilty of any criminal act? Were they sound of health, able to work? Did they represent a larger family willing to emigrate? Did they own a suitable change of clothing? Could they speak English, read or write?

“This fund pays for the transport, but encourages

any contribution you are able to make," Gaskell explained. "You boys own those fine horses that carried you here?"

"We are servants at Meirliún, working for our board," Lewy quickly answered. "The master had us pick up a new horse in Oughterard."

Gaskell gazed at their rough shirts and stained breeks. "We have more applications than we can grant, you see, for a ship that holds 800 destitute families."

"We haven't a schilling between us, and we are family. Cousins," Lewy added, shifting his shoulders as he glanced sideways at Robbie.

Gaskell cleared his throat, looking from one ruddy face to the other before he cracked a slow smile. "Yer not the usual sort that comes here, but that's not entirely unfavorable. Ye look healthy an say ye have no need fer clothing like some of the poor devils who come to apply in the only set of rags they own."

Unconsciously, Robbie's hands brushed his knees below the table.

"Better credit to you both—is knowing how to read, write and speak English."

After adding their names to a large list on blue paper, Gaskell made out their passage tickets and presented them with a warning, peering again over the rim of his spectacles. "The tickets are void now if yer named for owing a debt or committing a crime. Mr. Tuke and his committee are very diligent about comparing names with miscreant lists presented by all district and local authorities. Final check will be boarding day at Galway, so it behooves ye both to stay clear of trouble 'til then." They both nodded soberly.

Firmer handshakes and smiles exchanged, the lads

pocketed their tickets and left, chattering across their horses over most of the fifty kilometer ride back to Meirliún. Robbie was beginning to get caught up in the adventure Lewy proposed.

Chapter Thirty
A Six-Pound Send-Off

April 1, 1883

Will Turner stood ready at the master's carriage to drive the boys to the port in Galway. The carriage horses were restless in their dual hitch, unaccustomed to the restraint after long months of winter inactivity. A young shepherd stood at their heads, soothing them in a low voice, respectful of the sendoff in the dooryard. A few tenants, along with household servants formed a line at a right angle to family, shaking hands, hugging and saying goodbye, many with tears and the Irish catchword of good luck, *ádh mór*.

Even the master of Meirliún stood on line to wish them God speed and send them off with three pounds each. Lewy's mum had packed them a basket filled with tins of tea leaves, dried strips of mutton, brown bread and bannocks, berry jam, hard-boiled eggs and a small crock of buttermilk. Sarah gave Robbie a few of his favorite books, writing paper, pen, and the photo of his father, along with a list naming people she vaguely recalled in America, next to their last known locale. With her last tearful hug, she whispered something in his ear and pressed her jet rosary into his hands. "Take this and don't forget your prayers, son."

"I can't take your…" She closed his fingers over

the gift. “Aye, you can. The beads are worn by touch—your grandmum’s first. Her spirit…and mine will keep you safe on this journey.” She dabbed at her eyes with the ends of her shrug. “Whenever you have a care, think of us—just a rub away.”

He kissed her cheeks and held her tight. She smelled of spring and new wool. April blooms were already pushing through soil shot with green fuzz, damp and fragile in the thin morning light. Standing on tiptoes, her arms clamped around his neck in a grip he might never feel again. When had she become so slight? He could almost feel her bones beneath the plaid woolen shawl she wore.

When she stepped back with a final sob, he noticed that the master reached out to take her arm after shaking Robbie’s hand once again. Conal O’Brien wore thick spectacles now that made his dark eyes look beady, and he often used a walking stick outdoors. His black hair was touched by gray at the temples, but though he had aged as a widower, he lost no bearing of authority. There was still an energy about him that Robbie always expected. Conal leaned on his cane, inches away from his housekeeper…his mother. The picture they made inclining toward the other gave him pause for a few seconds and a wave of melancholy took hold of him. He would miss the two people who had most defined his life.

As the carriage moved along the drive, Robbie looked back and waved, imprinting the memory of Meirliún. It was not the great mansion he remembered from his youth, but the stone manor house was built like a small castle, solid and still sturdy enough to house another century of O’Briens. The stone falcon that gave Meirliún its name had a patina of age, and despite a chipped wing, still guarded the entrance in a small cove above the heavy entry. The Blackthorn bushes in the garden were already budding with white flowers, which would eventually drift like snow onto the walkways and bank against the junipers and yews that formed a wind barrier.

The thatched barn was also built of stone, as well as the little croft he knew as home. He could still see his mother, strolling down the drive for a last view of the carriage, arm in arm with Lewy's mum, the two women solid as two living falcons who belonged to Meirliún, guarding it fiercely, as each had guarded their boys for twenty years. Sarah's hair had loosened by the wind and a long tendril crossed her face. Would he remember that face, see it again in his lifetime?

Further down the road, he spied the O'Brien cemetery, stone-fenced on a rise beneath two lonely Hazel trees. There was a wide new gate at the entrance now, black iron bars with the O'Brien name on a post topped with a newly carved falcon. The newest grave was still covered with the rusty remains of spruce and holly laid there at Christmas. Livy's work. She was good about the old tradition—dutifully tending the resting place of ancestors over the festive days of *Nolag*.

He had given his mum one last letter for Livy, this one more of farewell than a last plea for forgiveness. She had promised on the rosary he now possessed that Livy would read it. In an odd moment of sentiment, he had enclosed a small twist of hair in the letter: A dark lock of his, bound with a few long coppery strands of hers found in his boots the morning after their guilty night of passion. Wrapped in a scrap of worn linen, and kept for months close in his pocket, the faint scent of ash chafed his memory with the reminder of that bittersweet night.

Lewy stretched his long legs on the carriage seat, marveling at the craftsmanship of upholstered seats and doors with brass knobs. Both of them had cleaned the carriage many times, but never rode in it. Lewy was clearly up for adventure and chattering like a magpie.

"'Tis grand to feel like gentry, is it not, boyo? The O'Brien was kind to send us off so well."

"Kind to part with six pounds." Robbie smiled.

"He was almost like a grandda, was he not?"

"I used to think he was, knowing him since we were babes. I remember how I cried when mum told me he was not just a cousin who shared our name—but a guardian angel in the flesh. When I was six, I followed him about, trying to make out a flutter of wings beneath his coattails. I didn't want him to fly away."

Lewy laughed. "I remember when he called us into his study and like a great Lord, knighted us with an old sword after we pledged to look after the tag-along."

Robbie felt his throat constrict as it always did with reference to Livy. He had not said goodbye to her, except in that last letter. A permanent goodbye, lettered in ink that smeared the paper with drops of hesitation. He held out a hope that he might see his mum again, perhaps convince her to emigrate once he was settled and prosperous, but he knew in his heart that he would never see Livy again. His mind had long ago adjusted to a life without Livy.

Chapter Thirty-One
Cushins in Boshton

Robbie and Lewy were among the last to arrive at the wharf in Galway, lugging their valises down to the quay to await gunboats and hookers transporting immigrants to the huge steamer in the outer Bay. A brilliant sun was already dominating a blue sky feathered with white clouds, and the sea sparkled like a carpet of emeralds. Sandwiched between sky and sea, the *S.S. Nestorian* spread over 300 feet across the horizon, riding high as an iron mountain with a single funnel and three masts with reefed sails.

Emigrant families lined the quay—generations who stood in clusters or sat on brown and red cases or strapped bundles containing everything they possessed for the trip, chatting and joking as if this was not a farewell, but a gay holiday they were embarking on. Robbie guessed that Galway today could not be mistaken for the harbors of tears that must have characterized emigrant ports during The Great Famine. He knew the people he saw in this line had freely chosen to leave behind their bleak and sterile land. Like Major Gaskell explained, the famine hammered the West almost beyond recovery. The fact that multiple generations of a family were gifted the option of a new life by the Tuke Fund made the exodus all the sweeter: Fewer relatives and friends left behind to miss.

It was a minor complaint that Robbie overheard from an elderly man ahead in line. "Me plot's going to be taken by farmers from Scotland."

"They will know how to work the soil," his companion assured him. "God help them, the Scots can squeeze blood from a dead turnip."

Most of the families were dressed for the weather in new wool and poplins, soft-brimmed hats, and new shoes furnished by the Fund through clothing stores and cobblers even as far away as Dublin. It was hard for Robbie to fathom the kind of poverty that deprived people even of necessary clothing. His mum was right about their blessings from Meirliún.

The family that straggled along the quay behind them was conspicuous for their dress, demeanor, and lack of a patriarch. An old woman in a kerchief with a face dark as a dried apple was helped by two lean women, all of them clutching threadbare shawls and cloth sacks shouldered against the wind. Two girls in red flannel skirts, one carrying a baby, and two grimy barefooted boys not much over ten or twelve trailed after the women. The younger boy clutched a shifting bundle wrapped around his long shirt at the waist. The older boy wore a buttonless jacket with sleeves hanging below his fingertips and a wrap around his waist that fell to his knees, instead of britches. He jabbed the smaller boy with an elbow when he began to mewl, and whispered something fierce into his ear. The younger boy scowled with a shoulder-bump response. None of these people gave the appearance of a family on holiday.

Robbie offered them bread and bannocks and jam from the basket he held and the two women gave him a silent sign of blessing before breaking the bread and distributing it first to the old woman, then the children. The youngest boy dipped two fingers into the jam, licked one and poked the other into his bundle. He took a large bite of his bannock and shoved the remainder into his bundle as well.

Lewy pulled on Robbie's coat sleeve whispering loudly, "What are ye doing, boyo? They will be fed on the ship. 'Twas said in the paper, meals will be served by day and gruel at night. That's me mum's bread you're givin' away so freely."

Robbie shrugged him off with a fierce glare. "I've never seen your mum begrudge beggars. By the looks of them, these women and children have not had the breakfast the others were given this morning, and they certainly didn't have the oat cakes and eggs we both enjoyed before our sendoff." Lewy rolled his eyes and backed off.

As more hookers packed with emigrants shuttled to the *Nestorian*, the line on the quay grew shorter, until the last boat made snug room for Lewy and Robbie and the family of eight with their scant belongings. Nobody but Robbie seemed to notice the bundle transfer between the two young boys—or hear the plaintive cry blocked as the bowsprit groaned and the jib sail flapped in the wind as the two fishermen expertly guided the thirty foot hooker out of the harbor.

The boys gawked at Robbie when he leaned between them with a hand on each shoulder. "Is a cat allowed?" he whispered. The older boy put his arm around his brother when the boy's chin began to quiver. Neither of them spoke, but the gesture and look was as unmistakable as Robbie's defeated sigh. It wasn't up to him to ferret out a stowaway pet.

The *Nestorian* seemed to perch above the outer sound a mile away. Robbie had never seen such a large ship close up. Over seven hundred souls and their baggage had only tickled the Plimsoll line on the ship's bow. Once hoisted aboard, they were guided alongside a rope drawn across the deck. The ship's purser and agent stood on one side with some of the Tuke committee, while ship and shore doctors stood ready to examine each immigrant on the opposite side. Each head of the family received his ticket paper and as the people were cleared, sea kits, blankets, and mattresses piled on deck were distributed before passengers disappeared through the hatchway into the hold.

The family of eight was scrutinized closely when the name Hugh Skerret brought on a spate of keening among the women, a low mourning Gaelic that nobody in authority seemed to understand. Robbie was not fluent, but he knew enough Gaelic to recognize key words. His offer to interpret was hesitant. He guessed that the Irish keening was for the absence of Hugh Skerret and offered a probable explanation that the family "head" was most recently dead.

The keening rose in volume when Robbie loudly repeated the Gaelic word for dead. "*Marbh.*" The purser and agent observing this checked the ticket paper and counted the remaining heads. When Bridget's name was shouted, the younger women stopped keening long enough to point to the old woman who worked her chin like a cow chewing its cud. In turn, each family member responded to their name or was prodded by another to respond until all eight were accounted for, including baby Jerome who had joined the keening with a healthy wail of his own.

Holding a hand clapped over one ear, a tall man beside the purser shouted above the din. “A male head of the family…or someone in Boston…can vouch for these people…if they pass examination.” With a tight face, he surveyed the group. “Look at their dress.”

One of the women must have understood what was said. She began to wail louder and her voice carried above the clatter of activity around her as seamen began climbing the masts to shake out the sails and the steam engines below deck shuttered to life. Robbie held out his hands and searched the family faces for one who could best understand his attempt to communicate. The women and girls avoided his eyes, but the elder boy spoke up at last in halting English as he waved his cap. “I head. Cushins,” he gestured at the group and flashed ten fingers. “Cushins in Boshton.”

“They have ten cousins waiting in Boston,” Robbie quickly related to the purser. “Surely you can see how destitute they must be.” Mottled faces with eight pairs of eyes, hollow from anxiety and grief-renewed, brought home Robbie’s message when they all turned to face the committee.

The purser and two Tuke agents on the opposite side of the rope conferred in whispers before one of them asked Robbie if he would substitute for the family head since he managed to interpret best. “Your English is gifted with barely an accent and ye seem to be able to relate to these people.”

The purser agreed with the agent. “We are sorely pressed for interpreters, young man. God willing they pass the physical, we shall accept the poor souls with your voucher.”

The agent added, “There are two large bundles of clothing set aside for such contingencies.”

Robbie nodded and taking the boy aside explained with more hand signals than Gaelic that they would each need to be examined to pass final inspection. The boy straightened up, related the message to his family and when they understood, there was a change in group demeanor. The old woman lurched at Robbie, grabbing his head to plant a noisy kiss on each cheek. “*Dia leat, dia leat.*” God’s blessing sputtered between missing rows of stained teeth.

Miraculously, after a cursory exam, all the Skerrets passed down the hold, with the ship doctor prescribing baths as their best medicine. Lewy was not as lucky.

“*A rash?*” Robbie exclaimed. “What do you mean, a rash? Where?”

Lewy fanned his hands down his chest and dropped his head.

“Idgit! What does that mean?”

“No voyage…this crossing.” He looked up, red-faced. “The doc said he couldn’t be sartin sure it was no gaol fever or bed rash, mayhap some reaction to poison weeds. Me mum would know of a plaster cure.” He shook his head vigorously. “’Tis no typhus or French pox.”

Robbie cursed, barely able to check his anger. “This emigration was your idea, not mine.” He growled, with a storm in his eyes that matched the color of the sea.”

“I’ll follow ye over next crossing—or so soon as I may be cleared.” He held out his hand for a shake.

“Geezus, Lewy!” Robbie clenched his fists, ignoring Lewy’s hand. “This was your idea. What am I supposed to do in Boston alone?"

Lewy reached in his pocket and shoved his three pounds at Robbie. "You are now six pounds rich." He smiled weakly. "When that runs out, you might use your gifted mouth to snag a job, boyo."

Robbie grabbed the rail with both hands. He wanted to punch Lewy. *Punch something.* "I don't believe this."

Seamen were swarming the deck, starting to crank the giant winch that hoisted the anchor and relaying commands from the bridge to the crow's nests. Two of the men in the Tuke Committee and a seaman approached with three other passengers who failed their physical.

"The last hooker is waiting to board back to Galway," one of them said, grabbing Lewy's arm. "Let's make away before the ship scuttles it in the wake."

With a last defeated look at Robbie, Lewy was led away like a prisoner.

The waiting hooker bobbed like a cork in the water aft of the ship as each man descended to it. A sea wind was already picking up, and Robbie gripped the rail harder to stop the vibration he felt from the steam engines churning the deck underfoot. Or was that merely his body twitching with emotion? He watched his friend slink into the boat and brace himself before he looked up. When their eyes met and held, Lewy tugged on his cap.

Robbie leaned over the deck and cupped his hands around his mouth. "Take care of her," he finally yelled. "Take care of her."

He watched Lewy fight for balance in the shifting

hooker. Shuffled between the noise of engines and the shouts of deckhands, Lewy's repeated response carried upwind. Desperate assurance contorted the face of his best friend. "I will…I will, *caraid.* I will." Lewy vigorously waved his hat, pausing now and then to swipe his eyes and nose on the sleeve of his jacket.

Robbie stood at the rail watching the distance grow between the little hooker and the monstrous ship preparing to cast off on the outgoing tide. Nearly half an hour passed before the dark red sails of the hooker disappeared beyond the stone walls of Galway's Bay.

Chapter Thirty-Two
Erin Go Bragh

From his vantage point high on the quarterdeck, Robbie could see the arched bridge of Galway in the east, the colorful warehouses lining the Bay and the stone walls that snaked around the city. Tiered uphill from the fish market, with a purple haze of the Connemara Mountains crowning them, he could still pick out the narrow streets, tiny shops and houses of weavers, bakers and tinkers, even miniature horses and stick figures moving between. The sign above Dooley's Pub was an orange pinprick on the horizon.

One memorable day four years ago, he and Lewy earned two pence and a Dooley draft for cleaning the plank floors after a fisticuff that drew blood and puke. They were bound for home with a wagonload of dry kitchen supplies when Jack Dooley himself hailed them down.

"Nobody will sit for a pint with the stains and stench of a fight reeking about them," he declared. "Me wife and lassies refuse the cleanup, but there's a job for two thirsty boys, I'm sartin."

Robbie nearly added to the mess once inside the tavern. Particularly after he mistook a glass eye for a boiled egg and stopped Lewy from taking a bite of it. It took them two hours to pick up chairs and scrub tables and floors, with several breaks in between to fill their lungs with seaside air. Two of the Dooley girls joined them on their wagon outside while they nursed their quease with a heady draft of Guinness. The girls were shameless flirts who parried easily with Lewy's more shameless baiting. It was near dark when they arrived back at Meirliún, both of them silly and smelling enough for a bath in a barrel of sea water with a bar of lye soap.

****

A tug at his coat broke the reverie.

It was the oldest Skerret boy—almost unrecognizable—cleaned up and sporting his new clothes and shoes. With gestures and odd Gaelic words, Robbie figured he was wanted in the hold. The *Nestorian* was built twenty years after the Famine began, an ironclad steamer capable of accommodating up to 800 passengers in the hold. Quarters for men and women were separated by the engines, with each section laid out in six-foot square grids—portable "rooms" with adjustable wooden pallets that could be filled with straw or laid with 2x6 foot mattresses. Long tables and benches were set up at both ends of the hold for dining at four set times during the day.

The Tuke Emigration charters were a far cry from the smaller coffin ships his mum spoke of—with crowded steerage and scant food or water—sending immigrants to the certainty of a new life or an eternal one. Because Robbie was pressed to be the new Skerret family interpreter, he was also appointed temporary guardian of the two Skerret boys in the men's section. Frank Skerret, the eldest boy had already picked up Robbie's mattress and blanket and was eager to lead his new protector down to their quarters. Liam Skerret waited on his lower bunk with one of the blankets offering a privacy drape from the bunk above. Robbie found the boy cradling his thin furry stowaway with tears streaking his face. The gray striped cat they somehow managed to smuggle into the hold was dead.

****

A slight wind and a drizzle didn't deter most of the passengers to come on deck after arranging bunks and baggage and touring the set-up for men and women. The family separations whipped up several protests from crying children who drew quick admonishment from parents who may have shared their disappointment. To Robbie's unpracticed ear for regional dialects, one of the scolds sounded something like "'*Tis the quiet pigs that eat the meal.*"

A cheer went up when a green flag of Ireland imprinted with a faded gold harp was hoisted on the mizzen mast. "*Erin Go Brach*" was the common refrain heard on most lips. The ship slowly turned southwest and rounded Black Head to enter the South Sound. In due time, it glided past the Aran Islands and the stark beauty of the Cliffs of Moher, catching the late afternoon sun. Hags Head poked out of the sea mist at sunset, and the coastline and the sea that buffeted it was set ablaze with fiery streaks of orange. When the dinner bell rang, most of the passengers filed down the hold in respectful silence.

****

For a final view of the homeland, Robbie guided his two young charges up to the quarterdeck. Twenty years of memories flashed before him as the shapes and colors receded. Ireland, for all its sharp-edged cliffs, low mountains, sterile rocks, and Burren was well-named as the Emerald Isle. He would always remember the green—bright emerald to dusky gray by season and light, plush by rainfall and mists. Impossible to understand how such land could deliver famine for so many years? *Would he ever see his homeland again?*

The sails caught in the southwest wind, pushing the iron steamer into prime speed as Ireland disappeared. With steam, sail, and the hope of good weather, they would make Boston in less than a month. Robbie and the boys remained huddled against the rising wind that cooled their faces and dried their eyes. In the dim light of riding lanterns, young Liam was hoisted enough to clear the rail and drop the sack he carried. They all watched it pierce the dark water and sink like a stone. Frank put an arm around his brother's heaving shoulders, whispering something to comfort him.

Robbie squeezed a hand on each boy's shoulder, drawing them back from the rail. "*A Dhia ár sábháil*" he muttered. He reached into his pocket for a touch of his mum's rosary. "Yes, God will protect us." His mum's last words rang in his ear.

Part Three

To Have and To Hold

Chapter Thirty-Three
Safe Territory

"Bananas and bacon?" Mitch gave me his walleyed look, so familiar over the last few weeks. He had a lot to compare from life as he knew it and life in the twenty-first century.

I took a big bite of the banana I held, and offered him the remainder, along with a rasher of crisp bacon waved under his nose. "Your son loves them both as finger foods, loves them even more blended into his morning oatmeal," I explained.

Without using his hands, he snapped the bacon like a fish to bait and chewed thoughtfully. "Aye, but I'll take my porridge straight, if you don't mind."

"Aye Aye," Scout chimed in from his high chair, banging on his empty bowl with a spoon. "More," he said, licking the last of the oatmeal from the corners of his mouth.

We both chuckled at the mimic while I dished up more oatmeal. "Let me guess. You've been reading Goldilocks and his pirate books again…aye?"

Mitch sucked his lips into a straight line. "Pirates? Oh aye, but Goldilocks?"

"She ate the bear's porridge, and wanted *more.*"

"Cheeky little lass."

"I figured you would cheer for the bear." I smiled, thinking of all the bedtime stories he'd read to Scout, even when it wasn't bedtime. Winnie the Pooh and Dora the Explorer didn't exist in his day. No Little Golden Books or pirate picture stories to capture a child's imagination. Mitch was amazed, in fact, by the number of books in my house—not only for children. I often caught him thumbing through one of my novels in the swivel rocker near the fireplace when Scout was down for the night. Modern books were a far cry from the Leatherstocking tales that had a place of honor in his old cabin. Language, setting, illustrations—even the print and quality of paper had changed in 130 years.

"Do people today write like this," he asked just last night as we both cozied up to the firelight with reading material and a mug of beer.

"Like how?"

"Like the front of his head was missing and his brains rolled over his face like jelly."

I laughed out loud. "Let me guess. You're reading Grisham?"

He nodded, his green eyes blinking wide with reflecting firelight. "You have other books here, that uh, with passages, uh, that describe things people do…"

Even in the firelight, I could tell his face colored. "Romance is a popular genre among women," I explained. "It rivals mystery and suspense. Did you find it offensive?"

He squirmed a little, avoiding my gaze. "Back a century or two…in my time."

"Well, it's not Jane Austen, to be sure. Even the modern take-offs on Pride and Prejudice might give Jane a good roll in her grave."

He gave me his narrow look. "You don't find that offensive, then?"

I set down the new craft catalog I was checking out and did a mental edit. He questioned me often with a gesture or look of confusion, less often verbally. I knew he was weighing my answers along with a personal assessment. "Stimulating, maybe. I think that's what today's writers try to do—hone in on a theme or topic that stimulates the mind, breaks barriers that may shock, even. Some open-minded people under seventy might even call it refreshing…honest."

He rolled his eyes. "Well, that pegs me, since your calendar tells me I'm well over 150."

I chuckled. "Well, you don't even look a third of that."

There were changes in his voice and appearance, however. His hair, now crew cut length was not the raven black I remembered. More dark brown, and his lashes were shorter, his teeth a little more discolored. He was still handsome, but the five o'clock shadow that I once found so attractive was patchy and thin even with a few days growth, but then I told myself that a new diet or a shock and injury can easily distort and discolor. I had a teacher once who lost his whole family in a car accident, and his hair turned white overnight.

When we went back to the hospital to have his stitches removed, Dr. Hawley was happy to see that his patient had gained weight and assured us that the long scar that trailed from the shorter lobe of Mitch's left ear down his neck would fade—or be better concealed when his hair grew longer. The scar gave him a fiercer look, but his nose and eyes were just as I remembered, his hands as worn and rough, his legs as long. I did miss the sardonic curl of his mouth in his trademark half-grin, and his self-assured teasing had all but evaporated.

I thought adjusting to life in this century might be like getting sea legs. For a time traveler, everything was off balance. I knew all about that first hand, though I conceded that falling back in time was easier than springing ahead.

I wondered how many changes he had seen in me. I wore my hair shorter, used more makeup now, and of course, favored tight jeans and sweaters in season, even boots with a fashion heel when I wasn't wearing my fuzzy leopard slippers in the house. I was keenly aware of the scrutiny he gave my clothing choices, and began to look for approval in his expressions. His eyes usually gave away his feelings—as they always had in the past. Wide to narrow, light to dark, steady or blinking. Without a word between us, I knew if I passed muster or not. It was almost a game—each of us studying the other—perhaps looking for something familiar. We tried not to be obvious about it, but I could feel his heated gaze, and I could tell when he was playing with Scout or picking at the computer that he knew I was watching him as well. With furrowed brow and eyes orbiting up to the right, I could even tell when he was mentally calculating—or trying to recall something.

Last night, emboldened by a rare mug of beer, I asked, "Do you remember your birth date?"

He was silent for a long minute, gazing now at the fire while his jaw clenched the way I always remembered. Finally, he shrugged and turned to look at me for assistance.

"I only remember we shared the same birthday month. May. In our summer together, I made you a peach cake and gave you a pair of Levi's from the post."

"The post?"

"Fort Laramie…the sutler's trading post."

He gaped at me, wide-eyed.

"You remember Fort Laramie?"

He rose to poke at the firewood with an andiron. In profile, this time I could see the color drain from his face.

I moved to the edge of my chair, thinking I stirred a memory. "It's changed since we went there together, but some of the buildings still survive. The sutler's store and Old Bedlam are probably among the oldest buildings left in Wyoming. In fact, the Visitor Center even carries some of my soaps—just like the sutler did in 1886." Encouraged by his sudden reaction, I told him Fort Laramie was now a National Historic Park, complete with a campsite and tour guides. "It might jog your memory if we visited…"

His response was quick and confusing. "Think that would help? After all this time, I doubt anything will help."

"All this time? It's only been a few weeks. Doc Hawley said it could take months for memory to return after a concussion."

He turned with the andiron in his hand. "Or maybe never," he said sharply. "Maybe it's best to leave the past in the past."

That was perfectly okay with me if the memory of Jessamine never came between us, but there was Tallie, his daughter with Jessamine. He was a good father to her, and so far, was amazing with Scout. Could a loving parent ever forget his children? I once read we may forget people, but never how our feelings swell around them—for better or worse. Sweet Tallie was a 'can do' child, easy to love, hard to forget. I even saw little signs in Scout that reminded me of his half-sister. In our last night together in his cabin, he told me a child was considered a *'gift'* by his people. Didn't he tell me soon after he met his son that Scout was the greatest gift of all?

We had skirted issues like we skirted each other since then. Though we were once intimate enough to create a child, bridging time and a century of change had turned us into polite strangers, focused now around the child we conceived when he thought I was his wife. Cold weather kept us indoors most of the time—in a small house where it was almost impossible to avoid contact. I felt Mitch needed time to heal and adjust to all changes before we had any come-to-Jesus talk about the future. I was not known for my patience, and often found myself biting the inside of my cheek or whispering my new mantra—"Take it slow Jessica."

Some of my questions were doodled over the borders of my craft catalog. *How did you get here and why were you stalking me?* He didn't come through a stone monument in Scotland—or appear from a genie bottle. It had to be the teacup. The mysterious cup that transported me into the past and back to the present. It was the last thing I had in my hands before I exchanged places with Jessamine, putting each of us back into our rightful century.

Most of my other questions revolved around Jessamine. Did he leave her for me? Did he want to go back to her, resume his life with her and Tallie? I knew from reading the history of our family in the family journals that Jessamine had re-married twice more after Mitch had suddenly disappeared. She even bore a son, who became my great grandfather. Unless history could be changed, Mitch was not scripted to return to her. If he had, I might never have been born. I would eventually tell him about his Tallie—what I read of her success fighting for Women's Rights in her time. He would certainly be proud of her accomplishments. But was that enough?

As I cleaned the oatmeal from Scout's face and hands, I decided to bring Jessamine into our conversation, picking up on the book theme from last evening. "Jessamine read *Pride and Prejudice*. I saw the book in your old cabin. Do you remember that?"

He looked startled. "Aye, I know of the book. I can picture it in a large bookcase…somewhere."

I pulled Scout out of his highchair and set him on the floor to toddle over to his toy box across the room. "Your memory is coming back then."

"Flashes—maybe like pictures on your TV when the sound is mute."

"Do you remember Jessamine?"

"Tell me about her." Frowning, he sipped his coffee while keeping an eye on Scout.

I sighed. We had broached this conversation only once before. Of all the things I hoped he would remember of our summer together, recalling the wife I briefly replaced was not one of them. This kept me from introducing him to the little chest in my closet that held the keystones of their life together.

The only man I ever loved was here…with me now, with our son. We needed him. How could I tell him that Jessamine had moved on, finished her life without him? Was I driven by concern for his feelings or for my own? I recognized the fact that I was jealous of my own great-great-grandmother. I poured too much milk into a fresh mug of coffee and after licking my oatmeal spoon, stirred it thoughtfully. *Lost in Time* was the slogan on my mug. Appropriate.

"Well, she looked like me, or rather I looked like her, with only a few minor differences. I had bigger feet for one. Same hair and eye color, same height, though. Jake told me once that I could have been her clone."

"Her clown?"

I smiled into my cup. "No, a clone is a plant or animal that is grown from one cell of its parent and contains genes nearly exacting as its parent."

His mouth hung open when he stared at me. "They do that with humans now?"

"Not yet, but lots of plants and even some animals have been cloned. I think a sheep named Dolly was cloned many years ago, but she aged prematurely and only lived for six years."

"A sheep? A blackface ewe?"

"I think she was all white, but you can find her picture on my computer." I had already given him cursory lessons on my laptop and cell phone, and how to switch TV channels and use the CD player for music. He was amazed by all the technology and eager to learn—asking me specific questions I couldn't begin to answer. Referring him to Google and Siri saved me from embarrassment. It also made me wonder how much I took for granted, seeing modern life as I did now—through his eyes. His green eyes. Reflecting wonder, they gave off a hue I didn't remember from our past. In his day, they had registered confusion, worry, fear, pain, anger and my two favorites—amusement…and love. I had yet to see much beyond confusion, wonder, and worry.

Our son was safe territory, the one subject that at least drove the focus away from unanswered questions. My own memory was vivid, recalling our final night together in 1886. *"The child will be the link that bridges our time,"* he whispered to me that night. As we did so often, our gazes shifted now to Scout who was pulling two fire trucks out of his toy box. He ran with them to Mitch and looked up at him with his green eyes wide and eager.

"We play firemen now, Dapa?"

Mitch pulled him onto his lap and smiled at me over his head. "Did you hear that? He's throwing more words together. Do you think he meant to call me Dada or Papa?" After he kissed the top of Scout's head, a broad smile split his face and two pairs of green eyes sparkling with unmistakable joy brought a glaze to my own eyes and a few extra beats to my heart.

Chapter Thirty-Four
Room for Evidence

It was supposed to be a solo morning trip to Wheatland, with a case of my holiday soaps to restock at a few stores, a trip to the bank and a grocery pick up for Thanksgiving. Jake and Meredith were joining us for the feast, and I wanted the occasion to be special—for particular reasons. I wasn't sure if Mitch had ever celebrated the holiday in the late nineteenth century in the West. The date was, after all, supposed to be a presidential proclamation instituted first by George Washington, then by Abraham Lincoln to set aside a day of thanksgiving for victories in war. Wars confined to the Eastern states. A turkey feast with historic tales of Pilgrims and Indians, referring to the First Thanksgiving came later.

I thought it was ironic that Indians played an important role in the first Thanksgiving, yet I remembered Mitch telling me on the 4th of July during our summer together that his people never celebrated white holidays. Every Indian battle won or great buffalo hunt was excuse enough for a feast in his childhood.

Presuming Jessamine influenced changes after they married, my Thanksgiving table would be compared to hers. I was beginning to feel thankful for some of his current memory loss. I may have resembled my great-great-grandmother, but I knew I could ultimately be only an inferior version of her—the accidental four-month "wife" exchanged in an aberration of time. Just as I had in his time, and now in mine, I was driven by comparison that generated a need to impress.

"Well, well, Mrs. Mitchell, how fortuitous we meet again." At the bank, I stopped endorsing the checks I had picked up for my soaps and followed the voice to Sheriff Clyde Lewis across the table.

I could feel my pulse quicken. Our last contact at the hospital had not gone well. "Sheriff Lewis, we meet again." I tried to smile.

He dipped his cap and got to the point. "I think we may have recovered your missing gun last week. Could you stop by the station to identify it this morning?"

"My gun? You mean the one missing from my glove compartment?"

"You have other guns?"

"Oh…no, of course not. Where did you find it?" I set aside the pen I held and wiped my sweaty fingers on my parka sleeve.

"It was used in a convenience store robbery. We were able to trace the registration to you."

My mouth dropped open. "You don't think I…?"

He smiled. "No, of course not. The video tape showed it was a young man in a dark hoodie and cap with a blue logo we couldn't make out. The revolver was found in a nearby ditch by one of my deputies. I was going to call you about it after the holiday."

After cashing my checks and stuffing the money into the envelope with my grocery list, I followed his car back to the police station a few blocks away. The evidence room was the size of a large bedroom with floor to ceiling shelves and no windows. Numbered and dated cardboard boxes of various sizes lined the shelves. He went directly to a small box on a low shelf and took out the gun, encased in a plastic sleeve.

"Yes, this looks like mine," I said, after hefting it in my hand.

He pulled a manila envelope out of the box. "It's already been photographed and dusted for fingerprints."

"Then I can take it home?"

"Ordinarily, we keep weapons used in a crime here until the case is tried in court. But the gun was empty when found. No fingerprints were found on it and no bullets were fired in the robbery. The convenience store was robbed of $185 with an empty revolver."

"It probably didn't work. I told you it seemed to explode in my hand when I used it."

"Oh, it worked all right. We tested it with a new load." He smirked. "You must have spent all your ammo in your bear hunt."

I winced, feeling heat creep up my neck.

"By the way, how is your husband?"

"Recovered, except for a temporary loss of memory."

He scratched the back of his neck. "Probably best in this case. Shooting your husband for a bear could have some grizzly effects on a loving relationship." He stopped laughing when he saw I didn't find humor in his play on words.

I took a deep breath and repeated tersely, "I can take the thing home, then?"

He cleared his throat and nodded. "If you promise to lock it up and let your husband do the hunting from now on." His lips quivered a little when he handed me the gun. "And I'll need your signature on the release form. If the robber is ever found, we may need the weapon back, but since no one was physically harmed, it will be considered a petty crime, most likely committed by a juvenile."

After signing the release, I shoved the gun in the deep pocket of my parka and turned to leave.

"Oh, Mrs. Mitchell," he called after me.

He winked when I turned back. "You have a happy Thanksgiving."

****

Mitch helped me unload the groceries when I got home, and noticed my change of mood. "You don't like grocery shopping?"

After determining that Scout was still napping, I took the gun out of my pocket and plunked it on the kitchen counter.

He looked from me to the weapon and back again, then hiked up his shoulders. "You robbed the grocer?"

I managed a chuckle. "Probably the other way around. Fresh turkeys and cranberries were not on sale at my favorite store." I opened the refrigerator and took out a half-empty bottle of wine and began to chug it down.

His eyes flashed with amusement as he took the bottle from me. "What happened?" After I told him about my encounter with the sheriff, he pulled a long draft from the wine bottle, himself, and was silent for a minute. The playful scenario was not lost on either of us. We sat on the counter stools, knees almost touching as we faced each other with the bottle between us. "He doesn't believe your story, then. Is that it?"

"Well, it is rather unbelievable, but the real story would be hard for anyone to imagine."

"The real story?"

I looked away from his green eyes and drummed my fingers on the counter. "Time traveling. Me…you. How we met is something straight out of fiction."

He spread his hand over my fingers. Looking down, he finally whispered, "I'm glad we met."

"So am I." I could feel his fingers tighten over mine and the warmth of our contact shivered up my arm. I wanted him to take me in his arms, tell me he remembered our summer, the way we were on our last night, and most of all, assure me that everything would be all right and he was here to stay.

Take it slow, Jessica. Take it slow. The voice in my head became suddenly distorted.

"Mama?" We turned in unison toward the little voice of Scout, rubbing sleep from his eyes before he ran across the room to me. "Where you go?"

It was the first time I had left him alone with Mitch for half a day. I swung him into my arms and twirled around while Mitch hid the gun in a drawer.

Until our separation of days while Mitch was in the hospital, Scout and I had never been apart for more than a few hours of daycare since he was born. When the cost of daycare became prohibitive with my income, Jake stepped into the breach and never considered payment, even if he had to take off time from his job to babysit. Most of the time, I lugged Scout with me when I delivered soaps or introduced myself to potential customers. My son was a charmer to all, perhaps the impetus even, that drew business. I was keenly aware of the possibility that people bought my soaps and lotions out of charity—identifying a single mother's struggle to make a living. Whatever the case, as long as we were together, I didn't care.

"Did baby miss mama?"

He pressed a pudgy finger into my lips and giggled when I pretended to bite it off.

Chapter Thirty-Five
Laughing Turkeys and Talking Mice

On Thanksgiving Day, I woke to a cacophony of frenzied gobbles, giggles, and clucks. I pulled on my robe and found Scout and Mitch at their bedroom window, watching a flock of eleven wild turkeys pecking around the Burr Oak tree in our dooryard. The hens in the garage were responding to the sounds of a wilder species, and Scout found the commotion incredibly amusing.

"Birds laughing mama," he cried out when I joined them at the window.

"What are they eating?" I asked.

"Cheerios," Mitch said. "Scout dumped a box of them out there this morning after I told him that the turkey in the fridge is for dinner today."

I laughed, ruffling Scout's hair. "We used to feed birds and deer and watch them eat as we sat on the porch swing last summer. When we ran out of birdseed, we scattered cheerios for several days which drew a mother turkey and eight poults."

I noticed Mitch was wearing Jake's old plaid bathrobe. Scout was still in his pajamas and blue bunny slippers, now stained and damp. "You guys went outside dressed like that?"

Mitch looked a little sheepish. "The lad escaped the breakfast table while I was in the bathroom. I thought he went to your room, but when I peeked, you were sound asleep—alone. I searched the rest of the house, looking in closets, even the garage before I noticed the front door knob was smeared with grape jam."

"Oh Lord, he is opening doors now." Not long ago he had mastered a crib escape and Mitch had modified the crib rails into something that resembled a toddler bed with a low guardrail. We both laughed when Mitch reported it now enabled the little monkey to climb down from his bed and tiptoe over to wake Mitch, reaching up to squeeze his nose.

"We'll have to be sure to lock the outside doors and pick up some of those kid-proof plastic locks for low cupboards."

"There is such a thing?"

"Necessity is the mother of invention. How did you keep Tallie from getting into things that could harm her?"

He gave me a blank stare. "Tallie?"

"Your daughter." He cocked his head, staring past me with the familiar wrinkle between his eyes. "You don't remember her, do you?" I asked with more snap than I meant, and could see the frustration cloud his eyes. "I'm sorry. I just hoped…"

He sighed deeply. "Recall is my hope, as well." He stared out the window, rubbing his finger over a spot of vapor from Scout's pressed mouth.

I carried Scout to the bathroom, cleaned, and dressed him, feeling even more anxious for a day that had all the potential for stirring up emotional reckoning. In a Thanksgiving observation, a famous talk show host once declared, "People travel thousands of miles to be with people they only see once a year. And then they discover once a year is way too often."

Right. Thousands of miles. What if one of the guests has traveled 130 years? I was nervous about the meal, more so about the company. Jake and Meredith were coming, and I wondered how to explain the "new man in my life" to the woman in Jake's life. Was it only a month ago that Jake and Meredith last came to dinner? She would naturally wonder how a single mother could meet a new man and invite him into her home and family in such a short time—especially since it took Jake over a year to achieve such live-in status.

I decided on dinner at four o'clock. Maybe an early supper would lead to early retirements and a minimum of questions. I was banking on plenty of wine and turkey with all the trimmings to generate polite conversation from well-behaved guests muzzy from wine and tryptophan from a twenty-pound turkey.

My own memories of the holiday were bittersweet. My parents died in a car accident nearly twenty-five years ago—just two weeks before Thanksgiving, and I went to live with Gran and Jake, my nearest relatives. Gran tried to make the holiday special for both her orphaned grandchildren, but I wasn't very cooperative that first holiday. I spent most of the day sulking in my new pink bedroom until dinner. I felt twelve-year-old Jake resented his new "sister," and I didn't like sweet potatoes or cranberries. My mother never forced me to drink milk without a spoonful of chocolate syrup mixed in it, either, and I pointed that out to Gran. She laughed, pretending not to be annoyed, and made a game of rhyming our favorite foods. Jake wanted to play Crazy Eights after dinner, with pie before bedtime, and a tradition was born. I ate very little that day, but the game and pie made me think I could get used to my new home. I crawled under my pink rosebud sheets that night and left no more tears on the pillowcase.

As we grew older, Thanksgiving Day became associated with feast and football. Often, the overeating made us even too tired to play our Thursday night game of Crazy Eights before bedtime. The last few years before Gran died, Jake fell asleep watching football while Gran and I cleaned dishes and packed up leftovers.

I plunked Scout in front of the TV in my bedroom and found a suitable channel of cartoons for him to watch while I dressed for the day in brown tights and my favorite paisley tunic, then settled on my bed to text Jake on my smartphone. We had to synchronize our stories for Meredith this afternoon.

At the Wheatland hospital, I attempted to explain to Jake that *Mitch* was the married man who was Scout's father. I tried to tell him that my look-alike ancestor, Jessamine, and I had switched places three summers ago and I fell in love with her first husband, Mitch. Since then, we had several conversations about time travel, and how such an affair affected our ancestry. We knew we had different grandfathers, which ruled out the incest factor, but it was still hard for him to process it all. I had *slipped* time and now Mitch had *skipped* time to find us. Jake—who knew me better than anyone—reeled over the truth. I would always wonder if he truly believed my story or decided to humor my fantasies to protect Scout. We squared the situation by salting it with a little humor. I banked on Jake's trust in me, and his own good nature to eventually accept Mitch as part of our small family circle—a family with a secret we could never share with outsiders. And we both understood that Meredith was an outsider.

—Since UR providing the tryptophan, I'll bring booze.—

—That'll put 2 of us 2 sleep. What about others?—

—Time 4 Scout 2 play host?—

—Very funny. What if we just told M the truth.—

—Not funny. Sanity at risk.—

—Only that he's Scout's father, staying…temporarily.—

—Temporarily?—

—Can't say yet.—

—There's hope he will disappear again?—

—B nice now.—

—Always 2 U. What about saying he had been deployed in army?—

—The Civil War or Indian Wars? Only conflicts he might remember.—

—Memory still gone? That works.—

—Soldier with PTSS could B reasonable.—

—Sounds good—would explain mental fog + scars.—

—No need 2 mention how he got scars.—

—losing reception. Got what?—

—Scars. Shooting Bear.—

—Roger. Shoot…—

—C U soon!—

****

Mitch asked if he could join Scout to watch *Mouse on the Mayflower* on the portable TV that could have been wheeled in its stand to the living room. I gave him permission to cross the line into my bedroom. He was fascinated by the TV and how it worked. It used to be a fixture in my bedroom, mainly for news or an old movie at bedtime, but since Mitch came, it spent half of the time in the living room when we could get any reception at all. Living miles outside of town, the only channels we got were local to Wheatland or Cheyenne.

After I stuffed and buttered up the turkey for his trip to the oven, I made a list of what needed to be done—in order. After mixing batches of dough for yeast rolls and pie crusts, I prepared the pie filling, then defrosted a large bag of green beans from my garden for the casserole Jake loved with mushroom soup. Aside from mashed potatoes and yams, cranberry orange relish completed my simple menu.

When Mitch emerged from the bedroom alone, he asked if he could help. He didn't flinch when I handed him a potato peeler and a bowl of potatoes and yams. After several tries with the peeler, he asked for a paring knife.

"Scout fell asleep on your bed," he said. "I nearly joined him."

"Oh?" I understood what he inferred. "It's a memory foam mattress—easily adjusts to the body weight."

"Better than straw," he muttered.

I stared at him. "Straw? Wasn't your old mattress horsehair and hemp?"

A wrinkle between his brows deepened as he thought about it, "It wasn't always. What is the mattress in Scout's room made of?"

"Springs and padding, I think. Personally, I needed something…more cuddly."

He nodded with a quick little grin and concentrated

hard on the potato he was paring almost down to a fingerling.

"How was the Mayflower movie?"

"Bright colors. I still don't understand how all those moving pictures are made."

"The technology requires lots of art work."

"But are they faithful to real life—like portraits?"

I chuckled. "Well, aside from a talking mouse, I think the artists try to simplify accuracy."

"Do you think they sketched a true replica of the ship?"

He was amazed when I opened my laptop and showed him how to google a picture of the Mayflower. "You can google anything, even old paintings and some photos of ships that might have been used in your time. Shipyard specifications and passenger journals from centuries ago even provide enough dimensions to recreate a true picture of what ships looked like."

"*Mo Dhia*," he muttered.

"What did you say?"

He stared at me, his green eyes wide with wonder. "Did it take you long to learn all this?"

I laughed. "You are in the information age, now. I think when you're born into it, well, maybe it's like learning to speak. Progress over the last 130 years may seem overwhelming to you, but most of the technology was born before I was." I shrugged. "Maybe with exception to smartphones and electric cars."

His eyebrows squished together as he rubbed the back of his neck. "Electric cars?"

I patted his hand. "A lot has happened between our times."

He grunted.

"Consider how it makes life easier."

"Or complex," he muttered.

I understood what he might be feeling. In his time, I was lured to the simplicity of life. What I missed most, however, was indoor plumbing, music on demand, and of course, the medical knowledge that extended life. Giving birth was a risk for women, and children often died before their first birthday. Scout…or I might not have made it in 1886. I smiled when our eyes met. "Do you think you could get used to…all the complexity here?"

I offered him some of the mixed nuts and candy corn I was putting into a fluted dish to set on the mantel. He picked out a few pieces and tossed them in his mouth, grunting again like a caveman.

He nodded without a word when I told him what Jake and I had texted earlier, and agreed to the storyline for Meredith, though I don't think he was comfortable with it. We might all be hauled away to the Funny Farm with the truth, I added.

"'The Funny Farm,'" he repeated in an uncertain tone.

"Just a kinder phrase for a loony bin."

"A loony bin?"

His face cleared when I got to the point with insane asylum.

"Maybe I could just hide in the hen house," he suggested, "or join Scout's flock of laughing turkeys." With a grimace, he rubbed the back of his neck.

I swallowed a nervous laugh and offered him more of the nuts.

Chapter Thirty-Six
Is this Thanksgiving?

The table was set and dinner almost ready when I heard the truck pull up. It wasn't Jake and Meredith, however. When I opened the door, Sadie rushed inside and made a beeline for Scout—who squealed with delight when the dog washed his face with her tongue. Chuck Beaverwood pulled off his black cap and winced. His gray hair was rumpled and I could tell even through his coke-bottle glasses that his eyes were strained and puffy. He fingered his hat and shifted from foot to foot.

"I, I should have left her in the truck, but she started whining when we came up the hill."

I hesitated briefly, then gave him a hug and invited him inside. "Happy Thanksgiving, Chuck."

He pulled away and stared at me. "Oh my God, is today Thanksgiving?" When he noticed the table setting, he backed away and tried to grab Sadie's collar. "I, I can come back tomorrow."

The dog dodged him, trailing after Scout who was already pitching a ball into the hallway.

Chuck was not a man who stuttered. I knew he had something on his mind that couldn't wait 'til tomorrow. I invited him to join us for dinner. "There's a very large turkey in the oven—enough to feed you and the boys if you'll stay. After what you did to help me out with

Mitch, I owe you more than a turkey dinner."

He rolled his cap around in his hands and his mouth quivered when he spoke. "The boys are gone."

"Gone?"

"They took off about a week ago. Left me a note saying they wanted to see the ocean and spend the winter in warmer climes."

"Oh, Chuck, I'm so sorry. Have you heard from them since?"

"Not a word. They cleaned out their savings and took our old coupe. If I wasn't out with Sadie that day, they might have taken her, too."

He collapsed in my easy chair and sighed deeply. I didn't know what to say. When Mitch emerged from a steamy bathroom in a robe, drying his hair with a towel, Chuck sprung awkwardly out of the chair. "Oh, I didn't mean to interrupt…" His gaze drifted between Mitch and me, then settled on Mitch, who looked equally uncomfortable in Jake's old plaid robe that bared his long legs to the knees.

"I'm glad to see you've survived," Chuck finally said.

I formally introduced them, with a condensed version of their initial encounter in the woods. Mitch had been unconscious on our race to the hospital, and probably oblivious to Beaverwood's help getting him to the hospital in Wheatland.

Mitch offered his hand first. "Thank you," he said simply before we were all distracted by Scout and the dog still scampering after the ball that was leaving a trail of doggie drool on my wood floor. Mitch excused himself to get dressed and quickly retreated to his room.

I stood before the fireplace, knowing the hot rush

of heat I felt didn't come from the cozy fire in the hearth. "He loves the steam shower," I said lamely.

With a quick little grin, Chuck pulled on his ear. "The bear has recovered, I see."

"He is Scout's father," I said, hoping that would stifle any other explanations. "Can I get you something to drink, Chuck? Coffee or something stronger?"

"Scout's father?" His face was a blank, trying to recall, I suppose, our conversation about raising children alone. Finally, he shook his head. "I'm intruding. I didn't remember it was Thanksgiving."

After offering more reassurance and a shot of brandy, Chuck slumped back in the chair and fished in his jacket to hand me something. I quickly threw back the scant shot I poured for myself as I stared at the unflattering picture on my driver's license. "Where did you find this? I didn't know I had lost it."

"It was in a box of trading cards I found in Tommy's room after the boys left. I was searching for any notes or an address that would clue me into their destination."

"But why would Tommy have my driver's license? It was in my…" Suddenly it dawned on me. I kept the license in my car's glove compartment—where the gun was supposed to be.

"Tommy had a crush on you, Jessica. He was amazed that you would bake us cookies, and offer lunch when we built your garage. We didn't get that treatment from other customers." His voice cracked when he added, "maybe your kindness reminded him of his mother and…he wanted your photo to remember? Tommy isn't one to think clearly."

I stared at the black cap he was again fumbling, the

one with the blue BB logo—for Beaverwood Builders and something the Sheriff said when I retrieved my revolver this week suddenly registered. *The robber in the video tape showed it was a young man in a dark hoodie and cap with a blue logo we couldn't make out.* Of course, I couldn't share this information with the suffering man in my easy chair—a man who had lost his wife to cancer and now, maybe his sons to something surely as life altering.

I moved across the room to take his cap and help him out of his jacket. "Well, kindness between neighbors is always an easy *pay-it-forward.*" Out of the corner of my eye, I saw Mitch now standing in the hallway, dressed and shaved. "We'd be honored to have you feast with us today."

Chuck took off his glasses and wiped them on his shirt when Sadie plopped the ball in his lap. "Well, looks like Sadie wants me to accept your invite," he muttered, rolling the sticky ball over to Scout.

When Mitch came to stand beside me, Chuck acknowledged us both with a silent nod of thanks. I was relieved when the two men began to engage in small talk while I checked on the turkey. Weather turned into tentative questions about the new garage and the construction business in the area. I couldn't help interjecting how pleased I was with the hen house, and added that Mitch was an experienced builder himself, recalling, of course, how he built his own cabin and most of the furniture in it. Mitch gave me a sharp look before I rattled on. Had the shot I consumed with our guest already loosened my tongue? Jake had promised to bring wine. I could handle that alcohol content without feeling muzzy. On the other hand, *muzzy* might get me through this day.

Jake and Meredith arrived in the breach of our silence, and the atmospheric pressure in my modern cabin soon elevated, as Jake grimly wedged his way inside with a large box in his arms. Meredith held the door for him with the pasted-on smile of someone who had just won an argument. Introductions made, a pall settled over the room until all focus turned to Scout and Sadie, now having a tug of war with one of Scout's rubber super heroes. Sadie was growling and Scout was doing a credible job of mimicking. I intervened, removing the toy before tug elevated to chomp on either end. "How about a drink before dinner?" I gave Jake a specific help-needed look after he picked up his nephew and kissed him on the cheek.

Jake caught my drift and quickly responded, setting Scout down before he began pulling bottles out of the box and lining them up on the island counter like soldiers facing a firing squad: Brandy, Crème de Menthe, Rosé, and Moscato, tonic and soda along with a six pack of dark draft beer. I handed him a corkscrew, muttering under my breath, "A sale at the depot?"

As we bumped hips retrieving glasses from the cupboard, he muttered back, "Insurance for the *happy* in Happy Thanksgiving."

Jake filled an ice bucket and played bartender while I basted the turkey and siphoned off enough juice for gravy. Meredith offered to help, and I put her to work mashing potatoes, a task she approached with jackhammer resolve. Mitch and Chuck continued their chum strum, ignoring everyone else, but Scout and Sadie.

When everyone was served a drink of their choice,

I rang a little bell calling for a toast. “To a happy day,” I cried, fervently hoping this was possible. Everyone raised a glass, glaring as if cued toward someone responsible for such an outcome: Meredith at Jake, Jake at Mitch, Mitch at me and after a sweep over each guest, I stopped at Chuck who was lovingly focused on the Old Fashioned he held.

Chapter Thirty-Seven
Dead Soldiers

After a heartfelt dinner prayer of thanks, all eyes centered on me. Smiling faces so far. *A good sign.* This was my first Thanksgiving dinner as hostess and cook since Gran died. Jake and I had dined out together the last few years, knowing how hard it would be to replicate the traditional meal Gran always engineered. When we were little, and picky over food choices, it was always fun to see what novel idea she would come up with to make something we couldn't resist eating: Baked potatoes or rolls with a turkey head or a pilgrim hat, yam tarts with marshmallow snowmen.

One year, she bought a wooden turkey at a garage sale and drilled several holes in its backside. Into each hole, she stabbed a colorful sucker and promised us one-a-day if we cleaned our plates. I had that turkey packed away somewhere. From the way Scout attacked his food, however, it didn't look like I would ever need a clean plate bribe.

Meredith had brought a small floral arrangement in a ceramic turkey, but there was no room for it on the table with the real thing. She passed the meat platter to Mitch sitting on her right and leaning over asked if he preferred leg or breast. Mitch's face turned almost as red as her gaping blouse as he glanced from the platter to the décolletage she presented. He quickly chose a drumstick and passed the platter to Chuck who was near enough to ogle, even with coke-bottle glasses. "I do prefer the breast," I said with strangled amusement.

Jake was cutting up a chunk of meat for Scout and missed the reveal. "You always grabbed the white meat," he said. "Gran and I were forced into the dark side."

I shot him a narrow look. "I always thought you preferred it that way?"

"I settled." Jake waved a fork at me. "Doesn't every man with two women in his life have to settle?"

In the silence that followed, I dared a quick glimpse of Mitch, noticing the thin scar running down his neck stood out a little brighter. After everything else was passed and plates filled, we all settled into the business of eating with few attempts at polite talk that didn't involve a wine refill. I asked Meredith how business was going.

"It's always slow over the holidays and even into the New Year. Things usually pick up in the spring. This is a good time to study up trends and take in a few conventions."

"The same with building," Chuck said. "Only inside projects this time of year."

"Do you have many lined up?" Jake asked, waving a large drumstick.

"A few, but now with my sons gone…" He took a gulp of wine and left the sentence hanging.

"His sons are wintering in warmer climes," I finished.

"Sounds like a plan," Meredith murmured. "I'm thinking along those lines, myself."

"Well, let's drink to that," Jake said a little too

loudly. He drained his glass and reached for the half-empty bottle of wine at his end of the table.

Meredith gave him a scorched look, then turned to Mitch. "I understand you've been serving our country. What branch?"

"*Army,*" I said, in unison with Jake." We grinned at each other while Meredith shuffled a glance between us and Mitch.

"Infantry," Mitch muttered as he wiped his mouth with a napkin.

"Did you say *Cavalry?* I didn't know they still rode horses in the army." Meredith jerked her attention back to Jake who, I figured, must have kicked her under the table. "Well," she continued perplexed, "Jake told me you've gone through a lot to get back here. I think every serviceman should be properly thanked for their sacrifices, especially today, with the endless turmoil in the Middle East and terrorists popping up everywhere."

Chuck lifted his empty glass, nodding for a refill. "We can all drink to that."

We all complied, but a kick under the table wasn't stopping Meredith. After a minute of silence, she turned again to Mitch. "So, is your leave permanent or do you plan to go back?"

"Meredith, you missed your calling." I worked hard to smile. "You should have been a journalist."

She sipped her wine and shrugged. "Well, of course, I know decisions like these are not always in a soldier's hands. The government, or a significant other…with his child…has to sway any decision like that." She smiled sweetly at me, licking a bit of marshmallow from her bottom lip.

"Yes, yes it does," I said tartly. Out of the corner of

my eye, I could see Mitch playing with the last of his sweet potatoes and Chuck buttering his second roll. I was about to add something nasty when I felt a tap from Jake's wandering foot beneath the table.

"Well, this is quite a banquet, Jess. Gran would be proud of you." He held up his glass. "I say we all toss…I mean…*toast* the chef. He whispered something into Scout's ear and my son raised his tippy cup and leaned over to bump my wine glass hard enough to empty the contents onto my plate, creating red rivers of cranberry sauce that tinted my mashed potatoes pink.

"Mama good," he said, with a baby giggle.

"Well, that's a compliment I can relish." I spooned up a runny mouthful of cranberries and wine, and when I vowed it was a recipe to remember, everyone else laughed. I leaned over to spoon some of my pink potatoes into Scout, who made a face over the new taste. Thankfully, the rest of the meal continued in relative silence until I rose to rinse off my plate. Mitch took my cue and also jumped up, getting a wet cloth to scrub Scout's little hands and face…under Jake's grim supervision.

I knew Jake must have felt deprived, probably even jealous of his obvious replacement. It was the first time he had seen Mitch react with Scout. I caught his eye and winked. Knowing him longer than anyone else in the room, we said more with a wink or a gesture than most siblings.

Nobody had room for pie just yet. Chuck asked if he could dice up a dish of meat and gravy for Sadie, while Meredith and I cleared the table and stacked the dishwasher. Mitch offered to bathe Scout and put him in his PJs. When Jake volunteered to help him, I pasted on a smile and rolled my eyes. Jake threw me a "don't worry look" but twenty minutes later, he emerged from the bathroom carrying Scout. Mitch followed them, wearing his own version of a pasted-on smile.

Since it was a beautiful fall day, sunny, and warmer than usual, I opened the front door to let in some fresh air, and Sadie immediately ran outside. Meredith followed with a pack of smokes, and Jake, still holding Scout, volunteered to keep an eye on the dog. Chuck pulled Mitch into the garage to explain the design points of the hen house he built while I put on a pot of coffee brewed with a raw egg contributed by one of the hens this morning. Alone in the house, I put on an easy-listening CD, stepped out of my shoes and—with an open bottle of Moscato—plunked into my easy chair and took a swig from the bottle. With eyes closed, I had trouble distinguishing between the music, hens cackling in the garage and Mitch and Meredith's pitched voices coming from the front porch. Maybe Jake was right, referring liquor to insurance. I had never consumed so much of it, but the muzzy feeling it gave me helped to dilute my worries.

With everyone united inside, pie and coffee was still deferred over the crème de menthe Jake brought. Mitch announced rather curtly that he was going to read to Scout, and Sadie followed him into Scout's bedroom after Jake made a half-hearted suggestion to play Crazy Eights. Chuck decided to sit by the fire to nurse a mug of coffee laced with brandy. That left me and Jake explaining the card game to a less-than-enthused Meredith. "You-know," Jake slurred, "this is a lot like Uno."

"This is not very challenging," Meredith observed,

shielding her breast with her cards, while her manicured forefinger dipped into her cleavage to scratch.

"It is when you've washed down a turkey dinner with a lot of boobs, I mean *booze*," I remarked with a little burp.

Jake winked at me with both eyes. "Jess an' I played this every Thanksgiving with Gran," he explained to Meredith.

While the two of them bickered over rules, I struggled to order the cards in my hand. I envied Chuck who had fallen asleep in the chair and was snoring softly. I also envied Mitch, keeping company with Scout and probably Mickey Mouse or Roger the Pirate. *I needed a nap and it was still early evening.*

Time for coffee. I insisted Meredith and Jake drink theirs black before leaving. While Meredith spent fifteen minutes in the bathroom, Jake and I shared a piece of pumpkin pie.

"How did Gran ever do all this?"

Jake looked at me with half-lidded eyes and held up two fingers. "There were just the three of us, Jess."

I gave him a third finger. "And a lot less to drink," I added.

"Ss-sorry about that. I thought it would…tranquilize the beast in everyone."

We both looked at Chuck, slumped in his chair and snoring like one of his buzz saws. "Well," I giggled, "it sure worked for him. I think he's down for the count. I'll drive him home in the morning."

Jake nodded. "Maybe this party just had the wrong guests."

I gave him a fish eye. "You don't mean Mitch."

"He's good with Scout, I'll give him that."

"But…?"

"But maybe Meredith asked what we all wondered. Is he here for the long run?"

I sighed. "Unanswered questions."

"I hope you know what you're doing, Jess."

"Doing a crash course in patience right now."

"Maybe the bigger question is do you still love him?"

The sudden welling in my eyes might have been from too much wine consumed. "He's Scout's father—a little different than I remembered, but this isn't his world." *Does he still love me?* That was the better question. Mitch still slept in Scout's room each night, sometimes sharing his bed with his son and a pile of storybooks they were reading together. I knew it was important for them to bond if Mitch was back in our lives for good. For good? Well, that was only one of the questions I couldn't answer.

"He hasn't…forced himself on you?"

"No, just the opposite. We are dancing around the issues until his memory returns."

Jake leaned close, his breath toxic with brandy, and kissed my forehead. "Jess, y'know I've always got your back." He patted the cell phone in his pocket. "Big bro's only a call away if y'need me."

"Well, I'd say I'll drink to that, but it looks like the liquor store is closed here." I waved a limp hand toward several empty bottles lined up on the counter.

"Dead soldiers." Jake chuckled.

After insisting Meredith drive when they left, I covered Chuck with the brown and gold afghan Gran had knitted for me in Wyoming U colors, then collapsed in my own bed.

Chapter Thirty-Eight
A Reason to be Thankful.

Even before something damp nudged me awake, I was dreaming I could smell fresh coffee and bacon. My head throbbed when I opened one eye and found a large black nose parked on the edge of my bed. Two open eyes revealed the rest of the dog, and a familiar giggle directed me toward the little green-eyed boy crouched beside her.

"Okay, team." I dragged my legs over the edge and pushed myself up. "You got me!" For a second, everything blurred when I rose. I wiped my eyes and straightened my wrinkled tunic. I had fallen asleep fully dressed. The wake-up team trailed after me to the bathroom where I washed my face with cold water, cleaned my teeth, and tried to rid the sour taste in my mouth with a gargle of mouthwash. I ran a brush through my hair and assessed myself in the mirror before I followed the aroma drifting from the kitchen.

Mitch, with a dishtowel tucked in his waist, was flipping eggs and frying bacon at the range. Chuck was sitting in the easy chair he'd slept in, this time nursing a steamy cup of black coffee in one of my favorite mugs, inscribed *Coffee Before Talkie*. All the empty soldiers were gone, the counters wiped clean and even the dining table—clean and stripped of all but the ceramic turkey and flowers.

"Good morning," they said almost in unison when my presence was noted.

"This looks like a very good morning." I smiled, glancing up at kitchen clock. "You guys are up early." It was half past seven.

"The dog woke us. We hoped you would be able to sleep a little longer."

"They teamed up on me." I nodded to Scout and his furry friend wrestling on the floor.

"Well, that's one of Sadie's lesser virtues." Chuck squinted a little at a shaft of morning light reflecting down from the loft windows. "She's an early riser. Good for me when the boys were in school and I had work to get at."

Mitch set up the counter with three plates. "The wrestling team has already eaten," he said. "I didn't think you'd mind if I fed Scout and started our breakfast," he added with a questioning glance at me.

"Not a bit," I said with a grin.

"I feel terrible for putting you guys out like this," Chuck said, rubbing the bridge of his nose. "You should have chased me out of here last night."

I shook my head. "You weren't in any condition to move—even out of that chair last night."

Chuck grunted. "Well, I displaced your man last night. At least I could have kept Scout and Sadie company, so he could sleep in his own bed."

Mitch looked down, with a tiny twist at the corner of his mouth, but said nothing. I could feel the heat creep up my neck as I poured myself a mug of coffee and added too much sugar.

The bacon was crisp, the way I liked it, and the fresh eggs were perfectly seasoned. Chuck launched into his theory about which kind of hen lays the better eggs and how he could usually tell by the shape, which hens gave them up. Mitch looked impressed, nodding at me.

"I bartered my hens from Chuck—part of the garage deal," I explained.

"My mum always found the best eggs…" he started to say before Chuck interrupted, offering me a couple more hens.

"I've got more eggs than I can eat, now. The boys and I could polish off a half dozen or more each morning."

My heart ached for the man. "Your boys are young yet, Chuck. They'll be back. Jake craved independence when he was even younger. At eighteen, he threatened to go off and join a circus that came to Cheyenne—to see more of the country he said. Our grandmother was wise to fund a rafting trip on the Green River for him, instead. He swallowed a lot of rapids that summer and came home with a new thirst for college. Maybe your boys just need a break to swallow up some new scenery before they settle down."

Mitch studied me with quiet intention, leaning against the counter, sipping his coffee, from my *Choose Happy* mug.

Chuck removed his glasses and stared off in space, his gray eyes damp as morning dew. "I hope you're right, Jessica. Raising children alone…" He shook his head and drilled a look at me with a nod to Mitch. "I'm glad you won't have to do that now."

From the porch, we watched Chuck Beaverwood depart in his pickup with plastic containers of turkey leftovers and pie, Sadie riding shotgun beside him.

Scout had refused to say goodbye, thumb in mouth, clinging to my hand with a deep frown. The dog had been equally conflicted, whining as she squeezed her nose into the two inch opening in the cab window.

When Scout broke loose and started running after the truck, screaming “No, no leave me,” I ran after him. Mitch ran faster, scooping him up while he flailed his arms and legs screaming like a siren.

My son had never thrown a tantrum over anything and the scene had me holding my mouth, choking back my own emotion. Twenty feet down the drive, the truck stopped suddenly and Chuck let Sadie out. “Take her,” he yelled in a shaky voice. “She needs a boy to play with.”

Sadie whimpered a little when the truck took off again, then turning full circle, she bounded up the drive to reunite with Scout in a scene that could have been a trailer for the Humane Society.

Mitch glanced at me and shrugged. “Looks like the lad has a dog.”

“Oh God, how can we keep her? Chuck needs her company now more than ever.”

“I’ll bring that up to him tomorrow. He offered me a job.”

I dabbed at my eyes with a wad of old tissue I found in my pocket. “ A job?”

“Aye, when we were looking at the hen house, he told me he has some commitments he’ll be needing help with.” He gave me a toothy smile. “To be sure, we haven’t seen the last of your woodman.”

My heart began to flutter. A job meant commitment. I knew Mitch to be a hard worker, a proud man, and proud men needed to have control in a foreign world. We sat on the porch swing and watched boy and dog solidify their reunion. "Sadie loves me," Scout sang, swiping his chubby hand under his runny nose. "Mama, Sadie loves me."

"Yes, darling, everyone loves you." I used my wet tissue to wipe his nose.

Mitch squeezed my shoulder. "Maybe Chuck needs to be alone for a while, to think things through."

"I've never seen Scout react so. If we have to give the dog back, it'll break his heart."

"We can always go for another dog."

"A replacement is never the same."

He gave my shoulder another squeeze. "It can be."

I studied him. His hair had grown out lighter and curlier than I remembered. He hadn't shaved yet, and his new whiskers shadowed the face I remembered. I pictured him in a cowboy hat, riding tall on an Appaloosa. *Clint Eastwood in his Italian westerns? Minus the steely gaze, of course.* His eyes, bright green in the morning sun, were unreadable when they locked on me. When he shifted position, and caught me staring at him, I felt the usual hitch in my chest.

"Thank you for yesterday," he said.

"Yesterday," I chuckled. "If there's any thanks to the day, it has to come from a higher power."He seemed surprised. "A great meal, great hostess. Your little story about Chuck's boys and Jake's river rafting journey brought it all home to me this morning. You held the rudder steering us all through some narrow channels yesterday."

I chuckled. "Jake's liquor probably held more sway in that ride."

"Jake." He rubbed his chin. "Your brother is…"

"Protective. I know. Jake was the only man in my life…until you."

"His face colored a little. I think he'd like to keep that role."

I curled my right leg under me and pushed the swing into motion. "Why do you say that?"

He grinned at me. "Sure you want to know?"

I nodded vigorously.

"Well, he told me if ever I did anything to hurt you or Scout, he would kill me—in your world or mine."

"Oh, my God! You can't believe that."

"A man who cares deeply is most believable."

"Well, my brother can be deeply dramatic. We shared everything, growing up. We were the only birds in Gran's nest. The three of us were a force.

He scanned the distant mountain range. "A force of three. Yes, I can understand that."

"If you had a sibling, you might understand. You can see how it is with Chuck. Family is important. Thanksgiving always brings that home…for almost everyone."

"You are very wise for your age. How old are you, anyway?"

"Younger than you. Nearly thirty three now."

He looked surprised. "How old do you think I am?"

"When I left your world, you were forty three, but you didn't look that old, and you haven't aged at all since then."

"I don't feel that old."

"Hey, forty is the new thirty in my world. With better medicine, vitamins, and exercise, we live long and prosper in this era."

He patted his stomach. “I could use a little exercise after your Thanksgiving feast.”

After pulling on warmer outerwear, we all trooped down the gravel drive to the river and checked for mail in my box along the road. It was a pleasant day, crisp and cool enough to see vapor cloud around our mouths. Gauzy clouds ringed the distant mountains, as if they also took breath. The headache I woke with was gone and when Mitch took my hand, I felt new energy course through me. Scout and Sadie bounded ahead of us with a joyful spurt of energy.

When we crossed the little foot bridge, I hesitated, then pointed down the river of thin ice to the large flat rock that once played a memorable role in our life back in 1886. I could almost visualize us at the summer site that marked the first time we made love. I asked if he remembered the rock.

“Should I now?”

“You would if your memory came back.”

His jaw tightened as he steadied both hands on the wooden railing and scrunched his face into deep concentration. “Nothing.”

“You know, you once told me when I pretended to lose my memory that it didn’t matter anymore to you, and that we could make new memories.”

“You *pretended* to lose your memory?”

“Well, I did after I recovered from a nasty bump on the head. You thought I was your wife. I had to lie to protect my virtue.”

“Protect yourself…from me?”

“I was thirty years old, still single, and never had a boyfriend. In your day, that defined me as a, a spinster, and I also happened to look like your wife.”

He stepped back from the rail, rubbing his neck. "My…*wife?*" A slow smile creased his face. "So, what became of her?"

"We exchanged places…in an aberration of time."

He sputtered a laugh. "You've been reading too many fairytales to Scout."

I shook my head. "I know it sounds crazy. I was only hoping the rock…well, maybe the rock would jog your memory." A deadly silence almost kept me from the next question. "How did you get here?"

He stared at me with the familiar wrinkle between his eyes and the tick in his jaw. "I walked."

"No, I mean when you found you were transported to this time, this century, what were you doing?"

He stared off in space. "I wish I could say." A small tempest was brewing in the green, something I never saw in him until that day, in his time, when I forced him to believe I was *not* his wife. It was the only time I had feared him.

I turned away, suddenly realizing Scout and his new dog were out of our sightline. He followed my gaze, and must have come to the same conclusion. "They can't be far. We parted in opposite directions.

"The ice, Mitch," I called after him. "I don't think the ice will hold if they try to cross."

His assurance didn't convince me. "The stream isn't deep this time of year."

I called, he whistled—that strong shrill signal that brought back more memories. He once teased me for not being able to whistle, but I still didn't have the hang of it. I hadn't run far along the bank when I tripped over a root and fell on a sharp rock that cut through the already worn knees of my jeans. The call of a red-tailed hawk circling above blended into distant barking and a different tone to Mitch's whistle. Gingerly, I retraced my steps around shrub and rocks and found them waiting for me at the bridge. Mitch had hiked Scout up on his shoulders, oblivious to the muddy red boots dangling over his shoulders. Sadie stood beside them, licking at the mud on her paws. I hobbled toward them. "Thank God, you found them."

"What happened to you?" Mitch pulled Scout off his shoulders and set him down beside Sadie with a "Stay" command that forced their attention.

I inched my way forward, hanging onto the rail. "I'm fine. Just tripped on my big feet."

"You're bleeding," he said, pointing to the bloodstains blooming on the knees of my jeans.

In one swift move, he had me cradled in his arms, moving across the bridge and shuttling the mud babies to follow us back to the house.

"They weren't far," Mitch explained, "but lads and muddy water are magnetic, you know."

I hugged his neck and peered at them over his shoulder. "They weren't in any danger?"

"Nah, water was a trickle. Sadie barked when she heard me coming."

I chuckled. "Sadie will make a good babysitter. We may have to keep her."

"You both need a keeper…or two."

A pair of soft green eyes met mine and instinctively, I kissed him on the cheek. "Thank you."

He blushed. "I should thank you."

"What for?"

"For giving me a reason to be thankful." Our eyes locked and for a minute, I was lost again in time.

Chapter Thirty-Nine
Suds and Pie

We triaged baths. Sadie was first, being the muddiest, and most likely to track up my floors. Mitch washed her feet in a bucket of water while I washed my hands at the kitchen sink, picking out small bits of sandstone from my palms. After I peeled off my jeans, Mitch insisted on doing my knees. I sat on the kitchen stool in my panties and robe, while he crouched on the floor cleaning away dried blood and dirt with gauze pads dipped in iodine. Sadie and Scout stood beside him watching the procedure in silence that matched his intensity.

"Mama has ouchies," Scout whispered to his new dog.

The left knee was only skinned and sore to the touch, but my right knee had a small open cut. When I overplayed the drama, wincing loudly from the sting of the antiseptic, Mitch apologized profusely. His wide-eyed expression made me giggle. Had the light-hearted banter we once enjoyed also run off trail on memory lane?

"I think I'll live," I reassured them all, reaching over to pat Scout who was suddenly sucking his thumb. "A long soak in a hot tub is all I need. And if necessary we can close the cut with liquid stitches."

Mitch narrowed his eyes. "Liquid stitches?"

"Yeah, I have a small bottle in the medicine cabinet. In carpenter terms, it compares to industrial glue."

"Glue?" He looked horrified.

I reached over to pat his head. "Modern conveniences."

****

It was several weeks since I had enjoyed the luxury of a leisurely bath. The jets in the tub sent watery fingers into aches I didn't know existed, and with a little help from a bottle, suds that smelled like lavender were swelling all around me. I used the hand spray to wet my hair, then shampoo and rinse it before wrapping it in a dry towel, turban style. With another towel wadded behind my neck, I leaned back and closed my eyes, until a loud knock at the door broke through the rhythmic hum of the motor.

"All right in there?"

I sat up quickly, sputtering when I noticed suds had ballooned up to my chin. I could taste the soap on my lips.

Before I could answer, the door flew open and in rushed Mitch. One look at the suds cascading over the edge of the tub and he skidded across the wet tile to turn off the running faucet.

When he plunged his hand into the water to grab my arm, I slithered out of his grasp. "I'm ok. I'm ok," I yelled over the hum of the jets. "Just get more towels!"

He skated over to the towel rack near the shower, grabbing every towel in sight to blanket the wet floor while I opened the drain with my foot.

His eyes were nearly the size of his mouth, competing to be heard over the sounds of the gulping drain and the bubbling jets. "Where did this come from?"

I punched the jet control, shutting it off and pointed at the bottle of bubble bath on the edge of the tub. "Bubble bath. Soap in a bottle! You've seen bath suds before!"

"Not like this." He shouted again, as if the jets were still humming.

I peered over the edge of the tub to survey the water damage. "I must have fallen asleep," I muttered, assessing the tile puddled with at least an inch of water.

"Aye. There's a downside to all your modern conveniences." He squinted now and the corner of his mouth twitched. *A bubble of amusement?* "I know of drier places to nap."

With the drain open and jets off, the foamy bubbles were shrinking, and my orange-hued knees poked into sight when I drew my legs up to my chest. The cut on my right knee blinked open and stung from the soap, but it didn't bleed. He sat on the edge of the sink and after slowly removing his wet shoes and wringing out his socks, he smirked at me with his arms crossed. "Would you be wanting some help getting out now? You don't want to bleed that knee again."

I shook my head. "You can leave now." There was nothing graceful about rising from a deep Jetta tub covered with patches of foamy bubbles. Mitch exited the bathroom, wearing a smug grin while I made a clumsy attempt to rise. The large wall mirror above the sink was parallel to the tub and as I stepped onto the wet carpet of towels, I could see my bubble collar glide down my torso to nest in the springy wet triangle between my legs. With handfuls of suds, I covered each breast and impishly assessed the blushing pink woman in the mirror—adorned in a foamy bikini. My robe hung on the hook on the door, and when I reached for it, the door creaked open a little. I snapped my eyes back to the mirror and in a reflected slice of the hallway, there was a fleeting shadow of movement. I slowly closed the door and pulled on my terry robe, belting it tight as my grin.

After brushing my hair and pulling it into a twisty, I wrung out the wet towels and draped them over the edge of the tub. He was right about needing a nap. A hot soak in my tub was usually a prescription for a good night's sleep, but it wasn't even lunchtime yet. When I exited the bathroom, I could hear Mitch reading a Jolly Roger story to Scout in the living room. I tiptoed into my room and pulled on a T-shirt and clean underwear before slipping under the cool sheets on my bed for the luxury of a short nap in a *dry* place.

****

I could see the lighted face of my digital alarm clock when I woke, and for a minute, I wondered if it was 7:25 in the morning or evening. With shorter days, the charcoal sky outside my window gave no clue. I pulled on my robe and padded down the dark hall to Scout's room. With his nightlight on, I could see that he was asleep, sprawled on his stomach, with Sadie sprawled on the rag rug beside his bed, her golden head pillowed between her paws. She sensed my presence and lifted her head to gaze up at me with whiskey-colored eyes that gleamed in the dark. "Oh, Sadie." I sighed, knowing without a doubt that my son had acquired a new guardian angel. Mitch's bed was empty.

The open living room was lit only by the fireplace

and a pillar candle on the island counter beside a single place setting with half a sandwich, a large pickle, and a glass of wine. When I chuckled, Mitch startled in the easy chair blocked by the portable TV pulled up close enough to touch his bare toes. "Oh, you're finally up," he said, wheeling the TV cart to the side. "I didn't want to wake you, so I turned off the volume on this dancing show."

I glanced at the screen to catch a tango twist executed by the dancing stars. "It's more entertaining if you can hear them move to the rhythm of the music."

"Well, I didn't want to wake you or Scout."

"It's early for Scout to go down, isn't it?"

"I wore him out with another outdoor walk this afternoon."

"And you fed him…twice?

"Aye. We finished off most of the leftovers, but I made a turkey sandwich for you. White meat." He gestured toward the plate on the island, rubbing the back of his neck as he shifted from one leg to the other.

I couldn't help smiling. "Very thoughtful."

"Well, I, uh, I ate half the sandwich, thinking you might sleep through the night." He shrugged apologetically. "You must be hungry."

I climbed on a stool, noticing there were no dirty dishes stacked in the sink, and he had used a colorful Christmas napkin for my placemat. The sandwich, however, was missing a spread of mayo or even butter. I squeezed the pickle between the sliced turkey and bread and took a large bite while he watched me intently. "Delicious," I squeaked, watching his eyes light up. "Is this the last of the wine?"

He nodded, confessing it was probably diluted by

the ice cubes he had added to keep it cold.

"I helped myself to a bottle of beer left from yesterday, too."

"Did you like it?"

"Aye. The dark is scoth."

I shook my head. "Not scotch, it isn't scotch. Jake likes dark lager. I prefer sweet wine." For a second he opened his mouth as if to speak, then jammed his hands into his jean pockets when I sipped my diluted wine, then pushed it aside. "I'm not much of a drinker. Another day like yesterday and I could sleep like a hibernating bear."

"Well, speaking of bears, what happened to my bearskin poncho?"

"It's in the garage."

"Might make a good fireside rug."

"Oh, isn't that remade from the one you had? It would be hard to forget…" I stopped when I saw the look on his face, hoping a memory of us on the rug didn't put the scowl on his face. He turned toward the TV and changed the subject.

"Do people dance like that today?" We watched the silent finale of another dance pair that had the man sweeping the floor with his partner before she curled up his leg and bent over his arm.

I laughed. "Not usually. Maybe in contests, or in theatricals."

"Do they dress like that to dance?"

I glanced at the glittering costume the woman wore. It didn't suffer from too much material drag, and the man's outfit bared an equal amount of flesh, though he wore a bow tie and skin-tight vest.

"Dress today is, uh, more revealing I guess." I

pulled my robe closed at the neckline and propped my legs on an empty stool.

He turned off the set, pursing his lips as his eyes flicked over my bare legs and feet, sticking out of my robe. "Your knees look better."

I finished my sandwich standing up. "Is there any pie left?"

He crossed to the refrigerator and took out two pieces of pumpkin pie, already plated. "One for each of us."

I grabbed the aerosol can of whipping cream from the fridge, shook it and sprayed a glob on each piece. He stared at the pie, horrified.

"Why would you do that?"

"You don't like whipped cream?"

"Whipped cream?" His cheek twitched. "This isn't your bath foam?"

Laughing, I squirted some in his open mouth. He licked his lips, then grabbed the can and squirted some on the tip of my nose. I dug my fingers into the pie and pushed a chunk of it into his mouth, then retreated around the counter. He chased, catching the back of my robe. I wiggled out of it and ran to my bedroom, slamming the door on his foot.

"*Áigh*," he cried, hopping on one foot to collapse on the edge of my bed.

I tried to swallow my laugh as I licked my sticky fingers. "I didn't mean to do that."

"Aye, you did." He grabbed me when I bent close enough to survey the foot damage, and I fell flat into his chest, knocking the wind out of him with a loud grunt.

"I'm sorry, I'm sorry." When I pushed myself up on my arms, I could see that his eyes reflected the red light from my digital clock, but his lips curled in a faint smile. Humor rising? He raised his head and licked the cream off my nose. For a few seconds we became still life, adjusting to the darkness, sinking into the foam mattress, listening to the sound of heavy breathing before our mouths slapped together with such force my teeth hurt.

My heart was thumping out signals shooting through my body when our tongues began a tentative dance. I could taste pumpkin and sweet cream. His hands stroked my back and when they slipped under my T-shirt and traveled down the keys of my spine, I moaned. He was back, the only man I loved was back and memories of our last night together in his cabin bed flashed through my mind like streaks of lightning. When his hand dipped below my panty line and cupped my buttock, he seemed to hold his breath, and after catching my own breath, my mouth traveled to his shoulder tasting him in little nips. Suddenly, I felt the heat of light sting my eyelids.

"Momma, no bite, no bite!"

The little voice of our son sliced us apart like a saber. With a hand, I shielded the beam of light from my blinking eyes and saw him standing a foot from the bed, training his Halloween flashlight on us. Sadie was sitting beside him, panting with her mouth opened in what I could swear was a doggie grin. Mitch pushed me aside and we quickly popped up to sit on the edge of the bed, looking at one another like two shamed children.

I was the first to move, smoothing my long T-shirt down when I stood up. "Give mama the flashlight, Scout. That's a good boy. Did we wake you?" The stupid little flashlight was missing the pumpkin head once screwed over the light source to dull the intensity of the beam. Briefly I scanned the light over Mitch and could see at once that even fully dressed, he was not ready to stand up. The scar trailing from his ear was white as lightning against the stain creeping up his neck. He pulled my bed quilt over his lap.

While I read Scout a bedtime story that put him to sleep again, Mitch took a long shower. We later met in the kitchen, both of us now clad in pajamas and robes, red-faced and subdued as we finished off the remains of the pumpkin pie. I noticed he was limping before we parted in the hall, both of us managing awkward smiles as we retired, each to our separate bedroom.

Chapter Forty
'C' Words

Chuck kept his word to Mitch and put him on the payroll remodeling a room in an old tavern in Guernsey, a small town near the North Platte River about fifteen miles away. The railroad, historic sites, and a state park with a reservoir defined the town's perimeters, providing maybe enough jobs to keep more than a thousand residents there. Register Cliff and wagon ruts carved into the old Oregon Trail also put the town on the map for tourists. It boasted a new school, a golf course and bowling alley, small shops and two motels. Main Street was a couple blocks long, with old shotgun buildings that resembled a western movie set meant to depict life in the 1880's. One of the blocks was exclusive to bars and restaurants.

Dooley's, the bar that boasted a drive-up window, had just changed hands and the new owner was anxious to alter its reputation from Saturday night fights to Saturday night dances featuring local bands. Opening up the bar room to a smaller adjacent room, and refinishing the floor to accommodate dancers and tables was on the Beaverwood work list.

I could tell that Mitch was excited about the job, even more when he heard the bar was named Dooley's, for some reason. He was dressed and waiting on the porch when Chuck picked him up early Monday morning. I was slugging down my morning coffee when they hauled a large dog bed inside, along with bags of dog food, dishes, leashes, and toys that belonged to Sadie. When I asked Chuck if he was absolutely certain about parting with her, he shrugged.

"I know she's in good hands, and will get the attention she deserves." With a brave smile, he patted her on the head and hurried back outside.

Mitch glanced at the kitchen clock, then saluted me and Scout as he dodged after his new boss. Scout paused over his breakfast to wave his spoon, flinging oatmeal on the floor around his highchair. I noticed every third spoonful was intentionally targeting my floor and Sadie's tongue was the mop.

I filled one of Sadie's dishes with dry dog food. "Okay, team. Listen up." I explained to both of them who eats what and where, after placing the dish and another filled with water on a vinyl mat that was part of Sadie's *luggage*.

Scout was at the window several times during the day watching for Mitch, even after I reassured him that he would be back for supper, but I found myself watching the clock just as often. I knew Mitch to be a diligent worker and for the most part, tools hadn't changed much in a hundred years, barring the use of electric saws and nail guns.

After wrapping bars of cured soap in silver Christmas tissue with my decorative JB label, I tied a small blue ribbon around each bar. My online order for holiday scents, paraffin, and lanolin came weeks ago, but in my preoccupation with Mitch and Thanksgiving, I hadn't made my usual supply of votive candles and lip gloss for the holidays. With Christmas just a month away, I was already behind and my bank account was drifting toward red alert.

The sky was thick with the threat of snow by late afternoon, and my crockpot was simmering with a hearty stew when Chuck dropped Mitch off. He smelled of sweat and beer, and his hair and jeans were flecked with sawdust. Sadie kept her distance and Scout backed away after an enthusiastic greeting, holding his nose. "You smell," he said, in the guileless way of children.

Mitch threw me an apologetic look and headed for the shower after noting the savory smell of something else in the house. I set the table, using Christmas placemats and a whimsical snowman candle as a centerpiece, then took time to comb my hair and dab a little of my favorite cologne on my wrists.

Clean and shaved, he came to the table and attacked supper like it was the last meal of the condemned. Halfway through, he noticed me watching and complimented my effort with a boyish grin. Were we beginning to channel TV sitcom families at mealtime? "So, how was your day?"

He told me they had taken down the wall that separated two rooms and sanded the floors. "We tried to keep the mess confined, as the owner still expected regulars tonight. A large bin outside held what we demolished."

"A dumpster."

He looked at me in wonder. "So that's what it's called!"

We both laughed when Scout piped up with "dumb truck?"

"I don't think Chuck could do this alone. He gave me a large iron mallet to attack the wall, and carried some of the wallboard and wood out to the bin, but I did most of the heavy stuff." The pride in his voice was unmistakable.

"You might identify with some of the fixer-upper shows on TV."

He gave me a blank look.

"That's a popular craze now." I explained. "People fix up or remodel old homes to re-sell at a profit—thousands of dollars, usually."

His eyebrows shot up. "A living, then?" He thought this over, then added, "Chuck said he'd pay me by the job, and the owner wants it done as soon as possible. She's already lined up a band for week after next."

"She?"

"Odd, I know, a lass ownin' a bar."

"A lass?"

"Aye, but it seems to be the way in your time. Women doing men's jobs."

I bristled, wondering how to respond. "Does this trouble you?"

His voice was guarded. "Nooo, unless…maybe…it robs men of a job."

"Welcome to my century. Today's woman has more use than the three C's Henry Garrett said she was good for."

"*The three C's?*"

"Cooking, cleaning, and conceiving." I wiped my mouth with my napkin and threw it on my plate. "I suppose you don't remember your sexist neighbor, Henry Garrett?"

"Henry Garrett?"

"Well, there's a good "C" for your memory slip.

Convenient." I scraped my half-eaten stew into Sadie's dish and rinsed off my plate at the sink.

He joined me at the sink, looking sheepish as he handed me his clean plate to rinse. I grabbed for it, but he hung tight to the plate until our eyes met and I could acknowledge the flutter of confusion in his. "If I said something offensive, I'm sorry. Your…your Irish is up."

"My Irish? There's very little Irish in me, but I know what that means. I also know you are half Irish and from another century, but you were never chauvinistic…before you lost your memory."

He rolled his eyes. "Another 'C' word?"

I rolled my eyes. "Chauvinistic means you feel gender superiority."

"You think that of me?" He abruptly let go of the plate and it slipped out of my grasp to shatter on the floor.

When we both stooped to pick up the pieces, he stilled my hand with a soft touch. "You are a rare woman, Jessica. You've mastered all of those, those 'C's', have your own house, a business, a car…everything a man…from any century might envy."

With a sigh, I turned away from the green. "I don't have everything."

"What is it you miss, then?"

Glancing back, I saw the apprehension in his face, and didn't know how to answer. We were both caught up in a net of 'C' words. This was our first full day apart since I shot him weeks ago, and we still hadn't talked about contingencies. How did he pass through time? What had happened with Jessamine and Tallie?

Was he here to stay? I thought he needed time to recover, time to restore some memory, but I was losing patience. If his memory never returned, we would eventually have to make choices that would affect both of us…and our child.

He turned my hand in his and studied my palm for several seconds, as if reading it like the gypsy once did in his century. The lifeline, the love line, the fleshy mount of Venus at the base of my thumb. Did he remember what it meant? I blinked away the sudden dampness I could feel in my eyes, before I pulled my hand away and sighed again. Silent words fell between us like the shattered pieces of the plate I began to pick up.

Take it slow, Jessica.

Chapter Forty-One
A Date with a Cowboy

Mitch was paid in cash for a week of work and insisted on taking me out to celebrate with dinner and dancing in Guernsey. “For all you’ve done for me, this is poor payback, but something I must do,” he insisted.

We had been tentative and careful with each other since the supper of ‘C’s, falling into a routine. Chuck picked him up early each morning and drove him home before dusk each evening. He showered and we ate together, exchanging small talk or focusing on Scout and Sadie. After supper, I cleaned up the kitchen while he cleaned up Scout, getting him undressed, playing with him or reading his favorite Pirate stories.

Scout was now potty trained, with only an occasional overnight mishap. Once he was asleep, Mitch and I watched TV together when the reception was good. Sometimes we even recounted our day, like an old married couple might have done. Only we weren’t married. Not even friends with benefits. I left my bedroom door unlocked, but the last time he crossed the threshold of my room was the day after Thanksgiving when Scout interrupted us with his flashlight.

Jake had agreed to take Scout—and even Sadie—home with him Saturday, saying he wanted to show off Torrington’s Christmas lights, and maybe drop in on

Santa at the Feed store to have their photo taken together. He approved of our new family addition, admitting the dog would be good protection for Scout and me. What I knew he meant was protection from Mitch.

He and Meredith were "taking a break in their relationship," and I think Jake also wanted to show off his nephew to Louisa Johnson, still running the gift shop at the Bunny's Café. He also took the remainder of my Christmas soaps and candles to disperse at the gift shops that carried them and offered to pick up payment for items already sold.

I knew Mitch was excited to show me what he had accomplished at Dooley's and I knew Whistler's, the restaurant just a few doors away, served great home-cooked meals. I was also excited—nervous as a girl on my first date, conflicted over what to wear: My maxi skirt or good jeans, a sweater or blouse, western boots or strappy heels? I played with combinations for days. When I saw his double-take over the silk paisley blouse I chose, along with tight black jeans, silver hoop earrings and western boots, I knew I had made the right choice.

His mouth hung open after he whistled. "Those jeans are pretty tight," he said, studying my backside.

"Jeans are meant to be tight…on men as well as women." I smiled. He was wearing his black jeans, cowboy boots, and the pale green shirt we bought at the Emporium in Wheatland. "You look good, yourself, cowboy."

He slicked back his hair, now a shade darker with a liberal dose of tonic that smelled as minty fresh as his aftershave. Squirming a little under *my* scrutiny, he rubbed his chin. “Maybe I should shave.”

“No,” I cried, a little too vehemently. “I, I like the five o’clock shadow.”

Grinning, he fingered one of my hoop earrings as he helped me into my jacket. “You pass the sniff test, yourself.”

“Rose water bath, and JB lotion.”

“Well, you have a customer, here.” He pulled on his own jacket and the cowboy hat he seldom wore.

I waved off the compliment. “These are women-scents. I’m still working on a men’s line.”

A groundcover of snow had accumulated during the week, but my car had good snow tires. “Dates who pay also drive,” I said, handing him the car keys in the garage. His eyes flicked approval as he straightened his shoulders. A loud send-off from roosting hens made us both chuckle. We were both primed with nervous excitement for what our first date night might hold.

****

We were also dressed appropriately for dining at Whistler’s. The restaurant was long and narrow with only six tables that seated four people and a few tables for two. With only half of them filled, we chose a table with a top laminated over colorful True West magazine covers from the 1980s. The room’s wood paneling above horizontal steel wainscoting was decorated with horseshoe hooks and framed western pictures and memorabilia. A block cutout sign above the door read: *We support our military.*

The young waitress recited the special of the day when she handed us menus, but Mitch told her we’d have two Wet Willies and Kahlua Lattes.

“I knew you’d want that.” She smiled at him,

jotting it on her pad.

Ordering for both of us surprised me almost as much as the waitress's parting comment. When she left, I asked him if he had eaten here this week.

"Chuck treated me to lunch a few times."

"I've heard about their Kahlua Lattes, but what's their version of a Wet Willie?"

"Roast beef and cheese on a French roll au jus and cowboy potatoes." When I licked my lips, he looked relieved. "I knew you'd love that, but the only liquor they serve is in their coffee specialties."

"I always love fine dining," I chuckled. "Especially when I'm not the cook."

"They have good pie here, too, but not as good as your pumpkin pie." He winked at me.

"Oh, so, you've tasted their pie, too?"

"Comparison shopping, Chuck called it. He agreed with me—about your pie."

Bemused, I leaned back in my chair and studied him. Only a week of gainful employment had changed him, giving me a glimpse of the confidence I remembered. He was more talkative, too. *Amazing!*

He had also put on some weight, and his hair was now long enough for sideburns that helped camouflage his shorter ear lobe and the scar that trailed from it. His jeans were tighter and even the green shirt he wore fit nicely across his shoulders. The color highlighted his eyes. Even wearing a cheap version of a Stetson, he looked like a cowboy you might find on a True West cover, not the half-Indian, half-Irish settler I remembered in his time. "Do you know what a wet willie is?" I asked, after our dinner was served.

"I'm eating it," he mumbled with a mouth full.

I laughed. “Well, it’s a clever name for a sandwich, but not what Jake described to me.”

“Jake knows about this place?”

I nodded. “He and Meredith come here often, I think.”

“Why don’t we leave Jake out of this date tonight? I mean, aren’t dates in your time s’posed to be between two people?”

“Aye, aye.” I saluted him, using his favorite pirate expression and finished my latte with a loud slurp. He was right about the sandwich, and tackled it full on with as much gusto as everything else he ate. We skipped dessert and followed the muted sound of music to Dooley’s just a couple doors away.

Their small parking lot was full, with the large dumpster still taking up space. Holding hands, we threaded our way around small groups of people inside. Two guitars and a drummer were set up with bulky floor amps and a strobe light at the far end of the new room, playing an Eagle’s song that two couples were trying to dance to. Most of the pub tables and high wooden chairs lining the dance room were occupied, but Mitch guided me to two stools at the L-shaped corner bar and ordered us both a tap beer from a rosy-cheeked bartender wearing a Santa hat. We took off our jackets and draped them over the back of the stools. The smell of new varnish was overpowered by the yeasty aroma of beer and strong whiskey. Over the noise and music, Mitch had to lean close, explaining with broad gestures how he and Chuck took out the wall and shored up the beams dividing the rooms.

A buxom blonde in a low-cut blouse and jeans that fit like a second skin approached and slapped Mitch on the thigh, tipping forward enough, I thought, to give him a peek at her navel. “Glad ya made it,” she cried above the din. Mitch introduced me to Kelly Caffrey, the bar owner, and after a cursory nod to me, she hailed the bartender and with her hand still on Mitch’s thigh, shouted that his tab “was on the house.”

Mitch thanked her, looking a little embarrassed by the attention when others at the bar turned to notice.

“We got this man to thank for the expansion,” she announced, in a gravelly voice. “Done it in record time with his partner.” She leaned in again to ask Mitch if Chuck was coming to the Grand Opening.

His shrug turned into a cringe when she swore. “Goddamnit, the old man could sure use a lift these days. He told me about his sons leaving when I asked him if you was his son.”

Mitch drew on his beer bottle and raised an eyebrow, shaking his head.

“Well, his truck said Beaverwood and Sons,” she explained. “I jest figgered.” She turned to scrutinize me, finally removing her hand to pull on her ear. “This your woman?”

I could see color creeping around the collar of his green shirt. He nodded and then pulled on his beer again without looking directly at either of us.

“Well, celebrate the night,” she said, slapping his leg again, “and don’t be a stranger here. I’m sure yore gonna get more work in this broke-down town. And if ya ever need a reference…”

I sighed and took a long draw from my beer when she moved on, greeting two preppy-looking men at the end of the bar wearing brown and gold Wyoming University sweatshirts. Mitch finished his beer and ordered a Guinness for himself after checking to see if I wanted anything. I deferred. The only two bars I had ever been in were surrounded by a restaurant or hotel, to celebrate a birthday dinner or holiday with Jake. I had never been in an actual neighborhood bar that catered mostly to locals. It seemed more like a club where the bartender knew everyone by name. From the look of things, Blonde Kelly was the friendly hands-on hostess of this club, ginning up business by sashaying some of her assets.

When the Guinness was served, Mitch collected our jackets and ushered me to an empty pub table for two near the band. The music was great but the noise level prohibited normal speech. Almost in sync, we both leaned back against the wall, nursing our beers while watching the band and dancers. It occurred to me that, aside from TV, he had never seen people dance in the flesh, generally unconnected to a partner, shuffling feet, swinging shoulders and vibrating to the guitar twangs and drum beats of a rock band. When a slow song was played, more couples rose to dance, eliminating space between them as they rocked tight in each other's arms. If he had ever been to any of the dances at Old Fort Laramie in his time, he might have remembered the compromise between the two styles he was witnessing now.

He leaned toward me and shielded his hand over his mouth. "Do you know how to dance like that?"

I slipped off my stool and slapped him on the thigh. "Let me show you, Cowboy." Grinning, he shook his head, but relented when I insisted. He was stiff and awkward, watching couples swaying around us in their own space. I told him to put his hands on my waist while I hooked my hands over his shoulders. “Just rock back and forth ’til you feel enough rhythm to move your feet in a slow circle.”

We moved in inches until I could feel his grip on me relax. He was shorter than I remembered—not quite a head taller than me when my temple brushed against his chin. “How am I doing?” he whispered.

I glanced up at him, moving a hand to the back of his neck. “Great. Just drop that steel rod out of your backside.”

“What did you say?”

I giggled. “Stop looking at our feet. You’re doing just fine.”

“I’m looking at the floor,” he said. “These were planks from a box we snapped together after we leveled the old floor. It turned out pretty solid, don’t you think?”

I stopped moving to bounce a little on my toes. “Amazing.”

Out of the corner of my eye, I noticed one of the men from the bar approach, in his WU sweatshirt. He tapped on Mitch’s shoulder. “May I cut in?” he said.

Mitch turned slowly, giving him a venomous look.

“It’s okay.” I patted his arm. “You can watch us dance.”

The man swept me away, leaving Mitch in the middle of the floor, still glaring darkly.

“Wha’s your name, darlin’,” he slurred, spraying me with a strong whiff of whiskey. “I haven’t seen you here before.”

I turned aside, pulling in a deep breath of air. “Jessica.”

“You with that cowboy?”

I nodded, straining my neck to track the cowboy marching to the bar for another beer.

He squeezed my fingers in a tight grip. "I didn't notice any rings."

I saw the band's strobe light reflected in his dark eyes, and noticed how stained his teeth were when he grinned.

"Cleaned. It's being cleaned," I lied.

"So, you don't mind steppin' out with someone new, then?"

"Actually, I do, but I was hoping you would help me demonstrate slow dance moves to my cowboy."

"Yeah, I noticed he was no great shakes on the floor."

Whiskey Breath shifted into high gear, twirling me around with a few fancy moves before he clinched me against him with a grunt. His hands slid down my back and cupped a butt cheek when the dance ended and he attempted a final dip that had us both crashing to the floor leaving me pinned beneath him in a whoosh of air. *My air.* I was sandwiched between a new wood floor and a hard belly hidden behind a collegiate sweatshirt. Suddenly, he flew off me backwards, and when I braced myself on my elbows, I could see that Mitch had two hands buried in the back of his shirt, flinging him across the floor to careen into another couple who bumped into yet another couple like dominos. Women were screaming, men cussing and somebody yelled "fight," as I scuttled like a crab out of the way of falling bodies.

My dance partner scrambled to his feet and took a wild swing at Mitch, hitting him in the stomach, while his buddy from the bar lunged at him from behind, holding him around the neck. Three other men came to Mitch's rescue and a flurry of fists were connecting with jaws and guts as punches were thrown indiscriminately and others emboldened by drink eagerly joined in the fray.

The band's guitarists started playing the old ACDC song, "Thunderstruck", stamping their feet to drum beats, while sidelined spectators cheered and stomped along to the music. Kelly, the bar owner tried to pull a couple of fighters apart, screaming shrilly above the noise, until the bartender pulled her out of the melee and dragged her behind the bar. The strobe light crashed to the floor, stroking the ceiling with flashes of colored lightning.

I stood on a chair, watching Mitch give and take throughout the skirmish. The two men in the WU sweatshirts were still throwing punches, wobbling now on their feet. Whiskey Breath already had an open gash above his eye and blood splatters decorating the front of his sweatshirt.

I fished in my pocket for my cell phone to dial the Guernsey Police, but someone must have beat me to it, yelling, "Cops on the way!" Shifting around tables to make my way toward the door, a chair skittering across the room tripped me and I fell with my cell phone in hand, gouging my cheekbone. A large hand gripped my arm, pulling me upright and when I saw it was Mitch, I blurted, "The cops are coming." He grabbed my hand and pulled me through a doorway past the restrooms and out Dooley's back door. We could hear police sirens clearly now and see red lights bouncing off signs and billboards around the parking lot. Doubling back the alleyway to Whistler's, we made our way to my parked car.

I insisted on driving and he was in no shape to argue. Both hands and one eye were swollen and his shirt was torn and bloodied. He lost his hat, and his hair was matted with sweat. I took the back way out of town, driving slow with no headlights through snow-covered side streets to get to the bridge that crossed the North Platte on Hwy 26. Moonlight guided me until we were far enough away to flick on my lights and push the speed limit the rest of the way home. Aside from insisting he buckle his seatbelt, I couldn't trust myself to speak. But for the sound of heavy breathing, it was a twenty-minute drive of deadly silence, until I pulled into the garage and the hens began to cackle. Mitch was motionless, his head lolling against his right shoulder and the door. Thinking he had passed out, I left him in the car and slammed the door with a vengeance.

Chapter Forty-Two
Like Riding a Bicycle

I locked myself in the bathroom, tore off my clothes and took a long hot shower to scrub off the smell of beer and sweat, along with a veneer of anger that made my skin crawl. How could a "date" that started out so perfect end like this? I hadn't been in a bar since college days. Bar brawls were something seen in movies with macho actors dramatically bursting with testosterone. This one began with Mitch and probably ended with a full house at the Guernsey jail. What had possessed the peaceful man I once knew? He was throwing punches like an amateur boxer, even appearing to enjoy it…until the police were called.

One look in the mirror and I could see the cellphone blow to my cheekbone was creating a bruise that was close to my eye. Still shaking, I dried off and slipped into a warm flannel nightie and rubbed my wet hair in a towel. The house was dark and cold when I went to the kitchen to make an ice pack for my eye, stopping first to throw a few logs onto the grate in the fireplace and kindle a decent blaze with old newspapers.

"I'm sorry about the *troid.*"

The thick voice startled me. In the flickering light, I searched the room and found him sitting at the counter holding a wet dishtowel over the left side of his face.

He must have revived in the car and tried to clean up at the kitchen sink. He wore only his jeans, dusty with sawdust and dappled with stains. His slick hair was ruffled like duck feathers, his feet were bare and Gran's afghan was draped over his slumping shoulders.

I approached him slowly, taking a deep breath, guarding myself against feeling any pity. "The *troid*?"

"Fight. Sorry about the fight."

"What were you thinking?"

"That man was mauling you."

"He was a harmless drunk dancing with me."

"He had no right."

"He cut in. Surely, you've been to dances—even in your time—where men cut in to dance with a new partner?"

Avoiding my eyes, he looked down at his clawed hands in silence. I followed his gaze and saw that his knuckles were raw. He peered up at me, his voice a little sharper. "Do men in your time generally end the dance belly to belly on their partner?"

"*Dipping*. It's called dipping. He was trying to show some fancy moves…and…and I slipped out of his hands."

"His hands were all over your back. Men in my time had more respect for women in public, they knew where to put their hands."

I snorted. "Yes, men in your time also frequented brothels all over Wyoming. Remember the three-mile ranch? Three miles from Fort Laramie. I don't think any of the customers there worried much about where to put their hands."

Even in the low light, I could see his face color as he stood up. "You are not a soiled dove."

I stepped closer. "And I'm not your property, either."

"We could change that."

I tossed him a hollow laugh. "Slavery ended long ago."

"Aye, but commitment didn't." He slapped the damp towel on the counter and stood up.

I searched his face for a long moment. It was a proud face. Handsome, even battered with one green eye swollen to a slit, the corner of his mouth opened with a cut, and thanks to me, one ear lobe shorter than the other. In spite of my anger, I picked up the wet towel to dab the corner of his mouth and ended up in his arms.

He winced a little when we kissed, tentatively at first, but when I feebly struggled, his arms tightened around me. His kiss deepened, pulling on my lips, exploring my mouth with his tongue, until my arms slowly snaked around his neck and my head tipped backward. I could taste beer and a coppery hint of blood in his mouth, and when we broke apart, I gasped at the sight of blood coalescing on his lower lip. With my forefinger, I dabbed his lip. "Your mouth is bleeding again."

He waved it off with a shake of his head and kissed my bloodied finger. "I'm in love with you," he responded, in a voice deep and thick, slurred by drink and maybe something else.

My breath hitched and my heart drummed in my ears. "What about…?"

He stopped me with another long kiss that must have been even more painful. Pressed against him, I could feel the throb of our hearts beating nearly in sync.

I was dizzy and breathless when he paused to catch his breath and gaze at me, his swollen green eyes filled with such longing, an unbidden tear rolled down my cheek, slow as a drip of honey. Wordless now, we moved as if in a trance, sleepwalkers drifting out of the firelight and into the dark cocoon of my bedroom, lit only by the red numbers on my digital alarm.

Choreographed by our heavy breathing, I slipped out of my robe and nightie and could hear the sound of his zipper and the ring of his belt buckle as his jeans dropped to the floor. We fell on the bed and groped for each other like drowning victims lost at sea, clinging inside a drifting lifeboat. In storm-tossed waves of emotion, we rolled on the bed, our legs tangling in sheets that bunched between us. I heard the soft thump of a pillow hitting the floor and another hitting my clock, setting off a slow beep and a steady blink against the white pillowcase. He paused with an impatient curse while I reached across him to shut off the alarm.

When I rolled back into his arms, he framed his hands around my face and kissed me tenderly, slowing the pace as his mouth traveled a route from temple, ears, eyes, nose, neck and when our mouths latched again, enclosing the yeasty scent of beer. I was doubly intoxicated. Like his mouth, his hands were warm and caressing exploring my body more slowly this time, and when he found my breasts and belly, I jerked with a shock of electricity that spiraled through my core down to my clenched toes and ricocheted up my throat in a deep moan.

Quid pro quo. I returned the caress, skimming his chest and lengthened my reach, until I coaxed his groan, deep and visceral. It had been over three years since we laid together that last night in *his time…his cabin…his bed*. I was the one, then, who said, "I love you," adding I would never love another man. And just as he couldn't respond in kind then, something stopped me now from repeating those three words again. Maybe then—as now—it was the specter of Jessamine. Or maybe it was all those unanswered questions swallowed by long delayed lust and inhibitions loosened by drink. I remembered how we agreed then: "No guilt, no shame" before we fell into that final intimacy, both of us knowing our parting was hours away.

I opened myself to him now as I did then, trusting now that we might have a future together. Trusting that he had willingly come back to me, not knowing what I knew—that history couldn't be changed. My existence proved that. He had disappeared in his time. Jessamine had remarried—to a man that became my great grandfather, which made Jake and I cousins through Jessamine. And when my great grandfather died, Jessamine married yet another man she outlived. Mitch couldn't know the history of his first love, but if his prior memories didn't come back, I knew I would have to give him the family journals to read, so he would know the secret of the teacup and the stories behind all the other treasured family keepsakes.

We quickly fell into a rhythm of love that transcended time. Like riding a bicycle—once learned, the act was something one never forgot—even after years of abstinence. Arched against him as one, I could feel a mutual urgency, like we were finally fighting the same fight, both of us straining toward a thunderous applause of the heart. A new explosion of warmth coursed through me like a transfusion, and we both shuddered and purred in little aftershocks. For a long time we lay hip to hip, sated in the sheltering silence of the house, meting out our breaths as we held hands to keep our attachment. Until I heard the metric whisper of his sleeping breath, I was finally able to give in to my own euphoric dreams. *He was here, in my time, my home, my bed, and...he loved me.*

****

He was in the shower when I woke and stretched in my bed, smiling at the memory of the night, in spite of a dull headache. I could hear him sing an unfamiliar ditty as I dressed and started a full pot of coffee. A strong dose of caffeine would clear heads for all that needed to be discussed. Even so, it would take more than one morning to answer questions and decide a future after one unforgettable night.

We also needed ice compresses and a good explanation contrived for Jake when he delivered our son later today. Surely, he would notice the black eyes we both sported, and wonder why we bubbled with joy.

Chapter Forty-Three
The Right Man?

We were married two weeks later by a Justice of the Peace in Torrington. Chuck was our best old man, Scout was our best young man, and Jake was the grudging man who handed me off to Mitch after a quick kiss on my forehead and a whispered, “You sure?”

I hugged him, crushing the boutonniere pinned to his lapel. “Trust me,” I whispered back, smiling when we parted. A few white petals fluttered to the floor between us.

When Jake brought Scout and Sadie home the day after the Dooley fight, and saw my eye, his fist flew to his mouth and I had to talk fast to keep him from attacking Mitch when his assumptions went wild. When he saw the greater damage to Mitch’s face, and heard my hasty explanation, he was almost gleeful.

Confused by the drama, and our black eyes, Scout ran to his room. When everyone calmed down, he emerged with his *Randy the Raccoon* book. Even Jake chuckled before reluctantly conceding Dooley’s had a reputation for Saturday night fights.

“Perhaps small town locals need a venue to throw off their testosterone,” I mused.

“Isn’t that kinda like women who go out for coffee…or protein shakes at a spa?”

“Jake, women don’t throw fists and chairs

afterwards. We gather to gab and exercise."

"Same thing." He smirked quickly before pulling me into a protective hug.

In two weeks, my bruising had become a faint yellow line, invisible under makeup, but Mitch was still sporting violet arcs he refused to conceal with anything but sunglasses or a small pirate patch Scout offered from his last Halloween costume. The patch humored Scout and brought on a lot of "Aye-mateys," and pretend sword fights with wooden spoons. The sunglasses humored me, giving him a mysterious secret-service aura that I thought was sexy. He preened a little over the flattery after I explained secret service men protected powerful leaders like the president.

"Fitting," he said, bussing me from behind while I flipped eggs one morning. "I'm protecting you."

I twisted in his arms, still holding the spatula and gave him a look. "From what?"

"From anyone who wants to steal your heart." He winked with his good eye. "It's mine, now.

I laughed, grateful for the return of the quip master I remembered. There was a new easiness between us since we were intimate, and the morning-after discussion cleared up a few of my biggest concerns. He was here to stay…in my century…happy with his new family. And because he still didn't remember Jessamine or Tallie, we were off the hook with comparisons, which made me happy, because I knew I still couldn't live up to my talented ancestor. If he never remembered his life with her, he might never regret a future with Scout and me.

****

For our hasty wedding, I wore the only dress I ever

owned that needed dry cleaning, a navy wool jersey with a draped neckline and a narrow silver belt. We had shopped for dress slacks, a blazer worn over a white shirt, and navy and green striped tie for Mitch. I carried three red roses in a bed of baby's breath, and all of my men sported white boutonnieres. I could tell Mitch was nervous, solemnly concentrating as we repeated our vows. His hands shook as he held both of mine, never taking his eyes from my face, even when Scout loudly announced he had to go potty. I heard Jake whisper something to him and after a brief pause, the priest hurried through the liturgy with a smile in his voice.

We had previously decided to exchange plain wedding bands for economy, but I was surprised when my white gold band turned out to be two carved hands holding a heart topped by a small crown. Trinity knots completed the circle. When Mitch caught my surprised look, he squeezed my hand and I responded with a grateful smile.

After the short ceremony, and a visit to the restrooms, Chuck insisted on treating us all to dinner at Deacons Restaurant. I thought he might have felt guilty about the fight at Dooley's that resulted in our black eyes. In his mind, we wouldn't have been there if Chuck hadn't hired Mitch for the remodel. Of course, we had given him the same laundered version we gave to Jake, blaming the fight on two inebriated college students. With only a few days off, Mitch had helped Chuck with two more minor jobs in Torrington that required building outdoor decorations for Christmas.

Both of us were astonished when Jake gifted us with a wedding night in The Torrington Inn and agreed to take Scout for the night. Since Jake lived just a few blocks away, I wondered if his gift was meant to keep me close by, in case I changed my mind about Mitch. But he seemed to be genuine when he congratulated us both, giving Mitch a firm handshake and even the hint of a grin when he added, “I hope you deserve her.”

Mitch graciously thanked him, returning a grin that didn’t match the thoughtful look in his green eyes. “My hope, as well,” he said softly.

The most expensive hotel in Torrington featured amenities found in large city hotels. Mitch especially wanted to see what an indoor pool was like. He stooped to touch the water , commenting on how blue and clear it was, and asked what the board at the end was for. Before I could explain, a nubile girl in a bikini bounced on the edge of the diving board, then dove in headfirst, bobbing up sleek as a seal, at the far end of the pool. He watched her, mesmerized as she emerged and began to towel off. Muttering something about swimming in underwear, he turned away abruptly, pulling me with him toward the exit.

I tried in vain to control my giggles when he braced himself in the corner of the elevator, watching the lighted numbers as we rose to the top floor. We were the only ones in the elevator. “You’ll see a lot of bikinis at a summer beach or pool—maybe even topless sunbathers in this century,” I told him.

He rolled his eyes. “Nothing, then, is left to the imagination. Do all females dress like so for water sport?”

“I suppose if they are confident about their body, they might. Some men wear swimsuits just as tight and brief—leaving little to the imagination there, as well.”

He gave me a stern look. “Well, that’s different.

Lewy and I always swam naked, but the water was never that clear or warm."

"Lewy who?"

Fixed again on the elevator lights, he muttered, "A childhood friend."

I wondered if memories of childhood foreshadowed memories to come?

When we found our room number at the end of a hall, he fumbled with the plastic card he was given to open the door. I flicked on the inside light to an explosion of red and green. The king-size bed had a red brocade spread that matched the drapes covering sliding doors that led to a small balcony. The carpet was dark green with a gold and red Turkish design. Two gold striped club chairs and a burgundy leather settee formed a sitting alcove in front of a low wooden table holding an ice bucket with champagne and a basket with glasses, fruit, cheese wedges and fancy chocolates nestled in a bed of evergreen.

We gaped, thunderstruck, taking it all in, before we both simmered in laughter.

"Well, Merry Christmas," I squeaked, feeling a rash of hiccoughs coming on.

The bathroom featured a glass-walled shower, a large round tub, a marble double sink displaying an array of soaps and lotions, two matching white terry robes and plush towels on a heated rack. I gulped down a glass of water to quell the hiccoughs.

Mitch gaped at it all. "Is this what all hotel rooms look like?"

I shook my head. "This suite must be Jake's idea of a joke. I've never seen a room like this, except in movies."

"The card in the basket says Congratulations Mr. & Mrs. Mitchell."

"That must be compliments of the hotel. This is probably a bridal suite or a room reserved for dignitaries."

"Dignitaries in Wyoming?" He loosened the knot in his tie and unbuttoned the top of his dress shirt before popping open the bottle of champagne. The cork flew across the room like a bullet, bouncing off the headboard of the bed. A fizzle of foam erupted from the bottle, and we each grabbed a glass to scoop up the overflow.

I sipped thoughtfully, mopping up excess spill with a linen napkin. "Who could afford this kind of luxury?"

"Maybe that's Jake's intended message; never could I afford to give you this."

"Jake isn't that devious. And even if he was, this isn't me, Mitch. I've never had luxury and never been impressed by it. It only took me four months living in your era to understand the value of a simple life…and the importance of family."

He blinked, looking over my head. "Refresh me then, why did you leave?"

I blushed a little, explaining that I was told by a gypsy that Scout would not survive a difficult birth. "She was right. He came early and wouldn't have survived without preemie care that wasn't available in your era." I couldn't tell him there were other considerations that may have led to the same choice.

He made a noise of assent, watching me intently. "Aye, early babes never fared well in my day." We sipped the champagne while examining the contents of the basket for a few minutes when he turned to me shyly. "So, do you want another?"

"I think I learned my lesson from Thanksgiving…and Dooley's. I'm probably a one-drink gal."

He edged a little closer and smiling, slipped an arm across my shoulder. "I meant do you want another babe?"

"I haven't thought about it, but…I suppose a brother or sister for Scout would be nice. That decision may not be ours to make, however. I, I did have a complicated pregnancy."

His green eyes sparkled a little as he studied my face, taking in my answer before he squeezed my shoulder. "With God's blessing, then, we can try to make it happen…with no complications."

I kicked off my shoes and splayed the fingers of my left hand, admiring my new ring. "Well, we are legally wed now, with a future promised to each other." I looked sideways at him and could see his eyes shining with new emotion. "A future together…"

He tore off his loose tie and hooked it around my neck, seesawing the ends to pull me close. "A future tied up in the same era," he whispered before his mouth covered mine in a tender kiss. "I think I'm going to love being married to you," he murmured against my temple.

My heart skipped a beat whenever he warmed me with his heat-seeking eyes, green and clear as a crystal ball with every declaration of love. "I certainly hope so, Mr. Mitchell. The way you trembled through the service, I began to worry you were getting cold feet."

He slipped out of his new loafers and propped his feet on the low table, wiggling toes clad in striped wool socks. "Not in these newbies."

I laughed. "It's an old saying, Mitch. Getting cold feet about marriage means you want to give up the idea altogether."

"Give it up?" He gaped at me.

"Many couples decide it isn't a commitment they can keep. Some even split on their wedding day. Some take years before they give it up. A divorce today is easier to get than a driver's license."

"I would never give you up, Jess. I jumped through a century to find my place…with you."

My thoughts jumped to Jessamine, his first love. I decided this was not the time to point out his 1886 conflict when he asked if a man could love two women. *Jessamine was not going to ruin my wedding night.*

He cradled my hand palm-to-palm with his larger hand and we both gazed at my ring with a mutual sigh. I had never seen a wedding ring like it, and I asked him about it.

"Love, friendship, and loyalty. I like to think the two hands holding the heart mean every great love begins with friendship, and the crown above the heart represents our trust and fidelity." He brought my hand to his mouth and kissed my knuckles. "I know this pales against traditional diamond rings, but someday, when I've put away savings, I promise you'll have that diamond."

"Oh Mitch, I would never want to replace this." His eyes widened with a look of innocence that belied his years. Clean-shaven, and dressed in his new clothes, he looked far younger than the man I remembered, and I vaguely wondered if moving forward in time somehow affected the aging process.

"You like it, then?"

"It's perfect. I'll never take it off."

Smiling like a schoolboy, he bent to kiss the ring, then turned my hand to kiss the bowl of my palm. I reached up to buss his cheek and he moved his head to find my mouth in a kiss that was sweet and steady with a lingering taste of champagne. It wasn't long before leisure kisses became more urgent. We hadn't slept together since the night of the Dooley fight because of one thing or another. Mostly—because Scout was cutting teeth that had him waking with nightmares and a slight fever. He insisted on sleeping with me, and Sadie came with the package, hopping onto my bed, as well.

After nibbling on a few chocolate covered strawberries, washed down with the rest of my champagne, I excused myself to change into my new white nightie. In the bathroom, I brushed my hair, cleaned my mouth, and dabbed hotel cologne on all my pulse points. The bedroom was dark, with only the drapes pulled to let in some starlight. I could see the shadowy figure of Mitch almost lost in the King-size bed, propped up against several pillows, his hands behind his head. The red spread was folded neatly, hemming the foot of the bed. I twirled around the perimeter in graceful ballet moves, until I could tell he approved of the gown. It was modest by most standards, revealing nothing but my shape, until I demonstrated the slit up the side. He reached out to grab me, and we bounced on the bed like two children testing out a new mattress

"I could use some company in this garden," he said, holding me down.

"A garden, is it?"

He gathered something from beneath his pillow and drifted handfuls of rose petals over me.

I laughed. "That wouldn't be my rose bouquet from the ceremony, would it?"

"In the garden of the heart, plant naught but the rose of love."

I lifted my hand to stroke his cheek. "That's beautiful. Did you make that up?"

He grinned, taking my hand from his cheek. "Your internet has quotes for every occasion." When he kissed my wrist, he chuckled. "There's wildflowers mixed in the rose garden. A lot of wildflowers," he added, when his mouth found the perfumed notch in my throat.

I giggled nervously. "Cheap cologne is bait for a poor man."

"So, you've been looking up quotes, as well?"

"That's one I remembered when I studied scents. I did order this nightie online, though. Do you like it?"

His fingers drifted down my leg over the silky material. "Mmm. Frost in the garden. Why isn't it sewn on both sides, though?"

"The slit is meant to be sexy."

He laughed, slipping his fingers under the slit, opening the gown like an envelope flap to expose my legs. "Aha! The most beautiful rose in the garden has long, lovely stems."

I shuddered when he caressed my leg, feeling the electricity charge through me. His hands were warm and comforting, smelling of rose petals as they glided over bare skin and silky gown, tracing my curves in a tactile massage that made me purr like a kitten. He bent again to kiss my throat and shoulders and cup his hands over the bodice while he kissed my ear, tickling it with his tongue. The hotel sheets were cool and silky against my back as I wiggled out of the gown as gracefully as possible under his watchful amusement.

We were both naked now and I could feel goosebumps rising on my limbs. Maybe from nerves, maybe from a drafty window. It was a cold moonless night, but the stars were out, twinkling like diamonds in blue velvet, and the soft beam from a tall pole light in the parking lot hit the window at just the right angle. Enough to turn the white sheets into a gauzy blue florescence. I closed my eyes, imagining I was floating in water. He nuzzled my neck and ran his lips up to capture my earlobe again.

"Is that your version of a wet willie?" I whispered.

"What?" He grunted close to my ear. "You want to talk about beef sandwiches…now?"

I opened my eyes and pulled his head down to kiss his ear, then grazed the opening with my tongue. "Well I do like this version better. Usually, it's a wet finger in the ear."

He jerked away when I demonstrated. "That tickles."

Giggling, I brushed my fingers over his furry chest, pinching one of his nipples into a nub. "Where else are you ticklish?"

He clamped his hands over mine, chuckling softly before his mouth found mine in a distracting kiss that took my breath away.

When I felt something poke me in the small of my back, I jerked up crying out. He fumbled behind me and retrieved the champagne cork that had flown across the room when he opened the bottle. The bed vibrated when we laughed, imagining a few silly uses for a cork in a bed. I waved the cork, under my nose and could still smell the full-bodied sweet aroma, blended now with the scent of rose petals from our garden.

Making scented soaps and lotions had given me a sommelier's nose. I could pick out bouquets that lingered…and sold well. *Did sex have a scent, an aphrodisiac that could be bottled?* I waved the cork over us, then tucked it beneath my pillow, thinking it deserved a place in the memory chest Gran had left me. Two months ago, the memory of my wedding night was bottled only in my hope chest of dreams.

We stopped the playful prolonging, as if the cork gave us permission to surrender to raw emotion. Bent over me, there was a hitch in his voice when he whispered, "I love you," repeating the words in an unfamiliar language, probably from an internet tutorial.

I knew that kissing, caressing, exploring the boundaries of love was considered foreplay to the final thrusts of passion and when it came for us, I was transported to another world, not his or mine or the playground of a king-sized bed. Sweaty and shuddering in the aftermath, I closed my eyes and lay quietly beside my groom, floating in a sun-warmed pool edged by flowers and serenaded by songbirds while cottony clouds danced in blue skies above.

In the dark, Mitch groped for my hand and swung a long leg possessively over mine. His voice was muzzy with exhaustion when he mumbled, "I Love you, Liv," before he nodded off.

Chapter Forty-Four
Do Scars Ever Fade?

I woke early, and waited until the gray light of dawn morphed into an icy blue before I pushed aside the comfort of a fleece blanket, and rose to pick my nightgown off the floor and close the drapes. There was a small balcony just outside the sliding glass door and from my vantage on the top floor of the hotel; I could see that a thin blanket of frost had settled over the parked cars below. A midnight cover of snow also whitewashed the streets in the distance, snaking through town clean of all Sunday morning tracks at the hilt of dawn. I was tempted to dress and step outside to breathe in the fresh clean air, as I would have at home, but I needed to shower and I didn't want to wake Mitch, still asleep, sprawled over more than half of the big bed.

I plugged in the little coffee maker resting on a low chest of drawers and tiptoed into the bathroom to relieve myself and shower. As the hot water cascaded over my head and shoulders and I soaped my body, I permitted a measure of euphoria to wash over me. The night was everything I dreamed of—romantic and sensual—until Mitch uttered his last word. Did he mean to say Luv, instead of Liv? It was an emotional day. He was nervous in the ceremony, quiet in the restaurant, still wary of Jake, but attentive and loving when we were alone and even playful in bed. Was it true that sex drained men, mentally as well as physically—often sending them into a drug-like sleep afterward? He slept soundly the morning I left him in 1886, not even waking when I tearfully kissed him goodbye, thinking I would never see him again.

I was beginning to shampoo my hair when I sensed I wasn't alone in the shower. He put a hand over my mouth when I screamed, then laughed when I slapped him with my wet washcloth.

"Who did you expect, my luv?"

With the steam rising all around us, I backed into the tile wall. *My luv?* He said *'my luv.'*

"Can I wash your hair?"

I handed him the little tube of hotel shampoo. He was gentle and diligent, lathering my scalp while commenting how dark my red hair became when wet. The suds slithered over my shoulders and dribbled down my torso, and when he noticed, he caught them with his hands and began to soap the rest of me, massaging curves and sliding his hands down the small of my back, circling my hips until I stopped his hands with a mewling gasp.

"Can…can I wash *your* hair?" "Go for it." He grinned, handing me the tube.

He bent his head when I reached up for his hair, noting how his hair also changed when wet…straighter, darker…more like the hair I remembered. I wondered if he would let it grow long enough to favor his old style, pulled back and tied. I always thought it was his only physical concession to his Indian heritage.

His chin felt like fine sandpaper with new growth. "I like you better with a beard," I said, skimming his neck and jaw up to the missing lobe of his ear. The ear and the scar that trailed from it had healed well.

He was still and quiet, gazing down at me with his green eyes piercing through the foggy steam. He caught my hand and kissed my palm, moving his lips to the pulse pounding in my wrist. “Ummm, I’ll remember that.”

I pulled some of the lather off his head and soaped his chest, darker now with a thin trail of hair that divided his chest, pointing like an arrow to a thicker nest of hair. “Fair’s fair,” I murmured, sliding my soapy fingers around him.

The gentle hiss of the shower gave way to a deeper cacophony of noise as we rattled into the glass door and locked into the motion of a slow tide, managing slippery kisses and caresses that heightened sensation as the water purled over us—sealing us in warm bliss. I slid down the cool tile, boneless as a puddle and gasping for breath when passion was spent, wondering if anyone ever died from making love in a warm shower.

He might have shared the thought as he reached up to turn the shower handles until cold water rained over us and we both gasped again. “Ahhh.” I lifted my face to feel the cool water, thinking this must be how a scorched body sizzles with relief.

When the cold saturated us, we rose together and melted into a hug after I fumbled to turn off the stream. “You all right, my luv?”

Sufficiently cool and a little dizzy, I pushed open the shower door, and grabbed one of the heated towels. “I, I’ve never done that before.” I handed him a towel.

He wiped his face and chest and tucked the towel around his waist as he laughed. “I haven’t either.

Months ago, I never knew the feel of a warm shower, unless I ran through a summer rainstorm. Even then, the water was never that warm."

I tucked the heated towel around me, sarong style. "I didn't exactly mean the shower." I rubbed a window in the steamy mirror, and he came up behind me, kissing my temple. Our eyes met in the mirror.

"I know what you meant," he whispered. "I've never done that either."

I gave him a sultry look as I rubbed my hair with a towel. When he turned on the fan, and opened the door, the steam began to disperse and as the fog drifted, I gaped at him. "What happened to your stomach?"

He looked down at the mottled green and yellow bruise peeking over his draped towel and rubbed his belly. "This?"

"Yes, that." In the darkness of night, and with my eyes closed most of the time, I didn't notice his bruise. This was the first time we had been naked together in any bright light.

"Just a gut punch from the brawl." He patted his stomach. "It used to be black as coal."

My mouth hung open.

He laughed at my surprise. "It doesn't hurt…anymore."

"Why didn't you say something?"

"Nothing to be done for a gut bruise. I've had them before." He picked up a brush and began to brush his hair, looking in the mirror.

I gazed at him in the mirror, noticing something else. I had never seen him without a long shirt covering his arms. "What happened to the scars on your arm?"

"What scars?"

"Bird tracks. The little scars left after I stitched you up that summer…after the accident with the horse In your time," I added.

"*An accident with a horse?*"

"The Appaloosa. We were breeding the Ap when the runaway black stallion charged and you were dragged over the splintered fence. I pulled a large wooden splinter out of your arm and had to stitch you up to close the gap."

I grabbed his arm and rubbed my hand over the inside of it up to his elbow. No scars, not even a trace of a raised scar. A thin layer of fine damp hair glistened in the bright light above the mirror. "You complained when I used pink thread."

"Pink thread? You stitched me up in pink thread?"

"That isn't the point. How do scars disappear?"

"Jessica, I don't remember any of that, but can't some scars fade over time?"

I stared at him. "I never thought so."

He pulled me into his arms and kissed the top of my head. "Maybe scars do fade—like bruises…and memories. A wound in my time may have looked worse than it was, as you remember it. Time heals, and God knows, we've bridged more than a century to be together."

I studied our reflection in the mirror. The scar that ran from his ear had certainly faded in only two months. The black eyes we sported two weeks ago were nearly invisible. Maybe he was right. Maybe scars, like perceptions do fade even more in time travel.

He picked up the hairdryer and changed the subject. "Does this thing work like yours?"

I stared at him in the bright light of the bathroom,

thinking more of the past than the bright future we faced together, and was suddenly overcome by a dark thought. He still didn't remember anything of the past we shared. Would that ever change? *Had I married a stranger?*

Chapter Forty-Five
Chocolate Kisses

Mitch continued to work for Chuck, ticking off small seasonal odd jobs that kept him busy most days. I was also busy, filling soap orders for last minute shoppers at all my customer sites, including the one at Fort Laramie and all the touristy shops and spas a few miles from the historic Park site. Of course, I also had to intersperse some retail therapy in with business. Christmas shopping for Scout was tricky when he was with me, but I managed to sneak in a few small things for him, along with purchases for Mitch and Jake, and even something for Chuck, who was rapidly becoming one of the family since he still hadn't heard from his sons. Given the reliance and trust Chuck showered on Mitch, and the admiration Mitch returned, I could see a surrogacy developing. Mitch needed a father as much as Chuck needed a son.

The day before Christmas, we bundled up after breakfast for a trek in the woods to find a juniper or pine tree. I carried the saw and a coil of rope over my shoulder while Scout hitched a ride on Mitch's shoulders. Sadie bounded along beside us, kicking up snow, her pink tongue hanging out in a wide doggie grin that expressed our collective joy. We were a family, happy to be together, Christmas tree hunting in the crisp clean air of a bright winter day.

A clean blanket of snow had fallen last night, weighing down branches 'til towering evergreens resembled giant umbrellas half closed. Mitch and I shook the smaller trees we thought were possibilities, and snow cascaded over us like images in a snow globe. Scout thought it was great fun, laughing with his tongue catching lacy flakes that salted his face and caught in his eyelashes. Sadie circled us, sometimes rolling in the snow, then rising to shake off layers that clung to her. One of the trees might have held a nest. A bright flash of black and white flew up when we shook it and we recognized the alarming *"dee-dee-dee"* call of a wintering chickadee.

Mitch pointed out animal tracks—mostly from deer. And when we spotted a large doe pawing at the creek to release a bubble of drinking water for two smaller companions, Scout shushed us with a finger to his mouth. "Deer mama," he whispered as we crowded together behind a large tree to watch. I held onto Sadie and when she barked, the stately doe raised her head to look our way, assessed the danger, then darted off with the smaller deer leaping after her, until all three disappeared over a distant ridge.

We finally agreed on a perfect tree—a stunted pine about seven feet tall, and after it was down and trussed with rope harnessed to Mitch, he dragged it behind him, marking a path for Scout and I to follow on foot. "This is where a horse or mule would shine," Mitch panted, after hauling it a half-mile home.

I helped untie the harness. "I'd love a horse…or two, but you will do." I grinned, hugging him around the waist.

He peered down at me. "Who did this last year?"

"We had a small artificial tree on the table. Scout was climbing and getting into everything. We couldn't trust him around anything he could topple."

While Mitch set up the tree stand and righted the tree by a front window, I hauled out a plastic crate of string lights and ornaments. The three of us decorated the tree, accompanied by a six-disc cassette of Christmas music in my CD player. After I wound lights around the tree, Scout hung the lowest branches with simple plastic ornaments I handed him while Mitch was assigned more breakables to the top. I filled in the middle with some of Gran's favorites—a collection of Santas through the years. Every year, Jake and I collaborated on a special Santa for her, dated somewhere on the ornament.

"This is nice," Mitch commented as we stopped for lunch and observed our handiwork when I switched on the lights.

"You didn't decorate a tree for Christmas when you were a child?"

"I don't remember." His brow furrowed as he thought. "*Nollag* was more about festive food and drink…and special reverence to the Creator, I think. Maybe a few gifts were involved."

"Nollag? I didn't know the natives had a name for the holiday whites called Christmas."

He shrugged, taking a bite of his sandwich and chewed thoughtfully.

While Scout napped after lunch, I coerced Mitch to wrap presents I hid in my closet for Scout as well as the leather day-planner for Chuck and the beer-making kit for Jake. I finished making two last batches of Christmas cookies, the little spritz trees flavored with green jello that Scout liked and a new recipe using some of the eggs our hens were laying. More than I had anticipated since Chuck added two more hens to the roost.

We planned to attend Christmas Eve services in Wheatland, then open our personal gifts at home. Jake and Chuck were coming for a Christmas Day dinner tomorrow, but tonight was ours.

The spritz were done and the new meringue cookies were cooling on parchment paper when Mitch joined me in the kitchen. I had just melted chocolate bits to dip the little oval ends into before sprinkling them with chopped nuts. He watched me for a minute, then popped one of the cooled cookies into his mouth. "Mmm, what are these called?"

"Chocolate Dipped Kisses," I muttered, stirring the chocolate to prevent it from seizing up as it melted. "And they aren't decorated yet, so don't eat any more."

He laughed at me and popped another into his mouth. "I don't think anyone will miss two or three of these. Looks like you have enough for tomorrow."

"If you want to help, you can sprinkle the ends with nuts after I dip them."

"Aye, aye, captain." He saluted me with a crooked grin, and working together, we finished the job in minutes. I wiped my forehead with the back of my hand and thanked him for the help.

"Wait a minute, we missed a few," he said.

I scanned the rows of cookies. "No we didn't."

He turned me around, kissed each corner of my mouth, and licked his lips. "Chocolate kisses…can't get enough of your chocolate kisses, Jess."

I gave him a look, then licked the chocolate off my

fingers and scraped the bowl with the last of the chocolate and waved the rubber spatula at him. “You can lick the bowl if you like.”

He grabbed the spatula and deliberately smeared his lips with it. “Your turn.”

My laugh was smothered when he pulled me into his arms and slid his chocolate lips over mine. Giggles turned into something else as we sucked and licked the chocolate off our lips.

“Are you done here?” He breathed against my ear.

“Quite undone.” I whispered, gazing into his twinkling eyes.

“Wanna take a shower to clean up then?” He swiped a finger over my forehead, collecting a dollop of chocolate.

“We’ll wake up Scout.”

“Only if you squeal.” He grinned, showing chocolate-rimmed teeth. “I could gag you with a washcloth, but then I do love to make you squeal.”

“Have we created a monster here?”

He gave me a wide-eyed look of innocence. “You mean like a cookie monster—a bright blue cookie monster?”

I laughed again. “Not exactly.”

“Cookie Monster!” Scout growled, running to hug us both around the knees as we gaped at him in surprise.

Mitch picked him up. “Your timing is always pitch perfect laddie.”

Scout beamed at us both with a toothy smile, running a fat fist through sleep-mussed hair. “Purrfeck laddie!”

I gave him one of the cookies, rolling my eyes at

Mitch. "Have one of mama's chocolate kisses, Scout." I grinned at them both as I licked my lips. Chocolate was the great equalizer with the men I loved.

"I'll have one of mama's chocolate kisses later tonight." He smirked.

Chapter Forty-Six
A Memory like This

Weighing their reactions, the Christmas Eve candlelight service was impressive for both Scout and Mitch. Scout sat on Mitch's lap, and two pairs of green eyes had a deer-in-the-headlights glaze, absorbing the ceremony and the decorations, which included a very large tree lit with starlights and decorated with symbols of the trinity, including an alabaster baby Jesus. A small crèche was set up below the pulpit with cardboard figures of Joseph and Mary, angels and shepherds, and various farm animals surrounding a wooden manger containing a life-like naked doll laying in a bed of real straw. Scout seemed particularly worried about the baby, pointing and finally whispering loud enough for several pews of worshippers to hear, "Where are dat baby's pull-ups, mama?"

Two pairs of green eyes focused on me for the answer while I struggled to keep from tittering, along with several others in hearing distance. I knew if I looked at Mitch, I would lose all dignity, so I leaned over to shush him holding a finger to his mouth, then whispered that the baby probably just had a bath.

Scout wasn't going to let it go. "But where his froggy towel?" he said more urgently. Mitch transferred him to my lap, with a blank look that belied the subtle shake of his chest. Again, I pressed a finger to my lips, this time, hoping to seal the wave of giggles bubbling in my throat. A stick of gum in my purse finally distracted Scout, along with a crayon and a scrap of paper. He was occupied with drawing squiggles until the congregation began to sing "Away in a manger, no crib for a bed…" As I sung the words, Scout hung a finger over my lip and asked where the baby's crib was. I transferred him back to Mitch with a cross-eyed look.

We laughed freely on the way home, and notwithstanding the cardboard crèche, thought the service was real and meaningful. "Was it like anything you remember?" I asked Mitch. We hadn't attended any church in our summer together in his time, and I wondered if he even believed in one God, given the native beliefs he must have been brought up with. From what I learned from family journals, "the Indian," as they referred to him, was saved when he was sent to the Catholic orphanage in St. Louis for six years. Mitch had explained to me on our last night together in his time how he was exorcized of Indian ways and given an American education probably equivalent to that of any well-born white lad.

"Parts of it seemed familiar," he said, with a pensive look that matched his tone.

After a quick supper of our favorite macaroni and cheese casserole, Mitch followed our evening bedtime rituals with Scout while I cleaned the kitchen and did a little prep for the day ahead. When Scout was finally sleeping, we brought out the horse scooter and toy train, along with wrapped presents to pile under the tree. I put some Christmas music on the CD player and poured us each a small glass of raspberry liqueur.

"This is…nice," Mitch said, gesturing with his

glass as we warmed our backs against heat from the fireplace and surveyed the tree. "I've never had this."

I clinked my glass against his. "I had a bumper crop of raspberries this summer and found an old time recipe."

He tasted the liqueur and smiled with approval. "I meant all of this—the tree, so many gifts, making Christmas cookies, the candlelight service at church—all because I have a new family."

I thought of Jessamine and Tallie and the life he left. "Maybe it's not exactly as you remember."

He shrugged. "If ever I lived through a day like today—I may not remember it, but I think I would remember how it made me feel." His eyes met mine, glowing like emeralds in the firelight.

"I can't say I ever had a day like this either, spending it with those I love." I sipped my wine, until I was able to continue. "Ten years ago, I would never have predicted marriage, a child, a home in the country, and a job other than teaching. Even a dog would have been too inconvenient for a career woman who wanted no strings attached."

Mitch leaned over and we kissed softly. He smelled of raspberries and soap bubbles.

"I want you to open one of your gifts tonight."

"I thought we were going to do that in the morning."

"Just one seems appropriate to the moment." I set my glass on the mantel, pulled a large box from the coat closet, and ordered him to sit. Like a little boy eager to see what was inside, he sat on the floor and impatiently tore off the crinkly ribbon and threw the lid aside. I watched his face for a reaction as he pulled away the tissue and sank his fingers into the fur.

He looked up at me, expectantly. “What is this?”

“Your bearskin poncho. I had it cleaned and made into a rug to lay in front of the fire—like the one you had in your old cabin.”

He sniffed the fur before spreading it over the floor. It wasn’t as large as his old bearskin rug, and it was missing the head and paws. He grinned. “It smells a lot better, and it looks like it belongs to the room. What a great idea!”

“You gave me the idea. After Thanksgiving, you said it might make a good fireside rug.”

He pulled me down beside him and we both took off our shoes and socks, and sitting cross-legged, we ran fingers and toes through the soft fur. When I asked him if he shot the bear, his brow furled, deepening the little crease at the bridge of his nose. “I think so. I remember a dead bear…in a cave.”

I clutched his arm. “You’re starting to remember, things!”

He gave me a strange look, then gazed into the fire. “Maybe we need to focus on new memories.”

I sank back into the fur, closed my eyes, and rested my head on my clasped hands as I stretched the length of the rug, wiggling my toes. Maybe he was right. Could everything we already cherished about our first Christmas Eve together as man and wife, could it all unravel by memory restored? On this magical night, on a bearskin rug before a blazing fire, I cast aside my troubling thoughts and doubts as I felt his lips cover mine and linger in a warm kiss. In the arms of a man who loved me and Scout, this was the finish of a perfect day.

Chapter Forty-Seven
The Photograph

Scout was up early, snuggling between us while Sadie padded from one side of the bed to the other, nudging me, then Mitch with her cold black nose. A crowded bed in the morning was becoming *de rigueur* since Mitch moved into my room. Protesting the move, Scout had listened quietly to our simple explanation with a lip curled: "Dapa needs a bigger bed. His legs are too long for the one in your room."

Glancing from Mitch's legs to his own, Scout only deepened his pout.

Mitch was touched until he had to fight for leg room when Sadie joined the three of us and he had to literally put a foot down. "What if I roll over to tickle your ear and find myself giving Sadie a wet willie some morning?"

We both laughed at the theoretical image.

"It's temporary. Unless there were thunderstorms or Jake was here, Scout always slept alone before. Besides, he has Sadie now."

"Well, maybe we need to convince the guard dog to reign in her boy. I'm willing to share you," he whispered, "just not in bed."

I was touched. "Ten years from now, he'll insist we both stay out of *his* room," I said, giving him a quick kiss on the mouth.

He gave me a look of mock horror. “Ten years!”

I laughed again then gazed overtly downward. “Maybe it’s true that all boys are a little frisky…in the morning?”

Sticking through wisps of sleep-mussed hair, the tips of his ears turned red before he made an unfamiliar noise, sounding something like a curse.

I shared Scout’s anxious excitement, knowing he was finally old enough to join legions of children all over the country on Christmas morning, children fortunate enough to find something under their trees. He squealed over the little rocking horse and train and gleefully tore apart the wrappings of his more practical gifts. Socks and underwear were thrown aside with the wrapping paper, but he loved the little bear slippers I found at a Western store. Sadie ignored the balled up paper flung her way, absorbed in gnawing the end of a giant rawhide bone she held upright between her paws.

Mitch loved his new shirts and immediately modeled his plaid Pajama bottoms with a matching robe that actually covered his knees. I remembered something left in the closet when I saw him pull a pair of new wool crew socks over his bare feet. The house was always cooler in the morning, and we all dressed accordingly until the fireplace was cleaned and electric heaters engaged.

“Another present? This is too much,” he said, looking embarrassed. He pulled a small, badly-wrapped package nestled between the presents left for Jake and Chuck and handed it to me. I opened mine first while he watched expectantly.

The wooden heart-shaped box was etched with trinity knots surrounding the words “*Go Deo*” on the lid. Inside, a pair of tiny heart-shaped pierced earrings rested in a bed of blue velvet. The inside lid was inscribed with our wedding date and initials.

"Do you like them?" he asked, hovering over me.

"I love them," I said, when I could speak.

"I carved the heart from a chunk of butternut Chuck gave me, and the jeweler made it into a little jewel box with the inscriptions."

"What does *Go Deo* mean?"

"Forever, it means forever in Irish. The night before we wed, the words came to me in a dream. I googled them to be sure of the meaning and thought it was an omen."

I put the earrings on in front of the bathroom mirror. I knew the silver wasn't real, but I wouldn't have cared if the gift came from a box of Cracker Jack. He stood behind me and in the mirror our eyes met, both pairs shining with emotion. I turned in his arms.

"Merry Christmas, luv," he murmured in a deep voice against my temple. "You have my heart, Jess. *Forever*." Unable to speak, I cupped his face with my hands and kissed him tenderly.

The slippers in the last gift I gave him seemed anti-climactic beside the earrings, but he chuckled with appreciation when I told him they were made from remnants of the bear rug. Scout put on his new bear slippers and they modeled them side by side while I took a photo of them with my smartphone, and selfies of the three of us in front of the tree. After I showed Mitch how to use the app, he added several photos of me and Scout alone, even Sadie—still gnawing her new bone.

When I tossed crumpled wrapping paper into the

fireplace, I noticed the envelope in the box that held Mitch's bear slippers. The note from the shoemaker said the old photo inside was found in the lining of the bear poncho. Mitch studied the faded sepia of a man in uniform, then sat down heavily in his favorite armchair, still gazing thoughtfully at it.

I sat on the arm of the chair beside him. "Who is it?"

"My father," he mumbled.

"You had a photo of your father? I thought you never met him?"

"I didn't."

"Where did you get this?"

He didn't answer me for a long time. When I asked again, he pulled in a deep breath. "My mother gave it to me."

I carefully picked the brittle photo out of his limp fingers for a closer look. The man was studio-posed between two flags wearing a buttoned jacket with a high collar. A dark slouch hat with a rakish feather covered his hair, shading his eyes. No way to tell if they were green. There might have been a slight resemblance to Mitch in the set of his chin and the long nose. I turned the picture over and saw that something had once been attached to it, covering the word "DIM." I looked in the envelope and found a thin lock of dark hair held together with a cracked smear of yellowed wax.

"Your mother gave you this?"

He nodded, still staring into the fire.

"She had a photo of your father?"

"She worked for his family."

"Where, when? I thought she died in a massacre

when you were a boy."

He turned to me, stiff and pale, even his green eyes unusually cold. "I don't remember."

I left him alone with his thoughts, watching him anxiously as I fixed breakfast. Had my questions spurred on memories he thought were dead? He told me back in his time that his Sioux mother was killed by soldiers when he was twelve and he was taken to the St. Louis orphanage by a sympathetic General who orchestrated the massacre. He never met his Irish father who died before he left the orphanage six years later with a letter and $100 from him…but he never mentioned a photograph. *Given to him by his mother?*

I understood there had to be anger, maybe even prejudice, bottled up inside him. For that reason, I didn't want to be the bearer of sad memories, as I knew them. I didn't want him to remember happy ones with his first wife, either. I wanted to believe that he came back to me. Traveling through time, somehow, he returned so we could be together and make our own history, our own happy memories.

When Scout climbed onto his lap, wanting him to read a new Christmas book, he seemed to thaw out, and when he smelled bacon and eggs frying, he moved to the breakfast bar and ate with his usual gusto. He remained oddly subdued, however. And though polite and smiling, that never changed, even when Jake and Chuck arrived for dinner.

Chuck had good news. His boys had finally called him. Though they loved the weather in California, they admitted to missing home and were working at a convenience store to save enough money to return sometime in spring. "I didn't offer to pay their way back when they gave me their address," Chuck said, scratching his head. "They were gainfully employed and trying to save. I figured if I made it too easy for them, they might just stay where they were." He looked at all of us for a response. "Isn't that called *tough love?*"

We all agreed with his plan, and I hugged him fiercely, happy to see him so relieved. I thought of what Sheriff Lewis told me about the convenience store robbery here—when he returned my gun. Nobody identified the thief as one of Chuck's sons and I wasn't going to speculate aloud—for the sake of the old man who had become "family" to us.

Chuck clapped Mitch on the back. "When the boys come back, you won't be displaced," he assured him. "You can outwork two men from here to Sunday, and I've got new customers to prove that. You've got a job with Beaverwood as long as you want it."

Mitch smiled, giving him a thumb's up, but he said nothing.

Along with a plastic crate of gifts for Scout and me, Jake also brought good news. He had split with Meredith for good, even before she decided to move to Denver to join a bigger realty firm. And he was already dating someone else. All of us, even Mitch, toasted with the wassail I made. "Do I know the new girl?" I asked.

"Louisa Johnson, Bunny's gift shop gal." He smiled.

"So, why isn't she here today? You know I always make more than we can eat on holidays."

"Well, I didn't want to rush things, and being Christmas and all…she probably has traditions with her family. She invited me to the New Year's Eve Dance at the fort, though."

"You're going to the dance at Fort Laramie?" I glanced over at Mitch. "Maybe we'll join you."

Mitch gave me a weak smile, but said nothing.

We opened Jake's gifts when we noticed Scout had unwrapped half of them already. I rolled my eyes when Scout banged on the little drum set. The gift he handed me was silent when I shook it. "I hope this is earmuffs or plugs."

He tapped his nose and laughed, as I opened the box and found padded earphones. "This will help…one of you," he said, glancing over to Mitch. "They should connect to your smartphone, so you can listen to more refined music of your choice." He also gave me a book titled *You Can Shoot Like Annie Oakley*—which made all of us laugh, including Mitch. Jake pointed out the envelope stuck in the middle of the book. When I opened it, I gasped aloud and took a minute to catch my breath.

"Jake, this is too much." The card enclosed said the house loan was paid in full.

"I gave you incentive just a few months ago…if you ever got hitched, this would be your reward." He snorted. "Well, that'll learn me; there's no such thing as a safe bet."

I laughed when I kissed his cheek. "I don't deserve you."

Looking a little sheepish, he wiggled his tie. "Yes, you do." With a furtive glance at Mitch he added, "You deserve to be happy." With damp eyes, I surveyed the room and locked on Mitch with a bright smile.

I was embarrassed to give Jake a paltry beer-making kit, but he seemed delighted, and Chuck loved the leather day planner and the plaster mold of Sadie's paw beside Scout's chubby handprint.

Chuck brought a toy tool chest for Scout, a hard rubber mouse for Sadie, a bottle of whiskey for Jake and presented Mitch with a bonus check. Mitch looked at the check with big eyes, and handed it to me while he shook hands, vigorously thanking Chuck. It was for $100.

We all chattered easily over dinner while Christmas songs played and the tree lights flickered. Even Mitch seemed to perk up and look like he was enjoying himself. If there was any tension between him and Jake, I didn't notice it when Jake explained how the earphones worked. A playful easiness prevailed, and when I brought out a tray of Christmas cookies and refills of wassail, I curtsied to the applause. It was a family Christmas I would remember. When Mitch caught my glance as I munched a chocolate kiss, I licked my lips and pulled on one of my new earrings. He winked at me and licked his lips in response.

Chapter Forty-Eight
Fifteen Steps

The Christmas Eve party at Fort Laramie was for volunteers and staff. I was strictly part time, clerking in the Visitor Center—which carried some of my soaps—on selected weekends or days when Jake or Mitch could watch over Scout. I also helped out with re-enactments. Living history skits were becoming rare at Old Fort Laramie, though an occasional military re-enactment was still an attraction on some holidays.

Hors d'oeuvres and complimentary drinks were to be served in the old officer's club near the Park Entrance and the old mess hall in the ground floor of the Cavalry Building reverted back to a dance hall, just as it had in the homesteader's era after the military abandoned the base. It was still light outside when we arrived and parked in the newer parking lot near the RV campground. I thought Mitch might recognize some of the surviving buildings from his era—to jumpstart his memory. *I wasn't wrong.*

His color faded, reminding me of his reaction to the photograph of his father. Tiny lines between his eyes popped when he stood at the monument obelisk and surveyed the grounds. In silence he turned right, and began to hike past the officer's club and trader's store. I scampered beside him in my western boots, avoiding small drifts of snow until we came to the Old

Burt House where I had slipped through time in a tea party re-enactment that turned me into his "Accidental Wife" in 1886. Of course, the boardwalk was gone, as was the picket fence post that I had collapsed against, hitting my head and dulling my own memory.

"Do you remember the Burt house?" I asked. "I fell here and you carried me to the doctor's house next door." He tilted his chin and slowly shook his head, but his look was troubling.

Old Bedlam, the oldest military building in Wyoming, and the limestone remains of three more officer quarters formed the most complete perimeter of the parade grounds. The restored old and new guardhouses were the only structures looming in shadows of dusk on the opposite side of the open parade ground. His eyes narrowed as he gazed at the old buildings with a tic in his jaw. "A wool blanket was all…"

"What did you say?"

His shrug was more shiver, but he didn't answer.

"Amazing isn't it—seeing what remains of a bustling oasis a century and a half ago?" He nodded this time, still staring ahead.

We finally retraced our steps back to the soldier's bar and went inside to claim our complimentary drinks and appetizers. A huge buffalo head hung on the wall near our table, and I tried to make a joke about it as we nibbled Buffalo wings, but Mitch just gave me a lame smile. When a park employee costumed as an infantry soldier approached, Mitch stood up rigidly to shake hands when I introduced him as my new husband. Jim Mokol insisted on buying us a pitcher of birch beer, telling Mitch he was a lucky man to finally *corral* me. I laughed, wondering if he chose the verb because he took care of the small herd of horses and mules that lived at the fort, or if he once considered me low-hanging fruit stubbornly aging on the vine. Until Mitch, it was true. I had never considered marriage.

Jim was always impressed by my historic knowledge of Fort Laramie. I couldn't tell him that I had actually been part of its history for the summer of 1886, but I joked that we were both armchair time-travelers. He studied the Fort history, and loved wearing the uniform to embellish his guided tours. In the glory days of Old Fort Laramie, any single woman over thirty would have been described as "long in the tooth," an old saw originated by a horseman who could tell a horse's age by its teeth. Mitch seemed unusually preoccupied with the buffalo head while Jim and I exchanged small talk but he managed to nod or smile when I poked him under the table.

A large gibbous moon hung over the spreading peach leaf willow tree in front of the Cavalry Building when we left Jim in the bar. Several solar lights illuminated a triangular path between the parking lot, bar and dance hall, and more couples were streaming toward the lights, merrily greeting recognizable faces.

Christmas lights scalloped the second floor balcony of the Cavalry Building, twinkling like stars against the blue railings and pillars. Holiday music from a quartet of local musicians spilled into the night as doors opened. The end of the year was getting a spirited send-off.

Mitch needed to use the restroom midway down the long veranda beneath the balcony. While I waited for him on an outside bench, I texted Jake to see if he was on his way. He texted back within seconds that he and Louisa were just a few miles away. I replied back that I was excited to see her again, and told Jake we would meet them shortly in the Dance Hall.

Mitch had never met Louisa, but I filled him in on who she was and how Jake and I met her at Bunny's gift shop in Torrington. I could tell that Jake was interested and hoped Louisa felt the same about him. She impressed me far more than Meredith ever did. Jake deserved someone to make him as happy as Mitch made me.

However, Mitch's recent behavior was mystifying tonight, going back to the photo of his father found at Christmas. Was it the photo that triggered his recent aloofness? He never fully explained how his Indian mother acquired it. And why didn't he mention the photo when we were together in 1886?

Something was also off since we arrived at the Fort. Come to think of it, he was less than enthused about coming to the dance. Did the fight at Dooley's color his opinion of all dances? I thought we had practiced enough since then to resolve any embarrassment over his inexperience. Perhaps recharged memories were troubling him? It was over two months since I wounded him. The Wheaton doctor was pleased last week by how fast he healed, and predicted his memory return was certainly imminent. Was this *"opening night"* on the memory stage?

Ten minutes later, I went inside to warm up, sitting on worn wooden steps that led to the second floor. A tour-only No Admittance sign was posted on a chain at the top of the steps. When I heard a loud thump come from the floor above, I tiptoed up the stairway and stepped over the chain. Holding high the light from my cell phone, I scanned the reconstructed company quarters—two long rows of narrow beds perpendicular to the outer walls of the Cavalry Barracks. Mitch was lying on one of the bunks.

A high wall of Plexiglas separated the long room from a small viewing area. Moonlight filtered through six deep windows on either side of the room and two at the far end. I knew the historic display was the pride and joy of the Fort's tour, and even in the dim light, I could make out the circular rifle racks, two tables with benches, a barrel wood stove for heat, water barrels, chest benches at the base of the beds, clothing and equipment racks on walls at the head. Two unmade bunks with rolled up mattresses revealed four board lengths composing the bed base. The rest were covered by a thin mattress and pillow and a wool army blanket with U.S. stamped high above a navy stripe. Narrow black rubber buckets and a couple of long axes hung on another wall rack high above a barrel, probably once filled with water in case of fire. I knew some of the furnishings were authentic or at least re-created from authentic schematics of the era.

Mitch had pulled a wooden crate up to vault over the Plexiglas. I had more trouble getting over, until I removed my coat. He was oblivious to my approach, mumbling incoherently when I bent over him. The Christmas lights on the deck rail outside his window striped his pallid face and his green eyes were fixed and glazed. When he recognized me, he caught the hand I used to touch his cheek and squeezed it painfully.

"This was my bunk," he said in a monotone.

"What?" I pulled away my hand and flashed my

cell light over the nametag on the shelf above his headboard. Pvt. O'Brien.

"Cold in winter, hot in summer…"

"But you were never a soldier…"

"Never good enough."

"I don't understand. When?" The journals I read that included anything about Mitch or his connection with Fort Laramie had him employed as an occasional trail guide or interpreter, even a wrangler before he married Jessamine and became a rancher.

"*Sé bliana…*six years." He responded, trancelike, with a strange cadence in his voice. "From one shore to another. Six years a soldier."

My mind was racing. I could hear footsteps pounding up the stairs…a bright light blinding me from the viewing area…a deep voice demanding we leave the room at once. It seemed to bring Mitch back. He stood up, saluted and took my arm, helped me over the barrier while the security guard focused his flashlight on Mitch, then me. "Miss Brewster? Is that you?"

I recognized Ed Bradley as one of the night guards and apologized profusely. "I, I was giving my husband a personal tour and noticed someone had thrown a pair of gloves over the barrier and knocked one of the checkerboards off the table. He helped me over to set it right." I fished in my pocket for my driving gloves and offered them limply to the guard.

He narrowed his look at me after examining the gloves. "All the tour areas were roped off tonight, even for staff. If you had asked for special permission…?"

"I know," I said quickly. "Terribly impulsive of me. I thought a quick look wouldn't hurt."

He shook his head, and when he handed me back

the gloves, I knew he didn't buy my story.

Like a naughty child, I hung my head as we marched hand in hand down the stairs ahead of the guard. Under his breath, I could hear Mitch mutter, "Fifteen steps, fifteen steps."

The cold outside air revived me, jumpstarting my heart. The night was coming alive with couples streaming into the dance hall to the lively strains of a fiddle. Mitch even managed a smile when I apologized once again. Ed's tone was more sympathetic when he said he wouldn't report this, seeing I was staff and this was a holiday party. I wished him a Happy New Year and we shuffled along the veranda toward the music.

Jake and his date were huddled together on a bench outside the dance hall when we approached. "There you are," he said, standing up to give me a hug. "Jess, you've met Louisa from Bunny's Gift Shop."

I tried to smile while polite introductions were made all around. Louisa was even prettier than I remembered; rosy cheeked and sporting crystal snowflake earrings. She hooked her arm through Jake's and he covered her hand with his, possessively.

"Jake, we can't stay for the dance." It wasn't a lie when I told him I had a splitting headache.

He looked at me sharply, then at Mitch. When he kissed my cheek, he whispered, "You okay?"

I summoned up a gesture of assurance and smiled. "Happy New Year to both of you."

We walked to the car without looking back, solemn steps in discord with a medley of snappy Christmas music coming from the dance hall. Our silence was deafening on the long ride home.

Chapter Forty-Nine
The Sound of a Breaking Heart

Chuck was surprised to see us back so early. Once again, I used my headache as a curt excuse and went to find some aspirin. Scout was already asleep but Sadie was keeping Chuck company as he watched Time Square Festivities on TV. Originally invited to spend the night, he opted to return home and left hastily, no doubt sensing something was terribly wrong between the newlyweds.

We faced off in front of the fireplace. He was slumped in his favorite easy chair and I perched on the edge of the chair opposite—hands clasped tightly to prevent shaking, willing myself to sit straight and breathe through my nose. On the drive home, I had ordered my thoughts to build my case. He didn't have Mitch's scars or his raven-black hair. He seemed shorter, thinner, and slow to tease. In the throes of passion, he twice called out another name, even spoke in another language when he talked in his sleep. Awake, he used odd words and sometimes a strange cadence of speech that I assumed came from his Sioux heritage. Were they all clues I deliberately chose to excuse or ignore? I had to ask the question that burned in my throat and I felt like a prosecutor when I finally spoke. "Just who are you?"

His green eyes were dull, his expression slack

when he stared at me. "God only knows."

I snorted ruefully. "You remember. I know you remember."

He nodded. "I remember scraps, little things that gnawed at me for months. Red sails, an ocean, a tower, a stone falcon."

"Then you knew you were not Mitch…for months?"

"I wanted to be him. I wanted to be the man you remembered, the man you loved." His voice broke. "I prayed I was truly Scout's father."

I choked back a sob. "And you…you married me, knowing you weren't?"

He stared at the glowing logs in the fireplace, twitched when a loud pop of sap sent up a small display of fireworks. "There has to be some scrap of honor—even in deceit—when you, when you, love someone more than life?" He sighed deeply, then looked at me directly, his green eyes soft and glassy. "I fell in love with you, Jess…you and Scout."

I snorted again. "Well, at least you got my name right this time. Who is Liv?"

He looked at me sharply. "Liv?"

"You uttered the name in your sleep and twice when we made love."

He bent forward to cradle his head in his hands, bracing his elbows on knees that trembled. *"Ah Dhia*, we grew up together. She was a friend."

"A friend with benefits?"

He peered up at me. "What does that mean?"

"It means you fucked her."

He had the grace to blush, dropping his chin to his chest. "Aye, and I know the shame of it tore us apart."

Once again, his eyes met mine. "I was a boy, Jess, not even twenty years."

I thought of myself at that age. A girl betrayed by my high school crush. Young as I was, it became my crucible—weighed against every relationship. Jimmy Potter was why I declared I would never fall in love, never marry…until I slipped through time to find the one man to shatter my determination. *Mitch.*

"I didn't know what love meant, Jess. Not until you took me in, not until I saw you with Scout, with Jake and an old man abandoned by his sons, even with the dog. You care about those you touch, care about everything you do; cooking, making your little soaps, even teaching me to dance. And when you melted in my arms, I put aside the wretched liar I was to become a better man, the man you wanted to return to you." He paused to swipe the back of his hand across his brimming eyes. "Don't you see? I wanted you to love me like you loved him, Jess. I would have lied 'til I took my dying breath, if it only meant…if it meant I had your love."

We were both crying now. I rose to get a box of tissues and pour each of us a glass of something strong. The only thing I could find stashed in the cupboard was the bottle of raspberry liqueur—made last fall with cheap brandy and my garden raspberries. He gulped it down and wiped his mouth with the back of his hand.

I blew my nose and swilled the liqueur around in my mouth before I let it trickle down my ragged throat and heat the emptiness I felt in my core. The room was warm enough with the fire blazing, but a chill radiated through my bones and my hands were icy cold. I still had questions for him, but when I opened my mouth, the only thing that came out was nothing that mattered. “How old are you?”

“I don’t know anymore. Time has become queer, one year blending into another. I think maybe I am somewhere around thirty.”

“Thirty!” That surprised me. He had looked younger than Mitch, but not *that* much younger. That made me three years older than him. “Your eyes. Your eyes are like his,” I muttered. “It sets you both apart. More than anything, they made me believe you *were* him.” Unconsciously, I was twisting the ring on my left hand. And when it slipped over my knuckle, I warmed it in my palm before I handed it to him.

“I married a stranger. A man who can’t remember his own name. That alone makes our marriage invalid…a paper fraud at the very least.”

With a look of torment, he stared at the ring he gingerly held between trembling fingers. “I want you to keep it.”

“What’s the point? All the symbolism you explained it represents is a lie now.”

The tick in his jaw hollowed like a dimple—reminding me of Mitch. He looked at me, his chin up. “I didn’t lie about any of that. Friendship…love…fidelity.”

I threw my glass into the fire, startling him. The pieces shattered against the burning wood, sending up a sound that mirrored the break of my heart. “Fidelity. Isn’t that the same as trust?” My voice cracked as new tears brimmed in my eyes. “How does any relationship move forward without trust?” I bellowed. “Did you honestly expect to live a lie; pretend you were another man for the rest of your life? Pull me and Scout into the lie and use *love* for the excuse?"

With his penchant for appearing, always at the wrong moment, Scout padded into the room, rubbing his eyes. Sadie—ever faithful to her boy—stood at his side, not even wagging her tail. "You wake us."

A single sob tore from the throat of my nameless stranger. Scout ran into his arms, hugging him around the neck. "Why you cry, Dapa?

Watching them clawed at my heart. I rose, unsteady on rubbery legs, and grabbed the back of the chair. I couldn't focus on the weeping green eyes peering over Scout's head. He was a good father to Scout. He loved another man's child, and Scout clearly returned that love. I couldn't think anymore. I left them both to take care of each other and ran to my bedroom, locked the door and sobbed into my pillow.

Chapter Fifty
However long the day…

I woke to a steady thumping in my head, and realized that someone was pounding on my bedroom door.

"Mama, Mama," the little voice was panicky. When I unlocked the door, Scout threw himself at me, hugging my knees. His face was contorted when I took him in my arms, and he smelled like sour milk and something even more pungent. I felt the sagging wad in his pajamas.

"Did you have an accident, Scout?"

He looked at me, his green eyes filled with the same look of shame I recognized last night in another pair of green eyes. Rarely did he have even a wet pull-up in the morning. "Scout make asid-dent, Mama."

A half dozen sticky little kisses smudged my face after I reassured him that accidents do happen. Though my digital clock read 7:43 a.m., I could have easily slept another hour, still feeling drained and disordered. I set him down and we both crunched over a path of cheerios to the bathroom. Sadie trailed us, chomping up cheerio crumbs until she caught a whiff of what was in Scout's pull-up and went to sit by the front door. When I left him on his potty chair and went to find some clean underwear and clothes, he yelled out to me. "Where Dapa?" It was then that I noticed the unmade bed in

Scout's room and the empty hangers in the closet.

The letter was propped against my *Be Happy* mug by the coffeemaker. One of us always made sure the timer was set the night before, creating a ritual of waking to an aroma that brought us together for the morning jumpstart we both seemed to relish. The coffeemaker was empty, dry as my mouth when I unfolded the notepaper and began to read the careful script.

Jess,

In a wrinkle of time and circumstance, you took in a stranger, gave him a name, a home and kin to love for all these months. But last night opened floodgates of memories that were better lost forever. I recalled an Irish saying, "However long the day, night must fall." I was a fool to hope I could stand against the man you loved, even with our green eyes and Irish blood. Our differences are a long dark night that damns me to shame for the liar I am.

This is the truth I remember: My mum was a good, hardworking woman, a devoted servant who raised me with learning and hope for a better life. But when I learned I was born a bastard—on a ship to Ireland, all hope died. I was a stable boy, good enough to muck out horse cac for a highborn Irish master until I immigrated to Boston and took the only offer that promised me a living. I failed as a soldier, and went AWOL before I could be court martialed or hung for a crime I didn't intend.

After living like a wild animal in a cave for months, maybe years, I began to stray farther outside and came across your cabin last summer. Watching you from the woods, I thought maybe by God's grace or some huge mistake, I was at the gate of heaven. But you dressed different, spoke different, and drove a funny vehicle. Thinking maybe I was at another gate, being tempted and twisted, I had to get closer, and I helped myself to your garden, even took things from your porch just to see what would happen. I was nearby when I saw the dog and the child and thought the child was going to fall in the stream.

I didn't remember any of this when I woke up in the hospital and you told me I was your husband. I didn't know who I was or where I came from or what I had done. Please believe me when I say I never would have married you, never made you a party to such dishonor and deceit had I known all this then.

Forgive me, Jess. If I am lucky to stand before God, the only redemption I can offer for my worthless life is that I once loved a beautiful woman and her child with all my heart. Regardless, I will die happy clinging to the belief that perhaps a wee pebble of their love was returned—to a nameless fraud.

Mo ghrá,
Go deo agus lá

****

I re-read the letter twice more before I went to my laptop to google his last words and my heart skipped when I read the English to Irish translation. "My love, forever and a day."

A few minutes later, Scout crawled onto my lap, naked as the day he was born, and chained his little arms around my neck. "Don't cry, Mama."

I gazed at the worried pair of bright green eyes and pulled a Cheerio out of his black curls and popped it into my mouth. Even this small, soggy morsel felt hard as a bolt when I swallowed.

"Where's Dapa?"

Hesitating, I said the only thing I could think of in the moment. "He's with Chuck."

As I bathed and dressed my son, I prayed that I hit on the truth. Unless he was too proud, he might have walked the five miles to Chuck's place. If not, the $100 Chuck had given him for Christmas would not last long. He had no car, not even a license to drive yet. Otherwise, Guernsey and Wheatland were the closest towns to offer a room and maybe even a job.

Did I want to find him? Was it unfinished between us? A conversation, a plan…at least another chance for a better goodbye? I knew I wasn't ready to open a door that had slammed shut so painfully, but I still had questions that nagged me. Most of all, I couldn't believe that the caring man we lived with could have committed any crime he thought worthy of a hanging. A flawed imposter—maybe—but not a criminal. Like him, I had been a look-a-like imposter once. Mitch was fooled into believing I was his wife, and when he accepted the truth, he flew off into a drunken rage and was brought home in a wheelbarrow.

Was it karma that brought another green-eyed man into my life, only to do the same thing? With the same end result? There were some differences. Mitch was married, had a life to continue, unraveled in his time. If this imposter was telling the truth, he had nobody to go back to…in this century, anyway. How did he pass through time to get from Ireland to Fort Laramie to me anyway? His letter didn't explain that. Was it another mysterious teacup? Or were there other triggers that could transport someone through time? I had slipped back. He had propelled forward. *Were there were others like us?*

Unexplainable things that happened for good fell under the heading of Miracle. Was that what this was? Maybe the sub-genre of a miracle? And if so, was I blind to the possibilities of good? Had I missed an opportunity to do my part, play a role to engineer that good?

I called Chuck to ask if he had acquired a new roommate and was shocked when Tommy Beaverwood answered the phone.

"Tommy, so good to hear that you're back! Is your brother home, too?"

"Nah, he couldn't take off without losing his job."

After some hurried chitchat, I learned that Tommy decided he was back for good and Chuck was out giving some estimates in Wheatland. "Was he alone?" I asked.

"Nah, Wolfie is with him."

"Wolfie?"

"My new dog. I brought my dog home with me. Dad is going to have him checked out at the vet since he's been scratching his butt a lot."

"Good idea. I'm glad you and…Wolfie are back. Your dad missed the company."

"Really?" Tommy laughed. "I thought he was glad to be rid of us! He lost no time giving away Sadie." I heard a little resentment in his voice.

"He did it for Scout. You remember how Scout and Sadie took to each other? Sadie was a heartfelt gift from a very unselfish man. You're lucky to have a dad like that." I couldn't help snapping out the final salvo. "Appreciate what you have before it's gone, Tommy."

I thought about that long after we hung up. Did I appreciate what I had? My thoughts were running wild. Obviously, he had not gone to stay with Chuck. After lunch, I hit on something that had germinated with my suspicions the day after our wedding. Maybe there was something I could do—if nothing else—to satisfy my own curiosity. I looked online for DNA testing in Wyoming and found there was a lab about 45 miles away. With Scout and Sadie, and samples collected in a plastic bag, we drove north to Douglas.

Chapter Fifty-One
Research

"Saliva testing is superior to hair testing." The technician squinted at us through her wire rims, as if she was peering through a microscope. The badge on her lab coat identified her as Dr. V. L. Perkins. She tapped a painted nail near the samples on her desk. "Old hair clippings rarely test well. Results aren't guaranteed without a follicle, and it takes some time, even with priority status."

My disappointment must have been obvious. She smiled when Scout mimicked her, stretching to tap a small finger on her desktop. "Luckily, January is a catch-up month here. Vacations over, full staff now on board, we could put a rush on this if you need it soon for a paternity hearing." She glanced at my hands when I pulled Scout back on my lap.

I nodded vigorously, letting her think what she supposed to be true. There were no rings on my fingers, not even a mark from the wedding ring I wore for less than a month. She offered to hold Scout while I filled out necessary forms after giving her a saliva sample from Scout and myself.

It was expensive. I hoped the check I wrote wouldn't bounce. Hoping to speed up the process, I promised I would call her with the information I couldn't yet provide about one of the samples, but she said a name wasn't entirely necessary. The long drive home gave me a chance to plan a course of action. Firing up my laptop to do some preliminary research was first on the agenda.

****

With a magnifying glass, I studied the old photo of his father. *Had he left it behind on purpose?* I already decided the flag with the harp may have been Irish. That meant the man was Irish, or was in an Irish Brigade. I recognized the other flag as the Confederate Stars and Bars. Okay, that meant the soldier was from the South—one of eleven states that had seceded by 1861. Clue one and two: Possibly Irish and from the South.

The hat the soldier wore was not the typical little kepi commonly worn by soldiers of both sides. Googling Confederate uniforms and hats, I found a slouch hat that also could have been common for men of both sides, but the Confederates preferred it because the wide brim was cooler on sunny days. Using my magnifying glass, I could see that the emblem on the front of the hat appeared to be two crossed sticks with the numeral one above it. Regiment, brigade, division number? I knew that Companies always started with a letter, but it took me some time to establish that Brigades and Divisions in the Confederacy were named after Generals or commanding officers. Clue three meant the number "1" on the hat stood for a Regiment. Most of the eleven Confederate States had "1st" regiments of Cavalry, Infantry and Artillery. Without a name to find, this could be time wasted.

The crossed bars under the number could have been rifles, but when I looked online for Civil War hat insignias, only three were listed for both Union and Confederate sides: a bugle for Infantry, crossed swords for Cavalry and crossed cannons for artillery. I could definitely eliminate him from Infantry and possibly even Cavalry. Clue four: Cannons? Under my magnifying glass, whatever was crossed looked too thick to be swords. On notebook paper, I jotted down the clues, adding a smiley face next to the most positive or promising.

After studying types of Confederate uniforms online, I could see that colors on collars and cuffs made a difference. If the picture had been in color, I could have learned what rank the soldier held, and narrow my search. Though the picture was faded and lined, the shade of his collar and cuffs was too dark to be yellow for cavalry but blue for infantry and red for artillery seemed possible. Black cuffs designated medical, and I thought the photo contrast between a gray jacket and black cuffs would have been greater, so I eliminated medical. Clue five: Infantry or Artillery.

Chevrons and epaulettes were also clues to rank. I learned that a private or musician wore none, corporals had two stripes, sergeants, three. Higher ranks were determined by stars on the collar or epaulettes. No stars anywhere on the jacket, but there was a chevron visible on one sleeve. Clue Six: The man was a corporal.

Buttons on the jacket also held clues. I learned that the most common letters, A, C, and I signified Artillery, Cavalry or Infantry, but often, buttons were issued with state flags or seals depicted, and an eagle button was reserved for officers. My magnifying glass wasn't strong enough to capture the details on his button jackets, but I could eliminate the plain letters and even the eagles since he wasn't an officer. Clue Seven corroborated Clue Six: Not an officer.

What I learned about the mysterious young soldier in the photo was that he fought for the South, which made him a resident of one of the eleven states that seceded. He was in the lst Regiment of one of those states, possibly an artillery corporal. When I learned what was on his buttons, I might even know his home state. *Smiley faces were sprouting on my list.*

On another page I listed what I knew about this man's likely son. Bastard. Mother was a servant. Born on a ship to Ireland. Dark hair, green eyes. Six years a soldier at Fort Laramie who went AWOL for a crime. Presently about age 30. Whatever I could learn about the father might lead to the identity of his nameless son. Didn't everyone deserve to know their name and origin?

Mitch was also a bastard who never knew his Irish father's identity until he turned eighteen. His father knew he existed, however, and gave him a last name and $100 enclosed in a letter when he left the orphanage. I remember Mitch telling me that he bought a pair of boots and a horse with the money but vowed—within his power—his son would never measure his worth by what a hundred dollars could buy. That vow became mine when I first gazed into the green eyes of our newborn son. I also remembered Mitch's last words to me in 1886. *"He will be the link that bridges our time."*

My eyes felt the Google-strain when I shut down my laptop for the day. After soup and a sandwich shared with Scout, I bundled both of us up for some fresh air outside. Sadie and Scout frolicked around the burr oak while I watched them from the porch swing, air puffs circling their heads like cartoon speech balloons. It was already growing dark, but a full moon ascending behind the house cast a glacial blue over the snow cover. I breathed deeply, mulling over what I learned today and wondered why I was going to such trouble. When Scout finally joined me on the swing, we cuddled there like we often did in nearly every season of his life. "Where's Dapa?" he asked for probably the tenth time today.

"At work or with Chuck" wasn't going to cut it much longer. I didn't know how to reply with anything that could reassure either of us. "Do you miss him?"

He screwed up his face and nodded vigorously.

I kissed his forehead. "So do I." And suddenly, I knew why I was going to so much trouble to find the name of the man Scout called Dapa. The picture was a clue to the stranger we both loved.

Chapter Fifty-Two
The Equal of a Little Hope

I dropped Scout off at the Visitor's Center at Fort Laramie after Audrey Wells, who was on her lunch break, offered to entertain him while I met with the historical librarian. Audrey had a son about Scout's age and though we always meant to arrange a play date for them, life seemed to re-direct our plans. I needed Audrey now, and promised her I would reciprocate soon.

I needed Stella Lowry as well. My old supervisor, who had been in charge of costumes and living history skits, was now a part time paid employee of the Fort Laramie Historical Association and a Volunteer in Parks for the National Historic Site. Officially, she was the undisputed Research Librarian who presided over files from her office on the second floor of the Cavalry Barracks. The same floor that held the re-created bunkroom I transgressed at the holiday party.

Since I didn't have the name of the soldier I was looking for, she couldn't follow normal procedure to access the Name File on her computer. "That could be good or bad," she confessed, pushing up the cuffs of her red Fort Laramie sweatshirt. "There are nearly 40,000 files in the program, divided among military, civilian, Native Americans and even emigrants."

"I'm only interested in researching the military

record of a man who served here, but I don't know his name."

She gave me a walleyed look. "A soldier without a name?"

I bit my lip and nodded slowly. "I'm working on family research."

"Could you at least narrow it down to a date, then…maybe even a year in service?"

"He was here for six years, just before the fort was abandoned."

She sat down at a long table, and pulled her glasses an inch down her nose, drilling me with her deep brown eyes for a long moment. "The final troops were gone by March of 1890, so I suppose we could begin with files descending from that year. Was he Infantry or Cavalry?"

"I'm not sure. He said he…I mean I think he was quartered in this building, the Cavalry Barracks."

"That doesn't necessarily mean he was Cavalry. After 1883, companies C and E of the 7th Infantry were the only units left at the fort and they bunked in this building." She pushed her glasses back up and jotted down a few notes while she enlightened me, clearly enjoying the effort. "Congressional downsizing of military posts was happening all over the country toward the end of the 19th Century, you see. Most Indians were confined to reservations and most western migration was no longer done by wagons, anyway." She tapped her ballpoint on the table and sighed. "You see, The Union Pacific routed through Cheyenne a hundred miles south of us and several towns sprouted up like weeds along the rail lines. Fort Laramie was no longer the mid-point wagon oasis to California, and The

Black Hills were now U.S. property." Looking up, she took a deep breath and asked if I knew anything else about my soldier.

I cleared my throat. "Irish. He was Irish, and he wasn't an officer."

She laughed. "Most of the enlisted men were Irish back then."

I sighed, pulling off my hat and gloves. "I heard he…he went AWOL to avoid a court martial."

"A common trend back then, as well." She sat back in her chair and smoothed the back of her cropped white hair. "But it is a start. I can sort files for General Court Martial records and the AWOL listings for those years and see if we come up with some Irish names to narrow the search. Since the post was down to only two companies, there probably wouldn't be that many. If you have any idea of his age, we could narrow the search even further?"

I had already done a calculation based on what he told me, without knowing how long he was AWOL. "Mid to late twenties. He was probably somewhere between 24 and 30."

Two hours later, I left her office with a printout containing five names from the 7th Infantry, who between the years 1884 and 1890 had records indicating Court Martial or desertion. All were enlisted men within the age parameters, bearing Irish names.

Stella had warned me that while all of the officers could be accessed in the name file, the enlisted men were not always there. In other words, my man might not even be one of the five on the printout. Still, I was optimistic, running the names over my tongue all the way home. Liam Burke, Patrick McCarter, Robert

O'Brien, Martin Connolly and Joseph Donovan. All good Irish lads with tainted records. Was one of them the man I had married? I couldn't wait to rendezvous at home with my own computer, now that Stella showed me how easy it was to access military records and Ancestry.com. I even wondered if I would find my great-great-grandmother Jessamine in the Ancestry files, and trace her line through her marriages down to me and Jake through our different grandfathers. Descendants could enter dates and personal knowledge. Maybe there was something there about Mitch—particularly his date of death. Knowing that might shed some light on what had happened to him, and close some doors…or open some windows. I was beginning to mix and match memories of the two men in my life who—incredibly—shared the same color eyes. The pure green color so rare that only 2% of the world's population can claim it.

Scout rushed into the house ahead of me after I parked in the garage and unbuckled his car seat. The chickens, as usual, cackled a greeting and I could hear Sadie barking from inside the house. Still in his hooded jacket and boots, Scout didn't get further than the kitchen before he was accosted by his dog and lay giggling on the floor while Sadie greeted him with her usual tongue wash. After I peeled him down to indoor clothes, my heart hitched as I watched him run from room to room calling, "Dapa, Dapa."

Finally, the two of them went to the front window, where the Christmas tree once stood, and Scout pressed his nose against the cold pane. The image in one of his new storybooks came to mind. A boy and his dog sitting before a lighted Christmas tree. The caption read, *A whole stack of memories never equals one little hope.*

The house felt cold and empty, and I needed the cheery warmth of heat to lick my face. After I built a fire in the fireplace, I settled in my easy chair to gaze at the flames and weigh my own memories against a little hope.

It was then that I noticed the bearskin rug was gone.

Chapter Fifty-Three
Articles of War

I searched the house and garage for the bearskin rug…and anything else I could determine to be missing. Nothing personal that belonged to Scout or me was gone, but I couldn't be sure about a few other items—an old pillow and blanket, my last bottle of raspberry liqueur, the flashlight I always kept in the drawer with candles. And when Scout wanted me to read his pirate book at bedtime, I couldn't find it in his little bookcase and had to substitute with "The Snoopy Puppy."

For the rest of the week, I was chained to my laptop, navigating Ancestry.com and Find A Grave, hoping to eliminate four soldiers that couldn't be mine. Spread over the kitchen island, I even made room for the memory chest that held the family diaries and Jessamine's journals. Boxes I had hidden in the crawl space of my closet, which included my own small journal—written after I returned from my four month "vacation" in 1886.

I remembered what Mitch told me on our last night together about the father he never met, probably because of the sadness in his voice as he related the rejection of David Mitchell. His father claimed a "proper" family in Virginia, all unaware of the half breed he fathered. I looked up the only David Mitchell in Ancestry whose lifeline aligned with what I knew, and found a Col. David Dawson Mitchell was a famous figure in negotiating with Native Americans. Even some of his five wives were Indian, with thirteen acknowledged children sired among all of them. If this man was Mitch's father, the Mitchells of Virginia were a mixed tribe of their own.

Great-great-grandmother Jessamine also claimed some space in the Ancestry files, going back as far as her German and Irish grandparents. Her three husbands were listed, with two children, a daughter by Mitch and a son with her second husband, who became my great grandfather. Jake descended from the daughter's line, I from her son's. Proof positive that Jake and I were third cousins, raised by Jake's grandmother, preferring to think of ourselves as siblings. It was more confusing when I tried to figure out how Scout could ever be listed, even with dates often missing. There was no deceased date for Mitch—just the year of his birth in 1843. Jessamine was born November 30, 1856 and died December 2, 1956, two days after her hundredth birthday. I thought of all she must have seen in her lifetime. Inventions that must have seemed like miracles or science fiction—not just with medicine and electronics, but transportation. I wondered if I lived to be one hundred, would time travel be part of the changing transportation cycle. What havoc that would create for genealogy buffs!

As for the five soldiers I was researching, only two of them had possibilities, according to the clues I checked off for the man Scout called "Dapa." Patrick Owen McCarter and Robert Dawson O'Brien, 7th Infantry, Company H privates were both born in Ireland, both of them about the right stature and age and in service between 1883 and 1890. Both of them also had GCM and desertion charges in their military records. Their biggest differences came in the severity of their charges and where they enlisted into the army—McCarter in New York, O'Brien in Boston.

The General Court Martial charge brought against McCarter in violation of the 45th article of war found him not guilty of drunkenness on duty, but guilty only of conduct to the prejudice of good order and military discipline. His desertion was listed 5/9/1886 but he was apprehended a month later, fined with a pay forfeit and confined to hard labor for ten days.

O'Brien incurred two GCM's in the first few months of 1888 for violating Article 4: being found one mile from camp without leave in writing from his commanding officer. Additional charges for a criminal offense according to Article 78 were *replaced* in favor of Article 9 which prohibited striking or lifting a weapon against a superior officer. His desertion was dated 4/10/1888. If he was apprehended, it wasn't listed in General Orders. This was the most promising clue of all, but the record left me with some apprehension. Obviously, he struck a superior, which was serious enough, but I wondered what kind of criminal charges could be brought, then dropped. After googling the Articles of War from the 1800's, I found no specifics listed about criminal charges.

After emailing Stella at Fort Laramie with a few more questions, I searched through several McCarters and O'Brien's in Ancestry.com. Neither man with the birth dates or military description I wanted turned up in their files. I went to bed that night mulling the information and formulating a plan.

Chapter Fifty-Four
DNA Revelations

The girls in my garage roost were laying fewer eggs. I could have attributed the decrease to winter cold, but the hen hotel was well-insulated and ventilated and roost bedding of bubble wrap was topped by nest cozies made of terrycloth and filled with dry rice and beans. Even the walls of the outside run were covered by heavy plastic and duct tape and they all had access to a heated waterer. We rarely had to throw out frozen eggs gathered in the morning. Feeding the chickens, refreshing daily water and cleaning the sand litter everyday had been *his* job, along with collecting eggs each morning for breakfast. Scout loved to tag along, learning how to handle the eggs with care, and pet his favorite speckled hen.

My four-egg Blender Coconut Pie was fresh out of the oven when I got the phone call. The genetic compositional analysis I requested was already complete. To save time I had also requested the lab notify me so I could pick up the results in person. After a quick breakfast, Scout and Sadie and I drove north once again to Douglas. I deliberately set the pie in a covered pie caddy out on the porch to cool before we left.

Dr. Perkins, the same technician who took my basic information, ushered me into her private office to present the results. "Normally, we just mail out the results with a simple explanation, but clients still have trouble understanding what they see. We end up fielding questions by phone or email, anyway." She opened a manila folder containing several sheets with colorful bars that reminded me of crayons. "I'm glad you could come in person, because these results may be more confusing than usual." She gave me a weak smile. "They even confused me."

The first sheet compared my chromosomes with Scout's. Base markers. They were black but we shared large orange markers, which meant we were related, as expected, and she pointed out the mother-son relationship was easily identified because of the greater amount of shared color.

"Your son's paternity was questionable, however, because he also has markers that identify him with every one of the other samples you submitted."

I gaped at her. As part of the subterfuge to get a quick DNA chromosome account for the two soldiers in question, I submitted three other samples. Out of curiosity to gauge the accuracy of the testing, I had also submitted the newborn hair swatch that was in my family keepsake chest. I already knew that if that sample was from Mitch's stillborn son by Jessamine, it would share a match with Scout. They were half-brothers. Something I could never document officially was that they were born 150 years apart.

"What do you mean, they are *all* related?"

"The chromosomal DNA shows familial support on all the test figures by varied degree." She pointed to the blue markers in Scout's sample. "These show up in all the other samples, as well. More in the newborn's sample, less prominent in the other two. Generally speaking, this means he and the newborn could be as close as siblings, but you dated the newborn sample in the 1870's. That would make it impossible for the child on your lap to be his brother."

Not impossible in my universe. I took a deep breath. "That is strange." I knew the sibling connection was accurate, but how could Scout actually be related to the other two? The man he called Dapa, and his connection to the soldier in the photo was still uncertain.

"Of course, we are testing saliva vs. hair—ancestry keepsakes in two of the cases. We were lucky to get a marker on the older swatches, even luckier to find shared ancestors." She looked up at me, smiling. "You must have the luck of the Irish."

If you only knew. I returned her smile. "I think I do."

"Well, normally, DNA has limitations going back to identify relatives more than five or six generations. You wanted to know your son's paternity and the ancestry link of the others, as well."

I nodded eagerly. "Yes, the ancestry link."

She pulled up two of the test sheets and laid them side by side. "However, even I was surprised by the clarity of relationship found in two of your subjects."

I opened my purse to find a bag of cheerios to occupy Scout while I leaned over her desk to study the comparison and ask about the colored markers.

"The hair sample from a Civil War soldier with initials of D.I.M. is definitely the father of the toothbrush DNA sample," she concluded. "And the shared markers with your son could mean *both* of these men are ancestors, perhaps distant cousins to Scout.

I studied the black bars infused with common green bars and could feel my heartbeat thrum in my ears. I was hoping to have the father/son connection corroborated. With what I had narrowed down about the soldier in the photo, along with his initials, and the possible clues from Fort Laramie, I knew I was close to finding the names I needed. Their connection to Scout, however, was a surprise. *How was that possible?*

After a few more of my theoretical questions were answered, I left with the complete folder, thanking her profusely, just short of a bear hug. It was beginning to snow when we hit the highway to home, so I shifted into 4-wheel drive and shoved a CD of kiddie songs into the stereo. Scout and I sang along to the disc most of the way home and after we pulled into the garage, I found another surprise waiting for me.

The pie I set on the porch before leaving…was gone, the red pie caddy with it.

I circled the house, but found the snowfall had already filled up any footprints that might have been left. There was a partial print left on one of the steps, however. I stared at it, imagining the boot that made it, then scanned the woodsy horizon. Tree branches were already layered with heavy snow, a black and white fairyland—just like another day months ago when I desperately searched for Scout.

The day that changed my life forever.

Audrey Wells was excited when I called her to set up a play date for Scout with her son. "I'm home all day tomorrow. It's about time we got the boys acquainted. Your Scout is such a happy little guy, I'm sure he and Jamie will get on like macaroni and cheese."

Macaroni and cheese. Good idea. I mixed up a large casserole and refrigerated it for tomorrow, along with the new bottle of cheap Moscato I picked up with a few groceries on our way home from Douglas.

Later, I studied all my notes and lined the clues up on yellow post-its running along the breakfast bar. After Scout had a quick bath and bedtime story that evening, I opened my laptop and settled down before a blazing fire in my easy chair. I had one familiar name to check in Ancestry.com and if my new suspicions were correct, he and his progeny would be the key to a mystery solved. I was navigating the site with ease now, impressed by the number of additions found by relatives on a genealogy hunt. I could see how addictive it could be to trace lineage and map out a family tree. With the family journals I had hidden away for years, I could add to the records and give Scout an impressive history. One, however, that his descendants would discard as "fantasy."

When I found what I was looking for, I gave a little war whoop, then rewarded myself with a long, relaxing bubble bath. While I languished amid a collar of lavender suds, I planned my attack.

Chapter Fifty-Five
Love with the Perfect Stranger

I wasn't far into the woods when I began to see tracks in the glistening snow. It was a bright, clear morning, sunny enough to start a January thaw. Birds were trilling above me and a rabbit, nearly white as the groundcover, scampered across my path. I thought of Alice in Wonderland as I stopped to watch it disappear into a hollow tree. Was I on the edge of a new adventure? Wyoming Alice—armed and dangerous. Deer tracks were abundant, along with a few other prints I didn't recognize.

When I found the largest footprints, I removed my right glove and felt the cold steel deep in my pocket. I checked my bearings as I followed the frozen creek and then I saw it just ahead. The treehouse in the huge oak. In my memory, it had been smaller, a roofless platform, but I paid it fleet notice after I shot Mitch. Ladder-like boards nailed to the tree made the access easy.

When I climbed to the top, I noticed the plastic wrapped around the sides and flat roof, the kind of insulation used to wrap around my chicken run. The treehouse had a crude door and two small window openings covered by more thicknesses of clear plastic. I drew my revolver before I opened the door and saw the bearskin bundle curled up like a sausage on a pallet along with my missing blanket. I eased myself inside, cracking the door open for light and fresh air. The floor was about the perimeter of a Queen-sized bed with a plastic crate on one side. My red pie caddy, an empty bottle of liquor, some utensils, a flashlight, and Scout's pirate book cluttered the top of the crate. There wasn't enough headroom to stand, so I braced myself into a corner and kicked with both of my wet boots.

The sausage groaned.

"Get up soldier!"

His head snapped up at the top of the roll, green eyes blinking at the light beam pouring in the doorway. "What the…?"

I pointed my gun at him, affecting my best flinty look. "Reveille!"

He scrubbed his eyes with his fists and blinked again. "Jessica?" His hair was longer and as unkempt as the whiskers that covered his chin and neck, and he reeked of alcohol, sweat…and coconut pie.

With my free hand, I pulled at the bearskin. "You're a thief!"

He snorted. "You gave this to me for Christmas."

I wavered a little. "Well, you stole my pie." I nodded at the crate. "And a few other things that don't belong to you."

He sat up, bracing himself against the wall and the bearskin dropped to his lap. I was amazed to see that he was shirtless, though it was remarkably warm in the little space. I was distracted also by the shoestring tied around his neck, holding my Claddagh wedding ring. He smirked, running his fingers through his long hair. "I always loved your pies. Is that a criminal offense?"

I glared back for a long minute. When he asked if the gun was loaded, I told him it was and I had practiced. “I can shoot straight now.”

He snorted, and looked away. “Well maybe that’s frontier justice delayed. Kill the murdering thief and bastard.”

I lowered the revolver a couple inches. “You’re not a murderer.”

His eyebrows lifted as he rubbed his lower lip with the side of his finger. “You’ve been practicing other skills? Second sight, maybe?”

“I know what happened at Fort Laramie.

He gaped at me. “What? How do you know that?”

“Ancestry.com and Stella Lowry.”

He scratched his head and narrowed his eyes. “Ancestry wha…who?”

“The internet and the Fort Laramie historian. I did some research.”

“At Fort Laramie?”

“It’s all there in the records, and online as well. Your sergeant lived another thirty years, after you knocked him out.”

He gaped at me. “But Paddy told me I killed him.”

The gun went slack in my hand. “You might have been court martialed for striking an officer, or even discharged from the service, but you weren’t going to hang.”

He looked at me, through me, dazed by memories. “But they told me to run. The men cheered me on for putting the bully down, but they told me I’d swing for it. They brought me a pack horse, told me to run…run far.

“So you remember it all now?”

“Most of it, I think.”

“Then you know your name?”

We said it in unison. Slowly. "Robert Dawson O'Brien."

A wave of relief washed over me, and I could see new clarity in his face. He had remembered his name. "You were a private in Co. H, enlisting in Boston in 1883."

"Yes…Boston," he repeated, trancelike. "I roamed the docks there, looking for work after the Tuke ship landed. I had a valise, six pounds and the photo and list my mum gave me. Addresses to check out, connections to make, maybe find some relatives, even my da's people in Virginia."

He stretched back on his pillow, hands clasped behind his head, his eyes sparkling with a parade of images he was finally able to recall, and I was spellbound by his story. He remembered going to a Boston oyster bar and meeting a Sergeant there, a man who painted a glowing picture of life in the west, full of adventure and opportunity—all for $13.00 a month in military pay.

"I showed him mum's list, told him I had kin to find. The Sergeant bought me a couple drinks and the next thing I remembered was waking up on a train bound for Cheyenne.

"Sergeant Gleason was dozing beside me. He was annoyed when I woke him, told me to shut up and enjoy the smooth ride. We'd soon be bumping around in a freight wagon to Fort Laramie. When I protested, he showed me enlistment papers I signed. 'You're in the army Mick, welcome to America,' he said. I shoved my hands in my pockets and found nothing but lint there. My mum's list and the six pounds I carried from Ireland were gone."

"So you were shanghaied." I said quietly.

He gazed at me with knitted brows. "Is that what you call it? *A Dhia,* I was ripe, I suppose, and used to taking orders. Regimental discipline sounded like a fair trade for a green lad fresh off the boat. The army gave me bed and board, a job in the mill and enough change for a little gaming in free time, if I could avoid the Sergeant's fines."

"Is that why you hit him?"

"He flimflammed most of the men in our company and threatened us if we ratted him. Six years of it wore on me when he reported me off base without written permission—a court martial offense—just to keep me in line when I saw him sneak off to Three Mile to roost with the doves."

"The doves?"

He colored a little. "Soiled doves—sporting women—cribbing at Three Mile Ranch. It was popular recreation for a garrison of men so near."

I poked my tongue in my cheek, then blurted out, "So, did *you* roost there?"

He snorted. "There weren't many single soldiers who resisted."

I watched him shift his shoulders, look away, then rub the back of his neck. "Well now, you can't expect me to remember everything that happened…130 years ago."

"Your memory seems to be gushing like an oil well about everything else," I snapped.

He studied me in the dim light, looking rough and sexy, bearing no resemblance to the innocent twenty-year-old he just described. "I missed you Jess."

"We missed you too. Scout has asked me every day

when Dapa is coming home."

Again, he rubbed the back of his neck. "I didn't know where to go, what to do. I had no transportation. I had no car, and I didn't want to burden Chuck, especially with his son home now. The wood and tools to build up this treehouse came from him—supposedly to build an outside doghouse for Sadie."

I chuckled. "Sadie is talented, but not enough to climb a tree."

"Where is the lad and his shadow?"

"Sadie is at home and Scout is at a play date."

"A play date?"

"With a boy his age, the son of a co-worker."

"So there's no danger of the duo popping in to see what we're about?

I knew what he was thinking. "No danger," I conceded, working hard to bite back my grin.

He extended his hand. "Well then, if you've decided to let me live, and can forgive a remorseful liar and thief, can we celebrate with our own play date?"

"Here?" I looked around before I gingerly closed the door with the barrel of my weapon, then handed it to him.

While I pulled off my boots and slipped out of my jacket, he examined my revolver and saw that it was empty. "So you weren't going to shoot me after all."

"I would never shoot the father of my children."

He opened the fur wrap to invite me inside. "Children?"

I brushed my mouth against his maimed ear as we snuggled together. "Mmm. We are maybe seven months away from giving Scout a brother or sister."

Even in the dim light from two small windows

covered in plastic, I could see his face brighten with unmistakable joy. "Oh Jess, *mo grá*, you don't mean?"

"Yes, uh, Robert, that often happens when…" I gave him a meaningful look…"when two people fall deeply in love."

His beautiful green eyes glistened with tears when he gazed at me, repeating in English the final line of the note he left me: "My love, forever and a day." When he smothered me with tender kisses and a dozen questions about the baby, I soon forgot how cold I was or how really awful he smelled. His body was warm, as usual, and when there were no more questions, we answered the most basic need of all lovers, regardless of time or place. When I was properly heated and left shuddering in the circle of his arms, he crooned in my ear. "You can call me Robbie now—or Rob, if you prefer."

Chapter Fifty-Six
The Teacup

We walked home arm in arm with my gun in the empty pie caddy and his belongings wrapped in the bearskin—slung over his shoulders like a giant Santa sack. Sadie was glad to see us both, giving him a face wash with her tongue, then running to lap from her water dish. He took the hint and headed for the shower.

I watched with a sense of satisfaction as the clean-shaven man in his new Christmas robe wolfed down most of the macaroni and cheese casserole I heated up for him. He admitted he had been on more of a liquid diet since he left and had missed my cooking. I put on a CD of Celtic music and opened my new bottle of Moscato, and when we both cozied up to a blazing fire, it seemed like everything was old, and yet new.

It would take some time getting used to his name, but now I understood how the green eyes and smile had seduced me into believing he was Mitch. There were differences, however. Maybe because he had lost weight again, I noticed his face was slimmer, younger, and his hair curled against his neck and ears. Mitch's hair was never curly. I *had* made allowances for time and circumstance, desperately wanting to believe that it was Mitch who had come back to me.

The bearskin was back in its rightful spot before the fireplace. There were still questions left unanswered, a mystery yet to be unraveled, but I sensed the thrill of discovery—and maybe the wine—had mellowed both of us into moments of a new normal. From his chair before the fire, he toasted me for the research I had done to exonerate him from murder. "It all came back to me at the Fort Laramie party, the shame and terrible guilt over what I had done."

I sat on the bearskin near his feet, relishing the heat from the fire and the feel of the shaggy fur against my bare feet. "Anyone knowing you would know you weren't a killer." I lifted my glass to him and could see his eyes grow filmy as he studied me.

When he found his voice, he whispered, "Would any woman, but you, go to such lengths to prove that?"

I hugged my knees and gazed at the cheery fire. "Thank God, there are resources in this century to prove things like that."

He set his glass down and pulled me up onto his lap. "Jess, you are the only resource I ever want in any century. *Mo ghrá—go deo agus lá.*"

Yes. Forever and a day," I fanned my left hand, displaying the Claddagh ring once again in its rightful place. "I'll take this off only if I can have that engraved inside."

"Part of it already is engraved there. *Go Deo* means forever."

"But I want the whole phrase. Can't that be added? Gaelic to either side?"

He enclosed my hand in his and kissed the ring. "I'd have that phrase engraved on my forehead if it makes you happy."

I nuzzled my head beneath his chin. He smelled of the lime aftershave I loved. Lost in the comfort of our thoughts, we both gazed at the orange and yellow flames, dancing it seemed, to the haunting music of a Celtic harp. *Home.* In just three months he had found the home he was denied for thirty years. And I, at last, had found that home is more than a dwelling place. It was a journey of the heart.

"Do you remember how you got here? I mean, when did you know you had been transported to another century?"

He scratched his chin. "You know, I thought about that a lot up in the treehouse. How would anyone, alone in an unchanged wilderness, notice that—even if they believed such a thing was possible?"

He told me when he deserted, he found a cave about two days west of Fort Laramie and lived there for months before he noticed the fresh stream trickling through it took on a funny color. His horse eventually refused to drink from the stream.

"I always boiled my drinking water, like we did on bivouac, but decided it was time to move on. We rode into some rocky hills, looking for another cave or an abandoned shack near a water source. My mare was bitten in a coulee by a rattler. I tried bleeding her from the poison, Jess, but she died in just a few hours."

He paused to take a swallow of wine while I murmured something sympathetic. When he continued, he told me about the caves he discovered a few miles further on, near a river deep enough to fish and standing in the water was another horse.

"At first, I thought I was dreaming. It looked like a wild Connemara—a spotted horse with a dark tail and mane, like those in Eire. It was larger than a Connemara, though, with darker spots."

"An Appaloosa?"

He looked down at me, thoughtfully. "It could have been an Indian pony."

"Did his coat look like ink spots spilled over white?"

"Aye. And when I got close enough with a rope, I could see he wasn't wild at all, just old. He even let me pull some burrs out of his mane."

"Did you notice anything about his eyes?"

"Wide, intelligent, almost human like?"

I squeezed his arm tightly. "Definitely an appaloosa."

"You know the breed?"

I nodded. Mitch owned an Appaloosa. "What happened next?"

"He wouldn't let me rope him, but he didn't gallop away, either. I watched him drink from the river, then followed him after he had his fill. He headed toward one of the caves, with a tree nearly covering the entrance, and I could hear something yelping from inside the cave."

"A dog?"

He nodded. "That or a coyote, I thought. I loaded my shotgun, hoping it was just a horse and dog belonging to a hunter who took shelter in the cave. I found the man inside with a dead grizzly and a dog, black and white, like the horse."

A black and white dog? I sat up. "Did the dog limp?"

He shrugged. "The dog was protecting his master, even snarled at me until I let him sniff my fingers. There was so much blood on both of them; it was hard to tell who it belonged to. The grizzly had a knife plunged into his eye up to the hilt, but he was still warm, so I knew the fight must have happened within the hour."

My stomach was beginning to roil and I must have made a noise of disgust. He smoothed his hand over my stomach and asked if I wanted to hear the rest. I covered his hand with mine and nodded slowly.

"Well, I dragged the hunter clear of the bear and braced him against his saddle so he could breathe easier, then ran to the river for water to clean his wounds. He was licking blood from his lips and I gave him a drink first, then splashed his face with the water I brought back in my hat."

"Did you notice the color of his eyes?"

"One was nearly scratched from the socket, but in the dim light, I thought they were blue…or green."

I rolled off his lap, onto the rug and took a deep breath.

Immediately, he knelt beside me. "Jess, are you okay?"

I tried to pull myself together, thinking coincidences happen, he could have got all the colors wrong, but I had to know. I nodded again. "Go on."

His forehead wrinkled as he felt mine. "This is making you sick."

I tried a weak smile. "No, I want to hear what happened to the poor man."

"It doesn't fare well for him."

I pulled in a deep breath. "I have to hear."

He gave me a worried look, as I hugged my bent knees and braved another smile. "It's just a little morning sickness. Happens sometimes."

He looked at the clock on the mantel. "This is late

afternoon."

I shrugged. "Happens then, too."

He narrowed his eyes, skeptical, then continued, editing the narrative with fewer graphics.

"I pulled a couple of bear claws out of him and staunched the bleeding with scraps of material from his torn shirt after I removed it. He winced when I moved his arm, and I thought maybe it was broken, so I fixed him a sling and covered him with his saddle blanket. When I thought he was stable, I built a fire and tended the dog, carrying him down to the river to wash off the blood, and let him drink on his own. One of his ears was torn and he had a claw in his side, but otherwise, he seemed to be okay."

"Did he, did he limp?" I dared to ask, thinking of Finn, Tallie's crippled dog.

"When he ran back to the cave, he hitched up a back leg, and I thought maybe the bear had thrown or batted him in the attack, breaking his leg. When I joined him again in the cave, he was at his master's side, licking his hand. His leg was at an odd angle, but it didn't seem to trouble him."

My heart was beating faster and I thought I was going to be sick. I rested my head on my knees and pulled in a few deep breaths.

He rubbed my back, asking if he could get me something—water or something to settle my stomach. I shook my head. I had to know what happened next.

"The hunter was moaning or mumbling in and out of consciousness all night. He slept with a hand on the dog while I butchered the bear and roasted strips of meat over hot rocks around the little fire pit."

"You butchered the bear?" I said, incredibly.

He nodded. "With the hunter's knife. Indians at the garrison swore on Bear grease to keep bugs at bay, so I figured it couldn't hurt to apply it to wounds and keep the fire going as well. Living in the wild, you have to eat what you can find, Jess, and we had a convenience store lying on the floor of the cave. The dog and I feasted, but the patient managed only a little meat soup I offered, probably because of his neck wound."

"The next morning, the hunter was feverish, even more incoherent—muttering something panicky about a cut or a cup."

My stomach was churning and my heart was bumping in my chest. A cup…a teacup? "What did he say about a cup?"

"I showed him my tin cup, and tried to get him to drink from it, but his throat was swollen. His bad eye was swollen shut as well and when he tried to speak, it was garbled. It sounded like he was repeating 'just' over and over, sometimes 'tell' or 'tellee,' He grabbed my arm, then and with his last breath, he clearly said 'cup.'"

I vomited on the rug, macaroni and cheese basting in a few sips of wine, and held my mouth as I ran to the bathroom and locked the door, emptied my stomach and muffled my sobs into a thick towel. Robbie was pounding on the door, pleading with me to let him in, threatening to break down the door when I didn't answer. Even Sadie was barking wildly.

I turned on the shower, composed myself enough to shout that I was okay, just going to clean up in the shower. I didn't bother to undress, just stepped into the glass enclosure and let the water mingle with my tears until I felt drained and numb all over.

He was dead. I could have expected that. I *should* have expected that. How could there be another scenario? Immortality is a dream of the gods. But he didn't deserve to die that way. I tipped my head to feel the warm waterfall on my face, wishing it could wash away the last images of his painful death in that cave…pleading for the teacup…wanting to come through to my century? *To come to me and our son?*

I stepped out of the shower, removed and wrung out my wet clothes. After slipping into my robe, I dried my wet hair and studied my image in the mirror. A brown-eyed redhead glared back at me—a woman who had come late to love, bearing children with two very special green-eyed men of the past—all because of a teacup. Perhaps immortality was not a dream, just a journey to love.

He was waiting for me, outside the bathroom door, his green eyes filled with worry. I assured him I was all right and with one hand on the small of my back and the other capping my damp hair, he held me against his beating heart, telling me I was the love of his life—in every century of his life. He asked me to marry him again, under his rightful name this time.

Standing on tip toes, I twisted my head and kissed the ear I had maimed with gunshot. "Yes." I choked out the words. "Oh yes…Robbie, my love." We sealed the promise with short, sweet kisses, and ended up slow dancing to the melancholy strings of an Irish harp.

With his impeccable timing, Scout arrived on the scene, delivered from his play date by Audrey and her little boy, Jamie. Sadie alerted us even before the car honked in our driveway, and stopped barking only when Scout rushed into the house to hug her. From the porch, I waved my thanks to Audrey and when she saw me in my robe and slippers, she got back in her car and rolled down the window, laughing. “Every mom needs a spa day at home! My turn next!”

I promised to call her next week.

When Scout noticed Robbie, he rushed into his open arms. “Dapa, you home again.” He clapped Robbie’s chin with his chubby hands and planted a wet kiss firmly on his mouth. “I miss you, Dapa.”

Over his head, Robbie’s damp eyes met my damp eyes. “I missed you, too,” he said, hoarsely. I smiled at him, thinking how lucky I was—a woman who not many years ago had no time for any men—now living with two of them—multiple sizes of green-eyed passion.

Epilogue

In the months that followed, Robbie officially changed his name to Robert Dawson O'Brien Mitchell and legally adopted Scout. We married again, using my newly-engraved Claddagh ring, and this time we spent the night in our newly-insulated tree house.

Robbie and Chuck became business partners in Beaverwood Builders, even advertising chicken coops and all-weather treehouses. After I was able to hear the rest of Robbie's cave story, we burned the bearskin I fouled, replacing it with a soft synthetic fur rug.

He had buried Mitch in the cave, marking the site with an Irish blessing and the date etched in the wall beside the grave. When he finished, the black and white dog slept on the grave of his master every night and stood sentinel by day, coaxed away only to eat and drink. Finn, the curious little crippled puppy I saved that summer of 1886 had grown into a faithful companion and protector, fighting for life against a grizzly twenty times his size on Mitch's last hunting trip. Eventually, Finn died, maybe from the infection he developed, maybe from the heartbreak of his loss. Robbie buried him next to his master with wooden crosses marking both graves.

The Appaloosa also proved to be faithful, never straying far from the river or the cave, eventually allowing Robbie to halter and ride him for short distances at the pace of an aging stallion. He grew stiff and thinner as winter approached. Robbie built a sheltered pen for him outside, but like the dog, he was drawn to a history of companionship and wandered inside the cave on cold nights.

The dead bear was a commissary gift for Robbie, long after strips of dried meat were gone. He saved the smallest bear claws for awls, fashioned the largest into digging or scraping tools and cured the skin side of the pelt, letting it dry in the sun until he could use the fur pelt to guard against cold Wyoming nights. When snow covered the ground, he fashioned it into a poncho, and made a special pocket to hold the photo of his father.

Mitch's saddlebags held whatever gear Robbie expected to find from a man on a hunting trip. Ammunition for his shotgun, rope, flint and matches, a small hatchet, fish hooks, bags of oats, flour, coffee and salt, Utensils, a tin plate and a small skillet, extra socks and a shirt in a bedroll. He laid the inventory out on a large granite shelf, using all but one item.

"Odd," Robbie said, "unlikely to be found among anyone's gear." Wrapped in sheep's wool and packed in a case remade from a steel trap, he told me he found an old blue and white porcelain cup with a missing handle and several hairline cracks. Mitawin was painted on the bottom of the cup in bold indigo letters. I knew at once how Robbie was transported through time. The same cup had been my vehicle when I slipped time.

He only used the cup once, the night before he left the cave for good. He remembered "cup" was the last word on the dying hunter's lips, and thought it must have meant something special. Perhaps it was a cherished memento or prized keepsake given by a loved one—like the photo his mum gave him of his father. He meant to bury the cup with the hunter before he left, but just once, he wanted to see if the prickly pear tea he brewed tasted like his mum's tea once sipped from Irish porcelain.

Listening to the wind whistle through the cave, he imagined he was back in Ireland, hearing the gulls cry as they soared above the cliffs. And he dozed in his bearskin by the fire with the cup warm in his hands. When he woke in the morning, his hands were empty and the cave was nearly black as night, with no fire and only pinholes of light coming from the entrance. The tree in front of the cave had grown overnight, enough to force him to hack his way out with Mitch's hatchet, now spotted with rust.

Once outside, he noticed the river was smaller and trees larger—or missing altogether. The saplings were rotted in the outside pen he had built for the Appaloosa, and when he searched for days, he found no sign of the horse, not even a hoof print.

Of course, I knew what had happened, and told him how time had reversed what I saw when I slipped back in time. Comparing our experiences blunted the unreality that spun around us, like a fine invisible web. We could finally share the unimaginable with someone who knew it wasn't crazy or delusional. Did it happen to others? Our magical connection was brought home even further when I showed Robbie how to surf the internet for ancestry clues to the DNA connections between him and Mitch and Scout.

David Dawson Mitchell supposedly fathered Mitch, who fathered Scout. The Virginia patriarch also fathered Dawson Isaac Mitchell (D.I.M.)—who fathered Robert Dawson O'Brien Mitchell, the illegitimate son of Sarah O'Brien, the Mitchell's maid, who was Robbie's mother. Dawson was a key name in the links, a common practice in many generations to repeat a favored name. The DNA links made sense, then, with all the facts and clues we gathered. Mitch and Dawson were half-brothers, which made Scout and Robbie half-cousins through the same paternal line. Technically, Robbie was now raising his cousin as his son. The new baby and Scout would be connected by their splash of cousin-genetics, and still, remain true half-siblings, as I was the mother of children by both Mitch and Robbie.

Jake and I had a similar connection through our common ancestor, great-great-grandmother Jessamine. I wondered if it was all just coincidental, God's joke—or maybe a blessing—on all of us. In His unique timing, a magical teacup put us all in the same melting pot of ancestral history.

Mitch once asked me if I knew of any man in my time who had two women and split his soul with love for each. I thought, then, it only happened in fiction or movies. But I became the female counterpart of his query. I loved two extraordinary green-eyed men in the same family, five and six generations apart from me, and I loved them equally well.

****

Some people don't believe in coincidence. Fewer believe in magic. Nobody believes in time travel. When our daughter was born on a hot August day with a lusty cry and clear green eyes, Robbie and I laughed and cried, and kissed her fingers and toes.

We named her Destiny.

Coming Next from Cj Fosdick:

THE ACCIDENTAL HEIRESS

Olivia Moire O'Brien was an embarrassment to her parents. An only child, born in 1867, she was not the son and heir to Meirliún that Conal O'Brien needed. Not the demure daughter her mother expected. Even years of finishing school in Dublin couldn't trim the willful edges of Livy. As a child, she burned her dolls and insisted on wearing breeks to follow two older boys who were sons of servants on the hundred-year-old O'Brien estate in West Ireland. Robbie and Scottish Lewy called her "the *rua*," a red-haired albatross the master forced them to protect.

Undaunted, Livy grew up learning to straddle horses, fish the coves of Galway Bay, and hold her own in the company of "low boys," as her mum called them.

When Livy fell in love with one of the boys, she was determined to risk everything to win his affection. But when her mother died, remorse and guilt shadowed her spirit, and the ultimate shame she brought to her family banished her to the infamous Magdalen Laundries. Could she recover to eventually become the heiress she was meant to be, or would the rest of her life be entangled with mystery and betrayal in her search for absolution…and the child she bore?

A word about the author…

Born and raised in Milwaukee, Wisconsin, Carol Ann Johnson Fosdick has freelanced for over 30 years, writing stories and articles for local and National publications. Her stories are published in three anthologies, including Minnesota's "Blossoms & Blizzards." One of several other award-winning stories inspired her debut novel, *The Accidental Wife*. Her novel dreams are pursued on a wooded country hilltop in Rochester, Minnesota, with husband, family, and a menagerie of wild and domestic animals coloring her days.

http://cjfosdick.com

~*~

Other Books by Cj Fosdick
available from The Wild Rose Press, Inc.

Hot Stuff (part of the Candy Hearts series)

The Accidental Wife

Thank you for purchasing
this publication of The Wild Rose Press, Inc.

If you enjoyed the story, we would appreciate your letting others know by leaving a review.

For other wonderful stories,
please visit our on-line bookstore at
www.thewildrosepress.com.

For questions or more information
contact us at
info@thewildrosepress.com.

The Wild Rose Press, Inc.
www.thewildrosepress.com

Stay current with The Wild Rose Press, Inc.

Like us on Facebook

https://www.facebook.com/TheWildRosePress

And Follow us on Twitter
https://twitter.com/WildRosePress